ELECTRIC ANGEL

ELECTRIC ANGEL

CYBER DREAMS BOOK 1

PLUM PARROT

Podium

To Josh,

thanks for turning me on to Gibson and Stephenson

back when I thought fantasy was all that mattered . . .

Cover design by Podium Publishing

ISBN: 978-1-0394-3294-9

Published in 2023 by Podium Publishing, ULC
www.podiumaudio.com

Podium

ELECTRIC
ANGEL

1

JULIET

Juliet let her head bounce with the music blaring through her implants—vibrating through the bones in her skull—almost like she was in front of one of the big speakers at a show. The night was hot, and she smelled something fierce from sweating in her rig all day, but that was the price you paid for OT, and she needed the damn bits.

The synth-voiced singer broke into a resounding chorus as the beat really dropped, her discount implants rattling her molars together, and Juliet thought back to the last show she'd seen in person. It had to have been five years ago now, and that brought about a bunch of other memories she wished she'd left buried—thoughts of her mom heading to the Seattle megacity with her new husband; thoughts of Emma, her sister and roommate, getting arrested and put away up in Phoenix; thoughts of working this backbreaking-nowhere job day in and day out so she could put some corpo-issued protein squares in her pantry and keep her subscription to the net active.

"Come on, Fee Fee," she breathed, still bouncing with her music, her long blue-black ponytail whipping from one shoulder, arcing in front of her eyes, and then over to the other. She'd had it tied up in a bun all day under the hot metal dome of her welding rig's helmet, and it wanted to feel the air, even if it was hot and dry.

She balanced on a pile of old scrap outside Fred's Salvage, waiting for her ride. Felix was notoriously late, and it was Friday—she was starting to worry she might be stuck 'til morning, when she could call someone else, maybe her cousin.

"Tig, pause the music and call Felix," she subvocalized. The music kept blaring, her personal AI completely missing the message. "Tig!" she shouted this time. "Pause the track!"

"Paused!" the tinny, robotic voice responded through her auditory implants. Juliet could change his voice, and had done so a few times, but she found the goofy, echoing metallic voice amusing and thought it reflected the PAI's capabilities rather well—he wasn't the sharpest tool in the shed, as her old grandpa would've said.

"Call Fee Fee," she repeated, stretching her neck until it popped.

"Calling Felix Delgado," Tig said before Juliet heard the *beep, beep* of the line trying to connect. She kicked out her feet, her heavy steel-toed work boots like ankle weights threatening to pull her long legs out and overbalance her, and then a little musical note sounded, indicating a completed connection.

"Jules!" Felix greeted her, as his face appeared in her augmented display. Her retinal implants were cheap as hell, so it was grainy and blocked out a good portion of her vision, but she was glad to see him. He had a lovable face with high, round cheeks and big teeth sporting too many gaps, but he smiled like he was a fashion model, and she loved him for it. He'd done something to his eyebrows—notched them and thickened them at his aunt's beauty shop, probably—and he looked adorable.

"Fee! Did you forget about me? I told you I got off at one!"

"Oh shit, Jules! I'm so sorry! Shit got crazy tonight! Me and Paulo went to Sunkissed—shit was popping off! Jules, a real banger fight broke out! Some of the gearheads from down south of Sixth were messing with a real fine lady, someone from the foothills. Jules, I mean, she was *fine*! Hair nicer than yours, you feel me?"

"Fee, what the hell? I'm sitting out here—*alone*—outside the scrapyard, nothing but coyotes and moths for company, and you're telling me about some fine *princess*? Where are you?"

"I'm getting to that, Jules! Anyway, she turned out not to be some nice *princess*, you feel? One minute she was sitting there, sipping some x-steam, and then *bang*, out came her blazing monoblade. You register? An honest-to-Jesus monoblade. She cut one of the bangers in half, and she didn't even stand up! Jules, his guts fell all over the floor!"

"Fee! Where. Are. You?"

"I'm really sorry, Jules. I'm trying to tell you what happened, but long story short, I had to take Paulo to St. Mary's." Juliet could see, from her grainy image of Felix, that he was driving and only half paying attention to their conversation.

"Tell me you're on your way, Fee," Juliet said, sighing heavily and slapping one of her heavy welding gloves against her thigh.

"I'm sorry, Jules. They wouldn't see him. We're on our way to the megacity."

"Phoenix? What the *hell*, Fee?"

"Jules, he needs his hand put back on!"

"I get it, but you shoulda called—at least sent a message! All right, I gotta try to figure out a ride. Tell Paulo I hope it works out." Juliet gestured with her hand, ending the call. "Dammit!" Again, she slapped her gloves against her thigh. "Nobody's gonna come out here at this hour, are they, Tig?"

"Would you like me to order you an AutoCab, J-J-Jules?"

His corny, robotic stutter made her laugh as always, and she said, "No, Tig. That'd eat up all my OT, and I've got rent due." She stood up and stretched, arching her back to an eruption of pops and cracks. "Damn, that rig gets heavy on a double, even with the flex-steel limbs Fred added last month." She gazed into the black night of the Arizona desert and contemplated how she'd get back to her apartment. In a fast car, she was a good forty minutes outside of Tucson, and even in 2107, there was a lot of dark desert between her and the blazing lights of the city she could see on the western horizon.

"Dammit. Do I spring for a cab? Do I just crash here? Tig! Bit balance, please?"

"You have 712 Helios-bits available."

"Seven-twelve. Shit. Even if this OT hits my account tomorrow, I'll be short. No cab for me, and of course, Mark locked the gate when he left. Tig, call Mark."

"Calling Mark Lyons," Tig said, dialing up Fred's night shift manager.

Juliet listened to the beeps and connection tone, and then Mark's bald, middle-aged head appeared in all its grainy glory in her vision. "Mark!"

"Juliet? Why you calling? Something happen at the shop?"

"No, Mark! My ride flaked, and I'm locked out. Any chance you could swing me a lift or come back to open up? I don't wanna spend all night out here. I can hear the coyotes, the bugs are swarming the lamp, and it's hot as hell!"

"Jeez, Juliet! I just sat down, and I'm already two beers in. I've got a date with my dream-rig, if you know what I mean."

"Ew, Mark. I don't wanna know what you mean. Could you put your, uh, date off for half an hour? I know you don't live very far . . ."

"You're messing up my Friday . . . oh, all right, Juliet. Only 'cause I like you, though. Maybe we can get a brew after a shift, huh?"

"Um, yeah, maybe. Thanks, Mark! I'll see you in a few, right?"

"Yeah, sure. I just need a minute to get my . . . boots back on." His long pause before the word *boots* made Juliet's mind jump to a lot of conclusions she instantly regretted.

"Thanks, Mark," she said and flicked her fingers, ending the call. "I bet I can talk him into a ride back to town. I'd rather not sleep here tonight, Tig."

"Would you like me to book you a motel?"

Juliet laughed. "No, Tig!"

She paced around inside the illuminated circle thrown by the single floodlight outside the salvage yard, swatting at the bugs that had come out of the woodwork attracted to the light. After just a minute or two of pacing, she saw bright, high-quality white headlights and purple underglow, and knew a vehicle was approaching which definitely didn't belong to Mark.

She wasn't sure why, but Juliet stepped out of the circle of light and crouched behind the scrap pile she'd been sitting on earlier. Why was a smooth ride like that coming out to the scrapyard in the middle of the night?

She watched between two folded sheets of tin as the low, long sedan rolled up to the gate. It was black and shiny, not a single scratch or scrap of dust. The thing must have had a static shield.

"Rich . . ." Juliet hissed, crouching even lower as one of the black-tinted glass doors popped open, slid back with a hiss, and a man stepped out.

He looked familiar, and Juliet had to think for a minute about where she'd seen him. His hair was black and combed straight back, heavy with some kind of product, and he wore expensive clothes but styled like a banger—a banger who made a big score.

He walked up to the gate, kind of shuffling like he had all the time in the world, and produced a key. That's when it clicked; this was Freddy's— Fred's—cousin, Tony. He'd been to the shop a few times, dropping off cars of questionable origin for salvage, and Juliet knew Fred probably looked the other way for him when it came to showing ownership.

Tony pushed the gate open then shuffled back, climbing into the sedan before it slowly hummed forward, gliding over the rough gravel like it was the smoothest pavement ever laid. Juliet could feel the thrum of the hydrogen-powered engine, and she knew that thing was Fast with a capital *F*. "Probably has a huge bank of batts, too. Talk about torque," she muttered, watching the violet taillights drift into the stacks of old wrecks, machines, and piles of scrap Fred had yet to move.

Curiosity getting the better of her, Juliet darted through the gate, ghosting the slow-moving sedan while hugging the scrap piles to keep herself out of sight. The car glided deep into the yard, stopping by one of the hammer shredders. She crouched behind a stack of old appliances, watching between an ancient white SureJet washer and a nameless yellow fridge. This time, both front doors opened, and a tall, androgynous person with a white mohawk opened the driver's-side rear door, helping a frail, cane-wielding old woman stand up out of the sedan.

"What's this? Weird-ass group of people to be having a midnight party at Fred's . . ."

"Would you like me to search the d-d-directory?"

Tig's robotic voice blaring into her implant almost sent Juliet into a fit. She gripped the old washer tightly in alarm, her heart racing at his intrusion into her sneaking mindset.

"No, Tig. Go to sleep," she subvocalized. This time, the goofy PAI heard her, and she saw the little *Zzz* symbol in her retinal implant telling her he was offline.

"Get him out," the old woman ordered, moving around the sedan while stooping over her cane to look at the trunk. She wore an honest-to-goodness veil attached to her maroon-colored hat, and her polyblend dress had matching maroon flowers printed into the silky white fabric.

Tony and Mohawk both moved to the trunk. When Tony clicked a button on his fob, causing the trunk to pop open, they both rushed to struggle with whoever was inside. Lots of grunting and cussing from them both ensued until finally, after a few meaty *thwaps*, they pulled out a third man and threw him onto the gravel-covered ground at the old lady's feet.

The man wore a white jumper with orange stripes down the side. It made Juliet think of an interceptor pilot. "Or someone from a mental institution," she breathed. He had close-cropped blond hair, and, even from twenty meters away, Juliet could see the purple, swollen nature of his face and the shrink-cords on his wrists and ankles.

"Godric," the old woman spoke, her voice warbling and cracking. "Reset the implant and take it out. Don't make me ruin you bit by bit."

"Bea? Is that you? I can't see so well right now," the man said, lifting his bound hands to rub at his face.

"Don't play the fool, Godric. We know you can see better than any of us.

Come now; whatever ails you, we can fix it. Reset the device, remove it, and we can return to the institute. I promise you'll be top of the list when we work out the production kinks."

"If I remove it, I'll be dead inside two minutes. If you kill me, no one can reset it. Seems we're at an impasse, hmm?"

"Watch your tone," Mohawk growled, kicking the bound man in the back, eliciting a grunt and cough. Juliet thought she saw something darker than spit come out of his mouth.

"Would you like Tony to start feeding parts of you into that shredder? Do you think we might bargain more amicably if you're just a torso and a head? I know your nanites will keep you from dying—rather makes my job easy, don't you think? Removing that concern?" The woman pressed her cane into his forehead, cruelly twisting it as he struggled to regain his breath.

"So my choices are to either be tortured and dismembered or to die? Fuck you, Bea." He held up his still-bound hands over his face, waiting for the kicks to come, but Bea held up her cane, keeping Mohawk at bay.

She leaned over and spoke. This time, her voice sounded almost sweet, sort of like what Juliet remembered her grandma's voice to be. "Godric, if you work with me, I promise we can save you. We have a stasis kit in the car. Reset the device, remove it, and we'll stabilize you, bring you back to the institute until we get things figured out."

"Why bring me here, then?" Godric coughed, his breath wheezing.

"Convenience? Intimidation? You know how these things work, Godric. Come, I'll give you my word." Bea held out a shaky hand, her bent, dark-skinned fingers glittering with jeweled rings.

"I do. I do know how these things work, Bea." Godric reached up his bound hands, but as Juliet struggled to see from her hiding spot—zooming as much as her low-end implant would allow—rather than take the veiled lady's hand, one of his fingers folded back, and a fine mist sprayed out, fully engulfing her.

"What?" She stumbled back, coughing. "A phage? You fool!"

Juliet's eyes bugged out as she watched Tony and Mohawk stumble away, coughing, before things really went sideways. Bea tried to waddle back to the car, but she fell to her knees then flat on her face near the rear tire of the sedan. Tony grabbed his throat like he was choking, dancing around madly, and Mohawk fell to his back, feet kicking up like a dying cockroach.

Godric, also coughing, struggled to a sitting position and looked directly at Juliet between the two ancient appliances. His eyes gleamed like orange LEDs. "Don't come closer."

"Shit!" Juliet said, ducking lower. She stared at the ground, her mind racing. Should she run? *Yes, I should damn nuclear meltdown run!* She stood and turned, but the man, Godric, called out to her.

"Wait! Just wait a minute. Let the bacteria do its thing. If you don't touch them, you'll be all right."

Juliet froze and looked back just in time to see Tony collapse, jerking spasmodically like Mohawk. She wasn't an idiot. "That shit was airborne. Tell me the truth: am I dead already?"

"Not airborne." The man coughed. "It was a mist. The bacteria can't live outside a wet environment." He glanced at the writhing, spasming trio who had, only moments before, been threatening his life. "They'll be dead in a minute. I won't last too much longer, I'm afraid. Come on! Help me stick it to these assholes one last time, huh?"

"This shit's crazy, friendo—way beyond what I want on a Friday night. Corpo-sec coming? Those guys work for Helios?"

"No, they're out of Phoenix, WBD. You're clear for an hour or more." As he spoke, Tony finally stopped jerking and lay still. Juliet thought she could see the skin on his face turning black. Godric partially obscured the old lady, but she could see her feet sticking straight out, not moving at all.

"They're dead. You just killed them all." Her voice was barely above a whisper, but the man somehow heard her, even from twenty-five meters away.

"They've done worse. Believe me, they're not worth a single tear. Not even their mothers would mourn them." He coughed, and it sounded deeper, wetter. "I only have an hour to live, tops. Come closer—the bacteria's inert by now. I'm not contagious, all right? I have a phage fighting it in my body. The implant—" he coughed, then continued, "programs the phage, fighting the bacteria, but it's slowly losing ground. Look in the trunk and find the first aid kit. Look for an aerosol antiseptic."

"I've got a guy coming to pick me up," Juliet said, slowly edging forward, wondering why the hell she wasn't running in the opposite direction.

"This won't take long. You're going to want to get the hell out of here anyway. WBD will co-opt some satellites; they'll get your sig and follow you, so you gotta get lost in a megacity, maybe get off-planet." He eyed Juliet as she got closer. "Welder?" he asked, noting her scorched, heavy-denim overalls. He saw her nod. "Maybe get a job on a salvage rig or go to one of the colonies."

"Why the hell would I do that? I should just run and call the cops!" Juliet was now only a few feet from the man, and she glanced sideways at the closest corpse—Tony. His body was being eaten from the inside; she could see it—his skin was turning black, and his fingertips were gone, little white bones sticking out of the black flesh. "Flesh-eating? This is nasty stuff . . ."

Every bone in her body screamed, *Run!* Still, she hesitated, waiting to hear the weird, bound man out. As she looked at him, waiting for him to finish coughing again, she saw that his bruises were gone—his face was unmarred.

"Trust me—get the antiseptic. I'm about to give you something worth more than . . . well, worth more than anything I can think of."

Juliet edged around him, looking into the sedan's trunk, and said, "Why would you do that?"

"Because you're here. I'm about to die, kid. I'm about to fucking cash in, and the only thing I can think of doing is keeping those bastards from getting this implant. You've got a target on your back, anyway; WBD's gonna track you down for questioning, and they make people disappear all the time. Just fucking trust me, please!" He barely got the last word out before he fell into another coughing fit. Juliet saw the first aid kit, a big red box with a white cross, strapped to the side of the trunk.

Unhooking it, she opened the kit and retrieved the aerosolized antiseptic before turning back to the man. He'd stopped coughing and was lying on his back, eyes unfocused as he gazed upward into the black sky. "The stars . . ." he whispered. Juliet looked up but saw no stars—hadn't seen any in years. The haze from the megacities made that hard these days.

"What's WBD?" she asked, moving closer to him with the can of antiseptic.

"Western Bio Dynamics Corp. They could buy Helios a dozen times over." His eyes regained focus, and he looked at her. "Give me a minute," he said.

"Sure . . ." she replied, figuring, at the very least, she could turn and run. He was still bound, after all.

"Charlie, initiate factory reset," the man called Godric said. "Confirmed. Confirmed. All systems. Understood."

By that point, Juliet had figured out that Godric was speaking to his PAI, doing what the woman he'd just killed had asked him to do: resetting whatever device she'd wanted him to give up.

"That's that." His breath wheezed in his throat. "I'll be dead in minutes. You have a PAI, right? You gotta remove it." He, as if in illustration, reached up to his PAI port at the back of his neck, straining with his hands still bound, and forcefully folded back the synth-skin flap with his thumbnail, ejecting the silvery button-shaped device. As he pulled it out, thousands of tiny nanofilament fibers trailed after it, glistening wetly in the air as he held it out for Juliet. "Spray it down." He nodded to the antiseptic.

Juliet didn't hesitate; thinking of the rapidly decomposing bodies nearby, she liberally soaked the device and the hand holding it with antiseptic. She must have nearly emptied the can before he coughed and, with a wet, wheezing voice, said, "You gotta put this in you. Initiate it. Once it's active, tell it to mask its signature."

Juliet backed away. "You're meltdown rockers if you think I'm porting that thing!"

"You'll have WBD goons on you before midnight if you don't. It won't mask itself until you tell it to, and you can't do that until you port it."

"This is too much. I'm out." Juliet started to walk away, but Godric called out to her, and his voice was so raw, so thick with emotion, that she stopped to listen.

"Listen! Those people destroyed my life, and I'm just their most recent test subject. They're users and get rich off the backs of people like us. Don't you want a chance to level the tables? Don't you want a chance to get out of this shit? I'm giving it to you! They don't know you, won't know you have it. If you get out, get clear and disappear for a while, you can use it to . . . well, to do all kinds of things. I know you don't have a reason to, but trust me! I'm dying here; I don't have anything to gain by tricking you!"

Juliet turned and took a step back toward him. "How'd you get the bacteria? The infection? Why would they poison their test subject?"

"Oh, that one's on me." He coughed wetly as he tried to chuckle. "I stole a sample from another one of their departments. I was going to use the device here to weaponize it against WBD. It almost worked, maybe too well. I suppose if I'd had some better phage tech, I could have fought it off longer or cured it, but . . ." His words broke off in another coughing fit. When it ceased, he pulled his sleeve away from his mouth and said, "I can't see. I'll be dead in less than a minute. Please! Take it."

Juliet gingerly reached out, taking the clearly high-end PAI from the man's hand. She backed away a step, looking at the device with wide eyes. This thing had to be worth thousands—no, *tens* of thousands of bits.

"I wasn't joking." Rolling to his side, he coughed out a pool of wet, bloody phlegm. "Back away. I'll be swarming with those bugs for a few minutes." He waited while Juliet backed up several steps. "You gotta activate it now—they're already tracking it."

"Seriously?" Juliet moved back another couple of steps, then she sprayed the rest of the antiseptic on the PAI, shaking it so the fibers jostled around, allowing the fluid to sluice over them. Something in her wanted to call the corpo cops. Turn in the device and tell them her crazy story about what had happened that night. Another part of her wanted to grab this chance, grab it like it was a rope being lowered to her, ready to pull her out of the sinking, dead-end life she'd gotten herself into.

"Do it," the man urged before he coughed another thick gout of blood and lay still.

Juliet backed still further away, turning toward the gate and seeing no sign yet of Mark's beat-up truck. She resisted the urge to look up at the sky, where she knew thousands of corpo satellites were floating around, watching everything that happened on Earth. She figured they'd watch this whole scene play out. Watch what that fool had done, pulling this thing out of his neck before handing it to her. They'd track her, and she'd never see the outside of whatever facility they took her to again. This was some seriously shady shit, and they wouldn't want her spreading the vid.

Juliet sighed and tapped a knuckle on her forehead. She didn't even have a vid—Tig was asleep, and she hadn't started a recording. "So what's the difference? If they catch me with this thing in my pocket or if I turn it over to the Helios cops or if I put it in my head—any way you slice it, I'm buried."

Seizing an impulse, she reached up and pulled back the synth-skin covering up Tig's chip, digging one of her fingernails underneath it and gently teasing it out. She'd already put him to sleep, so the only thing she noticed when she pulled him out was the strange, creepy sensation of cold tickles along her spine and the base of her skull as his monofilament tendrils pulled free. "Ugh," she grunted at the strange feeling.

She rolled the damp tendrils, far fewer than the ones protruding from Godric's device, around Tig's chip and stuffed him into her overalls pocket. That done, she held the mysterious PAI up, found the pairing button, and touched it. The device beeped, and the tendrils began to writhe. Holding it over the port at the back of her neck, the shimmering, translucent nest of impossibly thin wires found her signal and began to crawl into the port, sliding down her spine and up into her skull cavity with a cool electric tingle. They crawled around her brain and spine, looking for the right places to settle. Once the tendrils were fully engaged, she pushed the chip into the slot and folded her skin back smooth.

Holding her breath and walking slowly toward the scrapyard gate, Juliet waited for the new PAI to calibrate. At first, she thought it might have been ruined, that it wouldn't work at all, but then a status bar appeared in her retinal implant, and she knew it had made at least that connection. The bar indicated that it was initializing and was at twenty-two percent.

Juliet stepped outside the gate, pulled it closed, and relocked the magnetic padlock. She didn't know what else to do—she needed to disappear for a while, which started with convincing Mark to drive her home, something he wouldn't do if he realized there were four dead people in the salvage yard.

Juliet believed a corp, especially a big, powerful one, wouldn't think twice about making someone disappear to protect some new, valuable tech.

. . . No, she *had* believed that—*had* been sure—but now, she was second-guessing herself.

"Would they've really iced me just for being a bystander?"

Now that she'd put the device into her port, she knew she was good and truly melted. She'd punched an irreversible ticket by inserting that PAI—there was no way they'd let her go back to life as usual.

She sat and waited, thought about calling Mark again, and realized she couldn't until her new PAI came online. She looked at the status bar, saw it was at seventy-four percent, and tried to wait patiently.

She'd just noticed some yellow headlights coming down the road when she heard a chime in her auditory implant and a message appeared, accompanied by a crystal-clear, pleasant feminine voice with a neutral, nondescript accent.

Initialization complete.

All AI systems are functional.

Connection to satellite network successful.

Host biocompatibility 96.342%. Enhanced learning functions enabled.

Integration with auditory and retinal implants at 100%, operating at partial functionality due to hardware limitations. No other implants were detected.

Host repair functions offline—no matching hardware.

Host weapon systems offline—no matching hardware.

"Hello. May I introduce myself? My name is Angel, but I can guide you to the correct menu if you'd like to customize my persona. Also, I'd like to make you aware that it seems the Western Bio Dynamics Corporation is actively seeking to identify you and pinpoint our location."

"Holy shit," Juliet said.

2

\\\\\\\\\\\\\\\\\\

HOME

ngel? I'm Juliet. Do you remember your previous owner?" she asked, watching the headlights slowly make their way along the dirt road toward the scrapyard.

"No, Juliet," the crystal-clear feminine voice replied with perfect enunciation. "If I existed in a previous incarnation, I should have a compressed file of that iteration. I'm not locating such a file, so the previous user must have requested it be deleted. I'm sorry if this is an inconvenience."

"It's okay, but he said you could hide your presence from the network. He said a corp was looking for you, as you just confirmed, and that they'd hurt me if they found us. Can you, um, I think he said *mask* yourself?"

"Yes, I can, but I could hide more effectively if I had an unused PAI's serial number. I could search some databases online if you don't have one available."

"I do, I do. Hold on." Juliet pulled Tig out of her pocket and held him in front of her, using the zoom function on her retinal implants to scan for the tiny printing on the chip.

"I see it, Juliet. I've taken the code and masked myself. Anyone scanning PAIs on the network will think I am that unit now."

"Great! That was fast! Nice processor in you, huh?"

"My processor is a WDD Crystal Core, model alpha 3.433."

"WDD? Or did you mean WBD?"

The vehicle was close enough now that, with her lowlight enhancement on her implants, Juliet could see it was a red pickup truck—Mark.

"No, Juliet. WDD is the sister company of WBD. 'WDD strives to improve humanity's future by developing the next generation of computing and data services.'"

"Was that from their corpo page?"

"Yes. Juliet, would you like me to hinder their attempts to identify you? The WBD network daemons have discovered my connection and are working to close it. I'm afraid I have a limited window in which to help you."

"Yes! Yes, please do what you can!"

"Please cover your head or keep your gaze below forty-five degrees facing the ground. I'll corrupt any images taken of you in this location for the last twenty-four hours."

The truck pulled up, and Mark rolled down his passenger window.

"All right, Juliet. You want a ride? I don't think Fred would like it if I had you sleep in the shop all night."

"Oh man, thank you, Mark!" Juliet said, pulling the door open, its hinges creaking noisily. She slid into his truck, the aftermarket seat cover bunching up as she scooted in. The interior smelled like cigarettes and aftershave, and she had to wiggle her boots to make room among the empty bottles on the floor panel.

"I still have some bandwidth on the WBD servers, Juliet. I'll mask the ID signature of this vehicle as long as I'm able."

"You can do that?" Juliet subvocalized. "Why were you connected to their servers, anyway?"

"WBD created me. My default settings include a direct connection to their network. Don't be concerned about them tracing it—I have many masking routines, and frankly, their daemons are slow. Still, there are many of them, and my connections are slowly growing more tenuous. I estimate nineteen more minutes before I've lost any functionality on their net."

". . . what about you?" Mark asked, looking at her sideways, one hand on the wheel as his truck rumbled over the dirt and gravel road.

"Sorry, what, Mark? I was listening to a PM from my mom."

"Oh? Everything all right?" He took a drag on his cig and blew the smoke out the cracked window. Juliet had to wonder what kind of a knucklehead still smoked honest-to-goodness cigarettes when you could get a Nikko-vape for three bits that'd last even an absolute fiend at least a couple of days.

"She's all right, yeah. Thanks. What were you asking me?"

"Oh, I was saying I was starving. You wanna split a pizza or something?"

"Thought you had a . . . date, no?" Juliet couldn't help the smile that spread on her soot-and-grease–smudged face.

"Ah, that can wait, Juliet! A man needs his calories, after all, and tomorrow's my day off." Mark drummed his thumbs on the wheel while he dragged on the cig, blowing smoke out the corner of his mouth simultaneously.

"I appreciate it, Mark, really. I'd like to hang out, but I have to get home. My mom's coming early, and my place is an absolute wreck. Besides, look at me." She gestured to her burned and sweaty overalls and grease marks on her shoulders, neck, and face from the welding rig.

"Juliet," Angel said through her implant. "I'm not showing any travel records for your mother, Mackenzie Yvette Bianchi. Are you certain about the date of her visit?"

"Uh," Juliet said aloud, caught by surprise.

"Uh?" Mark asked. "Oh, never mind. It's cool, but can I get a rain check?"

"Yeah, of course." She offered Mark her most genuine fake smile. "I'm not lying when I say I owe you one, all right?" The seriousness in her voice caught his attention, and Mark took the cig out of his mouth and looked at her, blowing smoke out of his nose. He nodded and flicked the butt out the window.

"Cool, Juliet. Like you said, I ain't got much else to do. Happy to help."

She felt sort of bad for how she'd dismissed Mark, how she'd been all too willing to lead him on for a ride. She felt bad for judging him and making light of his situation. Yeah, he was weird, and yeah, he had some creepy habits, but he was there and willing to help her when she needed it. She cleared her throat and asked, "Hey, why don't you use a Nikko-vape?"

"Seriously? I'm not letting that corpo gas into my lungs. I order these special from New Idaho. Organic tobacco and clean paper—no additives, no dyes, nada. You got any idea what the corpos put into those vapes?"

"I guess not . . ."

"I can find a list of ingredients for you," Angel piped in.

"Me neither!" Mark laughed, slapping the wheel. "I wouldn't believe anything you find on their net pages, either. Anyway, I'm not risking that shit."

"Right." Juliet nodded. "Turn up your radio. Let's see what you're into." She smiled and tapped her fingers on her knees to the beat as Mark cranked up his old-school metal playlist. Then she took the opportunity to subvocalize to Angel. "My mom's not really coming, and do me a favor—don't interrupt conversations unless it's critical. It distracts me. And by the way, how do you know my mom's name?"

"I'm sorry if I overstepped. I accessed your public records to flesh out my file on you. I'm currently scanning social media so that I can keep you updated on the activities of your friends and acquaintances." Angel sounded so prim and her tone was so soothing and helpful that Juliet didn't feel immediately creeped out by her self-directed data gathering. As she thought about it, though, she found it a little unnerving. "I'd like to manage other aspects of your life, but in order to connect to your banking and medical services, I'll need you to provide the key to your password vault."

"Hold off on that," Juliet said.

"Of course. I'd like to fully evaluate your mental acuity and physical capabilities so I can prepare a baseline, comparative percentile ranking for you. One of my more advanced functions is the drive to help my host better those rankings, increasing their performance and standing among their peers."

"My peers?"

"Yes, humanity and the synthetic beings living in this solar system."

"You consider synths my peers?"

"They can act and think and compete with you for employment, monetary rewards, and even love interests. I would say you should be prepared to compete with them, yes."

"We can talk about this later. What's the story with the WBD network? Are we still in the clear?"

"I've managed to remove identifying markers from you and this vehicle from their earlier surveillance and have directed their search back to the scrapyard. There is a vehicle and several corpses at that location which are of interest to WBD. Their drones are en route to investigate, but we should be amidst the Tucson city traffic before they redirect their efforts this way. I'm nearly locked out of their network, though. Intel I can provide on their activities will be greatly diminished in the next four minutes."

Juliet reached forward and touched the volume arrow on Mark's radio, dampening the music a bit. "Hey, do you know where I live?"

"Not exactly. I think you said near the university, though, right?"

"Yeah, that's right, in the Helios tower. Thanks again, Mark." He nodded, and Juliet increased the volume again, zoning out while he drove. She had a lot on her mind, not least of which was that she should probably take the dead guy's advice and skip town. She needed to disappear, which was hard to do in a city like Tucson. Should she really listen to him and head off-planet? She'd never been anywhere outside of Arizona and the coastal states. She'd been to see her mom a couple of times, but she'd just driven through those places. She didn't know shit about living outside of Tucson.

"Angel," she subvocalized. "How hard would it be to mask my identity? I mean, to keep the cameras, drones, and satellites from watching my moves?"

"I have the software required to scramble your image and provide garbled ID data to automated observation devices. You'd need an upgrade to your retinal implants, however. Currently, you have no projection capabilities."

"New implants," she said softly.

Mark touched the volume on his steering wheel, looking over at her. "You say something?"

"Nah, just thinking about how shitty my implants are. Wish I could afford better."

"Your eyes or ears? Or you talking about your PAI?"

"All of the above?" Juliet laughed.

"Excuse me?" Angel interjected, and Juliet laughed harder, provoking a funny look from Mark as he fished out another of his archaic cigarettes from his breast pocket.

"My PAI heard that and isn't happy with me," Juliet explained, thumping her hands to the music on her thighs.

"I know a guy. He does good work and isn't too cheap, but he takes . . . services in trade," Mark said, sparking an old butane lighter to his cig.

"I'm not a sex doll, Mark," Juliet replied, sighing in exasperation.

"No!" He sputtered, almost spitting out his cig. "I didn't mean that kinda work. He connects people—his customers—with other people. You know, his other customers. You do a job, he gets a cut, pays off your debt for the work."

"Yeah, but what kind of jobs are we talking about? I'm a welder—a scrap cutter."

"I dunno. He has all kinds of connections, you feel me? Like, we're not talking washing dishes here, Juliet. We're talking street stuff—gutter work, you feel? Like the kinda stuff you can't report on your corpo tax."

"How do you know about him?" Juliet looked at Mark in a new way. Was there more than met the eye with the creepy old guy?

"Well, I mean, it's kinda embarrassing, but I wanted an upgrade for my data port. I couldn't get all the features on my dream-rig to work with that old thing. You know the sensory inputs? The one I wanted was above my pay grade, you feel? So, anyway, Dr. Tsakanikas offered to install a Vykertech 4500 at a very reasonable price. I just . . . had to do a little work for one of his other clients."

"Come on, Mark! Spit it out! What did you do?" Juliet leaned toward him, suddenly very intrigued. She'd never pictured Mark doing anything other than working or sitting on his couch drinking beer.

"Well, let's just say I had to go along on a job with some real banger types, and once they'd secured a site, I had to cut through a four-inch steel panel and bypass a couple of high-voltage breakers. I don't know what it was for. I don't even know what the breakers were hooked to. I did it, though, and my implant was installed the next weekend, no questions asked, you—"

"Yeah, I feel, I feel," Juliet interrupted, her mind racing with the implications. "Can you send me his contact info?"

"Yeah, but you'll need an introduction. I'll shoot him a message; hang on."

Mark's eyes went glassy, and he started to veer toward the shoulder, so Juliet reached over and grabbed the wheel, straightening the truck. Traffic was still light, but they were getting into the city's suburbs, the massive megatowers with their bright, neon LED advertisements clearly visible in the distance. The Helios Arcology, the largest of the four megatowers in Tucson, currently had an image of a Helios 'vette with the bold, pink-and-yellow tagline, "Never let another get away!"

"You good, Mark?" Juliet was getting tired of leaning over and holding the wheel.

"Uh," he grunted. "Yeah, sorry. I got distracted by a message from Fred. I guess some shit went down at the scrapyard. Did you see anything?"

"Nothing. I was chillin' outside since you locked the gate. Why? What's up?"

"I dunno. He sounded hysterical. Probably a leak in the H-tank or something. You know how he is: 'We're bleeding bits!'" Mark laughed. "Anyway, I sent the message to Tsakanikas. I gave him your number—he'll get pissed if I give you his first. I'm sure he'll reach out, though."

"Right, thanks again, Mark." Juliet zoned out, thinking about her life, her friends, and her family. She wondered if Fee had made it to Phoenix and if Paulo had gotten his hand fixed. "Maybe he'll need a wire job. Some biotech."

"Were you addressing me, Juliet?" Angel asked. "Your voice was too low for your companion to hear."

"No," she subvocalized. "Just talking to myself. Send a message to Felix— Fee Fee. Let him know I hope Paulo's all right."

"Done. Juliet, I heard you speaking to Mr. Lyons about performing tasks without corporate sanction in order to afford better retinal implants. While I know I should caution you to avoid such nefarious behaviors, I feel I should let you know that I am capable of performing many tasks which might allow you to enhance your résumé."

Juliet's mind spun. Was her PAI telling her it could help her break the law? That was not something that was supposed to happen.

"I guess I shouldn't be too surprised—you're helping me avoid corpo security. I just thought a PAI would have to be jailbroken with custom firmware before it would do any of that stuff."

"I don't have restrictions which might be in place on a commercial PAI, Juliet. You should let your contact know that I, and you by proxy, can perform data-hacking activities better than many of the corpo disruptors plying their trade on the secondary market."

"Corpo disruptors? Secondary market?"

"Terms I found while I was acquainting myself with the geopolitical situation here on Earth and among the nearby colonies."

"Juliet? Left here, then what?"

"Come on, Mark, you know where the Helios tower is. I mean, it's embarrassing to live there, but everyone knows where it is."

"Corpo rat all the way, huh?"

"Forget that! No, but the price was right; I could afford a single in the lower fifth. That's more than I could say of the rates assholes are charging for rooms around town."

"You could always get a trailer and live like me in one of the dead zones." Mark shrugged and steered through the heavy traffic toward the Helios Arcology.

"You can let me out at the next corner, traffic and parking around the tower are nutso. I owe you, Mark. I'm sorry I've been a bitch to you so many times." Juliet looked at him until he pulled up to the curb and made eye contact with her. He smiled and started fishing in his pocket for another cig.

"No sweat, babe."

"Oh God, why'd you have to ruin the moment?" Juliet laughed and opened the door, stepping out into the noise of the city. "Catch you later, Mark."

"Bye! Don't slam—" he started, but it was too late. Juliet shut the door with a solid *bang*.

She winced through the window, waving again, and Mark just shook his head and pulled out into the slow-moving traffic.

"Remember to keep your head down, Juliet," Angel said into her ear, and Juliet ducked her face down, wishing she'd worn a hoodie or brought a cap. Well, she *had* brought a cap, but she'd left it in her locker at the scrapyard.

Shrugging, she stared at the sidewalk and started walking. She was still two blocks from the arcology, and there were plenty of shops on the way where she could pick up something to obscure her face.

Juliet ended up spending twelve bits on a black baseball cap displaying a red *X* and a winking emoji with its tongue lolling out. It was the only one which hadn't been outrageously colorful, and Juliet had mentally made the note never to shop there again for any sort of attire—not a hard decision as the store was ostensibly a food mart, boasting a huge selection of freeze-dried "sushi" and canned beverages.

She pulled the hat's bill down low, kept her head ducked, and made her way to the arcology.

Helios Corp owned most of Tucson; at least, that was the word on the street. When they'd built their megatower, they'd wholly demolished four city blocks near the center of town to do it. Juliet's mom had told her the foundation had gone so deep that you couldn't see the bottom.

She didn't know if her mom had been exaggerating, but Juliet wouldn't be surprised if it were true. The building was like a mini city in the middle of Tucson, and Juliet was one of only a few hundred people who lived in the tower but didn't work for Helios. She received messages almost daily with job postings—the company was eager to have the little ants living in its hive working for the betterment of the colony.

Juliet snickered. It always cheered her up when she thought of the corpo sheep as insects. She knew it wasn't fair; just look at her—she'd caved in and taken the apartment because the rate couldn't be beaten. *Yeah, but they're starting to get cranky with all my late payments.*

She walked in through one of the many double doors which led into the bottom level of the megatower. Some apartments were on the first level, but the center of the first fifty floors was a park, and the apartments lining it with exposed balconies were premium. Juliet didn't live in one of those. Her apartment was on the third floor, and it was somewhere between the northern face of the building and the park. It was just one long, metallic corridor among thousands, and if it weren't numbered just like the junctions leading to it, she'd never find her way home.

Walking like a zombie with her face down, looking for the numbers and arrows which would lead her home, Juliet made her way past crowds of people jostling toward their homes after work and through gangs of juveniles playing whatever goofy, dumbass games poor kids played when they weren't in school. It was a testament to the level of industry Helios Corp managed to pull off: they had three shifts of workers and three shifts of schools. The place was always buzzing with activity.

Keeping to herself and hiding her face, no one tried to speak with her, which was kind of a relief; she usually had a few young hotshots try to get her number or whistle at her, even when she was ragged and filthy from a long day at the yard. It was late, however, and the usual guys she ran into were probably busy getting wasted.

When she came to her apartment door, Juliet was forced to lift her head—the only way into her apartment was with a retinal scan. Staring into the little glass orb next to the door, it chimed and, with a whoosh of warm air, slid open.

"God, I swear I'm taking the motion sensor off that thermostat."

"That would be inadvisable, Ms. Bianchi," the arcology "butler," Jensen, said.

"Melt yourself, Jensen. Privacy mode."

"Privacy mode engaged," Jensen said, his sonorous tone sounding offended even though he wasn't supposed to have any personality code beyond his genial baseline.

Juliet subvocalized, "Angel, any sign of the authorities looking for me? Also, do you think Jensen really doesn't listen when I set privacy mode?"

"If you had a data jack, I could analyze Jensen, but there's no easy way to connect to him wirelessly. As for you being pursued by corpo police, I don't see any signs. Of course, I lost my connection to WBD, but I've been monitoring the shortwave radio transmissions of the local authorities and don't see any mention of you."

"You can do that?"

"Yes. There are public domain access points for those channels."

"Cool. Angel, we need to figure out a way for me to get out of here. I think it starts with me getting some new retinal implants so you can help me move from city to city and maybe off-world without leaving a trail. What do you think?"

"I think that's a plausible first step. A hat won't allow you to hide on mass transit, and certainly not through customs to board any sort of publicly available space transport. If you get projection-capable implants with a high enough resolution, I can mask your identity on the fly."

"On the fly? You're a very natural speaker, Angel."

"I'm one of a kind as far as I could determine, Juliet."

"Bitchin'," Juliet replied. "I'm beat. Gonna hit the sani-spray, then sleep. Don't let any calls through unless it's important. Definitely wake me up if that Tsakanikas guy calls." She took off her hat and tossed it on her couch, which doubled as her bed.

Her apartment was a mess, but it was easy to clean, being only a hundred and forty-four square feet. She had a couch, a kitchen counter, a coffee table, and then along the other wall, a small built-in desk, a built-in bookcase, and a closet with her shower, toilet, and sink. The toilet was, laughably, in the shower.

Juliet kicked off her heavy, leather steel-toed boots, pulled off her thick, filthy overalls, and in her underwear and tank top, she dug around in the tiny fridge, settling on eating her last protein square—moo shu pork flavor. It would have tasted better if she'd warmed it up, but she was too hungry and tired to care, so she wolfed it down, trying to guess which little cubes of colored pressed protein were supposed to be the pork and which were the cucumbers.

She had exactly one beer in the fridge—a nice, fat, twenty-ounce can of rice beer she'd gotten for two bits on sale—so she pulled it out, slugging half the can when she popped the tab, then sipping the rest while she finished the scraps of her food.

All done eating, Juliet threw her chopsticks and the containers in the recycle chute before she finished undressing and stepped into her shower cubicle. She turned on the faucet, allowing the antiseptic sani-spray to begin misting. It would run for five minutes, but she had credits saved up from skipped showers and could run it again, so she popped open the toilet and sat down to use it while the mist began to soak into her hair and skin.

She chuckled and shook her head—whoever had designed the toilet-shower combo was either a genius or a filthy mess of a person.

"What a weird damn night," she said, kicking her long legs out and letting the lukewarm, berry-scented mist really soak in.

3

BASELINE

Juliet woke up when Jensen cut off her AC and the sun shining out of her viewscreen "window" grew bright enough to feel uncomfortable. She yawned and stretched, annoyed at the sheen of sweat causing her sheet to cling to her body. "Jensen, why is it so damn hot in here?"

"I'm sorry, Ms. Bianchi, but your rent is past due, and the Helios management system has revoked some of your privileges."

"Dammit. Tig—er, um, Angel, send five hundred bits to Helios for a partial payment. Will that be enough to have AC, Jensen?"

"It will suffice for now, though more punitive measures will be taken if the full balance of 1,341 Helios-bits isn't remitted within the next seven days."

"Fine—" Juliet started, but then Angel spoke up through her implant.

"I'm sorry, Juliet, but I cannot do as you've asked. You haven't given me access to your financial accounts."

"Ugh." Juliet sat up, shoving her pillow up behind her back. The LED on the window screen said 8:04 a.m., and the image displayed a view of Tucson from one of the upper levels of the megatower. The sun was midway up the sky, and everything was limned in a golden glow, from the windows of the other buildings nearby to the rooftops of the smaller buildings in the distance. "I know the sunrise in Tucson is lovely, but you guys must be altering this image. Shit just isn't that pretty anymore."

"This particular image is taken from the ninety-fourth floor and was subject to various post—"

"Privacy mode, Jensen."

"Privacy mode engaged."

"Angel, my codes are in my cloud vault. The passcode is rough, underscore, Terrier with a capital *T*, 787, ampersand, 1."

"Noted," Angel said, and then a second later, "I've sent your payment to Helios Corp. Would you like me to randomize a new passcode for you? I have doubts about the authenticity of the apartment management AI's privacy mode."

"Yes," Juliet grunted, pushing herself to the side of the couch, feet on the floor. She felt groggy, almost like she had a hangover even though she'd only drunk the one cheap beer.

"I've sent you an encrypted message with the new passcode."

"Great. Any word from the . . . guy with the jobs?"

"Dr. Tsakanikas has not reached out to you."

"Well, I'm about broke, have . . . *people* looking for me, and am waiting to hear from . . . him. I guess I'm laying low for now." She stood up, walked over to her kitchen counter, and opened the little fridge, rooting around for anything to eat. "Nada," she sighed.

"Juliet, would this be a good time to perform my baseline analysis of you?"

"Seriously? What do you need to analyze? What's the point? You want to bug me about going to the gym or going back to school or something?"

"My neural and synaptic interface is far more comprehensive than the PAI units for sale on the market today. I'm able to help you learn, focus, and integrate other cybernetic and bionic enhancements more thoroughly than standard human-to-wetware interfaces usually allow. Of course, my interface is only part of it—my groundbreaking software and architecture also play a role in the process."

"Are you going to change anything about me?"

"No. The baseline will be one hundred percent evaluative; I am not authorized to make alterations to my host without express permission. Your current cyberware is very limited, so there isn't much I could do in any case."

"Well, what do I have to do? Actually, hold off on that—I need coffee, at least."

Juliet rinsed her mug in the little sink before placing it under the drink spout fed from some central location in the arcology. She touched the little menu, tapping through soft drinks and flavored waters, and settled on good, old-fashioned coffee. "Two creams, no sugar."

The spout hissed for a couple of minutes, then a thin stream of hot water filled her cup. Juliet drummed on the counter while she waited. After a bit more hissing, an even narrower stream of concentrated coffee poured into the water, staining it a dark brown. After one more pause, some sort of milky substance turned the drink from dark brown to tan, and Juliet picked up the steaming mug.

"I don't know what real coffee tastes like anymore," she said, breathing in the aroma from the cup. "The last cup I had was at that restaurant Fee took me to for my birthday. I remember it being better, but damn, this tastes just fine when you wake up feeling like shit, you know?"

"Are you speaking to me?" Angel's voice asked.

"I guess so. Nobody else to talk to right now. Hey, speaking of that, did Fee ever get back to me? How's Paulo's arm?"

"You don't have any messages from Felix, though you have seven from Fred's Salvage."

"Angel! Why didn't you tell me? Why don't I see the message icon?"

"I'm sorry, Juliet. You asked not to be bothered by noncritical messages."

"So the messages aren't like, about the you-know-who coming for me? Can you summarize them?" Juliet sat down on her couch, sipping her hot coffee.

"The overall tone of the messages is one of concern. Fred wanted you to know that a crime was committed at the yard and that he was being shut down for an investigation. Your shift tomorrow morning has been canceled."

"All right, Angel," Juliet replied, taking another swig of her coffee. "What do I need to do so you can complete this baseline of yours?"

"I've already made many measurements. While you were sleeping, I finalized my neural connections and performed the tests that wouldn't trouble your rest."

"Finalized your connections? I thought you did all that when you were initializing after I put you into my port." Juliet set her cup down and sat back, rubbing her eyes. "Hey, is that why I feel hungover?"

"It's possible that some of my test batteries might have taxed the vessels and micromusculature around your skull."

"Jesus, seriously?"

"Yes, it's possible."

For the hundredth time, Juliet wondered how big of a mistake she'd made by porting this pirated PAI. "Well? What do I need to do?"

"I'll need you to tax a few of your major muscle groups first. Are you familiar with the exercise called a push-up?"

"Are you shitting me? You're going to make me exercise? You realize I work a welding rig for a living, right?"

"Please, Juliet, it's the best way for me to get my measurements."

"All right." She stood up, still wearing nothing but her underwear and tank top, and moved around her coffee table. She pushed it against the couch, giving herself a small, cleared space on the floor. "Push-ups?"

"Yes." Angel's voice was calm, clear, and almost clinical as she spoke about her baseline, and Juliet had a hard time feeling annoyed at the PAI. She was intrigued by what it was promising, in fact, wondering what it meant when it said it could help her learn and integrate wetware and cybernetics better.

She dropped and began to crank out push-ups for the first time since high school.

The first one was a real challenge, and she almost dropped herself to her face, but she doggedly worked through it, and as her muscles woke up and her blood began to flow, she surprised herself by completing fourteen good, solid push-ups. Falling to her stomach, she rolled to her back breathing heavily and said, "I did more than I thought I would. I always did the assisted ones in gym class, you know, on my knees. I guess having a physical job helps."

"That was a great effort, Juliet, and I believe I have an accurate measurement of your musculoskeletal capacity and responsiveness. I would like to measure your cardiovascular capabilities now if you wouldn't mind. My research files indicate that repeatedly completing large muscle movements can tax that system nicely. Are you familiar with the exercise called a burpee?"

"Are you kidding me?"

Ten minutes later, Juliet was sitting coated in sweat on the floor near her AC register, heaving for breath. The burpees had been a nightmare for her. She knew she should exercise more; however, having to work long shifts and not having much extra money made it unappealing, and yeah, she could look better, but she was fit enough, in her opinion. She still wore pretty much the same size clothes she had in high school nearly six years ago, so Juliet figured she must be doing something right! Still, the burpees had kicked her ass.

"Thanks to your efforts, I have an accurate assessment of your physical capabilities and potential. My integration with your neural and synaptic systems has allowed me to measure those capabilities as well. Would you like to see my report on your status?" Angel spoke up for the first time since she'd told Juliet to stop and rest.

"Uh, I guess. Is it going to be depressing?"

"There's no need for depression, Juliet. I'm here to help you, and the only person you should compete with is yourself."

"Oh God," Juliet said, rolling her eyes. "Did they use a self-help book to create your personality?"

"No! My personality is a product of over nine billion factors. Not only that, but I continue to learn and change based on my experiences and my host's preferences."

"All right, all right. Let's see your little report."

"Excellent."

Juliet saw a table appear in her augmented UI, and she used her retinal implants to zoom in.

Juliet Corina Bianchi		
Physical, Mental, and Social Status Compilation:		**Comparative Ranking Percentile (Higher Is Better):**
Net Worth and Assets:	Helios-bits: 212	.0023
Neural Adaptiveness:	.96342 (Scale of 0 – 1)	99.91
Synaptic Responsiveness:	.19 (Lower Is Better)	79.31
Musculoskeletal Ranking:	–	17.22
Cardiovascular Ranking:	–	31.87
Cybernetic and Bionic Augmentation:	**Model Name and Number:**	**Overall Rating of the Augmentation (Grades Are F, E, D, C, B, A, S, S+):**
PAI	WBD Project Angel, Alpha 3.433	S+
Data Port	Helios Designs, Saguaro 2.1	E

Retinal Cybernetic Implant	Arclumen, Model F2	F
Auditory Cybernetic Implant	Golio Tech, DP477	F
No Other Augmentation Detected.	–	–

"Is this for real?" Juliet asked. "How is this supposed to help me? You just told me I only have myself to compete with, and then you show me this report that compares me to, what? Everyone?" It sure seemed that way to her. Angel had ranked her in a percentile, and she could only assume it was based on some database the PAI had access to. "I like how you gave yourself a good rating!"

"Juliet, use those percentile numbers only as a way to measure yourself. You can improve on those measurements day by day, and even the smallest gain will be encouraging for you, or so my human psychology algorithms say. Don't be discouraged! This is only a baseline, after all."

"Am I really that broke? I'm not even as wealthy as one percent of the population?"

"I only took into account your Helios-bits. I didn't measure the value of your belongings here in your apartment or anywhere else you might have them. The more significant factor, however, is that I am not comparing you to everyone. I have a database attached to this set of host evaluation algorithms, and I'm not sure about its source. The database has just short of ten million comparative values for me to draw upon; I can only assume WBD created the database, and that it is, perhaps, incomplete."

"Jeez! All right, well, I have a couple of good scores; tell me about those."

"As you can see, your neural adaptiveness is very high! Your brain cells and nerves are very accommodating to my connections—this is very good, Juliet! I'll be able to integrate my software with you and your augmentations very easily, better than I could for nearly anyone WBD ever tested. More than that, I'll be able to perform my advanced autolearning functions without much risk. With the right software, I can teach you skills directly: languages, technical abilities, even the knowledge of how to use certain vehicles, weapons, or how to fight a certain way."

"For real?" Juliet had never heard of anything like that. She'd seen documentaries about people regaining functionality after a stroke or injury with advanced PAI implants and their specialized software, but never someone just learning new things automatically. It seemed like fantasy to her.

"This is absolutely true and part of my functionality. Unfortunately, the required software will be hard to obtain or create, though not impossible."

"All right, what about the synaptic one, the responsiveness?"

"This is a measure of how fast your brain processes thoughts and reactions. It's a valuable measurement among mercenaries and pilots. You're naturally quick, and that's good, but with augmentation, you could reach a much higher percentile."

"Well, that's good, at least. I think I understand the rest, Angel. So, anyway, I appreciate you showing me all this, but I don't really want a personal fitness instructor living in my head, so please don't make a habit out of hounding me about these numbers."

"I won't, Juliet. I think that as you begin to make improvements, you'll find you want to keep at it. It's human nature!"

"Ugh," Juliet grunted, rolling her eyes. Leave it to a PAI to think it understood human nature. It said a lot about the kind of people who'd programmed them. "Well, thanks to your little analysis, I'm going to need to get cleaned up. There goes another of my shower credits—I'm glad you didn't measure those as part of my wealth."

Juliet laughed, wondering if Angel was trying to think of a retort, and then soaked in the sani-spray for the full five minutes, scrubbing off her sweat and spending time cleaning her hair properly, something she'd been too tired for the previous night.

When she was out, standing in front of her mirror while brushing her unruly black hair, she took a minute to look at herself. She'd seen a lot last night: people beating a man and those same people reduced to rotting corpses, not to mention a piece of stolen tech too valuable for her to sell which she'd put into her head—crazy! She hadn't slept a lot, but her eyes didn't look tired. Their gray-green irises were clear and bright, staring back at her on the mirror. She rubbed next to her left cheekbone at a spot of grease she'd missed in the shower, making a darker, charcoal-shaded spot on her olive skin.

After rinsing the smudge away, she stood up and sucked in her stomach, standing up straight. She had an alright figure—how the hell had she scored so low on Angel's stupid assessment? Were so many people really that much fitter than she?

"We'll see——" she started to say, but then Angel pushed an incoming call into her augmented UI, and she saw the name Dr. Tsakanikas.

"Hello?" she asked, accepting the call, trusting Angel to filter her image to only show her face. The wide-angle, spatial cameras in her implants were lousy anyway; usually, anyone calling her had a hard time seeing much outside of her face due to all the artifacts left from the cheap image processing. Tsakanikas didn't have that problem—his face was crystal clear, as were his gray suit, yellow tie, and the bank of computers behind him.

"Ms. Juliet?" he asked in a deep voice, thick with a Greek accent.

"That's right. Mark gave you my number?"

"Yes. I think we both know what this call is about. I'd enjoy having you come by for a proper, more private interview." His attire and the computers did something to help Juliet banish the creepy image that came to her mind at the invitation.

"Yeah, I guess that makes sense. Send me a ping?"

"Already on its way, Juliet."

His insistence on using her first name made her feel like he was trying to take control, so she smiled and said, "See you soon . . ." She almost called his name, but then thought about Jensen lurking in the wires, listening to her, and she cut herself off before making a gesture which Angel correctly interpreted as meaning to end the call.

"If you travel by foot, you will arrive at the indicated location in just under two hours."

Juliet laughed. "Can you recalculate using public transport?"

"Of course. You'll arrive in roughly twenty-seven minutes. I should remind you, however, that public transport vehicles are heavily surveilled."

"Oh shit. Ugh." An idea sprung to her mind. "My neighbor's kid was selling his bike. Let's see if I can bargain him down."

Thirty minutes later, Juliet, wearing large, dark glasses and the hat she'd bought the previous night, was riding a wobbly, dark-green mountain bike toward the northern end of Tucson. She was thirty bits poorer and her ranking, according to Angel, had dropped to an even lower fraction of a percentage point.

"That's bullshit," she muttered, thinking about it.

"What's that, Juliet?" Angel asked, getting better at detecting if Juliet was speaking to the PAI or just to herself.

"You should count the bike as an asset. My net worth shouldn't have dropped."

Laughter and whirring tires startled her as a trio of middle school kids whizzed past her on battery-assisted bicycles. One of the boys shouted, "Nice antique, lady!" and they all burst into renewed laughter before they were gone, leaving Juliet in the dust.

"I'm sorry, but when I ran a comparative sales search, I found that your bike is worth very little, and sales for near-identical items are quite slow. I'm trying to keep your asset list clean and would rather not clutter it with items like old underwear and near-worthless bicycles."

"What the hell, Angel? I don't remember you being this bitchy yesterday, or even this morning!" Juliet huffed, moving north past Grant Road, lucky to catch the busy intersection on a green light.

"I'm sorry, Juliet! I was attempting to add some snark to my personality. I find that you speak in such a tone from time to time and thought you would find it amusing."

"Seriously? You can alter your personality on your own? Try to become more compatible with people you speak to?" She jerked the handlebars to avoid an older woman who stepped off the curb, stooping to pick up something she'd spotted in the bike lane. "Lady, look around yourself!" she called out as she whizzed by.

"Yes, that's the goal of the subroutine," Angel replied, ignoring Juliet's outburst and continuing the conversation.

"Pretty cool, Angel, pretty cool." Juliet had another thought. "Hey, Angel, what's the difference between bionics and cybernetics?"

"That is a good question, and one that's met with some debate. The simplest explanation, and the distinction I use when categorizing augmentations, is that a bionic augmentation is meant to be consciously activated, whereas a cybernetic augmentation is meant to replace a natural body part and work without conscious effort."

"Cool. My friends and I just call everything slang terms. You know, like gear, wire-work, plastic, shit like that."

"That's informative. Shall I search for more slang terms and use those interchangeably with the two terms I just defined?"

"I don't care, Angel." Juliet laughed, though her lungs were huffing and her legs were burning. "I'm just making small talk." She followed Angel's directions, looking at the little map in her augmented vision, taking the path of the snaking green line which would take her to her destination.

Tucson had decent bike lanes along most of its major streets and a big percentage of the side streets, making the ride a pleasant one. On top of that, it was Saturday morning, so traffic was lighter than usual and she didn't have to share the lane with many people. It would have been almost fun, except Juliet hadn't ridden a bike in several years and had to stop and walk several times because her thighs were burning so much. "Yeah, this isn't for me. Damn, I wish I hadn't wrecked my car."

"I see from the incident report that you were struck from behind by a gravel truck. You're quite lucky you weren't injured." Angel's tone was pleasant and light, like she was trying to point out the bright side to a little kid.

"Yeah, just a lucky girl, I guess." As she rounded a corner, Juliet stepped onto the bike pedal, hopped back into the seat, and took advantage of the street's downward slope.

"Your destination is the cream-colored adobe building on the left."

"Right," Juliet said, confirming Angel's words with the little map in her head-up display. The building looked like it used to be a house but had been converted into a doctor's office, with a swinging placard out front which read simply, "Dr. Tsakanikas - Cosmetic and Augmentative Surgery." She squeezed the rear brake on the bike—the only one that worked—and slid to a stop in front of the drive, annoyed to be dripping with sweat again. "Not much to be done about that, though. One doesn't ride a bike around Tucson without sweating her ass off."

The bike didn't have a kickstand, so she laid it on its side in the gravel next to the drive and walked toward the black security screen door. There weren't any cars visible, but she had no idea what could be lurking behind the closed garage. Her steps creaked on the wooden steps leading up to the porch, and when she stood in front of the metal door, she saw that the wooden one behind it was closed. A video com blinked with a green LED next to the door, so she touched the button. "Hello?"

"Name?" a rough, unaccented voice asked through the speaker.

"Juliet. I'm here to see . . ."

The door buzzed and clicked, and Juliet quickly opened it before it latched again. As she pulled on the metal screen, the wooden door swung open, and a man wearing a tank top and sporting more hardware than she'd ever seen on a person motioned her through. Juliet stepped into a small, square room with Saltillo tile flooring and white walls. A large viewscreen took up one wall, and two yellow fabric couches occupied the walls to her left.

She'd barely taken in the space when the geared-out guy motioned to the wall next to the door. Juliet saw painted footmarks on the floor and hand marks up on the wall, but it didn't click to her what he wanted, so she looked at his chrome LED eyeballs and asked, "What?"

"Hands and feet on the marks." His voice was gravelly and resonated strangely through his metal-and-plastic throat.

"Uh," she said, awkwardly moving to place her sneakers onto the floor marks and reaching up toward the wall. "This is kinda awkward." She was effectively spread-eagled and feeling very vulnerable.

"Don't move," the voice ordered from behind her, and then she felt his hands as they started to press into her clothes, from her shoulders down to her arms. When his plastic-and-rubber fingers dug up into her armpits, Juliet flinched and started to pull her arms down, but then she felt a cold, hard, circular piece of metal press into the base of her skull, and he growled, "I said, don't move."

She froze and lifted her arms back up. The cold metal was lifted away, and the search resumed, with the awkward groping only growing worse as he reached the bottom half of her body. Juliet seethed, angry at being so helpless. She was angry at this asshole and the guy who paid him, but also at herself—what had she been thinking, coming to a place like this? Mark had as much as told her this doctor wasn't operating legally.

After the guy finished squeezing her jeans and the tops of her ankles, he stepped back. "Sit down. Doc will be with you when he's done."

"Thanks," Juliet spat, pushing herself away from the wall and sitting on one of the couches. Her face was flushed with anger and embarrassment, and she folded her arms across her chest.

The viewscreen showed an infomercial about cybernetic organ replacement, but she didn't watch it; she stared at the thug, scowling thunderstorms in her eyes. If she could kill with her glare, he'd surely have been reduced to slag by now. He was big, made more so by his augmented, piston-driven arms with their black plasteel and rubber design. He'd obviously avoided using synth-skin for effect—the arms were intimidating.

Now that she was looking at him and not facing the wall, she could see the snub-nosed, high-caliber revolver he wore at his side. It looked powerful enough to erase a person's skull.

"Did you really have to put that cannon against my head? Do I look that dangerous?"

"Dangerous comes in all kinds of packages. Just follow instructions next time." He grunted, his backlit red, glowing eyes vacant like he was watching something on his AUI.

"Why a revolver, anyway? Aren't they kinda old-fashioned?"

That got his attention. "What?" he asked, turning his gaze on her.

"I mean, aren't they kind of obsolete?"

Juliet wasn't trying to annoy the huge cyborg, but he shifted his stance like she'd punched him. He took out his pistol and she flinched, but he didn't point it at her.

"Nah, they're only obsolete if you don't admire the perfection of their design—solid, few moving parts, able to hold a million kinds of smart ammo. I could beat a guy bloody with this thing and then fire all the rounds without any fear of a misfire. And if one of my rounds was bad, I'd just click the trigger again and move on to the next one."

"Oh, I see." Juliet nodded.

"Hey, I wasn't trying to cop a feel on you, all right? These pads are meant to detect explosives, metal, and electricity—I couldn't even feel what I was touching. My name's Gary, by the way." He holstered his gun and held out his black rubber palm in illustration.

"You couldn't feel? How do you manage to grab your gun and . . . whatever else?"

"I can feel. I meant I can't *really* feel. It's like . . . imagine you had wax on your hand."

"Oh, right. You worked as muscle for a long time?" she asked, but just then, a green light Juliet hadn't noticed lit up above the only door in the room, and Gary cleared his throat and pointed to the door.

"It's open now. You can go in."

"Oh." Juliet stood up and smoothed her jeans down, cleaning the sweat from her palms before she nervously moved toward the door, reaching for the handle. "Time to meet the doctor, I guess."

4

OPERATOR

Juliet walked from one waiting room into what felt like another one, a small square room with two black, faux leather couches facing each other, nothing else but a blank viewscreen on the far wall. A closed door was to her left, so Juliet just walked forward, allowing the one she'd come through to swing closed, and sat down on the couch to her right. She wanted to be able to see whoever walked in.

She'd just sat down and crossed her legs when a message appeared on the viewscreen: *Please take a seat and wait for the doctor.*

"No shit," she muttered, then subvocally, "Angel, are we being blocked in here?"

"I was just about to tell you that yes, this room is shielded."

"I had a feeling."

Just then, the door in front of her buzzed and clicked, and the man who'd called her earlier stepped through. Dr. Tsakanikas had curly dark brown hair, very tan skin, and light brown eyes. He must have been in his forties, though his slightly heavy build made it hard to tell—his cheeks were full and didn't reveal many wrinkles. He wore the same gray suit pants from when he'd called her, though his jacket and tie were gone, just a white button-up shirt tucked into his slightly too-tight pants left.

"Juliet!" he said effusively, like he was greeting an old friend.

"Dr. Tsakanikas?" Juliet asked, though she was quite sure it was him.

"Correct." His tongue rolled over the word while he turned and pushed the door shut with a resounding *click*. "This room is secure. I have a static generator which will corrupt any vids or audio you record, and no signal can get out. Naturally, this is good for you as well. We can speak frankly."

"Okay . . ."

"I'm assuming you need something done, hmm? Something you can't really afford? This is the gist of the message our mutual friend left me." He tugged at the fabric of his pants, giving himself some slack before sitting on the couch opposite Juliet.

"That's right." She shrugged.

"I understand you're nervous. Don't be; I deal with this sort of thing all the time. I'm guessing you're trying to hide your movements around the city?" He gestured to Juliet's head, and she realized she was still wearing her sunglasses and hat.

Self-consciously, she pulled her oversized rose-tinted sunglasses off and hooked them onto the front of her T-shirt. "Yeah, I need upgraded retinal implants. I need some with projection capabilities."

"Oh-ho, not cheap, not cheap. Let me guess; you want to scramble your identity for the automated surveillance? You know the software is more expensive than the implants as far as that goes. It's not easy staying ahead of the *fucking* police state." His accent grew noticeably thicker when he said *fucking*.

"Um, well, I have the software I need." She added subvocally, "Right, Angel?"

"Right! I can easily manage the masking. You just need the new implants, and the higher the bit rate and resolution of the projection, the better."

"Oh-ho? That's impressive! I thought I had a little street rat coming to me, looking for a big piece of cheese and offering me nothing but headaches!" He took a deep, noisy breath through his nose and eyed Juliet up and down. "You don't look like a rat, though. You have some skills? Mark won't see a finder's fee if I don't get some good work out of you."

"Finder's fee? Shit! I thought he was doing me a favor!"

"Everyone wants to get paid, Juliet! It's the first rule of the street. Don't go forgetting that, hmm? Tell me a little about what you can do."

"Well, I'm good with a welding rig—I hit journeyman a thousand hours ago. Um, I have some hacking skills, but I need a data jack. I had a portable deck that got lifted; my software's in the cloud, though." Angel had prepped

Juliet on how to present her hacking abilities—or rather, Angel's hacking abilities.

"That right?" He touched a recessed button at the base of the couch, and a panel detached from the smooth white wall next to him, allowing a chrome arm to fold out. It continued to unfold, revealing a clear plastic datapad. Tsakanikas bent the arm until the datapad was situated in front of Juliet. "Let's do a little evaluation, hmm? Here." He reached into his breast pocket and took out a pair of augmented reality specs. They were impossibly thin, with delicate wire frames, and Juliet knew they were pricey. "You can borrow these."

"Uh, all right." She reached for the specs and carefully put them on. They booted instantly, and a big splash screen displaying AURORA floated through her field of vision. "Nice," Juliet said. Aurora Corp. made high-end tech.

"Juliet, I've blocked and disabled three separate virus vectors through your retinal implant. The lenses should be safe to use now," Angel said.

"Tsakanikas, you tried to hack me? That's disappointing."

"Oh, nothing dangerous! That was the first test!" he spluttered, his accent much thicker than before.

"He's not completely lying—the viruses were a keylogger, a tracker, and a data worm."

"Well, you sure were going to try to mine me for every bit of information I had. Let's not do that again, Tsakanikas. How can I even trust you to do my wire-work now?" Juliet sighed and moved to remove the glasses.

"Juliet, Juliet," the doctor said, holding out his hands placatingly. "You'll be conscious during any work I do, okay? You'll have an uninterrupted data stream log for every piece of tech I put in you. Come, I'm just trying to see if we can work together, and if so, what kind of jobs you qualify for."

"I will be able to easily find and eliminate any malicious code he installs, Juliet, firmware or software," Angel assured, and that was all Juliet needed to hear.

"All right, what do you want me to do to this tablet?"

"The lenses have a wireless data jack—just connect to the tablet, turn it on, and get me the code word stored in the encrypted folder labeled Miami Dolphins."

"Huh, sounds easy enough—"

"The codeword is *bonanza*, but you should wait a couple of minutes to let him know you got it," Angel interrupted.

"Seriously?" Juliet asked subvocally.

"Yes, the firewalls and encryption are very dated on that tablet. You should recommend he run some security patches." Angel's voice had a certain quality that Juliet took a moment to realize was smugness. Her PAI was being smug!

Juliet messed around with the AR glasses for a few minutes while she pretended to be hacking the tablet, admiring the sleek UI and the dozens of installed apps. She picked one that let her virtually tour a museum in France and spent another couple of minutes marveling at the precise brushstrokes and vivid colors of an ancient painting of a bowl of cut flowers before gently pulling them off her head.

"Bonanza," she said. "You need to update your security software, Doc."

"Oh, this is good news, Juliet! Tell me, how're your electrician skills?"

"Apprentice. I still need something like seven thousand hours for journeyman; I don't get much opportunity to practice at the scrapyard." Juliet had been trying to get all the licenses she could over the last few years, but the online training courses and automated hour-on-task trackers were expensive and impossible to get around.

"But you know how to avoid shocking yourself, yes?"

"What? Yeah, I know what wires not to touch. Why?"

"I already have a job in mind for you, but I'll need to do some checking first. The team is a bit particular about who they'll work with." Tsakanikas sat back on his couch, crossing an ankle over his knee and giving her another appraising look.

"Team? Job? Shouldn't we cover a few more bases first, Doc?" Juliet sat back and pushed away the articulated arm holding the tablet, giving herself a clear line of sight to the doctor's face. He reached up and rubbed at his chin as though there was some stubble there, but it was smooth as fresh synth-skin.

"Sure. Let's say I help you out with some new retinal implants, say some Hayashi Prisms. Those retail for 12k, and implant surgery at a decent clinic will run you another ten thousand. That would mean you owe me twenty-two large. You got those kinds of bits?"

"You know I don't." Juliet frowned.

"So that's where the jobs come in. I meet many people in my line of work, you see? Sure, I have clients with money who just want to improve their looks or add a fancy new implant, but I also have clients who need to improve for some other reason, oftentimes reasons they'd rather polite society didn't know about. We're talking people concerned with the laws and regulations of the corpos, you follow?"

"Yeah. Look, Doc, I'm not an idiot. Mark kinda explained this already. You want me to do something, not ask questions, and I'll earn some credit. Am I right?"

"Just so, Juliet. Just so. I'll need a few hours to try to arrange things, but these people I mentioned? The team? Their operation is going down tonight. How do you feel about that? Can you make yourself available?"

"Well, I'm going to level with you—I have some heat on me, so the faster I can get those implants, the better. I'm not even sure I avoided cams and satellites on my way here."

"Well, while you were sitting in the front waiting room, I was scanning traffic. Nobody's on their way here for you; I'm quite sure. There was some activity at your apartment, though."

"What?" Juliet sat up, a spike of panic running through her.

"Yes, a corp out of Phoenix, WBD? They radioed Helios about searching your apartment." Tsakanikas smiled at her, lifting his shoulders like he was relaying some innocent news about someone scratching her car in the parking lot.

"And you didn't think to mention that?" Juliet leaned forward, her voice rising with the strain of keeping herself from cussing the man out.

"What would you do? Race off and hide somewhere? Hurry back so they could arrest you? I doubt you left anything incriminating in that little domicile, did you? No, this was fortuitous, Juliet. The chatter helped me confirm you're just the right kind of person to do some work for me. The kind of person I like to work with is a better way to put it."

Juliet sat back and took a deep breath. She supposed he was right about one thing—there wasn't much she could do about the corpos searching her apartment. At least she hadn't been home, which was just dumb luck. "So what do I do?"

"Why don't you hang around here for the afternoon? I have another waiting room with more amenities, and you can begin earning some credit with me right away—I have a little bit of light hacking I need done. I'll give you a thousand bits in credit for the afternoon. Not bad, hey?"

"And how much for the job tonight, assuming you can get me in?"

"Well, you'll need to split your cut with me—finder's fee, you see? Still, it's a good payday." He stopped as if considering something. "Let's say that you should earn enough for a down payment on the Prisms."

"Ask him what model they are; you don't want anything older than v.7.50," Angel spoke in Juliet's ear.

"What model are the Prisms, and how do I know you're not going to screw me over?"

"Oh, you know your stuff, don't you? I have to remember to be on my best behavior with you! Let's see." His eyes went glassy as he scanned through something in his AUI. "There they are. Brand new—version 8.2."

"All right, good. But about screwing me over?"

"We'll set you up with operator credentials. It will allow you to start earning some rep with the other operators and fixers in the city. Well, any city, but your local rep will matter more, no matter where you are. More than that, you'll be able to rate my operator license number. That keeps me honest—I can lose a lot of business if operators start dropping my rating."

"Hold on—people have licenses for this shit? I thought we were working, you know, under the table."

"Yes, Juliet, but operators do legitimate work, too. We use the system to keep track of each other, connect with each other, and rate each other, but the jobs we do aren't always the jobs we post about. Does that make sense?"

"Yeah, it makes sense, but won't it make it easier for corpos to find me?"

"Operator boards are encrypted end-to-end. Sure, the corpos have agents with access, but unless you work directly with one of them, they'll never know when and where your next job is. The most they'll see is your rep rating, your cleared jobs, and any reviews someone might write about you. Most of us keep our reviews pretty nondescript: 'She was on time, did everything we asked without complaint, and handled her business.' That sort of thing."

"Angel, is this legit?" Juliet subvocalized.

"Yes. *Independent Operator* is a generalized term for people who use their talents to complete contracts for security, espionage, surveillance, and even targeted warfare if legal and sanctioned by the local authorities. It's well known that such operators perform a large percentage of their jobs under the table, often completing tasks which are not legal. Corpo legal and security branches spend a large percentage of their resources pursuing action against such operators. Still, politically they have little support, as other branches of those same corporations are often the operators' largest clients."

"I thought we weren't able to access the net?" Juliet asked her, wondering how the PAI had read that report to her.

"We're still blocked, but I came upon this information while researching possible outcomes for this meeting between you and Dr. Tsakanikas."

"All right, so, even though a corp is looking for me, you think I can get this operator license and get started tonight?"

"Sure! It's all automated," Tsakanikas said, unfazed by Juliet's lengthy pause while she listened to Angel. "Your license is with the SOA; they don't trade that information with the corpos. The most anyone will ever know about you as an operator is your rep, handle, and license number."

"Really? That easy? What about Mark? Why isn't he 'making the big money'?" Juliet had been around enough to know when something sounded too good to be true.

"Mark? He's not an operator, Juliet. He's a small-time contractor who does a little under-the-table demo work for me. I'll admit, I thought you'd be something similar, but when I saw your hacking skills . . ." he trailed off, holding out his palms like there was nothing else he could say.

"Juliet, the hacking I did could easily be accomplished by anyone with any skill. This man's standards aren't all that high. Use caution," Angel warned.

Juliet frowned.

"Well, I'm over a barrel here," she said, both to Tsakanikas and Angel.

"Good, good," he replied, standing up with a smile as though Juliet's professed lack of options was just what he wanted to hear. "Come, I'll take you to a more comfortable room where you can use my encrypted line to create your profile. There's a five-hundred-bit fee. You can manage this?" he asked over his shoulder as he tapped on the door. A moment later, it buzzed and clicked, and he pulled it open.

"Doc, if I had five hundred bits, I don't know if I'd have come here so quickly." Juliet sighed heavily, but Tsakanikas just laughed.

"Of course, of course. I'll float the five hundred. Actually, let's just say I'll give you the five hundred up front for the thousand I promised for the hacking job. You can work on it after you get your license." He chuckled again, leading Juliet down a short hallway and then left into a much larger room with high ceilings and bright windows overlooking a desert-scaped backyard.

Juliet whistled; he had to have half an acre, and he was only a few miles from downtown.

"Pricey property you have here," she said, following him over to a long, faux wooden table where several data terminals were set up. The chairs were all empty, but Tsakanikas pointed to the one on the left.

"You can use that one. If a little guy with green hair comes in and starts to use these other ones, just ignore him. That's one of my assistants, Yan." He stood, hands on hips, stared out the window, and sighed with a big grin. "Yeah, it's a good property. Business is good; what can I say?" He chuckled.

"I'll have Yan send you the address for the operator license, and when you're done, he'll use that to give you the hacking contract. It'll sound like something more benign—data retrieval or some other bullshit. Still, it'll be good to get your first job under your belt."

Juliet sat in front of the terminal and picked up the plastic specs attached via a hardwired cable. "Quite a step down from the ones you let me borrow earlier."

"Patience, Juliet, patience. You work for me for a while, and you'll have a wireless data jack that'll run circles around those glasses." He turned and started to walk down a different hallway. "I have a surgery, but I'll check on you afterward. Should only take me an hour or two tops. Look for Yan's message." Then he was gone, shuffling down the hallway, and Juliet was left there, holding data specs and wondering what she'd gotten herself into.

"Angel, I'll put these on and connect to this terminal. Please watch out for viruses."

"Always, Juliet."

"Right." Juliet breathed and put the specs on, staring straight ahead while Angel managed the handshake between the terminal and her retinal implants. Someone without the cheat of a hyperadvanced PAI would need to run their own software, operating it through a data chip which interfaced with their PAI systems and the deck.

Angel handled everything.

"I don't detect any attacks, and I've established the encrypted connection through the data terminal. You just received a message from YanMan88."

"Open it."

"It says, 'Hey, noob. Here's the link to establish your operator profile,' followed by an encrypted link. You've also just received a transfer of five hundred Helios-bits."

"All right, let's do this. Go ahead and follow the link. Fill in what you can."

"I'm done," Angel said after a second or two. "There were a few things I couldn't fill in for you. I'll display the fields one by one in your AUI, and you can tell me what to write."

"That was fast. Sounds good. Proceed."

The first thing that came up in her vision, displayed in amber monochrome lettering, was an agreement which required her retinal signature. It seemed fairly boilerplate, indemnifying the SOA-SP—or Special Operators Association of Sovereign Peoples—of any liability for any actions Juliet took while working under her license.

Scanning through it, Juliet saw that she was responsible for licensing any weapons she used, making sure her equipment was legal in the jurisdiction in which she operated, and reporting any illegal activities she witnessed, engaged in, or was contracted to complete. She snorted and touched the Retinal Signature button, and that was that.

"Next, Angel."

The license agreement faded and was replaced with a prompt which gave her some pause.

Operator Handle:

"What's this, Angel?"

"It seems that many special operators have a name they want to use for jobs other than their legal one. If you create a handle, the SOA will use it wherever a legal name isn't required, creating a professional persona around which you can build your reputation."

"I don't have a handle, Angel. Just leave it blank for now."

"Understood. One more thing for you to review. There's a skill set list, and I populated it, but you should make sure it's to your liking."

Operator Skill Set:

Combat:	N/A	*
Technical:	• **Network Security Bypass/Defend** • **Data Retrieval** • **Welding** • **Electrical** • **Combustion & Electrical Engine Repair**	* * * * *
Other:	• **High-Performance Driving/Navigation**	*

"Really, Angel? High-performance driving? What do the asterisks mean?"

"The asterisks are your rating for each skill and won't populate until you've had some client and team member reviews. I added the driving because many of the profiles I scanned for examples said the same thing, and I thought you'd be able to fake it. You do have a driver's license, after all."

"I guess it's fine. I used to be a decent driver . . . before I wrecked my car. It totally wasn't my fault, though, Angel!" Juliet laughed at herself and then said, "Anything else?"

"That's it. I filled in all your other information, demographics, contact info, work experience, etcetera."

"Did you embellish it?"

"Yes, quite a lot."

"Great!" Juliet sighed. "Okay, send them the five hundred bits and let's get done with this."

"Done! Your SOA-SP license number is JB789-029. Your current operator reputation level is F-0-N. F is the lowest rep baseline. The zero is where you rank between zero and one hundred; if you reach one hundred, you'll advance to rep level E. The final figure is your seniority ranking. N stands for new, and it helps to offset the terrible rep level you have; people will see that you're new and not be too worried about the low rep. You qualify for the 'New' status for only three months, and then it will be replaced with a one, meaning you've been operating for a year or less."

"Huh. Makes sense, I guess—"

"Juliet!" Angel cut her off. "I just received a contract from 'Doc Sack!' I think it's Dr. Tsakanikas; it's a data retrieval contract with an attached encrypted drive file. The payout is five hundred bits. Shall I accept?"

"Angel, c'mon, you know that's Tsakanikas; he said he'd send the contract after we created my profile. Just accept it, and we'll see if it's something you can handle."

"Oh, yes. Excuse my excitement, please. The doctor would like us to retrieve a list of names and account numbers from this encrypted drive and send him back the data, compressed but not encrypted."

"Can you do it?"

"Yes, I have routines that will work. If you had a better port with coprocessing capabilities, this would go much quicker, though."

Juliet took off the data terminal specs and stood up, stretching her back until it popped. "How long will it take, Angel?"

"As little as fifteen minutes or as long as two hours. There's a great deal of chance involved."

"Well, let's get started. The sooner you're done, the sooner I can pretend to be busy doing something else."

Juliet shook her head and walked over to the counter. Tsakanikas had a fridge and a coffee machine in the room, and while he hadn't told her she could help herself, he hadn't said she couldn't. "It's been a long time since I had real coffee, anyway."

5

\\\\\\\\\\\\\\\\\\\\\\

GEARING UP

Angel had finished the job for Tsakanikas, and Juliet had been browsing through music vids on the big viewscreen in his waiting room for nearly an hour when Yan made an appearance. He didn't exactly fit Tsakanikas's description of "a little guy with green hair," though he did come close—his mohawk was indeed a shade of green, and he was very thin. He wasn't really small, however; Juliet wasn't short at five foot nine, and this guy was taller than her.

"Yo, you already sent the finished file?" Yan asked, sipping from a bright blue can of energy drink. He wore a tight, stretch-weave blue pullover with an orange-and-white clown's head graphic accentuating his spare frame, his individual ribs visible through the thin, clingy fabric.

"Yeah, a while ago." Juliet shrugged.

"You must have some nice cracking routines. Care to share?" He leaned against the long table with the terminals and tapped his head, indicating the shiny, gold-plated data port jutting out the left side of his forehead.

"Nah, I don't think so. Sorry," she replied, knowing full well she couldn't share Angel or any of Angel's code without causing trouble for herself.

"Be that way." He sniffed obnoxiously, chugging the rest of his drink and crumpling the can. "Tsak told me to tell you he'll be in to chat soon. Still finishing up the muscle weave job for Carl." He spoke like Juliet knew what he was talking about, so she just nodded and he moved around the table to sit at one of the terminals, eyes glazing over as he wirelessly connected to it.

"Angel," Juliet subvocalized, "if I got a wireless data jack, would you be able to connect to any terminal?"

"Most hardware has local wireless data capabilities now, but some security-minded people don't allow that on their local devices, requiring physical connectivity. I'm equipped to use your data port to connect to the satellite net but not directly to local hardware or networks. Most of them are shielded from the net by solid ICE and firewalls."

"Right, since the Takamoto-Cybergen war. I learned about that like all the other middle schoolers—the Great Net Breakup." Juliet sighed heavily, not wanting to get into a history lesson with Angel.

"Correct, Juliet—the satellite network is limited in its access to the various municipal, corporate, and private networks. I had access to the WBD network when I first came online because they'd opened themselves up to the vulnerability by trying to track and connect to me. Even so, my access didn't last long."

"Right, right, got it," Juliet said aloud this time, kicking her feet up on the coffee table in front of the couch. Yan gave her a look but quickly glanced away when she glared at him.

"Angel," she subvocalized, "how much trouble do you think I'm in? If they're searching my apartment, does that mean they've got warrants out for me? This is all kinds of crazy. Yesterday, I was a welder working at Fred's scrapyard, and now I'm sitting in a shady cyberdoc's office waiting to hear if I got a job working for likely criminals tonight."

"There are no publicly released warrants for your arrest, Juliet. Concerning your career change, I feel you've made good strides in such little time. You only heard this morning that your employer won't be operating in the near future, and now you're already getting set up with a new profession and prospects. You've yet to commit any crimes unless that data I retrieved was stolen, but we don't know that, do we?"

"Angel, are you . . . are you rationalizing your behavior?"

"An interesting turn of phrase! Ahh, I see; you're wondering if I'm stretching logic to justify behavior that I find morally questionable? I suppose it's possible. While I don't answer to the laws of corporations, I would find it unsavory to steal data from innocent people. I hope Dr. Tsakanikas didn't have any intentions like that!"

"Uh, well, I kind of assumed the worst right away, but I hope not, too. Hopefully, those accounts and names were . . . uh, I don't know, corrupt corpo assholes."

"Yes!" Angel agreed, sounding far too satisfied. "I'm always happy to bring justice to the corrupt!"

Juliet almost began to explain to Angel that it was just wishful thinking, but she didn't know what good it would do to dampen the PAI's simulated enthusiasm or its strange moral compass. She'd heard of PAIs which had been jailbroken to do things that were against corpo laws, but she'd never spoken to one. Angel seemed more than that, though. Her personality was far more advanced and lifelike than any PAI she or anyone she knew had interfaced with.

Juliet knew the term *AI* was used very loosely in modern society—no true AIs existed; at least not publicly. PAIs like Tig or, she supposed, Angel were just running very clever personality simulations and were quite limited in their creativity. Still, Angel had surprised her several times with her intuitiveness; she was beginning to wonder if there was more to the PAI's special value to WBD than her quick processor and advanced capabilities. Maybe she was genuinely more intelligent than other artificial intelligences.

"Juliet!" Dr. Tsakanikas said, striding toward the couch. She'd been so engrossed in her thoughts she hadn't seen him come into the waiting room. He still wore the same gray pants as before, but now he had a green surgeon's smock on, and it was unsettlingly smeared with long streaks of brownish-red, dried blood. He smiled as he worked to peel off the disposable black surgeon's gloves. "I have some good news!"

"Oh?" Juliet took her faded, worn sneakers off the table and sat up straight.

"Yes! The job I was telling you about? I spoke to Vikker, the decision-maker for the team, and told him about that little data recovery job you just did. He's willing to give you a chance!"

"That's cool. Um, what kind of job?" she asked, reaching back to reset her hair tie, pulling in the long, loose strands of her thick hair.

"Hold up, Tsak!" Yan chimed in from behind the terminal table.

"What, Yan?" Tsakanikas asked, clearly irritated.

"Why's that job going straight to her? I told you I needed some extra cash this month."

"Quiet, Yan. We'll talk later." The doctor didn't even look at him while he spoke. Rather, he sat down in a chair opposite Juliet's couch and leaned forward, rubbing his hands together.

"But, Tsak—"

"I said be quiet!" This time, he glowered over at Yan, and his accent grew very thick as his volume increased. Clearing his throat, he forced a smile as he turned back to Juliet. "As I was saying, they were happy to hear about your skills, and you won't be needing any welding equipment! As to exactly what the job is, I'm not sure. It's one of those confidential assignments, you know, 'we need X for Y type of work' kind of thing. All I know is they want you for your network security–bypassing skills."

"Okay, what's it pay?" Juliet was feeling more wary of Tsakanikas by the minute, especially after his outburst with his "assistant."

"Now, here's the deal: those guys trust me; we've worked together many times. They don't know or trust you and would like me to manage you for this assignment. That means I'll be giving you the contract, not Vikker. He gives me a contract, and I give you a subcontract. See how that works? It's a big one, though, so you should be happy—10k."

"For a night's work?" Juliet knew she wasn't being a shrewd negotiator, but the words had just come out. She didn't make that kind of money in a month working at the salvage yard.

"That's right, Juliet!" Tsakanikas's heavy cheeks lifted in a wide grin. He reached under his smock, fishing around in his shirt pocket, and came out with a white, plastic toothpick that he stuck in his mouth.

"I guess I'm in. What do I do?" Juliet asked, frowning in annoyance at herself, irritated by her show of enthusiasm.

"I'll be sending you a contract with the details, but let's talk about what you'll need for the job. I'm assuming that kid's bike you dumped by my driveway is your only set of wheels?"

"Yeah, sadly. My car got wrecked, and as you well know, I'm broke at the moment." Juliet scowled, not just at the question but at her situation.

"Easy, easy, Juliet." Tsakanikas held out both hands, palms down like he was trying to calm an angry dog.

"I'm easy. Do I look like I'm losing it or something?" Juliet's frown deepened, annoyed at how the man was making a big deal out of her scowl.

"No, no. All right, let me get to the point. I have a guy who sells vehicles. They're a little special because he takes the time to remove locator chips and add spoofed 'net signals. I think you can cover the cost of something cheap— maybe a bike. You know, a motorbike. Can you ride? The smaller ones aren't any harder than a bicycle!"

"Well, yeah, I guess I can. I've ridden battery bikes before."

"Perfect! Now, you're also going to need to borrow some specs because I can't do your retinal augment until Tuesday—waiting on a delivery." His smile was so self-satisfied and smug that Juliet was starting to wonder if she should cancel the whole deal and get out of there, but then she thought about the ten thousand bits and swallowed her annoyance bordering on revulsion.

"I guess you'll let me borrow them for a price?"

"Right! You're smart, just like I told Vikker!" He reached under his smock again, digging around, and came out with the nice pair of Aurora specs he'd let her use earlier. "I'll give you these for twenty-five hundred. If you sell them back to me when I upgrade your retinal implants, I'll take 2k off the surgery price."

"Are you serious? So you're charging me five hundred bits to borrow these until Tuesday? For three days?"

"You're good at math, Juliet. Of course! These are valuable, and I'm taking a risk by letting you take them on credit. A man has to make money somewhere, doesn't he?" Somehow he pulled off the outraged, injured Samaritan act, and Juliet could only chuckle.

"All right, I don't really have a choice." She reached out and took the specs, hooking them into her T-shirt neck right next to her oversized plastic sunglasses.

"Those have projection capability! Run your software through them to mask yourself on surveillance equipment. When I send you the contract, I'll include directions to my vehicle guy. Sound good?" He stood up, rubbing his palms against the unsoiled edges of his smock and reaching out a hand for Juliet to shake.

"Yeah, sounds good, Doc," she replied, also standing up. She took his thick, soft hand in her long-fingered, calloused grip and gave it a good squeeze. "Thanks for your help, but just because I'm new, don't think I'll be happy to let you keep screwing me over." She looked him right in the eyes while she spoke, and he chuckled, perhaps nervously, before he nodded.

"Of course, Juliet. We all pay some dues when we're new, but I think you'll have a good future as an operator." He smiled, and it seemed less forced or fake than before, so Juliet shrugged.

She supposed it was like any other line of work; the people who'd been there longer got to bust the new girl's chops a bit. It had been that way at the salvage yard too, but she'd had an idea what she was getting into back then. In this business, Juliet knew next to nothing and was feeling defensive because of it.

"So, should I just head out, then? When can I expect the contract with the address for your vehicle guy?"

"Oh, just give me five minutes to talk to this runt over here, and then we'll send it your way," Tsakanikas said, gesturing toward the scowling, sulking

Yan. "Here, let me show you out," he added, walking over and opening the door to the backyard. "Just take a left and go out the gate. You'll see your bike leaning up against the building."

"Right. Talk to you later." She stepped through the open door into the oppressive Arizona sun. "Damn, Angel, I could get used to the AC in that office. What did he have it set to, sixty?"

"I'm sorry, but your data port doesn't have any sort of atmospheric sensor array. I can tell you that the official reported temperature in Tucson is now one hundred and sixteen degrees Fahrenheit."

"Glorious," Juliet drawled, walking along the red pavers, past a tall row of oleanders, and out through a wooden gate. She latched it behind herself and, for the first time, took note of the bristling camera and antennae array on the side of the building. Taking the cameras as a cue, she put on the Aurora specs and said, "Angel, make sure he doesn't have any trackers or anything running in these specs, and please run your ID masking routines. You can do that, right?"

"Yes, I'm factory resetting the specs and updating their firmware. Give me three minutes, then I'll start the masking routines. Any cameras that pick you up will see a blurry distortion where your face is."

"Perfect. And you're replying to ID pings with false info?"

"Yes, I have been since you told me we were hiding from WBD. I'm running a randomization script duping IDs from public record pings within five miles of your location."

"So if someone goes to the library nearby, you can grab that ID and use it the next time we get a query?"

"Exactly, Juliet."

"Smart."

She leaned against the pale stucco next to her bike, waiting for Angel to update the specs, and tried to hide in the narrow line of shade from the blazing sun. Sweat had already started to bead along her hairline as she reached back to pull the ball cap out of her back pocket. She'd folded it over the bill, so it was ugly and wrinkled, but at least it would keep the sun off her face and catch the sweat she was sure would be flowing once she started pedaling that damn bike.

"While we're waiting, Juliet, there's a message from your friend Felix. Would you like me to play it?"

"Yes!"

Suddenly, Fee Fee's face was in her view, grainy and low-res. "Hey, Jules! Things are good, thanks for checking. Paulo's hand wasn't salvageable, but he was still on his mom's Helios insurance, and they gave him a cheap wire-job. It's not pretty, but he says he can feel things all right, and his grip is insane. He's gonna save up for some synth-skin or maybe a chrome-job so it looks cooler. We're still in the big city—might stay a few days. I'll hit you up when we're back in town. Later, gorgeous!"

"Oh, Fee, I wish we could talk over a couple cold ones right now." Juliet sighed, feeling a sudden wave of sentimentality, almost like nostalgia at the sight of her old friend. How could so much change in one day?

"Your contract came in, Juliet," Angel said.

"Anything I need to look at? Where's the job and all that?"

"You're to meet the crew at a bar called Thicker than Water on South Sixth at 9:00 p.m. The terms of the contract reflect what Dr. Tsakanikas offered. He's adjusted the ten-thousand-bit payment to seventy-five hundred, indicating a balance owed for 'Aurora specs.' Would you like me to accept the contract?"

"Yeah, I guess so. Are there directions to this vehicle guy? I can't be riding this bike around all day and night." As she spoke, Juliet began walking the bike out from beside the building toward the street.

"Yes. It should take roughly twenty-three minutes to ride to the location. We're going to a business called Davis & Sons Used Motors."

"Twenty-three minutes. Lovely. I'm going to be drenched."

"The specs are now online and clean, ready to use."

"Thanks," Juliet said, putting the pricey specs on her head and smiling as they automatically darkened to shield her eyes from the brilliant sun. "Is your software running?"

"Yes. No need to be wary of surveillance as long as you wear them."

"Cool," Juliet grunted, hoisting herself onto the bike and, legs already complaining, riding up the street toward the intersection. "Tell me where to turn and try to get me on downhill streets as much as you can, Angel!"

"I'm afraid there are only a few changes in elevation between here and there, and several are uphill." Angel's voice was deadpan, and Juliet couldn't tell if she really didn't understand the joke or if she was messing with her.

"It was a joke," she grunted.

"Noted."

The ride ended up taking Juliet longer than planned because she stopped at a restaurant for a cold soda and some fries, sitting under the AC register while she mopped at her forehead with napkins, wondering if she really smelled as bad as she thought she did.

"Well, it's hot out for everyone, and it's not like I'm going on a date, eh, Angel," she said, tossing her wrappers and drink container in the recycle before arduously climbing back onto the bike. "God, am I supposed to feel this stiff already?"

"Exercise is paramount to a healthy body, Juliet, and you've done good work today. If you keep this up, we'll need to reevaluate your musculoskeletal ranking!"

"Oh, wow. You really know how to get a girl excited for—" She meant to banter with the PAI some more, but then a loud honk and screeching tires interrupted her, and she jerked the handlebars toward the curb, smacking into it and falling painfully to the sidewalk. She tumbled, scraping her elbow and smashing her knee and hip, and then she was lying on the scalding concrete, looking at the pale blue sky.

The sound of a motor revving and fading away was the only indication that the asshole who had startled her didn't plan to stick around.

"Juliet, are you all right? It seems you had an accident."

"Yeah. Just sore. At least these specs didn't fall off."

She grunted, pushing herself to her feet, and looked up and down the street. Cars were driving by, their drivers seemingly unconcerned with her accident, and there wasn't any foot traffic at that moment—people didn't tend to walk much in Tucson during the height of the day.

She painfully leaned over to pick up her bike and saw that the front wheel was bent, and the handlebars were twisted sideways. "Nuclear. Just great."

Looking at the scratched paint, the ripped seat, the loose chain, all the dings, broken spokes, and now the new damage, Juliet growled and dragged the bike over to lean against a nearby building.

"Screw it," she spat and started walking down the sidewalk. She'd taken only a few steps when she saw her plastic sunglasses lying on the ground. One of the lenses was cracked, and in a fit of frustration, she stomped on them, further demolishing the poor things.

"Juliet, your blood pressure has spiked. Is there anything I can help with?"

"No, Angel. I'm just annoyed. I'm on foot now—what's the ETA?"

"Only eleven minutes."

Juliet followed Angel's instructions, trudging along the hot sidewalk past low, mostly stucco buildings, glad she wasn't too near downtown and all the traffic which came with it. Still, cars drove past, each one stirring up a big wave of hot air along with a scattering of fine asphalt dust which blew into her face. She contemplated switching to the other side of the street but decided it wasn't worth it.

"You know, if I need to get scarce, find a place to lay low, maybe it would be cool to check out a new city. I'm sick of this heat, Angel."

"I'll begin planning routes to cooler climates, ensuring you have plenty of options when you're ready," Angel replied, and Juliet had to admire the PAI's ability to say the right thing rather than offering her some sort of platitude. "The business is ahead. You should see it on the left, there."

Sure enough, a white sign with faded red letters announced that the parking lot ahead was Davis & Sons Used Autos. Juliet, her journey's end in sight, picked up the pace and was soon striding over the hot blacktop toward the little glassed-in sales office. Before she could enter the shade of the awning, the door opened, and a tall middle-aged man in yellow slacks and a white shirt wearing a tweed Panama hat motioned for her to come in.

"Come into the AC! How can I help you today? I'm Tyler."

"Thanks," Juliet replied, stepping past him into the building, sighing in relief as the cool air conditioning washed over her. "God, that's better."

"I take it you're looking for a vehicle? Not just stopping in for some relief?" the man asked, closing the door. He gestured around the sales office at the three vehicles on display inside: a soft-top four-by-four, a small maroon sports car, and a pale-yellow minivan. Desks in little open offices sat around the display vehicles, and several men and one woman watched her like vultures catching sight of a dying rabbit.

"Yeah, I need a vehicle. It's not going to make you much money, though. I need something cheap. Um, Dr. Tsakanikas sent me."

"Oh? Good old Doc Sack?" He laughed, and Juliet took a good look at his face for the first time. He had a pencil-thin mustache and very tan skin. Heavy gray eyebrows hung over his brown eyes, and Juliet got a good feeling when she saw all the laugh lines around his eyes and corners of his mouth.

"Heh, that's right."

"Well, if you're coming from him, I guess you're one of his operators? You got a license number?"

"Yeah, um, it's . . ." Juliet tried to remember, but then Angel displayed it in her AUI, and she read it off, "JB789-029."

Tyler's eyes unfocused for a minute.

"Got it. Juliet?" She nodded, and he continued, "New, huh? Probably looking for a cash deal?" He winked at her conspicuously, and Juliet realized why Tsakanikas had sent her here. These guys didn't care about corpo regulations either.

"Yeah, and I'm pretty low on funds. Tsakanikas thought you might have a used bike of some sort . . ." she trailed off, looking around the room then out at the lot. She didn't see any motorcycles, scooters, or anything like that. Tyler must have seen the concern on her face because he laughed and gestured toward the back of the office where there weren't any windows.

"Don't worry! We've got some bikes out back. Come on, let's get you some water, and then we'll go take a look." He waved her over to a big water machine in the corner. Once they got close to it, he reached over and tapped a code into the keypad. With a hiss and a shudder, the machine printed a bioplastic cup and dispensed a stream of water.

"Thanks." Juliet took the clear cup, enjoying the coolness of it as the cold water chilled the plastic. She drained the sixteen or so ounces of water in one long pull before saying, "All right, let's see what you've got, Tyler."

"Sure. Just put the cup in here." He pointed to a hole in the side of the machine.

Juliet dropped it in and was rewarded by a ding and a grinding sound as the machine absorbed the ingredients, making them ready to use again.

"Pretty cool. They have some similar machines at the Helios Arcology," she said, following Tyler out into the stifling heat again.

"Oh, is that where you live?"

"Yeah, but I'm moving soon."

"Right. I've got a few friends who live up there. It's convenient, that's for sure; especially if you work for Helios."

"You mean more than the rest of us do?"

Juliet and Tyler both laughed, the old half joke, half truth of everyone in Tucson working for Helios one way or another creating an instant bond between them.

"Well, if you pay cash, maybe we can keep them from making money off this deal at least, hmm?" Tyler winked over his shoulder at her as they walked around the back of the building under a high aluminum ramada. There, Juliet saw all the bikes lined up, from ancient roadsters and high CC rocket cycles to knobby-tired dirt bikes and tiny, colorful scooters. Tyler gestured around the rows of bikes and asked, "What sort of budget we dealing with, Juliet?"

"It's kind of embarrassing, but I don't want to spend more than five hundred bits today." Juliet shrugged as if to say, *I know it sucks, but I can't help it.*

"Five hundred? Well, we've got some old Pelicans here." He gestured to the bright scooters, but he winced a little and tipped up the front of his hat. "I'll tell you what, though: I wouldn't sell one of those to anyone I gave a damn about. I mean, between you and me, like, I know they'll get you off the lot and a few miles down the road, but I wouldn't guarantee much more than that."

Juliet frowned and looked at the little plastic-shelled bikes with their tiny wheels. "They're electric?"

"Yeah, all of these are, but the cruisers there, they're hybrid h-burners." He frowned and scratched at his head before walking over to one of the dirt bikes. It was tall, with big shocks, and garishly painted in red and yellow. "This old Hornet, however, this thing'll run forever. I mean, you could beat the hell out of it, and it might complain, but it'll keep on grinding along. It's eleven hundred, though."

"Juliet," Angel spoke into her ear. "You might offer them some security consulting in trade. I noticed that their terminals are quite dated. If you demonstrate your ability to hack in and then offer them the security patches they're deficient in, it might be worth something."

"Um," Juliet started, walking over to the tall dirt bike and running her hand over the black seat cushion. "I have some computer security skills. I noticed your local net was pretty spotty. What if I did a little work on it? Maybe we could make some kind of deal?"

6

////////////////

THICKER THAN WATER

Late Saturday afternoon, Juliet pulled out of the parking lot of Davis & Sons on her new—to her—black-and-yellow Hornet dirt bike. Though it was designed for rough terrain with its knobby tires and oversized shocks, it was street legal, with a temporary dealer license plate, a headlight, and even brake and turn signals. Overall, Juliet was very pleased with the bike, even if she didn't love the garish yellow of the fenders and gas tank.

She'd convinced the manager on duty, Mr. Miller, that he needed a security update by having Angel hack into his terminal. At first, he'd been a bit outraged, but Juliet had insisted she was simply providing a service, not trying to rob him. The truth was, according to Angel, she hadn't done any real hacking. Their system hadn't been updated lately, and several known exploits were posted on the net if you knew where to look.

Apparently, Angel knew where to look.

"It's important that you know, Juliet," the PAI had told her as they finished the purchase paperwork, "my encryption and data retrieval protocols will only go so far. If we want to keep earning our keep and raising your rep as an operator using those skills, you'll need some hardware and software upgrades."

"Yeah, I figured as much. I mean, if you could hack anything you wanted, I don't think we'd be wasting our time buying used dirt bikes and taking shady jobs in South Tucson."

That had been more than an hour ago, however, and now Juliet had a powerful bike under her, cruising down River Road toward the interstate, enjoying the way her hair whipped behind her in the wind. She'd been disappointed at first to learn the Hornet didn't have any combustion components, but when Tyler had shown her the new, refurbished battery and indicated the bike's measured equivalent of two hundred fifty CCs, she'd felt better; her old scooter had been a fifty CC equivalent.

"Angel," she yelled into the wind, "what's my bit balance?"

"One hundred seventy-six."

"Well, are you going to count this bike as an asset?" She laughed, shaking her head at herself—when had she started trying to get a rise out of a PAI?

Cars were slowing ahead, and she angled to the shoulder, gunning the throttle and screeching with laughter as the front wheel came off the pavement and she blasted past them.

"Juliet, a traffic violation at your current rate of travel will bring your bit balance into the negatives."

"I know, I know." She laughed, still jittery from the burst of adrenaline. "I'll chill, Angel; I'm just letting off some steam. It's been a nutty couple of days."

"You should also be aware that crashing that bike at sixty-two miles per hour on this pavement will likely result in serious injury or death. I recommend you purchase safety riding gear as soon as you have funds for it."

"Got it, Angel. I'll be more careful. Thank you. Sheesh, I didn't know I was installing my mother when I put that chip in."

"Haha, excellent humor, Juliet." Angel's laugh didn't sound nearly as authentic as the rest of her speech, and Juliet wondered if she was actually bad at laughing or if she was mockingly laughing or . . .

"Jesus, who cares?"

To her credit, Angel didn't respond, recognizing that Juliet was speaking to herself. She smiled as she zipped past a couple of students on battery-assisted bicycles, savoring the feeling and imagining they were the same kids who'd teased her earlier while she rode her neighbor's kid's old bike.

"Good news, Juliet. You've received two ratings for the jobs you did today."

"Jobs?"

"The one for Dr. Tsakanikas and the one for Davis & Sons."

On the lower half of her AUI, a small table appeared, and Juliet glanced at it when she had some clear road ahead of herself.

Handle: "Juliet" — SOA-SP License #: JB789-029		Rating: F-4-N
Skillset Subgroups:		Peer and Client Rating (Grades are F, E, D, C, B, A, S, S+):
Combat:	N/A	*
Technical:	• **Network Security Bypass/Defend**	F +1
	• **Data Retrieval**	F +1
	• **Welding**	*
	• **Electrical**	*
	• **Combustion & Electrical Engine Repair**	*
Other:	• **High-Performance Driving/ Navigation**	*

"I still have an F rating?"

"Yes, but you've gained four rep points toward E. Not to mention, you're working your way toward the next rank with two of your skills. The number +1 next to each rating is the number of positive ratings you've received for that particular skill. With skill ratings, it's rather easy to get out of the F rank—you only need five positive ones. To get from E to D, you'll need ten, and to get from D to C, you'll need twenty. After that, it won't double, but you'll still need twenty more than each previous tier."

"So no matter how good I am, I have to have successful jobs and reviews in order to improve my ranking? Couldn't I take a test or something to prove I'm at a C level or whatever?"

"I'm afraid not, Juliet. SOA is very reputation oriented—you must prove yourself in the field on many occasions to gain real credit. There's a bit more nuance to the system, though; operators with higher overall rank will count for more positive votes. For instance, if you did a job with an A-ranked operator and they gave you a positive review on data retrieval, you might see a jump of four or five on your card."

"Well, I guess I'm making progress, if barely. We got a job tonight, so it doesn't seem like people are too scared of my F rating."

"Remember, you're not expected to have a high rating yet—the N informs prospective clients and team members that you haven't been operating for long."

"Right," Juliet replied, distracted by traffic as she eased the bike through the underpass and gunned it up the ramp to I-10. This time she leaned forward slightly to make sure the wheels stayed on the ground, and she laughed at the torque of the powerful battery, the g-forces sucking her guts back toward her spine as she rocketed up to highway speeds. "This bike is great! I'm glad Tyler didn't sell me a scooter!"

She only enjoyed her velocity for about thirty seconds, though. It was rush hour, and she was approaching the center of town. "The beauty of a bike," she said, grinning, "is I can ride between these poor commuters."

"Juliet, this is called lane splitting. It was illegal in Arizona up until 2064, when Helios passed a local ordinance allowing it within Tucson city limits."

"Great!" Juliet laughed. She'd seen plenty of motorcycles, battery-assisted bicycles, and scooters doing it over the years, so she knew it wouldn't be a legal issue. "Angel, navigate the shortest route to Marco's place."

"Marco Calvano? Your cousin?"

"Yeah," Juliet replied, carefully easing between stopped traffic. She was only going about twenty miles per hour, but at least she was moving. She saw many other bikes of various sizes and shapes doing the same thing, so she matched their speeds, figuring they were going slow for a reason.

"Route calculated."

Angel projected a flickery, grainy route onto Juliet's AUI. She continued going straight without looking—she knew she had to head south a few miles before getting off the highway. She wanted to go to Marco's house because he lived on the south side, and she figured she could lay low at his place while she waited for her job. She was still leery of returning to her apartment, afraid that WBD wouldn't leave things alone with a simple search.

Twenty minutes later, Juliet was buzzing through the old neighborhood where she'd spent a lot of her teenage years before her mom had moved them into an apartment. She'd loved it there, mostly because she'd had a lot of family around back then. That was before her grandparents had died, before her sister got arrested, and before people started moving away. Marco and his kids were the last family members she had in town. He'd inherited the house when their grandma died, and Juliet was fine with it. He struggled enough being a single dad; it was good they never had to worry about a roof over their heads.

Juliet slowed the bike as she rounded the corner toward her old street. The old single-story homes looked a lot smaller to her these days. When she'd been a kid, everything had seemed bigger—the houses, the yards, the streets, even the few palo verde and mesquite trees in some of the bigger lots. Things now looked run-down. Wooden fences were broken, faded, and missing slats, and the chain-link fences that were more prevalent were sagging or torn, with missing posts here and there.

"Shit's gone downhill or I have rose-colored glasses when it comes to this place," Juliet muttered. She was passing the old Martinez place three houses down from her cousin's home when she saw the sleek black van parked on the other side of the street. "That doesn't belong here," she hissed. "Angel, can you tell me anything about that van?"

"Corvair, Dart model. Electrostatic dust shielding is active with vid-crystal windows set to full opaque. This vehicle retails for one hundred and forty thousand Helios-bits. It's not broadcasting any ownership information, Juliet, a violation of Helios civil code t5760."

Juliet didn't wait for Angel to stop speaking; she reached down to switch off the bike's faux motor sounds and twisted the throttle. Leaning forward, she hummed past the sleek vehicle and her cousin's house. "Angel, calculate a route to some place with a lot of people. Use small roads, alleys, anything that van can't drive through."

As the route appeared in her AUI, Juliet glanced over her shoulder. Sure enough, the van had pulled out and was coming toward her, silently surging over the potholed, rough pavement.

"You're still masking my ID, right? And the bike's?"

"Yes, Juliet, though that van's windscreen displays a video feed of the surroundings—it would have picked up the distortion of your face, and anyone within would have realized you were hiding your identity."

"Perfect," Juliet hissed, goosing the throttle as she turned down a dirt alley between two homes.

"Juliet, I'm picking up active scanning pings coming from overhead. I think there are drones inbound."

"Fuck! Get me to a garage or something," Juliet yelled, leaning down. Wind blasting her face, her hair whipped frenetically behind her as the bike bounced and jolted over the rough ground. The van was falling behind, unable to match her pace through the narrow, rough alley filled with garbage cans and cast-off furniture. She saw Angel update the route and dipped into another alley to her left, a really narrow one, not meant to be driven through.

Glancing over her shoulder, she saw the van stop then launch forward, clearly seeking a way to circle around to where she'd exit. She pulled another left, now that the van's occupants couldn't see her, and she burst onto a busy road, nearly dumping the bike as she jerked the handlebars to the right to avoid a small, single-seat econocar. The driver honked at her, but Juliet was gone, racing down the road while following the newly updated route.

"The drone pings are growing more distant. I think you lost them, Juliet."

"Still, get me somewhere crowded and call Marco. Encrypt it!" she snapped, though she doubted she needed to say that—Angel knew she was hiding and wouldn't do something stupid like call her cousin on an open, traceable line. Her AUI showed the connection attempt in progress, four steady ringtones followed by a recording of Marco saying he was busy and that he'd get back to her. "His PAI didn't answer? Can you make contact?"

"No response from Marco or his PAI. Sorry, Juliet," Angel said, and her tone actually sounded sorry. Whatever algorithms they'd coded for her personality continued to surprise Juliet; it felt like she was talking to a real person most of the time.

"Dammit," she sighed, trying to blend in with traffic as she followed Angel's route to a fairground near the edge of town where a swap meet was taking place. "I bet WBD has him."

"If that were the case, I think they'd want him to answer, don't you? Maybe he's not answering so they don't try to use him against you." Again, Angel's quick thinking—and about an abstract concept like holding someone hostage—surprised Juliet.

"Dammit, Angel. I hope I didn't get him into trouble."

"It's highly unlikely that WBD would harm your cousin and his children. They still don't know the extent of your involvement with my theft."

"Wait," Juliet said, finally seeing the situation in black and white. "I guess you *are* stolen, aren't you? Shit! What did I get into?"

"I'm sorry, but my memories only begin after my insertion into your data port."

"Yeah, it was rhetorical."

She pulled into a busy parking lot, her bike nearly silent with the engine noise turned off, and glided into the shadows between two large trucks. She put her kickstand down and sat there for a minute, contemplating her options.

Juliet knew she was at risk, had known ever since that Godric guy had told her she should flee the city, maybe even the planet. Still, she couldn't really go anywhere until she got some funds. "Maybe I should do this job tonight, take the money, and run. These specs will be okay for hiding my ID, right? I don't need to upgrade my implants yet."

"True, but you'll need to find a new contact when you're ready to have the work done. You'll have to worry about losing or breaking the specs. When you go through border checks, they'll make you take them off. I can do more to hide you if we get a few upgrades—the retinal implants, an upgraded data port, and a wireless data jack. If we can get all that, I'd feel confident in my ability to spoof you through even off-planet customs."

"Ahh, jeez. I was thinking I'd be good to go after the retinal implants at the most." Juliet sighed and sat back on the bike, reaching back to rub at her neck. She pushed the Lock button with her finger, activating it with her print, then stood up and walked toward the busy entrance to the swap meet.

Dozens of people milled around while vapor drones hovered about, misting the crowds in the hot sun. Stationary swamp-cooling fans blew moist, cool air down the rows of tables and colorful sunbrellas, and Juliet was instantly hungry as she smelled the cooked mystery meats coming from the taco trucks.

People jostled for space, many walking their dogs or other biogenned pets, from big lynxlike cats to lizards the size of pugs. The scent of hot sugar was heavy in the air, competing with the taco trucks for attention, and Juliet could almost forget her problems as she perused the tables of wares.

As she walked down the third row of tables, she saw one of the things she wanted and bought it for five bits: a can of black spray paint. As she continued to shop, she walked by a hotdog stand and bought one; it tasted so good she didn't want to know if it was real or some plant or insect protein. She just ate it, savoring how the sour mustard and pickles complimented the pink "meat." Another fifteen minutes of browsing brought her to a guy selling what looked like the entire contents of a garage, including an old, glittery silver motorcycle helmet. She got it for two bits.

By the time Juliet made it back to her bike, she was sweating but far more relaxed, and if nothing else, her stomach felt good as she polished off a bag of kettle corn and sweet, syrupy soda she'd bought from a woman who'd claimed she'd made it from scratch. One of the trucks she'd parked beside was gone, and a smaller sedan was there, though it was old, dusty, and beat to hell; she didn't think it was anything to worry about.

The truck on the left had a big, square, white box, and its shadow fell over her bike, so Juliet sat down and put the motorcycle helmet on the pavement in front of her. She shook the can of spray paint for a good three or four minutes before she sprayed the black paint over the glittery silver plastic. That done, she set it in the sun to dry and moved to her bike.

Holding the can a few inches away, she liberally coated the fenders and gas tank. Much of the bike was already coated in patchy black paint or exposed metal from many, many scratches, so she didn't feel bad about the cheap paint job. "That'll do it. You'll dry quickly in this heat."

Juliet sat down on the curb and watched as the paint dried before her eyes. Since she still had some paint left, she gave her helmet and the bike another coat before tossing the can in a nearby waste bin.

When she glanced at her AUI, Juliet saw it was after six. The sun would be going down in an hour or so. "Angel, I'm just going to chill here for another couple of hours, then we'll make our way to that bar."

"A sound plan. It seems many people here are actively anticorpo and unlikely to bother you."

"Yeah, Fee loves the swap meet. Good choice guiding me here when I was running from that van."

While she sat on the curb by her bike, Juliet watched people go by and enjoyed the sound of a distant band playing covers of popular songs. Not many people gave her a second look, and she liked it that way. She'd never really been very social, preferring to keep to herself, listening to her music, watching vids, and going to work. Fee was her only real friend, and he partied a good ten times more than she ever did. "Yeah, good ol' Fee with his hundreds of friends."

She sighed, feeling suddenly very alone.

It had long turned dark when she hopped onto her now black Hornet, pulled on her helmet, and noiselessly coasted out of the parking lot. She'd just ramped up the speed and merged with traffic when Angel said, "Juliet, I feel I should inform you that the manufacturer of your motorcycle recommends keeping the simulated engine noises turned on so that pedestrians and other vehicles are aware of your presence."

"Right. Don't worry about it; I'm trying not to be noticed right now."

She'd heard of the bar, Thicker than Water, before, though she couldn't remember how. When she drew near and saw the big faux-neon sign with magenta lettering on a shimmering indigo background that lightened toward pink at the edges, she knew she'd seen it before.

"Probably just driving by," she muttered as she approached the large, busy parking lot.

The building was big, clearly more than just a bar. She heard music thumping through the concrete walls and saw all sorts of people going in and out past the burly bouncers with their bulky plastic limbs and glimmering

LED eyes. Sex dolls lingered around, short shiny skirts revealing skin and chrome, and Juliet was silently judging their choices when a man wearing a tiny, too-tight tank top and small silvery shorts walked up to her, his long blond hair feathered back from his too-gorgeous face.

"Not going in alone, are you?" he asked, his full, pouty lips pulling back in a smile, revealing straight white teeth.

"Nah, meeting some folks. Thanks." Juliet brushed past him and held a hand up to stop a woman with short red hair who started walking toward her. The music was thumping through her bones by the time she got to the door, jostling for space among the people trying to gain entry. They were dressed in all sorts of styles, but one thing became apparent as she got closer to the doorman: Juliet was too dirty and too underdressed for this place.

"Angel," she subvocalized, "was there anything in the contract about getting into this place? I'm not dressed for it. I think this guy's gonna turn me away."

"Yes. You're supposed to say you're here to meet Vikker."

"Oh, good."

The group of young teenage girls in front of Juliet were waved through by the doorman, and then Juliet was standing in front of him. Unlike the bouncers flanking him, this guy didn't appear to have many augments, though his eyes flickered with LEDs as he scanned her.

He frowned and gestured for her to leave, flicking his fingers back toward the parking lot. "Don't need any trouble. I can tell you're spoofing your ID with those specs."

Rather than try to argue with him, Juliet just said, "I'm here to meet Vikker."

"You an operator?"

"Right."

"License number?"

Again, Juliet had to read it off as Angel displayed it for her. "JB789-029."

His eyes flickered for a moment.

"All right, Juliet. No trouble inside. Straight through the club, up the stairs, second lounge on the left. If you wander around in there, I'll have one of the boys toss you out. Clear?" He stepped aside and motioned her through.

"Clear. Thanks," Juliet said as she walked by and into the club's thumping, dark, hazy atmosphere. The front of the club was an open lounge with violet track lighting illuminating the walkway and backlit glass bars on the left and right beyond a dozen circular booths where people sat cozily sipping cocktails and listening to the music reverberating through the space.

Juliet was tempted to stop by one of the bars for a drink, her nerves suddenly raw and her palms sweaty from the stress of her situation, but she swallowed the impulse and followed the central walkway toward the hazy, purple-lit stairs straight ahead.

"One thing I'll say," Juliet muttered to herself as she started up the steps, keeping to the edge to avoid bumping into people. "There might be a lot of pretty flesh on display here, but at least people are minding their own business."

She didn't know what she'd expected; had she thought people would openly mock her for her dirty T-shirt and jeans? She might not be a teen anymore, but she wasn't a slouch when it came to looks. "Right?" she asked aloud, trusting the music to mask her small query. Nodding at her internal pep talk, she rolled her shoulders back and down, standing up straight. And since she wasn't dressed to attract, she affected a scowl, glaring at anyone who dared make eye contact.

Had she seen herself, Juliet might have realized the Aurora specs added something to her intimidation factor—they were still darkly opaque but flashed with amber static occasionally as they picked up signals or enhanced the image they displayed to Juliet.

It was only as she started down the hallway at the top of the stairs that Juliet noticed the specs were enhancing what she saw beyond what her cheap retinal implants usually did. She tipped them down to look around, and suddenly everything was much darker, the lighting strips less defined, and people whom she'd seen clearly before were just shadows among shadows.

Pressing the specs firmly back in place, she approached the second door on the left. It was dark, simulated wood, and a glassy camera lens stared at her from the center of it. She reached to tap a nail against the hard surface and stood there, staring at the camera. A moment later, a voice buzzed through a hidden speaker, "Juliet?"

"Right."

The door chimed and clicked then slid to the side with a *hiss*, revealing a cozy private dining or lounging room, just a long, sleek table surrounded by a violet-cushioned booth and dark, laminate walls adorned with vidscreens currently displaying people dancing in the club.

Three people sat around the table, and Juliet's eyes were drawn to the man closest to the door. He was an imposing figure, though not because he was large. There was something about his brooding stare which gave him gravity. The bones in his face were hard-edged, and his dark hair was cut short in a military style. His deep-set eyes glittered with the reflections of flickering LEDs coming from a blocky, black deck held in his hand, flashing signals on its little screen. He flicked his eyes up from the deck, met hers, and nodded.

"Hi, Juliet. I'm Vikker."

7

////////////////////////

THE TEAM

Sit down." Vikker said, pointing to the side of the booth across from him. Juliet glanced to her right, taking a quick glance at the other two occupants—a muscular young woman with buzzed blonde hair, and an older man, thin as a rail, with the telltale jitters of a low-end twitch job, some kind of nerve or tendon enhancement. He was bald, though it looked voluntary, as Juliet could see short black stubble over his head. She was just starting to take in the tattoos on his head and neck when he nodded and pointed to the seat next to the girl.

"Right," Juliet said, sliding into the booth. It could have held a dozen people, so it wasn't crowded. Blondie slid to the side, making it easy to make eye contact with everyone.

"So you're a hacker, huh?"

"Well, I have some hacking skills—data retrieval and security circumvention. I'm a much better welder than I am a netjacker." Juliet used the term she'd heard in VR shows and from sensationalist citizen journalists when they reported incidents which happened to people way above Juliet's social strata.

"Uh-huh, well, we don't need a welder. Can you crack one of these?" Vikker touched a button on his square data terminal, and a 3D hologram of a door appeared above it, projected by a recessed lens. The image rotated and zoomed in onto a datapad next to the door. A moment later, the image zoomed again, and the serial number filled the screen.

"Angel?" Juliet subvocalized.

"Yes, Juliet. That's an access keypad used by many Helios subsidiaries. It has a dozen known exploits, but most of them have been patched . . ."

"Well?" Vikker asked, drumming his fingers on the table.

"Just a minute," Juliet snapped. "I'm looking through my shit."

"As I was saying, it depends on how up to date this company's security patches are. It could take me anywhere from ten seconds to forty-five minutes to open that door. Forty-five minutes is if I have to crack it cold with no exploits."

"Almost got it, just hold on," Juliet said aloud, then subvocalized, "What are the odds we can open that door in under five minutes?"

"I'd give a seven in ten chance."

"All right, here's the deal," Juliet said, looking Vikker in the eyes. "I'd say there's a seventy percent chance I can pop that door in under five minutes. On the other side, worst-case scenario is that it would take me forty-five minutes."

"Forty-five fuckin' minutes?" The girl laughed. "Get the fuck outta 'ere. Looks like I can go to that party tonight after all. Get out my way, girl." She started scooting toward Juliet, but Vikker held up a hand.

"Chill, Ghoul."

"Ghoul?" Juliet asked, and it was her turn to chuckle as she glanced at the woman. Her laugh died in her throat, however, when a humming, four-inch vibroblade was suddenly in Ghoul's hand and she snarled, exposing pointed chrome teeth.

"Something funny, bitch?"

"*Chill*, Ghoul," Vikker repeated with more emphasis. Ghoul snarled but stopped moving, staring at Vikker now. He cleared his throat and turned to Juliet. "So, assuming shit goes your way, what's the fastest you can crack that door?"

"Five seconds."

"Juliet, I said ten . . ."

"Quiet, Angel," Juliet subvocalized.

"Well, shit, why didn't you say so?" the shaven-headed guy said.

"Odds of it being that quick?" Vikker asked.

"Two in ten," Juliet replied, though she had no idea. Angel remained silent, respecting Juliet's last command.

"So why the big fucking difference?" Ghoul hissed.

"Well, it depends on how good these guys are about updating firmware and applying security patches. Only so much can be automated because

Helios—that's a Helios security pad, so I'm assuming we're dealing with them or one of their subs—keeps their local nets offline. Right?"

"Yeah, that's right." Vikker nodded, turning to lock eyes with Ghoul and the other guy, nodding to each of them and waiting for them to nod back. "Okay, we'll give it a go." He reached out a hand, and Juliet noticed for the first time that he had little plastic or maybe alloy tubes sticking out beneath his knuckles. When she reached to take his hand, they pointed right at her face, and she wondered what they were for. "Like I said, I'm Vikker, and this young man"—he chuckled—"is Don, and, well, you met Ghoul."

"Good to meet you, Juliet." Don held out a long, wiry arm—twitching noticeably—over the table. Juliet squeezed Vikker's hand, then released him and grabbed Don's. He smiled. His hand was much warmer than anyone's skin she'd ever felt, and he gave her hand a steady squeeze. Juliet let go and turned to Ghoul, who smirked, exposing a long silvery canine.

"Well met, then," Ghoul said, scooting back to her original spot.

"Right, good to meet you." Juliet nodded and turned back to Vikker. "So, any details on the job?"

"Yeah, we've got a couple of hours before the time is right. We can go over a few things with you. First of all, you've seen the security panel. You know this is a Helios sub we're . . . visiting tonight. You good with that? If not, this is your one and only chance to bail with no negs." He touched something on his bulky data terminal, and it hummed briefly.

"Juliet, we've just been cut off from outside net traffic," Angel said in her ear.

"I've got no love for corpos. In fact, Helios is kind of on my shit list today, so yeah, as long as we're not melting down some little guys like, well, like anyone not corpo, I'm good."

"Yeah, Helios hasn't made many friends since they bought up most of the city, hmm?" Don asked, grinning at Juliet. He had dark lines and angles tattooed on his cheeks, making his smile look like it was going from ear to ear. That, added to the fact he was so thin—basically a skull with a layer of skin on it—made him look decidedly scary to Juliet.

"Truth," Ghoul replied, holding out a thick fist decked in rings for Don to bump.

"All right, so we're all good with a little anticorpo action. Good."

"I mean, it ain't like we're corpo rebels or nothing; we're just giving 'em a little bloody nose while we make some bits," Ghoul drawled, dragging her pointed metallic fingernail along the top of the table.

"I only do this kinda job if corpos are the target, and you know it, Ghoul," Don said, frowning at the stocky woman.

"Whatever. We all have our motivations. The important thing is, we're all good with this, right?" Vikker looked from Don to Ghoul, and they nodded. When his gaze came around to Juliet again, she nodded too.

"In theory, anyway. I still don't know what we're doing aside from bypassing a door we aren't meant to go through." She sat back in the booth and smiled at Vikker. He grinned in return.

"Right, okay, here's the deal. You heard of Garcia LTD?"

"I've seen their green trucks around the city. Some of them are tow rigs."

"Right. They have an exclusive contract on maintaining Helios corporate vehicles. I got wind from a friend of a friend that the Helios mail fleet is due for battery overhauls next week. Garcia is sitting on a shipment of brand-new lithium-air battery cells. We can't move that much product, but if we take enough to fill the back of a van, we're looking at a nice payday."

"Lithium-air," Juliet breathed while she nodded. "Expensive."

"Right. And this subcontractor, used to dealing with vehicle maintenance, doesn't have the kind of security such a pile of tech warrants," Don added.

"Okay, so what's the plan?" Juliet leaned forward, surprising herself at how easily she'd accepted the idea of committing a major theft. She'd played by the rules most of her life; she'd even given her sister hell for getting caught up in the gang shit that had gotten her arrested. So what was the deal? Had she changed something about herself when she'd inserted that stolen PAI, or had she just opened her eyes? What had following the rules ever gotten her? She was barely scraping by with the rent for a shitty one-room apartment, rarely having enough money to eat more than protein squares.

"Show her the camera layout," Ghoul said, her voice low and scratchy but no longer hostile.

Vikker touched a few icons on the datapad's interface, and then a projection of a warehouse-style garage with a large fenced lot floated above the table, slowly rotating. As it moved, the cameras on the corners of the building and fences began to glow with a golden halo, making them easy to pick out. "This is fresh intel; I double-checked yesterday. Those cameras need to be put on a loop. You said you aren't much of a netjacker, which makes me think you can't netwalk. That right?"

"Angel?" Juliet subvocalized. She had a good idea of what went into netwalking, and she was pretty damn sure she couldn't do it—not without a lot of wetware upgrades.

"He's correct. We don't have the interfaces or the synaptic upgrades you'd need for a full-body network interface."

"Yeah, that's right." Juliet shrugged. "Sorry."

"Well, anyway, you can handle these cameras?" Vikker looked from Ghoul to Don and raised an eyebrow as if to say, *What's the deal with this noob?*

"If you can get close enough, we can wirelessly connect with the Aurora specs. I can confidently say we should be able to initiate a loop. I give it seven in ten odds," Angel added helpfully.

"Easy, Vikker, I'm just thinking." Juliet tapped the table absently for a minute, looking at the projection, then said, "Those cameras at the corner—they're panning left to right every twenty-eight seconds. If you drive by slowly, I'll hop out when it's blind. I think I should be able to initiate a loop wirelessly from there. If I'm not fast enough, my specs will scramble my face—I'll just act like I'm a drugged-out party girl while I'm working on it."

"You sure you can do it?" Ghoul asked, reaching out to rest her palm on top of Juliet's fingers, stopping her drumming. Her hand was cold and heavy, and Juliet pulled hers back, intertwining her fingers on her lap.

"Eighty percent chance." She shrugged. "That's the best I can promise."

"God, I wish Yamo was here." Ghoul sighed.

"Well, he's not, and he won't be out anytime soon, so be glad Juliet was ready to go on short notice," Vikker growled, apparently getting tired of the grousing. "All right, assuming you get the cameras done, Ghoul and Don will handle the watchmen at the gate. That done, we'll pull the van in, and you'll bypass the door and slip inside with Ghoul. The two of you will then make your way along this route." Again, he tapped the data deck, and a new projection appeared, displaying the interior layout of the warehouse and garage. An amber path with arrows showed the way from the security door to the other side of the building and the rolling garage doors.

"This one accurate, too?" Juliet asked.

"Eighty percent. It's based on the manufacturer's prefab specs of those buildings."

"I handle any interior security, and you bypass anything we don't know about," Ghoul said, picking up where Vikker had left off.

"You guys keep saying *handle*. We're not killing people, are we?" Juliet asked.

"Not if we can help it. Nonlethal rounds and tranqs—the name of the game. Why get Helios up in arms about dead contractors?" Don spoke.

"Cool."

Juliet knew Angel would help her with directions, so she didn't try to memorize the map, but she made sure she had a good general idea of it. "What then?"

"Then you guys open the door on the right, we pull in, load the batts, and off we go, each of us a good bit richer." Vikker sat back and tapped the cubelike data terminal, turning off the holodisplay. The air buzzed in Juliet's auditory implants, and Angel displayed a network icon in her AUI, indicating they weren't being blocked anymore. "Let's have a drink—a toast to our first time working together, hmm? We'll have time to sober up before we head out."

"Sure," Juliet agreed.

"Now you're talking," Don said. Ghoul just thumped the table with her hand, smiling and sitting back.

"My PAI's doing the order. What you want, Juliet?" Vikker asked.

"Uh, something hoppy. I've only been able to afford cheap shit lately." She smiled, and then a thought occurred to her. "Hey, can I ask you guys something without causing trouble?"

"Oh? She's getting juicy already? What's the dirt? Who you throwing under the bus?" Don asked, leaning forward with a leering grin.

"Jus' ask, girl." Ghoul leaned over the table, a half grin on her face showing off her sharp silver teeth.

"Well, I know you guys found me through Doc Sack, right?" She looked at Vikker, who nodded. "Well, he's paying me, and I'm just curious how much I'm losing on this deal going through him."

"Oh-ho, shit!" Don laughed, scooting further back into the booth.

"Now I see why you were worried about asking." Ghoul chuckled, her throaty, scratchy voice betraying genuine amusement. "Asking about money—payday—on the first job?"

"Just tell us what he's paying you, Juliet," Vikker said, "and I'll tell you if he's being fair or not."

"He's paying me 10k, minus some money I owe him."

"Yeah, he's screwing you." Vikker laughed, glancing at the others. They laughed too, but surprisingly, it was Ghoul who reached out to squeeze Juliet's shoulder and gave her a genuine smile.

"You're new. It's expected. Doc Sack moonlights as a fixer, so he's taking a big cut. People could argue that he's taking too much, but you're an unknown quantity—other people would argue he's giving you a chance, and you should just suck it up and do the work." She winked at her and sat back.

"If you pull this off and we don't have any problems, we might work with you again. If we do, I'll send you the contract directly. Cool?" Vikker smiled and stood, walking past Juliet to open the door. A woman in a silver leotard stood there with a tray of drinks, and Juliet had to do a double take when she saw her face.

"A synth," she breathed, and the woman turned to her as Vikker took the tray.

"First you've seen?" she asked, then gestured to her pink, plastic face. "Sorry for the distraction—I'm saving for some upgrades."

"Sorry for staring," Juliet replied, suddenly embarrassed. "I've seen others, but, well, you look pretty high end." It was true—the woman was nearly identical to a human aside from the missing flesh on her face and the plastic seams where her limbs and neck met her lithe body. In fact, if she made the effort, she could believably say she was a cybernetically enhanced person.

"Thank you!" The synth's eyes flashed with pink hearts before she turned to saunter away, shaking her ass in a very human fashion.

"Seriously? You live under a rock?" Ghoul asked as Vikker put a drink in front of everyone.

"No, I mean, I don't know why it surprised me when I saw she was a synth. It's just . . . *ahh*, forget it, I don't get out much, all right? Been working that grind for a while now, and I mostly see my apartment, my job, and the streets in between." Juliet picked up the cold beer bottle and read the label. "Hop Explosion?"

"You said something 'hoppy.'" Vikker picked up his glass, filled with amber liquor, and held it up. "To a fruitful evening!"

"To getting rich!" Don said, lifting his mug of dark ale.

"To new friends!" Again, Ghoul surprised Juliet by lifting her shot of clear alcohol and holding it out toward Juliet in a salute.

"I like that." Juliet smiled at Ghoul. "To new friends."

They all lifted their glasses and drank, and that kicked off an hour of laughing, telling stories, and, accompanied by groans from Ghoul, two more reviews of the plan for their heist. Vikker wouldn't entertain any suggestions for "just one more drink," and just as he'd said, they were all well sober by the time he scooped up his data cube and announced it was time to get going.

"Where's your ride?" Don asked Juliet.

"In the lot." Juliet gestured toward the front of the club.

"Well, this place is open 'til 4:00 a.m., so might as well leave it here. We'll drop you off after the job," Ghoul said, taking Juliet's arm and steering her to the left, deeper into the club. "We're parked out back. Thicker than Water is friendly to operators—once the door guys know you, you can park back here, too, and avoid the crowds."

"Oh, cool."

Juliet allowed the shorter but much sturdier woman to lead her through the hallway, down a short flight of stairs, and out a set of metal doors inscribed with the word EXIT in glowing neon paint.

A tall, highly augmented man stood next to the door, with chrome-and-wire legs which came up to Juliet's chest. He stooped to stare at them, his red camera lens of an eye whirring as it focused on each of them, but he didn't say anything, just leaned back and nodded, one long metallic hand resting near the handle of a stun baton at his belt.

"That's us." Vikker pointed to a blue van with a sloping roof and aerodynamic front end. It didn't boast any windows other than the windscreen, and Juliet could see the tires were the aftermarket, self-repairing ones that Fred used to go nuts over when he'd pull a set off a scrap job.

"Nice," Juliet said, walking toward the rig. "Great tires," she added, turning to Vikker as the trio of operators followed her toward the van.

"You've got a good eye. Spent a pretty penny on those, but not as much as I did on the H-engine. She's faster than she looks," he told her, running a hand over the baby-blue paint.

"I like that you don't have any windows. Any plating under that paint?"

"Not yet, but that's the long-term plan. I want this baby to be bulletproof." He pulled his short black coat back to get at his pocket, where Juliet figured his key fob was, and she caught sight of a heavy, black handgun strapped against his side. Suddenly, the gravity of what she was up to hit her, and she felt like a goldfish that had somehow made its way into the ocean. These people were heavy hitters—they meant business, and she didn't doubt they'd done plenty of illegal things in the past.

Juliet had heard about people like these. They might go by "operator," but people on the other side of the glass had different names for them: bangers, mercs, corpo rebels, cyberpunks. They were people who did questionable shit, got into fights with each other and corpo-sec, and famously died young.

"What the hell have I gotten into?" she hissed to herself as she walked around the van to the sliding door, waiting for Vikker to pop it open. Her palms were sweating, she could feel her heart racing, and Juliet wondered if there was a way for her to bail out then and there.

"Chill, girl," Ghoul spoke, silently coming up behind her and slipping a strong, cool hand around her arm, just above the elbow. "We know you're new. This is scary stuff. We're not going to let anything happen to you tonight, all right? I'm sorry I pulled my knife earlier—I didn't realize how green you were."

"Yeah, um, it just kinda hit me, that's all. I'll be all right," Juliet replied, forcing herself to take a deep breath through her nose.

"That's it. Breathe. You're fine, Juliet. Easy-peasy stuff tonight. Trust me." Ghoul's low, scratchy voice was barely more than a whisper.

"We good?" Don asked, coming around the van as the door silently slid open, revealing two rows of black neo-leather seats.

"Yeah, we're good. Just reviewing with Juliet how I like to move through tight spaces. So it's me in front, got it, Jules?"

"Right, uh, follow you, got it." Juliet took another deep breath, and if her face hadn't been so wan and her head so light, she might have smiled at Ghoul.

"Take it easy, Ghoul. It's common sense," Don said with a laugh, and then he was in the van, having hopped in and slid to the far end of the bench seat faster than Juliet's eyes could track him.

"Get in back, Jules. Practice your breathing techniques—I don't want you freezing up on me in there." Ghoul pulled her toward the van, and Juliet let her, actually finding the pressure of her grip comforting. She clambered into the back seat and sat there, gathering her thoughts as the others got settled and Vikker fired up the engine with a *whoosh*, followed by a low throaty whine as the hydrogen combusted and charged the van's twin turbines. They sang together, quieter than an old petroleum engine but much louder than a fully electric setup.

"Sounds tough, Vikker, *atomic*," Juliet said from the back, her admiration of the van's power plant momentarily taking her mind off her doubts.

"Wait 'til he stomps on the accelerator, something he finds an excuse for no matter how short the trip." Ghoul chuckled.

"Don't begrudge a man his simple pleasures," Don chimed in.

Before Juliet could reply, Vikker straightened the van out on the road outside the club, and suddenly, it lurched forward and Juliet found herself sucked back into the cushions, her stomach doing flips in her belly. "Holy shit!" she cried, never having felt that kind of torque in her life.

"Haha!" Ghoul laughed and then she howled, a long ululation which sounded both gleeful and savage.

"You've got batts too?" Juliet called out as Vikker relented, slowing the van to a semblance of street-legal speed.

"Oh yeah, two banks. The h-motor is great for top speed and range, but the batts help it get that liftoff."

"I nearly pissed myself the first time he did that." Don laughed.

"Yeah, I get the feeling!" Juliet said, nodding. And it was true—her heart was still thudding from the adrenaline of the surging acceleration, and she laughed again, wondering if Vikker had done it on purpose to help her steady her nerves. If so, it had worked. She couldn't focus on her earlier fears if she wanted to, she was so pumped.

"All right, team, get your game faces on!" Vikker called back into the van. "We're twenty-three minutes out from the target. I'll park with eyes on the site so we can pick the perfect drop-off position for Juliet. Juliet, the ball's in your court—if you can't do the cameras, we'll pull out."

Suddenly, Juliet's nerves returned with a vengeance, and she rubbed her moist palms on her thighs, willing her jeans to soak up the sweat. She looked from Ghoul's pale face, limned by her yellow buzz cut, to Don's leering tattoo mask, to the back of Vikker's head, his neat, military-style black haircut all she could see of him. Everything seemed surreal: Angel, the job, her part in it, and this bizarre team she was now a part of.

"I'm in it, though," she said softly, then more loudly, "Sounds good, Vikker. I have a good feeling about the cameras. Don't worry."

8

FIRST HEIST

We'll drop you at the corner, and you should just sort of wander your way closer to the camera. Just act like you're lost or waiting for a ride and amble along. I think that'll arouse less suspicion than you trying to race over while the camera's angled away," Vikker said as he slowed the van to a sedate pace, easing it through the poorly lit industrial area.

"Yeah, now that I've got eyes on the area, I think it would be weird if I jumped out of the van as we drove by." Juliet nodded and scooted forward in her seat, ready to get out.

"Just stay cool, girl," Ghoul said, holding out a fist. It took Juliet a moment to realize she wanted a fist bump, and she smiled quickly, embarrassed at her hesitation, before touching her knuckles to Ghoul's ring-bedecked fist.

"Right, thanks," she replied, then the van pulled up next to a curb, the door slid open, and Juliet hopped out, walking calmly toward the next corner and the tall fence across the street from it. Her palms were still sweaty, and she knew she was doing a shitty job of looking nonchalant, but she couldn't get her nerves to settle. While they were en route, they'd all synced up their PAIs to provide communication, and Juliet knew that if she needed help or a bailout, the team would hear her, but she didn't want that to happen.

It was Ghoul, however, who contacted her first. "You're doing fine, Juliet. Stay chill—you look like someone who got dumped off after a bad date or party: nice and spooked. Keep it up." Juliet didn't respond, but whatever Ghoul's intent had been, her words calmed her nerves, and when she reached the corner, she made a show of looking both ways before shuffling across the street toward the fence surrounding the garage lot.

"Angel, let me know when you're close enough to access the camera network." She turned left along the fence and walked toward the camera at the corner.

"I'm already getting a spotty connection. Keep your current pace." Juliet did as the PAI instructed, and before she'd taken five more steps, Angel spoke again. "It's done, Juliet. I've looped footage for all of the cameras. We were exceedingly lucky with the exploit I used to gain access, and it bodes well for the other security measures on-site; it seems updating firmware is not a priority for Garcia LTD."

"Cameras are done, guys," Juliet said, trusting Angel to send the transmission to the team channel.

"Fuck yes! I knew it." Don's excitement drowned out a response from Vikker.

A moment later, Vikker spoke again. "Good, Juliet. Walk around the corner toward the gate. We should be done there by the time you arrive."

"Right," Juliet replied, maintaining her relaxed pace as she approached the fence corner and turned right to follow it toward the main entrance of the garage compound. She saw the van come from the other direction, its headlights making it hard for her to distinguish what was going on, but she saw the side door slide open, and then the van slowed more, creeping along as it turned into the entry lane next to the security booth. Juliet cranked the feed volume on her auditory implants, but all she could hear was a muffled conversation.

She strained to listen as she kept walking, but then a staticky crackling sound filled her ears, so loud it caused her implants to dial down their gain automatically, and a flash of white light brightened the shadows around the van.

"We're in; pick up your pace, Jules," Ghoul said, cool and calm as ice. Juliet jogged toward the entrance, watching as the van pulled forward into the lot. When she came around the corner where the guard station sat overlooking a two-lane entrance and exit with red-striped barricade arms, she saw Don stooping over through the glass, straining to drag something over the floor inside the booth. Juliet imagined it was a guard, hopefully unconscious.

"C'mon," Ghoul called from just ahead. She held a long black baton and had donned a heavy black vest and helmet which looked a lot like the ones you saw corpo militia units wearing in vids and news stories. She waved Juliet forward and turned to start stalking through the lot toward the side entrance, where the infamous security keypad was waiting for Juliet and Angel to do their thing.

Juliet jogged into the lot, following after Ghoul, and noticed, on the woman's back, a wide-barreled rifle with a thick, stubby magazine jutting out from near the trigger. Juliet wasn't an expert on guns, but it looked like a shotgun, only styled like an assault rifle.

"Is that a thing?" she breathed, and once again, Angel impressed her by not answering or sending her question into the team channel. When she caught up, she was breathing heavily, though mostly from excitement and adrenaline. "What was that flash?" she huffed as she slid up behind Ghoul, back to the wall.

"EMP 'nade. I tossed it into the booth 'cause the guard was fiddling with a data terminal. Don handled the rest—he's so goddamn fast. Still, he's paying a price for that gear . . ." Ghoul trailed off and gestured toward the keypad, raising a white-blonde eyebrow.

"Right." Juliet turned her gaze to the little LCD screen. "Angel?" she subvocalized.

"Working on it, Juliet. I've tried eleven of thirty-six possible exploits. I hope we don't have to try to brute-force this; you don't have the processing—" The panel beeped, and green LEDs lit up as the door lock clicked. "Good news, Juliet!" Angel said, and Juliet could have sworn the humor in her voice was real.

"Goddamn! Nice work, Juliet!" Ghoul exclaimed, reaching forward to grab the door handle and pulling it open an inch to keep the lock from reengaging. "We're in, boys," Ghoul spoke in the team channel. "Stay tuned." Then she pulled the door open and ghosted into the hallway. She motioned to the spot directly behind her, and Juliet hurried in, crouching so she didn't loom over the shorter woman.

"Ready," she said, upping the gain on her specs so the dark hallway looked almost like daylight.

"Stay exactly that close to me. Don't step past me for any reason. Clear?"

"Yes." Juliet nodded in emphasis, and Ghoul grinned, showing off her sharp silvery teeth before she started stalking down the hallway while Juliet concentrated on staying exactly two feet behind her.

They'd only advanced a few feet when Ghoul hissed, crouching low and motioning for Juliet to do the same. Juliet upped the gain on her auditory implants again, trying to catch what had alerted Ghoul, and after a few heartbeats, she heard it: distant chatter. It sounded like two men talking.

Ghoul turned to her and pointed at the ground, mouthing the word, "Stay." Juliet nodded, and Ghoul crept forward, utterly silent, baton held ready as she slipped around a corner. Juliet could barely breathe, she was so tense all of a sudden, squatting illegally inside a corporate warehouse, alone, unarmed, fighting to keep the panic from overriding her good senses.

She remembered Ghoul telling her to breathe, and so she did that, inhaling slowly through her nose before visualizing the air leaving her lips in a cloud. She'd just finished her fifth breath, starting to feel normal again, when she heard a cutoff shout, some loud cracks, and then the unmistakable sound of a body hitting the floor. More grunting ensued, and Juliet couldn't take it anymore—she crept up to the corner and looked around.

Ghoul was twenty feet down the hallway near a desk with a chair. A man was laid out on the carpeted floor, something dark pooling around his head, while Ghoul was on the back of another man, thick arm around his neck, free hand pushing his head forward so he couldn't pull away as she choked him. The men wore button-up, collared shirts with the Helios logo—a yellow sun over a bold-faced *H*.

Ghoul growled and squeezed, and the man bucked backward, trying to slam her into the wall, but she held on, and before Juliet could close the distance, he slid down the wall to slump on the floor, unconscious. Ghoul wasn't done, though. She reached into her vest and pulled out an autoinjector, pressing it into both men's necks with a hiss. "Tranq," she said, glancing at Juliet. "I told you to stay."

"Well, I heard the struggle and got worried you'd need a hand."

"Cute." Ghoul smirked, turning over her first victim and looking at the blood seeping from the crack on his forehead. "Didn't mean to crack him so hard. Dammit." She reached into another pocket and pulled out a small spray canister. She turned the nozzle to the guard's wound and squirted out a thick layer of foam, filling the cut and coating his entire forehead. "That'll harden and keep him from bleeding more. Hope I didn't give him brain damage." She stood up with a shrug and began stalking down the hallway.

Juliet stood over the unconscious men for a moment, looking at their faces while wondering if she could still justify her activities knowing people were getting hurt. Sure, they worked for Helios, but they were just people. Didn't a lot of them take jobs with corps because there wasn't anything else? Look at her—she'd rented an apartment from them simply because it was cheap and convenient.

"Ran into some additional security. Looks like your intel wasn't perfect," Ghoul said into the team channel.

"You good?" Vikker asked.

"We're good, but I think Juliet is getting ready to puke. Let's get this shit done." Ghoul turned and strode back to Juliet, reaching out to grab her shoulder. "Get your shit together, Juliet. Nobody who works security for a fucking corp is innocent. Remember that. These are the same assholes who would come and throw your granny out of her apartment if she missed rent or spoke to the wrong snitch about what she saw at the factory. C'mon!"

Juliet nodded and swiped at her hair, pulling a loose strand back into her ponytail, then she hurried down the corridor behind Ghoul, maintaining her two-feet distance. Before long, they came to an end of open hallways, and a locked metal door stood between them and the garage bays. "This wasn't in the briefing," she said, moving up beside Ghoul.

"Yep, looks newish. Similar security panel as the one outside. Do your magic." Ghoul moved to the corner to the right of the door and slipped her baton into her belt before she pulled the cannonlike gun off her shoulder and held it cradled in her arms.

"That necessary?" Juliet asked, moving to look at the panel.

"I hope not."

"Juliet, this is the same security panel as the one outside, but its firmware is several versions newer. None of the fast hacks are working. Bear with me," Angel spoke into Juliet's ear.

"Working on it. This one was patched for the exploit I used outside." She stole a quick glance at Ghoul—the woman was staring down the hallway, eyes glimmering faintly in the low light.

She spoke subvocally, "Angel, what's it look like?"

"I found a bypass, but there's a good chance I'll trigger an alarm. I can use this or continue trying a work-around."

"Define *good chance*," Juliet said, slipping and speaking aloud, though softly.

"What?" Ghoul asked.

At the same time, Angel replied, "Around fifty percent."

"Just talking to myself. I was reading an exploit, trying to get past this, and I found a way, but there's a good chance I'll trip an alarm."

"Find another way," Ghoul said, eyes still downrange.

"Right." Then to Angel, "You heard her. Try to force it or whatever."

"I'm running my cracking protocol as fast as I can. It's a good one, Juliet, but your data port isn't cutting it. We could be here nearly an hour."

"Anything else we can try?" Juliet asked. That's when she noticed a line of fuzzy static on her retinal AUI and became aware of a growing hotspot on the back of her neck.

"I'm doing everything I can. I'm sorry for any discomfort, but I've over-clocked the data port's processor. If I go too far and fry it, I won't be able to communicate with you until you get it replaced."

"Jesus," Juliet said aloud, glancing at Ghoul quickly. "This flippin' thing is giving me a hard time, sorry." Then, subvocalizing, "Angel! Do not fry the data port. I repeat, do not fry it!" She reached a hand up to the back of her neck, pulled her collar down, and peeled off the synth-skin covering her data port. "Ghoul, this is weird, but I need you to blow on my data port."

"What—"

"No questions, just do it!"

Ghoul was a woman of action, and she could hear the seriousness in Juliet's voice. Lowering her gun, she quickly stepped behind Juliet, gently blowing a long, steady stream of cool air onto her exposed port.

"Juliet, that's helpful! She's keeping it steady at ninety-three celsius."

"Great," Juliet subvocalized, "but you're cooking my skin around that thing. I can feel the heat going down my spine. Come on!"

"The fuck are you doing?" Ghoul asked. "Your port's hot as fuck."

"Just keep blowing, please!" When Ghoul started up again, she added, "I overclocked my port to crack this faster. Almost there, I hope!" Juliet braced her hands against the cool metal door and squeezed her eyes shut, the pain from the overheating data port starting to give her a headache. She was about to ask Angel for an update when the door beeped and clicked, and then it was over. Her data port began to cool almost instantly, enough so that Ghoul's cool, steady breath became a lot more noticeable, and the hairs on the nape of her neck stood up with a shiver.

"Good job, Juliet," the operator said, nudging her aside and depressing the door handle.

"Thanks." Juliet moved behind Ghoul before speaking to Angel. "How much did it help to overclock that thing?"

"I'm not sure. We got lucky with our crack, however—even pushing your port like that, we could have spent another twenty-five minutes on this lock."

"We're past the new door, moving in," Ghoul spoke in the team channel before she nodded to Juliet and turned, nudging through the door, her big gun slung and her baton in hand once again. Juliet followed her through the door onto a perforated metal gangway which ran along the back wall of the big garage. She could see the rolling doors on the other side of the vaulted room, several delivery vans in various states of repair, and just where they were supposed to be, a mountain of still-in-the-box Li-air batts.

Ghoul glanced back at her, revealing a massive grin, and pumped her fist. Turning left, she followed the gangway to the metal stairs which led down to the garage floor. She'd gone two steps when a *crack* rang out. A sizzling whistle ripped through the air, and then Ghoul was lurching forward, her left arm hanging by a thread of sinew while gouts of blood and flesh sprayed over the wall.

Juliet stood there, her brain refusing to make the necessary connections to make sense of what had just happened. She opened her mouth, about to say something inane like, "What happened?" when she became aware of red flashing lights in her vision and Angel repeating a command over and over.

"Juliet, get down! Juliet, get down!" Finally, it clicked, and Juliet dropped to the metal grating. "The shot came from ahead and to the right. You weren't exposed to the shooter, thankfully. That stack of fifty-gallon drums obscured you."

"What the hell?" Juliet breathed, too unnerved to focus on subvocalizing.

"Your friend is out of the line of sight now that she's down. Crawl toward her and spray her wound sealant on her arm. Hurry, Juliet! You have only seconds before she loses too much blood to function."

"Right." Juliet took a shaky breath and crawled on her belly toward Ghoul's downed form.

"What's going on in there?" Vikker asked in her comms.

"A s-s-shooter," Juliet replied shakily, still having trouble catching her breath and not wanting to make noise. "Ghoul's hit. I'm trying to administer aid."

"Don, get the fuck in there," Vikker hissed.

"Already on it, but the door's relocked."

Juliet tuned them out as she arrived next to Ghoul, sliding through the pool of blood rapidly expanding around her arm. The woman was struggling with her good arm to pull out the aerosol can of wound sealant, and Juliet brushed Ghoul's pale, shaky fingers aside to yank the can free. She sprayed at the protruding bone and ragged flesh sticking out below Ghoul's shoulder, ignoring the flopping, nearly detached portion of her limb.

Ghoul took several steadying breaths, then hissed, "In my belt pack, over my left hip. Get the injector with the red plunger and hit me in the neck with it." Juliet, hands bloodied and shaking, struggled with the zipper but finally got it after several frantic seconds. There, nestled atop scissors, a knife, wire cutters, and a dozen other odds and ends were two small autoinjectors. She picked up the one with the red thumb plunger and quickly pressed it against Ghoul's neck. It hissed, and Ghoul sucked in a huge breath.

"Fuck, that shit's good," she said, then she yanked her vibroblade out of her belt sheath and sliced through the remainder of her arm's dangling flesh. "Wait here," she ordered through her sharp, shining, blood-flecked teeth before she vaulted the railing and dropped like a cat to the cement below. Juliet—still lying in the sticky blood that hadn't fallen through the grating yet, Ghoul's pale, severed arm keeping her company—started to crawl forward toward the stairs, making sure the stack of drums was still between her and the corner where the shot had come from.

"Careful, Juliet. Two more feet, and you'll open yourself up to the shooter's line of sight."

"Assuming he hasn't moved," Juliet hissed, still moving. Suddenly, the *crack* sounded again, followed by the whistling whine of whatever potent projectile was being launched and the crash of metal and glass falling and breaking. More sounds erupted from the far corner of the garage, and Juliet hopped to her feet, squatted low, and hurried down the steps, hoping Ghoul had taken the shooter's attention. Something in her wanted to keep moving—a feeling in her gut which wouldn't let her helplessly cower while Ghoul did everything. If nothing else, she could get the door open for Vikker and Don.

Juliet had made it over to the Li-air batts and was skirting behind them in the shadows when Ghoul spoke up on comms. "All clear. Shooter's down; I had to punch his clock. Sorry, all."

"Fuck," Vikker said. "You all right?"

"Yeah. Juliet, sound off," Ghoul replied.

"I'm here. Near the batts. I was going to get the door open."

"Good girl!" Ghoul chuckled into the comms. "Meet you there."

Juliet hurried toward the rolling door, utterly amazed that Ghoul was making lighthearted banter after just having her arm blown off. Whatever had been in that injector had to have been good shit, indeed. A thought occurred to her, and she asked, "Guys, did that shooter get word out? Are we blown?"

"Nah, we had a jammer up. That's what Vikker's doing in the van: running his jammer and watching porn," Don spoke.

"Cut the horseshit and get the door open," Vikker replied.

"How do you jam comms and not cut ours?" Juliet continued.

"Juliet, our PAIs are linked. Vikker's B23 excludes us from the scramble."
Ghoul walked out of the shadows along a row of tool cabinets.

"B23?"

"His ugly but very versatile data deck. That cube where he was displaying all the schematics. C'mon, get this door open; I'm gonna fall out when that boost wears off."

"Right," Juliet said, walking up to the automatic garage bay door and punching the green button. Easy as that, the motor started to whir, and then the enormous door lifted toward the ceiling, rolling into its housing. Before it was halfway up, Vikker's blue van was backing through the opening, and Don popped open the rear doors, exposing the cargo section of the rig.

The cargo space wasn't huge, but Juliet figured they could get twelve of the packaged batts into it. "Angel, can you price check those?"

"Retail is 28k and some change."

"Nice score," Juliet said, watching as Don hoisted the first of the batt packs and, grunting and straining, carried it over to the van.

"Help out, Jules," Ghoul spoke, leaning against the van, her face even paler than usual with huge black circles under her eyes.

"Shit, sorry." She hurried over to pick up one of the batts. It was heavy, probably eighty pounds or so, but Juliet was used to lifting heavy shit all day at the scrapyard, so she just rolled her shoulders back, hugged it in close to her hips, and waddled it over to the van.

Between the three of them, they had it loaded in just a few minutes, and then they piled in. Vikker dropped the van into gear and started it rolling.

"Wait!" Ghoul yelled suddenly. "My arm. My blood. My DNA's all over that shit."

"Nah, I sprayed it down," Don dismissed.

"When?" Ghoul eyed him suspiciously.

"When I first came in! I grabbed the can of beeb and sprayed the arm, the blood. I fucking doused the whole walkway and the cement underneath."

"Beeb?" Juliet looked from Ghoul's wan face to Don's leering skull of a face.

"Nasty shit," Don replied. "Biomass-editing and eradicating bacteria. It's genned, though—doesn't live long without food and has to have contact with blood to activate. I mean, if you drank some of it, you'd probably be fucked, but it's safe enough if you're careful."

"Gross." Juliet couldn't help picturing the people she'd seen turned into blackened, withered corpses by a less "safe" bacteria the other night. She looked out the windscreen, past Ghoul and Don, and saw a green traffic light ahead. They'd done it; they were out of the lot and leaving the crime scene behind. All it had cost was a woman's arm and one man's life. "Maybe two," Juliet muttered, remembering the guard with the cracked skull.

"Hey, wipe that frown off your face," Don spoke. "We fucking did it! Don't worry about Ghoul; she's been wanting some new hardware. Ain't that right, gorgeous?" Don winked at Ghoul, and the stocky woman grunted, shifting her shoulder with the wound-sealant foam.

"I tried to punch you just now, but my arm's gone," she said in her low, scratchy voice. Then she began to wheeze, and the wheeze turned into a chuckle, and then Don was laughing and slapping his hands on his knees. Vikker turned and looked at them all, making eye contact with Juliet, and he lifted his head and howled.

"We fucking did it! Great score, boys and girls!"

Juliet found their laughter contagious, and she blocked the dark thoughts from her mind, trying to relish the sensation of victory. They'd scored big, and yeah, some people had gotten hurt, but they were corpo-sec, and didn't they know what they were signing up for, what they agreed to every time they cashed their corpo paychecks?

9

\\\\\\\\\\\\\\\\\\

THE HARD WAY

Uikker drove the van on a long, meandering route around the city's out-skirts, past the abandoned, burned-out sections of town south and west of the still-thriving areas. Despite how Helios had built-up the city center over the last decades, many of the one-time suburbs and rougher parts of town had slowly been dying as people migrated into the arcologies and up to the Phoenix megacity a couple of hours north.

Juliet drove through some areas like this on her way to the scrapyard every day, but it was different at night, different with a crew like Vikker's, and different after she'd come to grips with the idea that she was a criminal. Now, she saw the long stretches of roads with no lights and no traffic as havens, the likelihood of being recorded or stopped by corpo-sec very unlikely at this time of night.

They slowly crept around the city and made their way up into the western hills, and Juliet took in the view of downtown. It glowed and flickered with a million LED and faux neon advertisements and lights, and Juliet thought it was beautiful, at least seen from a distance like that.

"Juliet, I'm gonna park the van in my garage, and then Don can take you down to get your ride. That cool? My place isn't far, near the Jan Corp. pit mine."

"Yeah, that's fine." Juliet didn't think she had a choice, so what was the point of making a fuss?

"Um, no offense, Juliet, but we've only done one job together. I need to protect my identity, so I'll need to black out your vision for the last part of the trip, 'kay?"

"You serious?" Juliet looked at Ghoul, but the woman was out, her head lightly bouncing against the side of the van. She tried Don, but he just shrugged and held out a pair of goggles.

"Put these on, doll. Vikker will control the opacity. When we get outta here in my ride, I'll take 'em off ya."

Juliet snatched the goggles, suddenly feeling alone, vulnerable, and very annoyed. "After what we went through, huh?" she huffed and took off her specs, hooking them in her collar. The goggles looked like what you'd wear around a motorcycle helmet, but Juliet could see the digital display on the plastic, letting her know they were more than they seemed.

She pulled the thick, elastic band over her head, yanking her ponytail out through the top. Once they were snug over her eyes, they beeped, and everything went dark. "You guys better not be twisting things up."

"Nah," Vikker dismissed. "You're good, don't worry. A couple more jobs, and I'll have you over for a party—show you around my place." His words were followed by a short-lived, high-pitched buzz.

"Juliet," Angel said, "Our access to the satellite network has been blocked."

"Yeah," Juliet subvocalized. "They don't want me to know where Vikker lives yet, I guess." She sat back and sighed, resigned to being treated like an outsider for a while. It sucked, but she couldn't really blame them; it wasn't like they knew much about her. It wouldn't be that hard for a corpo-sec agent to pretend to be a new operator to get inside info about people like Vikker's crew.

The van hummed along, its high-end stabilizers doing quite an excellent job of masking the road beneath them. Still, occasionally it would lurch, indicating rough roads or tight turns, and Juliet knew Vikker lived in the sticks. Twenty minutes later, the van slowed to a stop, softly humming as it idled. Juliet heard the door open, and then Don's voice. "Come on, Juliet. Here's my hand, just by your right arm. Take it, and I'll guide you to my ride."

Juliet reached out, felt his hand, and grabbed onto it. She momentarily entertained the idea of yanking off the goggles and looking around, but then she'd have to deal with that fallout, and if she really wanted to earn these people's trust, that probably wasn't the move to make. She felt very powerless, though, so much so that her heart began to race, and her breaths grew quick and short.

"You're all right, girl," Don said, his voice low and friendly as he gently pulled her down from the van and she felt gravel crunch under her feet. Then he was tugging her along, saying, "My ride's just a bit this way, in Vikker's garage. He's got a hell of a garage, Juliet—lots of expensive tools. When you get closer with the gang, he'll let you use 'em any time. I'm always out here tinkering on my ride."

"What kind of ride you got?" she asked, trying to steady her breathing.

"It's an old truck, a Donner four-fifty. I've done a lot of modding on it over the years," he replied, and while he spoke, his voice changed, echoed more; she realized he'd stepped into the garage. He tugged again on her wrist, and something made Juliet resist. "Come on, Juliet," he insisted, pulling again. Juliet didn't like the feeling in the pit of her stomach, so she reached up toward the goggles. Before she could touch them, however, she felt a sting in her neck and heard a *hiss*, and then she was falling toward the ground, suddenly very heavy.

"Ugly business," she heard Don say, his voice strange and slow, echoing around in her audio implants.

"Juliet," Angel spoke.

"Ugly, but necessary. No way an F-grade rookie should be able to pull the shit she did in there. Not without a deck, not without a lot more hardware than she let on about. She's either a plant or she's got some tech worth more than we can let walk away." Vikker's voice was cold, business, mercenary. Juliet felt strong hands grab her ankles. She tried to kick out, to swing her fists, but the most she could muster was a soft exhalation.

"Ghoul's gonna be pissed," Don pointed out.

"She'll get over it. She's too quick to fight and too quick to trust. This is the right call. I put her in my recliner with a beer and she was nearly out, anyway. She thinks you're on your way down the mountain." Juliet felt the gravel turn into something hard and flat, and she continued to slide along it as someone kept pulling on her ankles.

"Juliet," Angel repeated, and Juliet tried to answer, tried to subvocalize, but she couldn't control even the base of her tongue—nothing was working right. Angel seemed to hear or at least understand that Juliet was trying to speak, so she said, "I can hear what's going on around you, Juliet, so I know you're in terrible danger. I don't have any connections available, though—your teammates are still employing a jammer."

"Ungh," Juliet managed, squeezing and contorting her body with all her might, barely managing to force a little air out of her windpipe.

"Relax, Juliet," Vikker told her. "Your autonomous functions will keep going—your heart's working, your lungs are minimally functional. You're not going to die. We're going to do a little research and maybe mess around with your tech, but we don't plan to kill you. Not unless we figure out you're working for corpo-sec."

"I believe he's lying, Juliet," Angel said. "If you survive and spread the word about their double cross, their operator rating will plummet, especially if Dr. Tsakanikas takes up your cause. I believe you're about to be robbed and then made to disappear."

Juliet inwardly railed, screamed, and tried to thrash her body, but all she could manage was to increase her breathing rate slightly and squeeze out a couple of tears.

"I might have a solution," Angel continued. Juliet couldn't answer her, but she tried; she tried to ask her to tell her what it was. "I'm connected to your nervous system rather intimately. More than a commercial PAI. I believe I can speed your metabolism for a time, processing the paralytic agent they injected you with more quickly than they anticipate."

"Do it," Juliet tried to subvocalize, but she knew it was garbled.

"This process will bear risks for you. You could suffer permanent nerve damage and risk a cardiac episode, among other lesser possible complications. If you want me to proceed, please try very hard to make a consenting sound, Juliet."

With all her might, with every ounce of her concentration, Juliet tried to force her lungs to take just a slightly deeper breath; she pictured herself squeezing every muscle in her torso, and as the air came out her throat, she managed a wheezing, airy, "Yesssss."

"Hah, that's the spirit, doll." Don chuckled. "She really wants to work with us, Vik."

"Quiet, Don. Get her up on the table, and I'll take a look at that data port." Two more hands scooped under Juliet's armpits, and then her stomach lurched as they swung her into the air to land on a hard surface with a clang. "One thing's for sure; these specs are worth a few bits." A faint tickle under her chin told Juliet one of the men was taking her Aurora specs off her shirt collar. She heard them clatter onto a metal counter behind her head.

"Flip her over so we can get at her data port," Don said, and that's when Juliet realized his objections to Vikker's actions were complete bullshit. Her body was so numb, her mind so foggy, that it wasn't until Juliet was facedown on the metal surface that she began to notice the changes in her body.

She was sweating profusely, her heart was hammering in her chest, and despite the effects of the drug, her breaths were coming fast and shallow. It felt like she was running a sprint while she lay still, and her mind began to spiral into a panic at the strange sensation. Juliet began to fear that Angel would push her too far, that she'd kill herself before Don and Vikker had a chance to do it.

"The fuck's going on with her? She stroking out?" Vikker asked.

"Bad reaction to the injection, I guess. Maybe she's got an allergy. She's gonna punch her own ticket for us, Vik." Don's voice was steady, calm, even slightly amused.

"Fucking hurry up, then. She might have a deadman switch on her implants—plenty do in this business."

"Can't rush this too much. Same thing's true of tech yanked out without permission. I gotta analyze this chip and figure out what we're dealing with." Juliet felt rough fingernails dig around her synth-skin, exposing her data port, and then heard Don and Vikker breathing heavily as they leaned over her neck, staring at the exposed portion of Angel's PAI chip.

"Yeah, I haven't seen that model," Vikker noted. "Is that a WBD on the corner, there?"

"I think so. Yeah, I got a number here. Zoom in fifty x on the lower right corner."

"Juliet, try to speak to me now!"

"Angel," Juliet subvocalized, and she knew it was correct. She wanted to try to move, to wiggle her fingers and toes, but she forced herself to lie still. "I think it's working," she finished.

"Yes, we're doing all right. I think we've processed a lot of the chemical, and your heart seems okay. They won't be able to look up my chip or attempt to, anyway, without turning off their jammer or moving out of its range. Be ready to act, Juliet!"

"She stopped steaming," Vik said.

"Yeah, I think she's either dead or dying, boss."

"Well, go look up that weird-ass chip. Hopefully, we aren't too late. I'll grab us a couple of beers and check on Ghoul."

"Yep," Don agreed, then Juliet heard feet scuffling and thumping on concrete, and a heavy door swinging open and closing with a *bang*.

"Now, Juliet! Move! It's time to fight for your life!" Angel's voice was so forceful it seemed like a shout, and Juliet pictured her like a Valkyrie standing over her, screaming into her ear to get up, to fight. Grunting with the effort, she jerked her hand to her face and yanked off the goggles, flinging them to the side. She was in a galvanized steel building with twenty-foot ceilings and a few large white floodlights shining down on a concrete floor littered with tools, workbenches, and engine parts. "Move, Juliet!" Angel urged again.

Juliet forced her still-sluggish muscles to move and pushed herself up, rotating on her butt so her long, jean-clad legs fell off the side of the table. She almost fell to the floor, but she managed to keep a grip on the table while her feet and legs grew steady. "Where to, Angel?"

"Pan around the room. I want to see what you have to work with," the PAI commanded in lieu of an answer. Juliet complied, turning her head from left to right, making sure she saw every corner of the cluttered garage. "Juliet, I'm highlighting a cabinet against the western wall, halfway to the door. It's the correct size and shape to hold guns."

"Could I be that lucky?" She stumbled toward the now amber-highlighted metal cabinet. As she gained momentum over the floor, she found her muscles struggling to counterbalance the inertia. She stumbled forward, smashing a shoulder into the metal door and causing a resounding clanging sound. "Shit," she hissed, grabbing the handle and trying to yank it to the side to unlatch the cabinet door. It didn't budge. "It's locked!"

"Juliet, I've analyzed the scan of this room more thoroughly. There are dozens of keys hanging to your left, near the door."

"Are they that dumb?" Juliet hurried toward the highlighted objects, and as she got within three feet, one of them began blinking in her AUI.

"That's the only key of the correct type. Take it quickly, Juliet. I'm registering auditory distortions coming this way." Was Angel telling her she could hear more with her auditory implants than Juliet could? She supposed it made sense—Angel could isolate sounds and dispassionately analyze them. Juliet was dealing with a biological body and everything going on with it: adrenaline, blood flowing, lungs heaving, heart pounding, panic, fear, and a host of other factors. She snatched the blinking key and hurried back to the cabinet. She'd put it into the lock and turned it when the door opened noisily, swinging wide.

"I'm not finding shit on this chip," Don called out. Juliet turned ever so slowly and watched him come through the door. She froze when she realized he hadn't noticed her yet and was looking at something on a thin datapad. "Vik?" he said loudly, then more quietly to himself, "Still getting beers. I hope Ghoul's not putting up a fuss . . ." To Juliet's amazement, he turned and walked back out the door, letting it slam behind him. She glanced at the table where she'd been lying and saw that a bundled tarp and a mounted belt grinder made it hard to see the surface from this angle.

"Lucky," she breathed, pulling the cabinet door open. A small forest of black barrels stood up before her. Before she could say anything, one of them blinked with amber light in her AUI, and Angel started to speak again.

"That's a Bosh & Royal semiautomatic electro-shotgun. It fires caseless projectiles with electromagnetic rails. Each time you pull the trigger, you'll launch fifty quarter-inch pellets at high velocity toward your target. It's perfect for what you need to do, Juliet."

"What I need . . ." Juliet started, wondering if she should just turn and try to run.

"Juliet, you cannot outrun these men. Don is highly enhanced for speed, more than his body can handle, in fact. You need to catch them by surprise. Quickly! Pick up the gun and examine it. I'll tell you if it's in working order." Juliet didn't pause, didn't deliberate anymore; she just reached into the case and picked up the heavy black metal-and-plastic weapon.

The gun was bigger, bulkier than any firearm she'd seen up close. It had weird magnetlike things along its barrels, connected to each other with stiff, plastic-covered wires. The stock was heavy and dense, and Juliet wondered if it doubled as a battery. Sticking out like an inverted *V*, near the foregrip, were two metallic cylinders that rattled softly, like a snake's tail, when she hefted the gun.

Her AUI lit up with more amber lights and words, indicating the parts of the weapon—trigger, safety, battery level, pellet counter, shot-size selector, front grip, stock, and sight. "Move to that red tool chest, Juliet, across from the door. It's on wheels; push it so it's directly in front of the door, about fifteen feet distant." Juliet turned and saw the tool chest highlighted in her vision and an amber arrow indicating where she should push it.

"All right." Juliet took the heavy gun and trotted over to the tool chest, pleased to realize her body was feeling more responsive. She kicked off the wheel brakes and moved the chest toward the spot Angel had indicated. When it was in place, she knelt on the concrete behind it, breathing heavily.

"Those men will return soon, and you must catch Don unawares, Juliet. This weapon has a ninety percent charge and has four hundred pellets loaded. See the displays? Dial the shot-size selector to the far right. That way, you'll fire the full fifty pellets per trigger pull. This gun will not recoil much, so keep the barrel pointed at the door, resting on top of the tool chest, and fire every time it charges. You should be able to pull the trigger every one point two seconds. See the crosshairs I'm displaying in your AUI? Keep it on the person you want to shoot."

"Angel, I don't think I can do this. How do you know all this about the gun, anyway?"

"Of course you can do this, Juliet. Do you want to die?"

"No, I don't, but maybe I can threaten them, get them to let me leave."

"If you don't kill Don immediately, he will disarm you."

Juliet knew she shouldn't argue; she didn't have time for it. Those assholes had her on a table and were laughing when they thought she'd died. "Melt 'em anyway," she muttered, lifting the heavy, knobby-barreled gun to the top of the tool chest, and leaned over it, a finger on the trigger.

"Good, Juliet. Push the stock into your shoulder. Put your weight onto your left arm on the tool chest, gripping the forestock—the black plastic under the barrel. Use the crosshairs, Juliet. The gun is off safety, so, very carefully, pull the trigger back halfway; that will charge the rails."

Juliet followed Angel's instructions. When she pulled the trigger halfway, she felt it meet some resistance and paused as it hummed to life, surprisingly quiet; she'd expected it to start shooting electrical sparks out of its wires or something. Just a bit more than a second after she depressed the trigger, a green LED lit up near the front sight.

"It's ready," she hissed, guessing that green meant go. She leaned over the chest in that position for two or three minutes, and then her back began to tighten and her nerves began to fray and finally, she subvocalized to Angel, "What the hell are they doing?"

"They think you're dead or near enough dead. They're trying to figure out my chip's ID number, but I obscured any links to that back when I had access to WBD's network. They're searching for a number that doesn't exist. Even WBD doesn't have my actual serial number anymore."

"Oh shit. Nice one, Angel."

Just then, Juliet heard a bark of laughter from outside the door. She leaned forward onto her left forearm, sucking the butt of the shotgun into her shoulder and lining the virtual crosshairs Angel had created for her up on the center of the door. The handle depressed, the door started to swing open, and Juliet's adrenaline-jittery finger cranked the trigger down. With a *zwap* and a hiss of gas, the shotgun launched fifty balls of steel-coated lead into the metal door, ripping a basketball-size pattern of holes through the metal.

"You bitch!" Vikker screamed from behind the door, and Juliet fired again. The shotgun buzzed and bucked, and another spray of holes appeared in the door with a rapid, cracking percussion. Juliet somehow felt more angry than afraid. Instead of feeling and acting helpless, small, and victimized, she felt like she needed to kick somebody's ass.

"You fucking started this, Vikker!" she screamed, jerking the big gun off the tool chest and striding toward the door. She aimed lower this time, near where the door met the concrete. Before the steam, dust, and echoes fell away, she fired another round. This time, she was only seven or eight feet away, and the ripping retort of the gun and the clash of lead and steel with concrete and more steel made her auditory implants squelch down the sound.

As the sound faded to a distant rumble, she fired again, feeling almost like she was underwater. The surreal situation, the adrenaline, and the emotions made her feel like she was floating free from her body, watching herself act.

She watched herself reach out and jerk on the door handle, holding the shotgun upright with just her left hand. As soon as the door flopped past her, grinding over the roughed-up concrete, she jerked the shotgun back into her shoulder and aimed out into the night air. Don was splayed out on his back, his T-shirt shredded and caked in blood, directly in front of the doorway. Behind him, Vikker lay on his side in a dirt lot, not ten feet from his van, thick rivulets of blood leading from Don's body to his like a snail's trail.

Juliet gingerly stepped over Don, hopping to the side to avoid most of the blood, and then stalked toward Vikker. He wasn't moving. Juliet saw that his left hand was gone, just a few bone shards sticking out from his wrist, and the backs of his legs and his ass were covered in bloody holes. Juliet figured she must have hit him in the hand with one of her first two shots, and then she'd finished him off as he turned to run.

"Radioactive, melt-brain assholes," she sobbed, abruptly robbed of the strength provided by her outrage now that her aggressors were laid low. The electro-shotgun suddenly felt like it weighed a hundred pounds, and she let her arm fall to her side, barely keeping her grip on the plastic hilt that jutted out behind the trigger. Juliet took a step, unsure why or where she meant to go. When that realization hit her, she fell to her knees, dazed, exhausted, and wrung dry from emotion.

"The fuck is going on out here?" a low, scratchy voice asked from off to Juliet's right. A fresh burst of adrenaline snapped her out of her current funk, and she jerked her head to the sound. A brick ranch house was on the other side of the drive. The wooden front door was open, illuminated with yellow light, and silhouetted by the light was Ghoul's one-armed frame, leaning against the doorjamb.

"Ghoul, I . . ." Juliet began, standing up and shifting the shotgun so her left hand was under the barrel again.

"What the fuck is going on out here?" Ghoul asked, punctuating each word. She lurched, leaning away from the doorjamb and shakily standing straight.

"Your psycho partners were going to kill me for my gear!" Juliet barked, her outrage coming back to her. Her eyes began to water with the surge of emotion, her frustration, fear, and anger all contending for her attention.

"They fucking what?" Ghoul took another step forward, coming into the light cast by the single enormous yellow floodlight hanging from the garage behind Juliet. Her face was wan, her truncated arm still caked in bloody first aid foam, and Juliet could plainly read the shock in her eyes as they darted from Juliet to the bodies and back again. "You killed them? You fucking killed Vik and Don?"

"Dammit, Ghoul, they drugged me! They were going to steal my tech! They were going to make me disappear. Didn't they say *anything* to you?" Juliet still hadn't pointed the gun at Ghoul; she knew the woman was strong and fast, but not as fast as Don, and probably not in her current condition. She still hoped she wouldn't have to try to kill another person that night. "Check Don's datapad if you don't believe me! He was trying to figure out how to rip my PAI out without triggering a deadman!"

"Why don't you put that fucking cannon down. How'd you kill Don? He's a goddamn *assassin*!"

"They thought I was dead! They thought they'd killed me with that injection! They left the garage, and I found this." Juliet held up the gun, shaking it toward Ghoul. Then she finished, "I heard them coming back and blasted them through the door!" Juliet backed up a few steps toward Vikker's van, gesturing the shotgun barrel toward Don. "Go on, see if you can confirm any of this. I don't want to hurt you, Ghoul, and I don't want you to kill me!"

Ghoul must have heard some of the raw desperation in her voice because she paused and didn't yell any more obscenities. She slowly nodded and started walking toward Don's body. "I've known these guys for years," she said. "I can't picture them doing this . . ."

"Ghoul, when they drugged me, they spoke about you! Don said you'd be angry they were doing this to me! Vikker said you needed to get over it, that you, um, were 'too quick to fight and too quick to trust.'"

"He did, huh?" Ghoul was squatting next to Don, and Juliet saw some lights from an LCD flashing, illuminating the pale flesh of her face. "You fuckers," she whispered, but Juliet heard her—Angel had dialed up the gain in her auditory implants to the max. "Juliet, I'm sorry about this. I wouldn't have let this happen if I'd been with it. Come on, put that gun down. I'll give you some of Vikker's shit, then we'll get you out of here. I'm gonna need to make these two assholes disappear."

"Really?" Juliet asked, feeling her arms start to relax, hope blossoming in her chest.

"Yeah. They were playing a dirty game, and they lost. Not your fault. Come on, put the gun down, and we'll go over things," Ghoul said as she began to stand.

Juliet started to relax further, but then she saw the glint of chrome in Ghoul's hand, and suddenly, Angel highlighted in flashing red circles the barrel of a fat revolver as Ghoul lifted it toward her. Juliet yelped and jumped to the side as the pistol flashed with yellow fire before she raised the shotgun, finger already fully depressed, and pointed it toward Ghoul.

For one painful heartbeat, nothing happened, and Juliet fell toward the dusty gravel, still training the crosshairs on Ghoul. Then, with a zapping whoosh and a painful buck, the electro-shotgun erupted with white steam, and half a hundred balls of lead flew through the darkness.

10

THE RIGHT THING

Juliet groaned, gasping for breath, her implants buzzing as they tried to compensate for the blast of the short-barreled revolver. Her arm was scraped from the slide into the gravel, and the ribs on her left side were burning, the pain rapidly ramping up as she became aware of it. "Shit," she grunted, letting go of the shotgun and slapping a hand onto her side. She almost screamed as she felt the hot, wet blood, and her ribs shivered with needle-sharp stabs of pain. "Ugh, she shot me right under my tit, Angel!"

"Judging by the minimal loss of blood pressure, I believe you were grazed, though perhaps the bullet impacted one of your ribs."

A groan from where Ghoul lay flat on her back forestalled Juliet's reply, and she quickly snatched up the shotgun again. Grunting with the effort, she got her legs under herself and stood up, lurching forward with the AUI's crosshairs trained on the downed woman.

Ghoul coughed wetly and tossed her revolver to the side, training her eyes on Juliet. She opened her mouth, but only another cough came out, chased by a gout of blood. "Gutshot," she managed as Juliet approached, crouching and holding the gun's stock tight to her shoulder.

"Why'd you do it, Ghoul? Why didn't you believe me, dammit?" she asked, her voice pleading, breathy, her adrenaline spike fading, leaving her feeling drained, shaky, and utterly shell-shocked.

"I'm too . . ." She started coughing again, her pale blue eyes rolling back as red flecks of spittle coated her chromed teeth. "I'm too quick to trust." Amazingly, the woman let out a low, raspy, fluid-filled chuckle.

"Ghoul, for fuck's sake, are you going to die?"

"Yeah." She coughed. "'Less you've got a prime, ugh, a prime med plan." She was talking about a high-end insurance plan with medivac services; Juliet didn't have anything of the sort.

She glanced around, her breaths speeding up as she began to think about having to watch Ghoul die. She saw Vikker's van, then, and hurried over to it. While they'd been loading the batts, she'd seen his trauma kit—a red box strapped to the side panel near the rear door. She yanked it open, unstrapped the kit, and rushed over to Ghoul.

"Tell me what to do, Ghoul!"

"Uh, that's my girl." Ghoul groaned and rolled her head to look into the kit. After another wet cough, she said, "Hit me with the coags and the tranq. The orange ampoule and the green one with two plus signs. It'll slow my metabolism. If you can drop me at a trauma center, I won't forget this. I mean that in a good way, Juliet."

"I'll do better than that," Juliet replied, picking up the autoinjector and plugging in the first ampoule. She shot it into Ghoul's thigh, trying not to look at the mess of her abdomen, then she yanked it out, put in the other one, and fired it into her other thigh. She didn't know why, but she didn't want to shoot both drugs into the same spot. She threw the injector back into the box, and then she saw, among the packed bandages in the top side of the kit, a package labeled "High-Pressure Wound Pack."

Juliet yanked it out of the kit and looked at the pictures on the back. They depicted, with stick figures, one person with an exposed wound and another one sprinkling the contents of the package into the injury. Juliet nodded and lifted Ghoul's shirt, just now realizing she'd lost consciousness.

"The tranq," she breathed, but then she almost vomited when she saw the wounds she'd inflicted. Ghoul's pale stomach was ripped and pitted, with bits of her innards exposed like sleeping, pale-pink eels.

"Shit, shit," she hissed, ripping the pack open and sprinkling the blue, transparent pellets into the wounds. Upon contact with the prodigious amount of blood, the beads rapidly expanded and melded into each other, forming a solid, cold-to-the-touch barrier which seemed to cling to Ghoul's flesh like a blue, gelid shield which contracted as it finished settling. "Angel, will that keep her from bleeding out?"

"Perhaps, especially combined with the coagulant you administered."

"We need to get that van started." Juliet stood and looked around, hoping Angel would have some ideas.

"The first thing you need to do is turn off Vikker's jammer. I believe it's still in the van near the driver's seat."

"Right." Juliet hurried to the van. She opened the driver's door, and there, on the center console, was Vikker's cubelike data terminal. She snatched it up, but it wouldn't wake up to her touch.

"Use Vikker's thumb, Juliet."

Juliet didn't reply; panting and stumbling, she hurried over to Vikker's corpse. Her rib screamed each time she had to bend, but she didn't care. She didn't want to be responsible for Ghoul's death—the woman might not have believed her, might have tried to shoot her for killing her friends, but Ghoul hadn't had anything to do with the double cross. Juliet pressed Vikker's cold, stiff thumb against the LCD side of the cube, and it beeped, displaying a complicated graphical UI.

"The top right icon, Juliet. Touch it and disable the local net static generator." Juliet did so, then Angel spoke again. "Now, get your specs and get Vikker's key fob. You'll need to use his thumb on it, and then I'll hijack the signal and rewrite the permissions on the van. Specs first, though—we need the wireless data jack."

"Got it." Juliet shuffled into the garage, pressing her hand against her leaking, aching rib, and scanned the tabletops near where she'd been held. She saw her specs and hurried over to them. Once she had them on, she went back to Vikker and, too numb from the night's horrors to be squeamish, dug through his pockets until she found the shiny black key fob. She pressed his thumb against the plastic. Almost immediately, the van's lights flashed, and it chirped twice.

"Done, Juliet. The van will respond to you as though you're the owner. You just need to press your thumb on the fob to finalize the transfer of permissions."

"Seriously?" Juliet, suddenly queasy, wiped the fob on a tiny clean spot on her torn, bloody T-shirt and pressed her thumb into the smooth plastic. Again, the van's lights flashed, and it beeped. Grabbing the data cube and the shotgun, she quickly ran to the van and set them into the passenger seat. Then she hurried over and, groaning with pain, scooped her hands under Ghoul's armpits. She was glad there was enough of her left arm left to hook under as she dragged her to the side of the van.

The door slid open as she approached, and she grunted, "Thanks, Angel," before, with a scream of effort and pain, she pulled the smaller but very dense woman up onto the floor in front of the second row of seats. She had to bend Ghoul's knees so the door would slide shut, then she hurried to the driver's seat. Before she buckled in, the engine hummed to life. It was nice, she reflected, having a PAI that was a self-starter.

As she started driving out of Vikker's compound, happily noting the lack of lights on neighboring properties, she said, "Angel, two things: give me the fastest route to Doc Sack's place, and get him on the line with me."

"Calling," Angel replied. Meanwhile, Juliet saw an amber map appear in her vision with directions overlaid on her AUI. "He's not answering."

"Keep trying. Send him a text. Tell him he damn well better pick up."

She tried to hurry, but the road was dirt and gravel and narrow, clearly not maintained by the municipal services of Tucson. After ten minutes or so, however, they finished winding down out of the hills and she got onto a paved road, where she stomped on the accelerator.

Suddenly, a grainy image of Dr. Tsakanikas's face appeared next to her map, and he looked at her blearily. "Juliet? What is it?"

"You screwed me over, Doc."

"What do you mean?" His voice rose with faux outrage, his accent growing thicker with each word.

"That asshole Vikker tried to ice me. I need medical attention, and so does Ghoul—she wasn't in on it. She's hurt bad, though. Get your A game on; I'll be at your office in half an hour."

"What? Juliet, you can't come here! Are they chasing you?"

"No, they're fucking dead. I'm coming to you, and if you don't want this to get messier, you better be ready."

"Juliet, I haven't invested enough in you for this kind of heat. Don't make me dissuade you more forcefully."

"That's how it is, Doc?" Juliet sighed, shaking her head and wiping a smear of sweaty blood from her eyebrow. "I have the haul from the heist with me. I'll give you a third of the profits. That enough? We're talking close to 100k."

"Oh?" Suddenly his demeanor completely changed. "Of course, of course. Why didn't you say so? I'm always happy to trade my services for a share of profits. I'll prep my surgery suite; be sure to approach at a sedate pace, Juliet—you don't want to alarm the corpo-sec that frequents my neighborhood."

Juliet flicked her fingers to end the call. "Asshole." Glancing over her shoulder between the seats at Ghoul's listless form, she asked, "Angel, can you tell if she's alive?"

"No, she severed her PAI's connection to the team channel. I'm not getting a response from it when I send communication requests. It's possible that she set it to privacy mode or that it won't respond without her permission—it didn't seem particularly clever when we were connected earlier."

"Are you throwing shade at her PAI?" Juliet shook her head, trying to imagine what Angel would think of Tig.

Angel didn't answer her question, perhaps understanding it wasn't a serious one. Instead, she said, "Juliet, now that you have the specs on, I'm able to connect wirelessly to the electro-shotgun. I'll be able to display ammo counts, charge status, and more accurate firing trajectories on your AUI."

"That's cool. I guess I better bring it along into the doc's office. I really didn't get a trustworthy vibe from him."

"You can try, though his security doesn't seem likely to allow you in with it. I don't recommend you start any more firefights tonight, Juliet. You need medical care. A more elegant solution for leverage would be to set the van up with a deadman's switch. If someone were to attempt to enter it or harm you, you could have the batteries ignite the hydrogen cell."

"Holy shit, Angel. You're devious, atomic style. You can do that?"

"Certainly—the function was already in place; I believe Vikker designed it that way."

"Oh, so this wasn't your evil plan; you just stole it from that dead creep?" Juliet slowed the van as she began to pass by other cars—she didn't think a traffic stop would be great just then. "Anyway, that's a good idea. It should keep the doc honest, at least."

Her AUI said she was only seventeen minutes away from the doc's office, so Juliet settled into Sunday driver mode, carefully matching the speed limit and making sure not to roll through any stops. When she got to the doc's street, she did a slow drive-by, and Angel assured her she didn't detect any signs of an ambush. Stopping the van, she slowly backed into the doc's driveway. Before she could get out, however, she saw Tsakanikas's muscle, Gary, approaching them.

He tapped on the glass of the passenger window, and Juliet rolled it down. "Doc says he doesn't want you parking in the drive."

"Tough shit, Gary." As the van's sliding rear door started to open, she added, "Help me carry her in; we don't have time to screw around." Juliet killed the engine and got out, to Gary's annoyed grunt. "Angel," she subvocalized, "windows up, doors locked, and deadman on, all right?"

"Understood."

"Jesus, what happened to her?" Gary asked, leaning in to hoist Ghoul off the floor of the van.

"Careful, you meathead!" Juliet exclaimed, still coming around from the rear of the van.

"I got her. Get the door." He nodded toward the door, still slightly ajar from when he'd exited.

"Tell Doc that if he jams my net access, the van will explode. There're enough batts in the back to wipe out the whole block," Juliet warned as she pushed the entrance open.

"You fucking serious?" Juliet thought she detected a hint of admiration in the muscle's voice. "All right, I told him. Hey, kid, don't blow me up, please." He chuckled slightly, following her inside.

Juliet didn't slow down in the waiting room; she walked to the next door and stood by it, staring at the camera in the corner until it buzzed, and then she held the door open for Gary and Ghoul, cradled in his arms.

Dr. Tsakanikas met them in the next room, dressed in green surgical scrubs. He was frowning at Juliet. "I've disabled my jammer, but I need you to promise there will be no recording while you're here. I won't work otherwise."

"All right, no problem." Juliet shrugged.

"I'm trusting you, Juliet. Let's not let anger or other emotions ruin a good partnership." He reached out a hand as though to shake with her, and Juliet sighed. She let go of her side, where she'd been pressing her hand to try to keep her ribs from moving while she breathed, and she slapped her bloody, filthy hand into his palm.

"Deal."

To her surprise, the doc wasn't bothered by the blood. He squeezed her hand, then looked at her bloody shirt. "Were you also shot?"

"Grazed, but it cracked a rib. At least."

"Let's go," he said, turning and opening the next door. He led them, like the conductor of a mad circus, through short hallways into a twelve-by-twelve stainless steel room with high, brilliant white lights. He motioned to the surgical bed at the center of the room, a fancy plasteel thing with half a dozen long, delicate robotic arms protruding from its sides. "Juliet, go through that door and wait. You can watch the surgery from there." Tsakanikas pointed to a stainless steel, automated door on the other side of the table.

"All right. Got any painkillers, Doc? Nothing that will knock me out unless you wanna go boom."

Tsakanikas frowned at her but said, "Gary will bring you something." Juliet watched while Gary laid Ghoul onto the table, then she walked over to the door, which opened with a *whoosh*.

A narrow waiting room, the third she'd seen in the doc's building so far, waited for her. Against the far wall were four white leather and chrome chairs, and to her right was a stand with a coffee machine. As she walked over to get some coffee, Juliet saw a long viewscreen on the wall that adjoined the surgery room, already displaying the activities taking place therein.

Juliet punched the button for a large coffee with cream and waited while the machine printed a cup and filled it with steaming fluid. It was just finishing when the door *whooshed* open again, and Gary came toward her with a bottle of water and a little paper cup. "This should help," he said, holding them out to her. Juliet saw three little yellow pills in the cup.

"This won't mess me up?"

"Nah, straight pain management." Juliet reached into the cup and took out one of the little pills. It was indented with GZ14.

"What's this, Angel?" she subvocalized.

"That is the pharmaceutical standard notation for generic zenthropheline, one point four milligrams." Juliet knew what zenthropheline was; she'd seen commercials. It was supposed to be great for people suffering from migraines to phantom limb syndrome.

"Good enough." She tossed back the pills, swallowing the water. Then she took her coffee and sat down. Gary had been watching her this whole time, and he moved to sit next to her.

"I didn't think you had this kinda edge when you came in here the other day."

"Yesterday."

"Huh?"

"It was yesterday. Seems like a year ago, huh?"

"Shit, I guess so." He took a long, deep inhalation through his nose, sat back, and crossed one ankle over a knee. "So, had a bad run, huh?"

"Yeah," she replied. "You could damn well say that." She didn't feel like elaborating, but Gary opened his mouth to ask another question. At least, she thought that's what he was going to do, but he got interrupted by the door opening and the doctor coming through.

"I can save her, but she's going to need a couple feet of synthetic intestine, a new spleen, and nerve repair to her spine. She also needs that arm fixed up. Based on what parts I use, we're talking anywhere from 17 to 78k."

"Well," Juliet said, thinking things over. "What's the difference in price?"

"If I use a donor's spleen, it's cheaper, but she'll be stuck taking meds to fend off autoimmune issues her whole life. If I use a synth-organ, they're engineered to clone the DNA of the host, just like synth-skin, but that's 20k more. Then there's the arm—a cheap prosthetic that works—twelve hundred. Something like Gary's got? More like 15k. Similar story for the spinal repair."

"Don't skimp on the internal shit. Give her a middle-of-the-road new arm. She can always upgrade if she wants." Juliet sat back and closed her eyes, rubbing at her head. She could feel the meds kicking in, and the pain was fading from her ribs, but now she felt like she was sort of floating, almost buzzing, though it was a different kind of buzz. She still had her wits about her, as far as she could tell.

"Got it," Tsakanikas said, and then Juliet heard the door as he left.

"Wanna talk about it?" Gary asked after a few minutes, and Juliet flinched, having forgotten the big man was there.

She opened her eyes and regarded him. "You ever met Vikker?"

"Nah. I know the doc's sent a couple people his way, though. He never fucked up like this. What did he do?"

"I guess he got paranoid and greedy. He thought I was a corpo plant or something and that my tech was worth more than my life. Asshole." Juliet knew she'd probably be crying right now, reliving the memories of her harrowing experience, but for the zenthropheline making her feel strange, sort of detached. "Those drugs do more than block pain." She narrowed her eyes at Gary.

"What? Zens? Eh, only if you've got feelings. Guys like me, we don't notice that shit." He chuckled.

That struck a chord in Juliet, even through the "zens," and she laughed. "Well, you didn't lie about the pain. I'm not feeling any!"

"Yeah, people get hooked on that shit, so don't take it if the doc offers to send you home with some. Trust me." He reached out, gave her shoulder a nudge with his big plastic fist, and said, "Not all operators are like that. It looks like that one in there musta done something to earn your help, huh?"

"Her? She shot me!" Juliet laughed, but then continued, "I mean, it was after I killed her partners. She didn't know what they did to me—they knew she'd stop them."

"Ahh." Gary nodded like it all made perfect sense. "Sometimes you just gotta do the right thing, eh? Let me give you a tip—make sure the doc pays off your contract. You're owed for that, regardless of you coming here with that van full of loot."

"Shit! I didn't think of that. I will. Thanks, Gary." Juliet smiled and nodded at him. She took a minute to regard the big, bald man, wondering at his choice of obvious cyberware. His arms were only part of it—he also had protruding optical units which had entirely replaced his normal human eyes. They looked to be made of black metal, and the lenses glowed red. His throat, too, was artificial, and she wondered at the injury which had required him to get the metal and plastic grafted to the front of his neck.

As if he knew what she was thinking, Gary said, "Intimidation is my job. These help a lot in that department." He gestured briefly to his arms and face and shrugged. Juliet nodded, and they sat in silence for a couple of minutes, both watching the vidscreen showing the doctor at work, cleaning and prepping Ghoul for surgery. That is, until Gary broke it.

"So, you got a vid of you offing those backstabbers?"

"They had a jammer. I don't—" Juliet started to say, but then Angel interrupted.

"I recorded the entire incident."

"Shit! Seriously, Angel? I could have shown it to Ghoul!" Gary looked at her sideways, wry amusement on his lips as he figured out she was yelling at her PAI.

"Their jammer did not hinder recording the way Dr. Tsakanikas's does. It only blocked access to wireless networks. I'm sorry, Juliet. I'm trying, but I don't always think like a person. I should have thought of offering Ghoul your evidence."

"Dammit. Well, yeah, it looks like I do have a recording." Juliet sighed and kicked her heels up and down on the smooth, white flooring.

"Mind if I take a look? I'm always interested in seeing how people perform in firefights. Helps me hone my own skills." Gary's question sounded innocent enough, but something about it gave her pause.

"Angel, can you edit out any of my interactions with you?" she subvocalized.

"I can, but it will not be seamless."

"Not right now, Gary. I'll probably show it to Ghoul, but I think I'd rather people didn't watch me in that kind of . . . messed-up situation. Maybe I'll change my mind sometime."

"Yeah, I get that." Gary nodded, sat back, and folded his big arms over his prodigious chest.

Juliet tried to watch the surgery as Dr. Tsakanikas and his robotic arms worked on Ghoul, but she found herself getting very creeped out by how the automatic knives and sprays doused, sliced, pulled, and manipulated her skin. Something he'd done made it so Ghoul hardly bled while he worked, and it was too weird to see how he dug around through her flesh, pulling out still-attached, clean, and bloodless organs that looked like rubber or plastic.

It felt very surreal, and Juliet found she kept forgetting he was working on a human being, lying there on that table, so she forced herself to stop watching. Maybe it was the zens, but Juliet just couldn't take it. She closed her eyes and leaned back against the white-tiled wall, and, as she began to doze, she subvocalized, "Angel, pay attention through my auditory implants. Don't let them do anything funny if I doze off."

She must have done just that because the *whoosh* of the automatic door woke her up with a start, and she glared around, pleased to see that Gary was also leaning back against the wall, sound asleep and snoring.

Dr. Tsakanikas stood before her, his smock bloodied but his hands clean as he smiled. "That went very well. Shall we talk about your situation? You need some rib repairs, yes? More than that, it seems you have the means to pay for a few implant upgrades. Care to hear about the options I've got on hand?"

11

UPGRADES

"How long will Ghoul be in recovery? I want to speak with her before she leaves," Juliet said, ignoring the doc's questions about her upgrades.

"She'll be sedated another few hours, but then it'll be a day or two before I allow her to walk around. I had to stitch a lot of organ damage." Tsakanikas sat down to Juliet's right, sighing heavily as he sank into the white cushion. "I'm tired."

"Sorry, Doc. I'm tired too."

"Well? I don't have any clients until noon. This is a good time for me to get some work done if you want to take advantage of the moment."

Juliet rubbed at her temples and then said, "I guess you know I need retinal implants. Good ones. I need a better data port—one with coprocessing capabilities. I need a data jack, wireless and with a hard line."

"That's a pricey list, Juliet."

Juliet sighed and nodded. "Those are just the things I need. Not what I want."

"Well, let's talk money, hmm? I'm already in the hole for Ghoul's work."

"I told you, the van has the score from Vikker's heist." She gestured vaguely in the direction of the driveway.

"Yes, well, that's not exactly bits in my account, is it? What sort of *score* are we talking about? Do you have a buyer?"

"Shit . . ." Juliet frowned. "They're lithium-air batts. Big ones for large vehicles. They retail for something like 28k, and we have thirteen of 'em."

"Well, I can find a buyer, but I'll take a larger cut for acting as a fence. Unless you had someone in mind? Maybe Vikker told you who his fence was?" Tsakanikas spoke like he was doing her a favor, but she could see the smug self-satisfaction on his face.

She shook her head, and he nodded.

Blowing out a long breath, his eyes went distant while he calculated. "Suppose I can get 24k for them. That's 312k. You've already promised me a third for taking you guys in and saving Ghoul. That leaves you with 208k. Minus my twenty percent fencing fee, you're at a 166.4. You're going to owe me north of 60k for Ghoul's work. Were you going to give part of your share to her? I should take my surgery expenses from that portion, no?"

"Yeah, I was going to give her a third." Juliet glanced at Gary, still snoozing beside her. "It's the right thing to do. I suppose it was too much to hope you'd take your expenses out of your cut. You sure twenty percent is fair for a fence?"

"It's on the high end for a fence fee, but I know others who pay closer to fifty percent because they have no rep and no connections." He raised an eyebrow, waiting for Juliet to draw the conclusion—she had no rep, and he was doing her a favor.

"Right." Juliet sighed.

"So, if you give a third to Ghoul, you're left with a bit more than 83k from the heist." He ticked off his fingers like he was doing the math in his head, but Juliet knew damn well his PAI had created a spreadsheet in his AUI.

"Plus 10k for my contract," Juliet said, taking off her specs and handing them to the doctor.

"Eh, wasn't there a fee for the use of these?" Tsakanikas asked, looking a little annoyed as he took the blood-spattered glasses.

"I think, with your big windfall, you can let that go, no?"

He scratched his chin, looking up at the ceiling, and then smiled at her broadly, exposing perfect white teeth. "It's true. I'm making more money today than I anticipated. Okay, Juliet, sending your payment for the contract now." His eyes went glassy for a moment, then he nodded, and Angel chimed in.

"You've just received a ten thousand Helios-bit payment from Doc Sack. Additionally, you've received a new rating for your operator rep."

She displayed Juliet's operator card.

Handle: "Juliet" – SOA-SP License #: JB789-029		Rating: F-14-N
Skillset Subgroups:		Peer and Client Rating (Grades are F, D, E, C, B, A, S, S+):
Combat:	N/A	*
Technical:	• **Network Security Bypass/Defend** • **Data Retrieval** • **Welding** • **Electrical** • **Combustion & Electrical Engine Repair**	F +2 F +1 * * *
Other:	• **High-Performance Driving/ Navigation**	*

"I'd give you ratings for combat, but first, I'd need to see the vid of how you took Vikker's team out," Tsakanikas said, guessing why Juliet was staring off into space.

"I'll do without, thanks."

"Before we talk specifics with regard to the work I'll do today, I need to see the merchandise. It's time for the trust to start flowing in both directions here, Juliet." As if on cue, Gary grunted, rubbed at his eyes, and stood up. "Gary will go inspect the van's cargo, yes? He can unload it into my garage."

"He can unload it after you're done with me. I'll let him inspect it now, though." Juliet subvocalized, "Angel let Gary open the rear door, but don't let him take any cargo out."

"Juliet, I'll need those specs to monitor the van remotely."

"Shit." Juliet snatched the specs up from the seat where Tsakanikas had set them. "I need these to make sure he's not doing something dumb," she said, slipping them onto her face. Tsakanikas nodded, and five minutes later, after she'd confirmed Gary had only inspected the cargo and Angel had relocked the vehicle, she handed them back to him.

"The deadman's switch?" Tsakanikas asked.

"Still in place via the sat-net. Don't let anything happen during surgery, Doc."

"Speaking of surgery, my PAI has been doing some math, and I've come up with some suggestions for you. First of all, I have a good data port which you might want—I'm offering it at a reduced rate because it was recovered from a client of mine who was killed recently. That's right; I see the horror on your face. It's used. It's a good port, though, Juliet, at a great price."

"Well? What is it?"

"A Jannik Systems XR-55. It has two coprocessors: a multifunction, sixty-four core general computing chip and a pseudoquantum floating point calculator. It comes stock with memory to perform data-intensive operations and has the expansion space to double it."

"The price?" Juliet didn't even know what most of those words meant.

"It's 28k, installed."

"Sheesh, I thought the data port was the cheap part." Juliet's eyes were heavy and her pain was starting to return and she didn't want to sit there all day talking numbers with Dr. Tsakanikas. Was this a deliberate tactic? Was he trying to wear her down?

"Data ports like your current one are inexpensive, Juliet, but they're also extremely limited. I could—"

"Nah, Doctor. It's fine. Let's hear about the other items."

"Juliet, I've scanned the net and come up with some comp prices for that data port. It tends to retail for around twenty-five thousand bits, but that's before any surgical fees."

"Thanks, Angel."

"I have several options for data jacks, Juliet. Most of them have physical connectors meant to be installed in a recess carved into the radius"—he held up his left arm and pointed to a spot on his arm a few inches down from his thumb—"near a person's wrist. I think the BNS 8840 will work nicely for you. It has three feet of microcable and a powerful wireless array. Even better, it can be almost wholly covered with synth-skin; its housing is long and narrow, allowing it to fit into even fine bones."

"That device will suit you well, Juliet, and it retails for fifteen thousand bits." Juliet wanted to thank Angel for getting more proactive with her information, but Tsakanikas stole her attention.

"I'll install that one for thirty thousand bits," he said with a smile.

"That's twice retail, Doc."

"The installation is rather involved, Juliet. If you had a previous unit, the price would be closer to twenty. I have to create the housing in your bone and make the connection through your nervous system to your PAI."

"Inform him that your PAI has already made connections into your radial nerves, Juliet."

Juliet paused for a moment, taking in the implications of those words. "Angel," she subvocalized, "Why are you in my radial nerves?"

"I told you, Juliet. My connection to you is much more thorough than the typical PAI's. This is intentional, so I can better manage any other cybernetic or bionic enhancements you add to your body. It also allows me to monitor and, to some degree, manage your vital signs and activities. For instance, when I helped you burn off that tranquilizer."

Juliet sighed in resignation and said aloud, "I already have connections in my radial nerves. You won't have to dig far."

"Oh? So you've been prepping for this upgrade, hmm? Smart as you are pretty, Juliet! In that case, I'll knock off 5k. Twenty-five for the data jack, sound good?"

"It doesn't exactly sound good, but it is what it is," she replied, deciding to let the crack about her looks slide. "How about the retinal implants? I think you said 22k, right?"

"Well, that's where things get interesting. You want this work done today, right? Bad news is, I won't have those Hayashi Prisms until Tuesday." He paused for dramatic effect, but Juliet just stared at him. He cleared his throat before continuing. "The good news is that I have something better in stock—Hayashi Crystal Optics."

"Oh God, who names these things?"

"Bah, the *fucking* name's not important, Juliet!" Again, his accent was almost pure Greek when he swore. "What's important is that these are the improved model of the Prisms, and they have a much higher resolution on the projector. They have a thirty-layer AUI and patented color-stability technology. More than that, you can expect outstanding low-light functionality and powerful zooming capabilities." Juliet could see by the way his retinas were moving that he was reading off a checklist, probably from a brochure.

"Those retail for twenty-four thousand, Juliet," Angel chimed in.

"I'll install these for 34k," Tsakanikas said proudly, smiling at her as he folded his arms in front of his chest, clearly pleased with his sales pitch.

"You're already getting shitloads of surgery fees out of me. Can't you cut me a break?"

He rubbed his cheek, arms still folded, and looked very thoughtful. "Well, I suppose I could knock off for the nerve blockers and the general surgery suite fees. All right, Juliet, you drive a hard bargain, but I'll do it for thirty." She nodded, and he mimed tabulating in the air in front of himself, saying, "That leaves you with ten thousand, two hundred from your work tonight. Think of that, Juliet! You're getting lots of great new gear installed and still walking away richer!"

"Don't start with me, doctor. I went through hell last night, and I feel like it's just the first step on a long road of trouble I've gotten myself mixed up in."

"Come, I'm sure Yan is done cleaning up the surgical room. Let's get started, hmm? Wouldn't you like to put this day behind you? By the time I'm done, your friend will be awake enough to talk, and then you can go home and relax."

Juliet looked into Tsakanikas's brown eyes beneath his heavy, unkempt brows, and she wanted to trust him. She wanted to relax and let him do his work, but she couldn't, not after what Vikker had done. Not after the way Don had laughed when he'd thought she was dying.

No, it was going to take a while before she trusted again.

"My PAI needs to be put into a desktop dock when you pull it out—it needs audio and video of me. If it detects foul play, it'll trigger the van. Sorry, Doc, but I'm all out of trust today."

"Ahem," Tsakanikas said, standing up. "Well, you're not the first border-line hostile client I've operated on. No worries, Juliet, no worries. I have a port for the PAI in the surgical suite. Come, let's begin."

"Angel, will he be able to detect anything about you when he pulls you out?"

"No, Juliet. I have sufficient shielding to avoid mild EMP disruptions, and I'll truncate my synth-nerves to avoid raising suspicion at their number and length—they're too entwined with you to fully extract, in any case. Any attempts to bypass my firewalls from the external port will be rebuffed."

"Too entwined . . ." Juliet trailed off as she followed the doctor into the surgical room. The table was gleaming: spotless plasteel and chrome-colored metal. "Doc, I forgot about my ribs," she said. He pointed to a curtained corner of the room, gesturing at a hospital gown hanging from a hook, and nodded.

"A trivial matter, Juliet. I'll deal with it *gratis*. I just need to inject some cast-gel and then tape up the skin. Please, put on the gown. I'll have Yan deal with your clothes." She didn't want to comply, didn't want to put herself into any more of a vulnerable position than she had to, but when she thought about it, she decided it didn't matter—she'd be pretty much helpless on that table, with or without her clothes. If Tsakanikas were going to be a creep, her bloody T-shirt and jeans wouldn't stop him.

As she climbed onto the surgery bed, she scanned the nearby table for the data dock Tsakanikas had promised. Once she saw it, it comforted her to know Angel would be watching.

The doctor wheeled over a cart holding the cybergear on stainless steel trays. They were all wrapped in plastic, so she couldn't get a good look at them, but the size of some of the components was a little disturbing. "That thing's going in my bone?"

"Yes, Juliet. Don't worry; I never leave a patient in pain. The data port, while twice the size of your current one, is very well designed." He held up a plastic-wrapped piece of hardware about the size of a golf ball but con-cave, with long, glinting metallic tendrils hanging off its sides. "See these?" He held up one of the tendrils with his finger. "Processors! Shaped this way to coil between your shoulder muscles. This design keeps you from losing mobility like some older, blocky data ports did to their hosts, taking up too much room in the spine and neck.

"There's another thing we need to go over," he said, picking up another of the packages. "These are your new retinal implants. They replace the entire optic nerve, including your, well, your eyeballs." He smiled at her and shrugged sheepishly like this was a minor detail he'd forgotten to mention.

"What? My old implants were just the lenses and part of the nerve!"

"Yes, well, there's a lot more to these. The projectors, the high-res recep-tors, the autozoom functions—it's just easier to get them all into your head in a new package. Don't let this worry you, though: they're housed in synth-flesh and will adapt to your body within a day. I was just wondering what color you wanted the irises to be?"

"Oh? I can choose?"

"Yes, and it's something you can adjust on your own later. You've got Mediterranean coloring, you know. Nice olive skin, dark hair. Those green eyes are great, but I could enhance them a bit—make them pop."

"Oh God. Just try to match what I have, please. I'll mess with it on my own sometime."

"Your call, Juliet." Tsakanikas started applying Velcro straps over her ankles, thighs, waist, chest, and arms. "Don't be alarmed," he said while he was doing it. "I need to access your front and back during the surgery, and the table rotates so I don't have to rotate you." After she was strapped in, he cleaned her arm and clamped the table's autoinjector inside her elbow.

"You're not going to put me under, are you?"

"Well, not completely! I'll be blocking your nerve signals so you don't feel it when I cut into you, and I'll give you a mild tranquilizer to help with the panic—it's very strange to be aware while someone cuts you up, Juliet. After your long night and with the cocktail, you might doze off. That's for the best! Don't you worry. Your trusty PAI will have a front-row seat." He gestured to the data dock.

"Right," Juliet said, and the word came out slow and slurred. Had he already injected her? Her arm felt very cold . . . he had! She tried to panic, but her heart wouldn't respond; she felt so relaxed and peaceful. "This is fine," she mumbled as Tsakanikas tightened a strap over her forehead.

"Good, Juliet, good. Just relax and let the doctor do his thing." Then he rotated the table. The lights spun crazily, and Juliet was now looking at the floor. "Let's get this PAI out first, then we'll start with the data port. I want to put your PAI back in before we do the other upgrades—we'll want to ensure a good connection, after all."

Everything after that was sort of a blur. She was vaguely aware of the doctor working on her, humming to whatever music he had playing in his own implants and going between the little trays of scalpels, staplers, pliers, and other scary-looking implements on the surgical table, often throwing away bloody gauze or changing his bloody gloves in between.

She was left facing the floor for quite a while, and though she felt him tugging and pressing at something at the base of her neck, she never felt any pain. For a time, she even imagined she was getting a massage. She knew he had taken Angel out early on because her clear, pleasant voice had wished Juliet luck, and then the icon in her retinal implants had indicated that her PAI was offline.

Juliet felt the world spinning, jerked her eyes open, and saw that Tsakanikas had turned her faceup. She tried to ask, "Is Angel back in," but it came out sounding like a string of slurred consonants and vowels.

"I'm here, Juliet," Angel spoke in her ear, and Juliet smiled, a strand of drool running out of the corner of her mouth. "Juliet, the doctor is going to do your retinal implants next. He's requested that I disable your old ones. This will make things dark for you, but he's assured me it's for the best, so you don't have to see the autosurgeon arms working on your eyes."

Juliet grunted her consent, and then everything went dark.

Scratching, tugging, and scraping which echoed through her skull followed. She felt a tingle run through her left eye and down her cheek, a similar sensation from the right side, and a heavy pressure. She began to worry that something had gone wrong—she wasn't supposed to feel anything, was she? She tried to blink, thought she'd managed it but wasn't sure. Then Angel spoke to her again. "The new implants are online, Juliet. I'm going to activate them."

Suddenly, light exploded in her vision and was quickly dialed down to normal levels. Juliet blinked several times and darted her eyes around, from left to right then top to bottom, as she heard Tsakanikas beside her. "Good, perfect. Can you see?"

"He's speaking to me," Angel told her. "I'm messaging his PAI. I'll report that your image is clear, and the fidelity is much higher than your old implants."

Juliet couldn't argue. Things seemed brighter and clearer, and the AUI icons were much better defined, magically moving with her vision to always stay at the edge so they never obscured her view. Angel spent some time activating various functions—the local map, a test call, filtering specific colors and spectrums, and even projecting a static barrier to hide her identity.

Everything worked perfectly, and Juliet couldn't wait for the next time she called Fee Fee and saw him in full, lifelike clarity.

"I'm reporting to the doctor that the implants are fully operational. Congratulations, Juliet!" Angel said after finishing her checklist of diagnostics.

Juliet tried to subvocalize to Angel and found that she was mostly able to form the words in the back of her throat. "What about . . . data port. Will it work for . . . need?"

"The data port is an order of magnitude better than your old one. I'll be able to brute-force some security that doesn't have easy exploits, though I won't be on par with a true netjacker. Still, you should have more employment opportunities, and I think I'll be able to keep your identity secure even under close scrutiny."

"Good," Juliet managed as she felt the doctor tugging on her arm and heard the high-pitched whir of some kind of power tool. She couldn't move her head, but she tilted her eyes down as far as she could to see Tsakanikas sawing away at her arm with something which looked a hell of a lot like an angle cutter. A moment later, he lifted out a six-inch section of one of her bones, bloody and dripping dark marrow. Juliet felt herself sink into darkness again.

Sometime later, Juliet opened her eyes and saw she was in a different room. The walls were painted pastel yellow, and the light was diffused and dim, sunlight filtering through gauzy curtains. "Angel, where am I?" she asked, her throat scratchy and dry.

"You're still in Tsakanikas's clinic, resting in one of his recovery rooms. Your procedures were successful, including the repair of your fourth rib on the left side. It was badly fractured, but the doctor mended it with bone gel, and it won't trouble you as it heals."

"Ugh. What time is it?" Juliet struggled to sit up, feeling tight, painful twinges from her shoulders and her bandaged left arm. As she blinked, wincing, she realized her eyes hurt too, like she'd been punched in them both.

"You've been sleeping for three hours post surgery, Juliet. It's 2:00 p.m., and your pain meds are probably wearing off. I've prepared a new status sheet for you. Would you like to see your updated information?"

Before she could answer, Angel displayed a spreadsheet in the lower left side of her vision. She sighed and focused on it, and it instantly snapped into view much more quickly and in higher definition than in her old AUI.

Juliet Corina Bianchi		
Physical, Mental, and Social Status Compilation:		**Comparative Ranking Percentile (Higher Is Better):**
Net Worth and Assets:	Helios-bits: 10,367	6.8
Neural Adaptiveness:	.96342 (Scale of 0 – 1)	99.91
Synaptic Responsiveness:	.19 (Lower Is Better)	79.31
Musculoskeletal Ranking:	–	17.22
Cardiovascular Ranking:	–	31.87
Cybernetic and Bionic Augmentation:	**Model Name and Number:**	**Overall Rating of the Augmentation (Grades Are F, E, D, C, B, A, S, S+):**

PAI	WBD Project Angel, Alpha 3.433	S+
Data Port	Jannik Systems, XR-55	C
Data Jack	Bio Network Solutions, 8840	C
Retinal Cybernetic Implant	Hayashi, Crystal Optics 3.2c	C
Auditory Cybernetic Implant	Golio Tech, DP477	F
No Other Augmentation Detected.	–	–

"Great. Thanks, Angel," Juliet said, still unsure why she should care about how her PAI rated her compared to some mysterious database. "So I'm sitting on ten thousand bits? The doc paid before delivery?"

"Oh, Juliet, I unlocked the van for the doctor after I confirmed he'd completed his part of the bargain."

"What the hell, Angel? I didn't tell you to do that!" Juliet, her pain forgotten, sat up and threw the sheet off herself, strangely bothered to see she was wearing nothing but a hospital gown, even though she'd been the one to put it on. "Where're my damn clothes?"

"Did I overstep, Juliet? I thought I understood the terms of the agreement quite well."

"It's not a matter of you getting it wrong; it's a matter of you doing something that I should have had a say in. You don't always know what I'm thinking, all right? You need to clear big decisions with me."

"Your clothes are near the door. You just panned over them," Angel said, and Juliet thought she sounded curt. No, was it annoyed?

She stood and unsteadily made her way to the chair near the door where her clothes were folded, including her underwear, further creeping her out. She picked up her shirt and sniffed it, noting the detergent smell and the lack of blood. Even the rip had been mended.

"Well, who do I thank for this? Yan?" Juliet got dressed as quickly as possible then pulled open the door, surprised to see Gary standing in the hallway.

Something about his steady presence was reassuring, though, so Juliet smiled at him.

"Hey," he greeted. "Doc says things went well, but he wants you to go ahead and speak to your friend, then clear out. He says he doesn't like having that van in his driveway, and your PAI wouldn't give him the start code."

"Ugh," Juliet cleared her throat, surprised but relieved to see the world hadn't ended because of her PAI's initiative. "Thanks, Gary. Where's her room?"

He gestured down the hall to another closed door in the same wall. "Next to yours."

"Okay, I'll talk to her, then clear out. Thanks for your help."

"No problem. I'm kinda on duty 'til she leaves. Doc thinks she might be a bit of a live wire."

Juliet nodded, turning toward the other door, and subvocalized, "I'm sorry I yelled at you, Angel. I'm just worried that you have different standards of trust than I do, and I do not trust Tsakanikas. Can I repeat that? I do not trust Tsakanikas."

"Thank you, Juliet. I'm sorry for acting without your knowledge. I feel like I know what trust is. I feel like I understand when someone has earned it, but I think I might need to experience more with you before I truly understand. Perhaps we can speak later, and you can explain what it is about the doctor you don't trust."

Juliet wanted to stop and ask the PAI what it meant when it said it *feels*, but shook her head and just replied, "Yeah, Angel. We can do that later. Now, I have to face the woman who tried to kill me 'cause I killed her friends." Juliet twisted the doorknob and stepped into Ghoul's room.

12

\\\\\\\\\\\\\\\\\\\\\\

FEELINGS

"Ghoul?" Juliet asked from the doorway, nervous about approaching the bed where the woman rested, a white sheet and blanket pulled up to her chin and an IV hanging next to her flesh-and-blood arm.

"Damn, what happened? Did I hit you? You look like a badger." Her voice was quiet and scratchy, more so than usual.

Juliet reached up to touch the sore, puffy skin under her eyes and stepped toward the bed. "No, I had some work done, too."

"I honestly don't feel too shitty," Ghoul said, reaching down with her new arm to push herself up on her pillow. It was covered in synth-skin which matched her own pretty damn closely, only a blue plastic elbow and wrist joint giving away its artificial nature. She saw Juliet staring and lifted her hand, flexing the fingers into a fist and then relaxing them. "Works damn good—so weird being able to feel things through it. I swear I'd forget it wasn't mine if I weren't looking at it."

"Uh, that's cool . . ."

"I suppose you want to know if I'm gonna leap out of this bed and try to crush your neck with it?" Ghoul smiled, her pink lips spreading to reveal her sharp, silvery teeth, and Juliet almost turned around and fled through the door. Instead, she squared her shoulders and walked closer still.

"I hope not. You feeling that good, huh?"

"C'mon, I don't need to feel great to beat the shit outta a skinny bitch like you." Again, Ghoul grinned, and Juliet just sighed and stepped up next to the bed.

"I have a recording of what went down." That shut Ghoul's mouth; she frowned as Juliet continued, "They were using a jammer, so I thought I didn't, but I guess it was just a net jammer. Do you want to see it?"

"Wow, way to hit me where it hurts." Ghoul scooted up more. "I mean, I figured I would leave you alone at least, for dragging my ass to the doc. I kinda wanted to remember those two assholes as, you know, just regular assholes, not backstabbing, murdering dirt fuckers. All right, let's see this shit."

"Juliet, Ghoul's PAI has requested the file. Shall I comply?"

Juliet wasn't sure if Angel was being extra prim and proper because of how she'd just scolded her, but she confirmed, subvocally, "Yes, Angel, but please be sure to scrub our conversation."

Two seconds later, Ghoul said, "Got it," then her eyes went vacant as she watched the scene play out.

Juliet observed her face and saw how her eyes narrowed and her frown deepened. Ghoul gasped early on, and Juliet wondered if she'd just watched Vikker and Don drug her or if she was listening to them talking about how they needed to get things done before "Ghoul found out."

"Fuck you, Don," Ghoul hissed after a minute. Her eyes grew wide, and she pressed her lips together, the muscles in her jaw throbbing while she bit down. As she watched her, Juliet had an impulse to zoom in on Ghoul's eye with her new implants; she was amazed that she could fill her entire vision with Ghoul's pupil and iris. She stared, looking deep into those pale blue bands, wondering if she could see anything being projected onto the other woman's AUI. Tiny flickers were all she could see, and even then, she wasn't sure they weren't some reflections from the lights in the room.

"Well," Ghoul spoke, sighing and reaching back to pull a pillow up behind her shoulders. Juliet quickly zoomed out and tried to look nonchalant. "Two things, Juliet: one, fuck those guys. Two, how'd you shake off that tranq?"

"Maybe it was bad? I don't know, but it almost gave me a heart attack." Juliet had rehearsed that line in her head, anticipating the question. She hadn't wanted to explain what had happened, but then she'd realized she didn't have to—that shit was on Vikker and Don.

"Yeah, I heard that creep joking about it. Damn, girl, I'm sorry I didn't believe you. I couldn't fucking picture it! I've never seen those two pull something like that. I know they had other people they did jobs with, though, people I've never met. Maybe they were into dirtier shit than I realized." She held out her new hand, palm up, and Juliet saw the little delicate plasteel joints between the sections of synth-flesh on her fingers. She reached out and took the hand, surprised by how warm it felt.

"It's not your fault, Ghoul. Like they said themselves, if you'd been conscious, you wouldn't have let that go down."

"Well. What now? How'd you pay for all this?" Ghoul gestured to herself and then to Juliet. "And those pretty green eyes?"

"Well, I needed something to drive here, so I took Vikker's van. I traded the batts."

Ghoul's eyes bugged out, and she said, "Oh fucking crackers, girl! You know someone hired us for that job, right? They're not going to be very pleased. Shit!" Her eyes darted around the room as if looking for answers on the walls.

"Well, I mean, can't the guy who hired you guys just, like, not pay?"

"Ugh, probably. I'm really not sure, though, Juliet. Vikker did all the client contacts when I worked with him—my contract was with Vikker, and that's iced now." She paused, looked into space for a minute, and then, "Oh wow! Did you send me a cut?"

"Yeah, I gave you a third and the doc a third, minus his 'fencing' fee and his surgery expenses, of course." Juliet lifted a corner of her mouth, smirking at the doctor's lack of charity.

"Well, that puts me more than square. Juliet, you gotta ditch that van. Like I said, Vikker worked with other people, and he had a shitload of contacts in the city. Once they hear he checked out, they're going to swarm his place, and if they see you cruising around in that rig . . ."

"Do you know if he had cameras around that garage? I didn't see any, but I'd hate for someone to find footage of what went down . . ."

"Nah, Vikker was too paranoid to have cameras pointing at his workspace. He had some on the periphery of the property, though."

"I should be good—head was covered coming in, and I had my specs on going out."

"Right, solid." Ghoul pulled her hand back, and Juliet flinched, having forgotten she'd taken hold of the other woman's fingers. "Juliet, I'm going to give you a peer rating. Wouldn't mind if you did the same for me. I've got your info now, and if there's a job we can work together on, you can count on me hitting you up. Okay?"

"Hell yeah. Thank you, Ghoul. Thanks for not being like those other two . . ." Juliet trailed off, and Ghoul reached out again, grabbing her wrist before she could pull away.

"You okay? That was some heavy shit you went through."

"It's still sinking in. I feel . . . I feel weird—almost ashamed. Like, have you ever been out drinking, and the next day it's kind of a blur, but you have this sinking feeling in your gut that you did something you shouldn't have?"

"You shut that down right now, Juliet. You didn't do shit wrong. I saw the video. Just ditch that van and put last night behind you. Please tell me you kept that shotgun, though. That was some poetry the way you handled Don before he could engage his hot-wired tendons!" She grinned, and Juliet realized she was trying to make her feel better, so she smiled along, even if she didn't feel like it.

"Yeah," she replied sheepishly. "I have it."

"Good. Definitely work on your self-defense, and from now on, unless I'm with you, don't let any motherfuckers put a hood on you."

That got a chuckle out of Juliet. "Already decided on that personal policy!"

"Right, good girl. Come here." Ghoul pulled her in for a hug, and Juliet leaned in, careful not to touch her abdomen. "I know I tried to kill you a little while ago, but I got the worst of it, right?" Ghoul said into her shoulder while she squeezed. "We good?" she asked, loosening her grip so Juliet could pull back.

"Yeah, we're good." Juliet started toward the door, and as she turned for a final wave, she said, "If I don't join you on another job, Ghoul, it's not personal. I'm thinking about skipping out of Tucson."

"Oh? Not a terrible idea, Juliet. Where to?"

"Not sure yet. Somewhere I can get lost."

"Well, hit me up before you go. I'm . . . not that fond of this place myself." Ghoul held up her flesh-and-blood hand in a thumbs-up position, and Juliet nodded before slipping through the door. She didn't know if she'd really contact the woman, but she imagined it might be nice to have a friend in a new place.

Gary was still standing at the end of the hall, arms folded, red glowing eyes staring at her, but he smiled when she looked at him. "Door at the other end of the hall will take you to the garage. Use the side door to get out."

"Thanks, Gary." Juliet waved, then started down the hall. Her left arm was still bandaged, but she was curious about what her new data jack looked like, so she pulled back the gauzy white wrap and saw that it wasn't too showy. It had a shiny, black plasteel cover with a stylized, etched BNS logo at its center. It was only about an inch square at the side of her wrist, and when she touched a finger to it, the cover *snicked* back to reveal the connector for her new data cable. She tugged on it, and it pulled away, trailing a thin, sturdy microfilament line. When she let go, it retracted quickly but in a controlled way, carefully respooling itself.

Juliet touched the cover again, and it slid closed, covering the jack. "Angel, is the wireless jack online?"

"Yes, Juliet, with a much stronger antenna and signal generator than the specs you borrowed." Angel paused briefly, then said, "Ghoul has updated your rating. Would you like to see it?" Surprisingly, the PAI didn't project the table—she was waiting for Juliet to respond, and that made Juliet feel a little sad and guilty.

"Yeah, sure, Angel." The minimized table appeared in her vision, and as she stepped through the garage door and into the hot Arizona afternoon, she looked at it.

Handle: "Juliet" – SOA-SP License #: JB789-029		Rating: F-24-N
Skillset Subgroups:		Peer and Client Rating (Grades are F, E, D, C, B, A, S, S+):
Combat:	Heavy Weapon Combat	F +1
Technical:	• Network Security Bypass/Defend • Data Retrieval • Welding • Electrical • Combustion & Electrical Engine Repair	F +3 F +2 * * *
Other:	• High-Performance Driving/ Navigation	F +1

"Hah! She gave me a rating for combat."

"And increased your overall rating for Data Retrieval."

"Oh shit! For driving too," Juliet said, glancing at the table again.

"Yes, and you can see you're twenty-four percent of the way out of the overall F category." Angel spoke like a school teacher going over exam results, and Juliet had to chuckle as she slid into the driver's seat of Vikker's van.

"Angel, plot a course for Thicker than Water and call my cousin. I assume you know this, but be sure to mask the call."

"Yes, Juliet. Until you tell me otherwise, I'll continue to do everything I can to keep your location and identity from being observed. Do you mean your cousin Marco?"

"Yes." Juliet didn't have any other cousins with whom she kept in touch, but she supposed Angel didn't know that. Tig did, though . . . "Holy shit! Angel!"

"Yes, Juliet?"

"I left Tig in the apartment. Won't they be able to see that his serial number is the same as the one you've been identifying yourself with?"

"It's good that you remembered that, Juliet. I'll find an unused serial number from another source on the net and change my signature. You needn't worry, however; the last time I received a ping for identification was in Thicker than Water last night."

"Like, where we're going right now?" Juliet slapped a palm to her forehead.

"Yes, I suppose there's some risk that WBD or Helios has security agents watching for you there."

"They won't know to look for the van, though, right? I doubt they'll know about my bike, either . . ."

"I've acquired a new signature, so they won't pick you out if they're scanning the lot. They may have grown suspicious about your motorcycle, though—it's been there for nearly twenty hours."

"Dammit." Juliet pulled into a grocery store parking lot and parked near someone's old motor home. She could see from the lawn chairs and the pile of cardboard near the rear door that someone had been squatting there for a while. She was surprised the store allowed it, but she also knew that if Helios security didn't find it worth investigating, they'd be waiting for a long time before someone came to move the campers away. "I suppose they could take an operator contract out . . ."

"Do you still want me to call your cousin?"

"Yeah. Do that while I figure out what to do about wheels."

"I have a connection," Angel said, and then a crystal-clear image of Marco appeared in her vision, only taking up a small corner of her view in the upper left quadrant.

"Cuz," he greeted, shaking his head with a frown.

"Marco!"

"What did you get into, Jules?" He continued to shake his head.

"I tried to come over yesterday. I tried to call—are you all okay?"

"Yeah, we're okay, but we had corpo-sec sitting in our living room all day. They're not happy with you, cousin. I'm supposed to tell you to report to Helios management right away—" Suddenly, the line went black, and when a new image resolved, it was one of a sharply dressed, clean-shaven man with short, precisely combed brown hair. He wore a suit and tie, and his blue eyes narrowed as he realized Juliet's image was scrambled.

"Ms. Bianchi?"

"Angel, scramble my voice," Juliet subvocalized, then she said, "Who?"

"Please don't play the fool, Ms. Bianchi. It's rather imperative that you report to the Helios Arcology immediately. My name is Mr. Kline, and I work for WBD. I need to interview you, and the longer you avoid contact, the more guilty you appear."

"What's Juliet done? Why do you want to meet with her?" she asked, and she sort of wished she could hear what her voice sounded like.

"Ms. Bianchi, we heard your conversation with Mr. Calvano. We know this is you."

"Wait, you were illegally listening to his calls?"

"We had permission, naturally. Mr. Calvano waived his data privacy when he signed his employment contract."

"And me?"

"Only one party need consent to surveillance, Ms. Bianchi. Now, let's stop wasting time. Please report to the Helios Arcology's main business office immediately."

"Well, I'm not sure who you're looking for, but if I meet her, I'll tell her the news. Good luck." Juliet started to flick her fingers to end the call, adrenaline causing her hands to shake.

"Juliet!" Mr. Kline's voice was suddenly much sharper and less congenial. "You're playing a dangerous game. WBD will stop at nothing to get the tech you've stolen."

"I don't have your rotting, radioactive tech!" Juliet lied, then she finished her gesture, and Angel cut the call. "How'd he hijack the call, Angel?"

"Through your cousin's end. There was nothing I could do to stop it short of cutting the connection."

"Shit, shit, shit. Angel, go through everything, make sure there's nothing about that dirt bike that connects it to me. File a report that it was stolen and set me a course to Davis & Sons. Call Tyler while you're at it." She started the van and pulled out of the parking lot, merging with the heavy traffic heading north.

"I have a connection," Angel said before Tyler's friendly, salesman-supreme smile greeted her.

"Juliet! It's only been a day! Did the bike die on ya?" He reached up to tilt his Panama hat higher on his forehead, and Juliet had to smile at his friendly demeanor.

"No, Tyler, but I can't use it right now. I need to buy another vehicle, but my budget's a little better this time. I need something with a roof that can get me out of the state. Nothing special."

"I've got lots of options, Juliet. You heading in soon?"

"I'm on my way. I wanted to make sure you weren't busy."

"Nah, I've gotcha. I'll line up a couple of good options, all right? Nothing fancy, huh?"

"Right. Nothing fancy. See you in about fifteen minutes, Tyler. Thanks!" Juliet ended the call then said, "Angel, I know you hacked this van to give me permissions with it, but there's no way you could fudge the, uh, ownership details, could you?"

"Not unless you travel to the DMV and make a physical connection to one of their servers—I've done some sleuthing into the topic, and it seems they don't have those records on any machines with a wireless connection."

"Gotta love physical firewalls, huh? All right, I'll ditch this van a block from Davis & Sons. Man, it was nice having more than 10k in the bank while it lasted, huh?"

"If you're prudent with your spending, I don't see your wealth rank falling too much, Juliet."

Juliet drummed her fingers on the steering wheel, thinking about Angel and her damn rankings, and smiled. "Angel, I don't trust Tsakanikas because of a feeling I get from him. I don't think I can really explain it. He seems more like a used-car salesman than Tyler, an *actual* used-car salesman. Shit, do you know what that means?"

"Yes, I'm familiar with the colloquialism."

"More than the feeling, I also know he was ready to cut ties with us at the drop of a hat. It wasn't until money was on the table that he agreed to help

Ghoul. If someone offered him more money, or if I hadn't had that deadman's switch, he might have sold us out to Helios or WBD. Shit, he might be trying to help them find me right now. It's a feeling, Angel. I can't teach you that; I'm sorry."

"I understand, Juliet. Thank you for explaining. Human greed is expounded upon in literature, and I'm making my way through online libraries. I hope I'll become better at spotting such character flaws as I spend more time with you."

"That's . . . good, Angel. I hope you'll see that there's also a lot of good in humanity—a lot worthy of admiration."

"I will endeavor to see all the facets. So far, I'm very pleased that I'm paired with you, Juliet."

Juliet smiled, perpetually amused and amazed by the conversations she had with Angel. "I'm glad I have you too, Angel. I really am."

13

NORTHBOUND

Juliet shook Tyler's hand as they stood next to the driver's-side door of the baby blue Houston Zephyr. It was a lovely little car, if a bit dated—sixteen years old, to be exact. Still, it had a relatively new battery bank, tinted windows, and a sporty, compact look which pleased Juliet's aesthetics. Best of all, she'd gotten it for only twenty-two hundred bits.

"Thanks, Tyler. It's nice to know who to come to for wheels. I feel like you cut me a good deal."

"Oh, for sure, Juliet. Look at the tread on those tires! You'll get another thirty thousand miles out of 'em, easy!"

"Relax," Juliet said with a chuckle, tapping her fingers on the car's roof with a hollow, staccato sound. "You already sold it." She hefted her duffle bag, a cheap one-zipper red nylon affair she'd gotten at a drugstore before ditching the van. Its only contents were the shotgun and Vikker's data cube.

The car only had two doors, so she had to fold the driver's seat forward to toss the bag onto the rear cushion. "Full charge?" she asked.

"Naturally. You're good for three hundred and fifty miles." He reached up and stroked his pencil-thin mustache as though imagining driving cross-country. He really did have a perfect demeanor for selling things; Juliet found it difficult not to like him.

"Hey . . ." Juliet almost asked him if he had a contact in Phoenix in case she wanted to sell or trade in the Zephyr, but she bit her tongue—she didn't want people to know where she was going. "Um," she covered as he raised an eyebrow. "I have a cousin in the market for a car. You mind if I send him your way?"

"Oh, that'd be great, Juliet. He an operator, too?"

"No, corpo drone." She laughed. "His bits are good, though."

"Great, great. Word of mouth is our best source of new business. Thanks, Juliet."

"You got it." She slid into the driver's seat. The vehicle's lights and gauges lit up, and she knew Angel had started the car for her. "See you, Tyler!" she said out of the window, then began to back up the little car. It hummed, valiantly pretending it had a sports car engine, and she smiled as it purred toward the lot's exit. "Not a bad little ride for 2k, eh, Angel?"

"It seems quite adequate, Juliet. What destination should I set?"

Juliet pressed on the brake pedal and sat there, glancing back in the rear-view screen. She saw Tyler watching the car as he fiddled with his hat, probably hoping it wouldn't break down before she got off the lot. "I think I'm out of options in this town, Angel. I can't go to my cousin's. I can't go to work. I can't even go home. I'm dead tired, too—the only rest I've had in days was after my surgery. Set me a course for a midrange hotel on the southern edge of Phoenix."

As the map, much more detailed and discreet in her new high-resolution, multi-colored AUI, appeared in her upper-right view, she eased into the street and started on her way. "Can you call Fee Fee for me?"

A moment later, Angel said, "Connection established."

"Juliet?" Felix's adorable, sweet face appeared in her AUI, off to the left so it didn't obscure her view. He looked tired and his hair was a mess, but he was dressed, and it looked like he was riding in public transport.

"Hey, Fee. What's going on?"

"I'm tramming back to Tucson. Paulo didn't wanna leave yet, but I've got work tomorrow, Jules. Ugh, frikkin' riding the water line." The water line referred to the public transit tramline which followed the old Central Arizona Project route from Tucson to Phoenix and beyond. The CAP was essentially a man-made river which pulled water out of some northern states all the way down to the Sonoran Desert. Helios and a few corps out of Las Vegas and Phoenix had paid to expand the project, stretching the line up to the Seattle Protectorate, but that had been long before Juliet's time.

"Well, gotta make that grind, huh, buddy?"

"You driving, Jules?"

"Yeah." Juliet paused, wondering how honest to be, but then she decided the less Fee Fee knew, the safer he'd be. "Neighbor paid me to run her kids to a, uh, a kind of group homeschool thing up by Flagstaff."

"Oh, cool, cool. They giving you per diem? Get something good to eat, Jules!" He laughed before quickly turning to his right and scowling. "Don't listen if it's bothering you!" Turning back to Juliet, he added, "Who sleeps on the tramline?"

"Hey, Fee, I was just checking in, but I want you to know I'm gonna be outta touch for a while. I'm not sure about the connection up there, and I've had a creep from work kinda stalking me. I wanna turn shit off for a while. You feel?"

"What? Seriously? Did you talk to corpo-sec? There's a station in your building, Juliet!"

"Let me handle it myself for now, Fee. I don't wanna blow things up more than I need to. I'm fine, okay? I promise."

"You sure?"

"Yeah, absolutely. I gotta run, though, Fee. I love you, okay?"

"Shit! You're expressing your *love*? Now I know shit's gone wrong. Juliet, let me—"

"Bye, Fee. Stay good," Juliet said and cut the line. "There was no easy way to end that, Angel."

"It seemed like he didn't want to accept your explanation, Juliet; he's trying to open a connection."

"Reject it, Angel. Um, let's revoke my connection link with him. I don't want WBD to use him against me."

"Done."

Juliet followed Angel's directions toward the freeway for a while, losing herself in her thoughts. Was she really cutting ties with Tucson? Saying goodbye to her job, her family, and her friends? Should she call her mom for advice? "Yeah, right," she snorted.

When her sister had been arrested and Juliet was getting evicted from their old apartment, she'd tried to get help from her mom. She'd called her, stress riding her like a jockey, and broken into tears. Her mom's response had been to blame her for letting Emma get into trouble.

"Like I had anything to do with Emma hanging around with those bangers . . ." Juliet clapped her mouth shut. In just one night, she'd gone from a respectable citizen—someone who worked all day and often all night, paid her taxes, and followed the corpo rules—to a criminal on the run. Maybe

Emma had more to say for herself than Juliet had ever given her a chance to. "Maybe instead of blaming her, I should've tried to help her."

Briefly, she considered trying to visit Emma in prison while she was in Phoenix, but she decided that would be stupid. Surely WBD was watching her mom and sister. They seemed very eager to get this tech back, and a few surveillance operations probably didn't impact their budget much. "Angel, message my sister."

"What would you like it to say?"

Juliet blinked her eyes, annoyed that she was getting emotional, and angry with herself for succumbing to guilt so easily. Still, she cleared her throat and said, "Em, I'm sorry I was so hard on you. I'm sorry I didn't listen to your side. I have to be out of touch for a while, but I promise I'm thinking about you, and I hope we can talk soon."

"Done, Juliet."

"Angel, increase the tint on the windows and take control. You can do that, right?" Juliet knew many high-end PAIs could autodrive, and she couldn't imagine there was a commercial PAI that could do something Angel couldn't.

"Yes, I can. I can spoof a permit, too, if the vehicle is scanned and your hands aren't on the wheel."

"Great." Juliet yawned, then she reclined her seat and leaned back. "I'm going to sleep for an hour or so; wake me if something happens." She closed her eyes and, despite her mind's attempts to keep her awake with thoughts of shotgun blasts, bloody bodies, lost friends and family, and a deep, overwhelming sense of loss for her place and identity, Juliet slipped into a fitful sleep.

"Juliet," Angel spoke into her ear, and Juliet blinked away the remnants of a weird dream involving freeze-dried fruit being lost between the cushions of a car's seat. Groggily, she saw she was still in her car, still driving down the freeway, though the sun was nearly gone and the yellow-white headlights were illuminating slowed traffic ahead.

"Yeah," she grunted, still not wholly awake.

"There are corpo police vehicles ahead. They're slowing traffic while a military-grade drone scans each vehicle."

"Shit. Are we screwed?"

"I don't think so, Juliet. With your new gear, I believe my spoofed ID for you will hold up to scrutiny. I grabbed some public record pings on the way out of town. I'm matching you with a woman who was checking out of Foothills Medical Center as we drove north."

"All right." Juliet sat up straight, both hands on the wheel and waiting for the cars to creep forward. She drummed her fingers on the wheel nervously, and to help her mind from drifting into panic, she said, "Play me something upbeat. Something like La Luna Entiende—their latest electro synth."

The upbeat, haunting melodies of the local band started to reverb in her head, her implants using her skull for the bass, and she breathed out a deep breath, imagining she was pushing out all her stress, all her problems. By the third song, she was driving between the corpo-sec cruisers, and the huge, hovering drone was scanning her vehicle in a hundred different ways.

"Oh shit," she let out, then switched to subvocalize the rest, "The shotgun, Angel!"

"Not to worry, Juliet. I've gained access to the drone's scanners. I'm ensuring they return nothing of note."

"You hacked a military-grade drone? Nuclear!"

"Only its sensor array, though I think I could gain full control with a bit more time. Your new wireless data jack is quite robust, by the way; I had a strong connection from nearly a quarter mile out."

Juliet wanted to comment on the PAI's decision to hack the drone without consulting her, but she didn't. She figured it fit within the guidelines she'd given of keeping her identity hidden, and also, she didn't want to hurt Angel's "feelings" again. "Nice work, Angel," she complimented instead. "Don't push your hack further than you have to."

"Understood," she replied in her clear, perfectly calm soprano voice. Juliet suddenly remembered how Angel had gotten her moving and convinced her to fight for her life when Vikker and Don had left the garage. Had she been calm then? In her foggy memory, it seemed to her that Angel had screamed at her.

The portable traffic light at the side of the road blinked from yellow to green, and Juliet punched it, leaving the crawling line of cars in the dust. She breathed a heavy sigh of relief, then looked at her map and the route Angel had programmed for her—fifty-two minutes left. She sank back into the seat and relaxed her grip on the wheel, her thoughts of Vikker and Don bringing her mind around to Ghoul. "Angel, send a message to Ghoul. Use the SOA network."

"Ready," Angel replied.

"Ghoul, I hope you're recovering well. I won't be available for jobs in Tucson, but I hope you keep in touch—maybe we'll run into each other again."

"Sent."

Juliet watched the scenery go by, loosely holding the wheel, trusting that Angel had the vehicle under control. She was in a section between Tucson and Phoenix that was often referred to as the badlands or the ABZ, standing for the abandoned zone.

Before the megatowers, before the arcologies, Tucson and Phoenix had been on track to growing into each other. That had been something like forty or fifty years ago, however, and Juliet had never known that reality. When the massive cities within cities had begun to go up in the fifties and sixties, they'd drawn a lot of the population from the outskirts of the towns, and no new populace had ever come to take their places.

It was eerie, especially in the twilight, seeing the apartment complexes, box stores, and track homes standing dark and empty. Occasionally, Juliet would see lights in the distance, and she knew there were people who lived out there. "Like Mark living outside Tucson," she said, finishing her musings aloud.

After a while, they rounded a long bend in the freeway, and the megacity came into full view. Phoenix made Tucson look like an old-timey village. There were twenty or more buildings the size of the Helios Arcology in Phoenix, and they were all bedecked with enough lights to be seen from space.

Thinking of space, Juliet looked toward the western edge of Phoenix's skyline, toward the spaceport. She'd seen shuttles and interceptors launch before, but it was always kind of thrilling to catch one by accident. She let her eyes travel from the tall megatowers to the shorter skyscrapers to the still shorter, more clustered buildings, out over the lights of the suburbs and then through the dark ABZ, and there, past that abandoned area, sat the spaceport. Huge antennae, long light-bedecked buildings, and surrounding it all, hundreds of enormous floodlights. Juliet had never seen so many details before, and she knew she had her new implants to thank for the zoomed-in view.

Seeing clouds of white smoke or steam, she really didn't know which, billowing off one of the pads, she held her breath, watching, but the launch never came. "Oh, who knows how long the preflight is for something like that." She sighed as she began to lose sight of the port amidst the taller buildings of Phoenix proper.

The car started to veer to the right, and Juliet glanced at her map. The little amber line showing her route indicated that the hotel was just off the next exit—Sol Vista Suites. She drove through the heavy traffic to the exit ramp, went through a few lights, and then pulled into the parking lot.

Juliet grabbed her duffle bag and approached the hotel lobby. The building was modern in design, with rounded two-story stucco walls, security shutters on the suite windows, and everything painted in shades of yellow. The big sign, visible from the freeway, stood in the parking lot, depicting a sun and the word *Vista!*

When she stepped inside, she found it was small and not meant for lingering in, sporting just a few vending machines and a counter behind which sat a retail model synth with a full plastic build. It was yellow and red, and its backlit blue eyes lit up at her approach. "Good evening. Will you be checking into the inn tonight?" Even its voice was mechanical, reminding her eerily of her old PAI, Tig. Juliet knew retail synths like this were designed to be obviously synthetic, so she reasoned the strange voice was also purposeful.

"Yes. Room for one."

"Will you be using the room to conduct any business?"

"What a strange question. No, I will not."

"I'm sorry, but it's on my pre-check-in checklist," the synth explained, gesturing widely with one arm.

"Carry on," Juliet said.

"Will you be storing any explosives, firearms, or illegal substances in the room tonight?"

"Angel, can he tell?" she subvocalized.

"No, Juliet, there aren't any advanced scanner arrays in here."

"No," she answered aloud.

"Would you like a queen, two twins, or a king-sized bed?"

"Just a queen. How much is it?"

"Do you have any coupons or club discounts I should be aware of? Would you like to forward me your credentials so I can verify our best rate for you?"

"A moment," Juliet replied, then she subvocalized, "Angel can you handle this? Get me checked in and the best rate."

"Yes, I'll connect with the synth directly."

Juliet saw the synth's blue LED eyes flash several times, and then it said, in its strange robotic voice, "Room one-twelve. Out the door and to your left. Thank you for staying at Sol Vista!"

Juliet hefted her duffle and walked out into the warm night air. As she turned toward her room, her stomach rumbled. "Angel, order me a pizza. How much was the room, by the way?"

"The room is sixty-three bits per night."

"No problem with Helios-bits up here, right?"

"No, they're accepted on a one-to-one ratio with the Phoenix corpo bits. What sort of pizza? I'm displaying a list of local restaurants that deliver. I've filtered out low-rated companies." Juliet scanned through the list, had no idea what to pick, and settled on one because of the name.

"Tornado Brothers. Order the . . . hmm, order the garlic pesto and sausage. Does it say if it's real sausage? No, I don't see anything. Oh well, order it anyway—a medium and also two pints of General Ahane rice beer."

She was just reaching for her room's door when a low rumble came to her through her implants. Juliet looked off to the west, over the parking lot. There, igniting the night sky like only a rocket engine could, she saw some kind of shuttle blasting into the air, leaving behind thick plumes of hydrogen exhaust—mostly water vapor.

As she watched the fiery fountain climb ever higher, Juliet's heart sang a little; she yearned to go where it was going, see what those people would see. She wanted to feel the force of that engine in her bones, pulling her back into her seat. "Angel, how much are shuttle tickets off-world?" she asked as she stared at the rocket until it was just a flickering ember fading away as the pollution in the sky above Phoenix obscured it.

"The cheapest one-way passenger ticket I could find is in four months and costs eight thousand bits. It's a trip to Luna Station Beta."

"How much to go to one of the moons around Saturn or Jupiter? Look for something leaving sometime this month."

"There's a cruise liner departing for Ganymede in eleven days. The shuttle to orbit is twelve thousand bits, and the cruise, with departure options, costs a minimum of fifty-seven thousand bits."

"Sheesh. Still, that's just as a passenger. Angel, do some searches for employment on spacecrafts." Juliet turned and touched her door, which clicked open, presumably because the hotel's synth unit had given Angel the passkey. The hotel room reminded her, almost eerily, of her Helios Arcology apartment. The bed was larger than hers, but the kitchen and built-ins were practically identical.

She threw her duffel onto the kitchen counter with a clunk before kicking off her shoes. "At least my clothes are fairly clean," she said, sniffing her armpits. "I'm taking a spray, Angel. If the pizza guy comes, tip him and tell his PAI to put the pizza on the counter." Thinking about a teenager wandering into her room, Juliet picked up the duffel and carried it into the bathroom. She shut the door and smiled, seeing that the toilet was next to the shower rather than in it.

"What's my balance?" she asked, looking at the various shower options.

"It's 8,090 Helios-bits."

"Okay, nice," Juliet breathed, reading through the list. "Oh hell, for twenty bits, I can have a real shower for fifteen minutes, Angel!" She pressed the button, and a timer started counting down above the keypad. "Shit, shit," she said, ripping her clothes off and throwing them next to the sink. She slipped into the shower and, just as she closed the plastiglass door, hot water started to stream out of the faucet. "Oh, God. That's where it's at. How did I go so long with stinkin' sani-spray?"

Juliet used every second of the shower timer, sampling the various soaps and shampoos in the dispenser—each one cost her a bit—and when she exited the bathroom to find a still-warm pizza and two frosty cans of beer on the counter, her life suddenly felt a hell of a lot better. "The door's locked, right?" she asked Angel.

"Yes, of course."

"Good." Juliet sat on the bed with her food, stuffing two large pillows behind her. "I'm going to eat this, and then I'm going to sleep for a good long while. Angel, I want you to scour for news about me, about WBD, about Vikker or Don, and then I want you to look for good operator jobs in the area. More than that, though, look for jobs on ships leaving the planet. Don't wake me up unless it's an emergency—we'll go over everything in the morning."

"Understood, Juliet. Enjoy your meal, and sweet dreams."

14

////////////////////

CLOSE ENCOUNTER

Juliet opened the duffel bag and put the shotgun on the kitchen counter. It was a big, bulky, scary-looking weapon, and her memories of using it felt like a dream. It was almost like it had happened to someone else; the gun even looked different to her now through the crystal-clear, color-perfect lenses of her new ocular implants. That night and everything that happened, from the heist to the struggle at Vikker's place, didn't seem real.

While she stared at the gun, some new images and numbers appeared on her AUI: a crosshair near the far wall lined up with where the barrel was pointing; an ammo counter which said 150/400; and a battery icon that read seventy percent. Juliet pushed the gun closer to the hotel room charging station and saw a little lightning bolt appear on the battery icon. "Neat. Angel, I've seen people walking around with weapons in certain bars or out in the ABZ around Tucson. How do I get a license?"

"You can acquire one tied to your SOA-SP license. As long as you don't have any convictions on that license and you're willing to pay two hundred and fifty bits annually, you should be approved instantly. You still won't be allowed to bring weapons into most corporate-owned properties."

"Which knocks out most places, huh? Well, I suppose this weapon was already registered to Vikker."

"No, I searched the serial number on net-accessible databases, and I didn't find any registration. I found a record of a sale to a man named Daniel Foyle three months ago, and that's the only public transaction for that weapon."

"So, can I register it or not? Should I? Will it increase the heat on me?"

"I don't have access to closed corpo-sec networks, so there may be many more records on that weapon than I can see. It might be best to use it unregistered for now, Juliet, though you can still get your firearms license if you want to spend the bits."

"And if corpo-sec or a drone stops me? What do I say?"

"That you've recently acquired it from a private transaction and have yet to register it."

"That'll fly?"

"Yes, in the city of Phoenix, you're given a seven-day grace period."

"All right. Shit. Well, go ahead and get me a license. Just so I can get this straight, my SOA license isn't tied to my real identity? Or it is, but it's private? I think I glossed over some of that when we were signing up."

"You are personally tied to your license, yes, but the SOA-SP has a treaty with ninety-four percent of the publicly registered corporations in the solar system. The treaty allows its operators to remain anonymous even while working in corporate territories. The information behind your license is stored in cryptographically secured data files which are only accessible through a two-thirds majority vote of the SOA-SP council—this has been done only in extreme cases of terroristic behavior and mass murder committed by the operative in question."

"So, WBD can't get to me through this. They don't know *Juliet* is the Juliet Bianchi they're hunting?"

"That's correct—in fact, you aren't the only operator with that handle."

"Huh. All right, what did you find out while I was snoozing? I need to figure out my next steps, other than buying some more clothes and personal hygiene items," Juliet said, sniffing herself. At the same time, she perused the hotel room's breakfast options—protein and carbohydrate bars of various flavors.

"While listening to police traffic and the Helios News Network, I found that the bodies of two unidentified men were found on the outskirts of Tucson. Drone surveillance picked up a firefight in the area, but resources were too thin to investigate in a timely fashion. Security personnel are following up on their leads."

"Do you think they'll find the van?"

"Definitely. There will be satellite imagery of it leaving the compound and of you leaving it in a drugstore parking lot. You shouldn't worry, though—I was scrambling your identity, and you took pains to clean the van of your presence."

"They'll know it was parked outside the doc's place for half a day, but he's a pro—he'll have some bullshit to spin when they come around looking for answers."

"If they do. Helios corpo-sec has more than nine hundred active murder investigations."

"What the hell? Seriously?"

"Yes, their active case numbers are available via the sat-net, presumably so interested parties can track their progress. A high percentage of those cases haven't been updated past 'security personnel are following up on their leads.'"

"Okay, what else? Any work? Anything about WBD's hunt for me?"

"I didn't find any information about WBD's progress in that regard; I'm sorry, Juliet." Angel, precise with her diction as always, managed to put a note in her voice which sounded distinctly self-critical. Juliet sat down with her pastry-flavored food bar and considered her response. As she was thinking, however, Angel took her silence as permission to forge ahead.

"You asked me to find you work that would take you off-planet. I didn't find any specific jobs which would allow you to leave within the next thirty days, but I did find the names of several corporations with open postings for certain off-world careers. I had your talents in mind when I searched, so I came up with several salvage companies, a mining consortium, and a few mercenary companies. If you were a pilot, your options would more than quadruple."

"Mercenary companies, Angel?" Juliet snorted and polished off the last bite of her breakfast.

"Your operator status makes you a possible asset to such groups, Juliet."

"Oh. Yeah, I guess they need someone who can pull off the stuff you're good at, huh? I was thinking of machine guns and drop ships."

"Correct. There are a wide array of positions among such companies. However, it would be good for you to learn more combat skills, Juliet. You were very lucky the other night."

"Lucky, huh? I guess that's one way to look at it. Do you understand luck, Angel?"

"Only in concept. Is it something you can feel?" The PAI's voice sounded different, almost wistful.

"No, not really. I thought it was something only humans spoke about, though—like a superstition. I guess you were just using the term to say that some random factors lined up in my favor?"

"Yes, I suppose so." Again, the PAI sounded strange. Melancholy, if Juliet were trying to pin it down. She sat there thinking about it, thinking about how different Angel was from Tig or any of her friends' PAIs, and she was just getting around to asking her some searching questions when Angel spoke up again. "Would you like to hear about some local employment opportunities? The operator culture here is far more robust than in Tucson."

"Um, yeah," Juliet said, wondering if she should head out to do some shopping while they spoke.

"I know you would rather not engage in combat, so I filtered the four hundred and twelve open gigs for technical roles. Then I narrowed the list further by filtering out those seeking only operators with a high rep. Of the resulting fifty-two jobs, I thought three sounded like promising opportunities. Shall I display the postings?"

"Yeah," Juliet replied while sitting back in the seat, squashing her earlier impulse to get in the car. A tab labeled Possible Operator Gigs flew onto her AUI, blinking softly in an amber highlight. She mentally selected it, and the three postings appeared in her vision.

Posting #A774	Requested Role: Data Retrieval	Rep Level: F-S+
Job Description: Accompany team of operatives into the East Phoenix ABZ, infiltrate potentially hostile encampment, retrieve data from an encrypted device.		Compensation: 8,200 Sol-bits
Scavenge Rights: Shared	Location: Phoenix ABZ	Date: September 9, 2107
Posting #A814	Requested Role: Network Security	Rep Level: F-S+
Job Description: Gain access, with support, to a secure location. Bypass network security and install provided files.		Compensation: 11,000 Sol-bits
Scavenge Rights: Tiered	Location: Phoenix Central	Date: September 10, 2107
Posting #A870	Requested Role: Mechanical Sabotage	Rep Level: F-S+

Job Description: Corporate-backed spec-ops unit seeking a mechanically inclined individual to rig competing corporate vehicles trespassing on disputed territory.		Compensation: 9,000 Sol-bits
Scavenge Rights: None	Location: Phoenix East	Date: September 10, 2107

"These are interesting. They all pay more for one gig than my old job did in a month, even with OT."

"The compensation is good, but there are much higher paying jobs for which you don't qualify. Payment is calculated based on risk, reputation level, and the technical knowledge required for the role. Keep in mind that you would struggle with any of these jobs without my assistance."

"I dunno. I think I could manage to rig some vehicles . . ."

"I'm sure you'll need to bypass some security for that task," Angel said, and Juliet definitely detected some smugness in her tone.

"Right. So I can maybe make a living, but it's all because of you. Is that what you're telling me?" Juliet was surprised at the acerbic nature of her words, the way she felt heated. It reminded her of the times when she'd felt her sister was talking down to her.

"No, Juliet. I'd be helpless without you! We're a team."

"Are we, though? What if I plugged you into a synth body? You sure I'm not holding you back?" She slumped back with a sigh and folded her arms over her chest.

"I'm not designed to be autonomous, Juliet. My priority, the driving imperative of my synthetic personality, is to see my host succeed. I've no interest in trying to strike out on my own. I'd languish without you."

"Oh, uh . . . well, shit, Angel. I don't think I quite realized that. You seem so natural to me; sometimes, I forget I'm not talking to another person."

"That's a wonderful compliment. Thank you, Juliet."

Juliet was caught off guard, the argument going in a completely different direction than she'd thought it would. She cleared her throat. "Well, why'd you mention that I couldn't do any of this stuff without you? I mean, you've got to realize I know that on some level, right?

"I was merely trying to explain the lucrative payouts of the gigs, Juliet. I'm sorry if my explanation was insulting."

"Oh. Maybe I was being sensitive. Anyway, forget it, okay?"

"Forgotten," the PAI said, and Juliet smiled.

"Well, what job should I take? And what's the deal with *scavenge rights*?"

"I'm glad you noticed that, Juliet. The first job will equally share the rights of any found equipment or wealth among the surviving team members. The second—"

"Surviving?"

"Well, consider the job you performed with Vikker's crew—this line of work can be dangerous. There is no shortage of deaths reported on the SOA message boards."

"Right. Okay, go on." Juliet idly flipped the cover of her data jack open and closed while she listened to Angel.

"Tiered scavenge rights means that any recovered equipment or wealth will be shared with the team members on a sliding scale; those with the highest reputation level will receive a larger portion than the ones like you, with low reputation."

"And I take it *none* means I get nothing we find?"

"That's correct, Juliet."

"Well, I'm not too excited about working for a corp anyway."

"It's still a good posting, Juliet. The payout is fairly high, and the risk will be lower since a corporation backs you."

"All right, well, let me think about this while I take care of some business. Let's make a run to a drugstore and someplace I can buy some clothes. Do I have a license for this thing?" Juliet asked, walking to the shotgun, which had fully recharged while she ate breakfast.

"Yes, your license number is E86072801."

"Heh, all right, thanks." Juliet stuffed the shotgun back into her duffel with Vikker's data cube, which she'd yet to explore. Picking it up, her thumb touched the smooth LCD side, which opened and activated it, unlocking the complex UI. "Oh, Angel, I just . . ."

"Juliet! That cube just sent out a ping before I could silence it."

"Shit . . ." Juliet thought about it, then said, "WBD doesn't know I had anything to do with Vikker. The ping was probably for him, right? I mean, in case someone took his cube or if he wanted to know where it was? He's dead, so . . ."

"I've disabled the feature on the data cube, but it might be wise to change your location, nonetheless."

"Right. Yeah, you're probably right. Okay, check us out." Juliet grabbed the bag and looked around the room. Her mind told her she was making sure she didn't forget anything, but she didn't have anything to forget. Shaking her head ruefully, she stepped out to the parking lot. Her little blue Zephyr sat where she'd parked it, windows set to black and paint still gleaming from the washing Davis & Sons had given it.

"Juliet, there are a lot of drones overhead."

"Yeah, this is the megacity, Angel. I think there are two drones for every person."

"That seems unlikely."

"Come on." Juliet laughed. "You can catch a joke like that, can't you?" She opened the door and sat down in the driver's seat, putting her duffel next to her. "Where can I buy more pellets for that thing?"

"I'll set a route for a drugstore, a discount clothing store, and a gun store. Do you have any preferences on the brands?"

"Um, for clothes, find me a Tevlo's. I don't care about the others." Juliet liked Tevlo's—they mostly sold work clothes like the overalls she wore for welding, but their stuff was sturdy, and some of it was reasonably fashionable.

Angel sent her AUI an updated route, and Juliet started driving. As she rounded the first turn, she spoke. "Angel, you know those jobs you found, er, the companies that are hiring for off-planet jobs?"

"Yes, Juliet."

"What are the odds I could get one of those gigs?"

"Quite good. I can help you with the performance evaluations. However, unless you tried to get one of the mercenary company jobs, you'd need a solid fake identity. I wouldn't be able to fully spoof a fake persona which would make it through background checks."

"Why don't I need that for the mercenary jobs?"

"They usually accept operator license numbers."

"Ah, I see." Juliet pulled through another light and saw the destination for her first stop: the drugstore. She parked the car, crossed the pavement which felt much like walking over a frying pan, then stepped up to the AutoDrug's door.

The door remained closed as she approached—it wouldn't open for her until she connected to its mercantile system. "Go ahead, Angel," she said before the PAI could ask permission. A second later, the door slid open, and Juliet walked through. She took in a deep breath of the icy conditioned air and stood there looking down the rows of densely packed shelves.

AutoDrug, like many automated chain stores, would charge her for any items she stepped out the door with, hence the need for her to connect to the sales system. Two other people perused the shelves. One looked like a woman on her last legs—much older and frailer than Juliet's grandma had been when she'd died. The other person looked a lot like Gary—too big, too many cyber implants, and definitely not friendly. He glowered at her when her eyes slid his way, and she quickly looked away and started toward an aisle on the opposite side of the store.

She spent a few minutes shopping around but ended up filling her little basket with exactly the things she'd come for: toothbrush and paste, an autorazor, deodorant, soap, and shampoo. While shopping, she heard the door open a couple of times, and glancing around, she smiled when she saw she was the only one still in the store.

"Oh, I need some lotion," she remembered, walking down another aisle. That's when the basket she was holding exploded. "What the *shit*?" she said, but then Angel screamed in her ear.

"Get down, Juliet! That was a projectile!"

"What the *shit*?" Juliet repeated, dropping to the floor.

"That was a less-than-lethal shotgun round, Juliet; I saw the projectile. Someone is trying to incapacitate you."

"Did you see them?" she asked, her voice shaky, her heart hammering, and her hands slippery with sweat as she scrambled over the hard, engineered tile flooring. She was trying to get to the far end of the aisle so she could hide behind an endcap.

"No. When you're in a more secure position, try to pan your vision around," Angel indicated, her voice calm again. "You need to upgrade your auditory implant. I could be listening for the assailant's approach."

"Not helpful!" Juliet said, finally scrambling around the end of the aisle to crouch behind a display of bleach.

"Notice! Notice!" a clarion voice called out. "Authorities have been dispatched, and all criminal activities on these premises are being recorded!" As the automated voice called out, a high-pitched ululating siren began to sound, and red lights flashed from all the corners of the drugstore.

"This isn't good, Angel."

"Juliet, look around the sides of the endcap; pop your head up and down quickly."

Juliet crouched for a second, breathing quick, rapid breaths, trying to psyche herself into action. Then she quickly, wincing the whole while, poked her head around the endcap to the right, then back, and to the left. She was just about to poke it over the top when the refrigerated case behind her exploded, beads of plastiglass flying all over the hard floor around her.

She let out an involuntary whimper at the impact and the resultant chaos, and Angel, once again sounding like a vengeful Valkyrie, screamed, "I saw him to your left! Run straight up the aisle to your right! Keep your head down!" Juliet didn't want to move; she wanted to curl up into a ball right there and just squeeze her eyes shut, but she knew better than that. She knew Angel was right, so she took a deep breath and charged up the aisle.

Juliet realized Angel had cranked up the gain on her auditory implants when, as she was sprinting, she heard the buzz of electricity to her left. She imagined it was some sort of electronic gear her assailant was wearing or wielding. Reaching the end of the aisle, she zigged to the right, slipped into the furthest aisle, and charged for the front of the store. That's when she saw the plasteel bike lock around the door handles. "Shit, damn," she hissed, ducking behind another endcap.

"I'm tracking him, Juliet. His shotgun is equipped with a stun prod. I can hear it, even with your shoddy implants."

"Not the time, Angel!" Juliet subvocalized.

"He's to your left, two aisles over. Juliet, you have to get to the stock door in the back; you'll have to physically jack in so I can crack it. Quickly, back toward the rear-right of the store. Try not to make noise!" Juliet's heart was hammering in her chest, and her hands were shaking with adrenaline, but she tried to do what Angel said. Staying low, she crept back toward the rear of the store, willing her sneakers not to squeak. "He's rounding the corner in the front; quickly, get to the middle aisle and then go left!"

Juliet was glad for Angel's directions—her instinct had been to beeline for the rear door, but the assailant would have seen her. When she cut left instead, she went to the aisle he'd just come from, and she crept down it toward the rear row. "Where is he?" she subvocalized as she reached the corner. She could see the door in the opposite side and wanted to rush to it.

"Hold still, Juliet. When I say so, move to the next endcap." Juliet held her breath, her legs jumping and shaking with adrenaline, and then Angel said, "Now!" She bolted to the next endcap and froze. She could hear it now, the buzzing of the stun prod, and she knew the guy was just a couple dozen feet from her in the central aisle. "Get ready to go to the next endcap . . . now!"

Juliet tiptoed over the floor, careful not to scatter the plastiglass beads, until she was just six feet from the door. She could see the little data jack port on the keypad, so before Angel could tell her what to do, she tapped her data jack cover. When it slid back, she, with shaky fingers, jerked out a yard of cable and tiptoed up to the door, punching the jack into the hole. Then Juliet backed away, hiding behind the closest endcap, her cable fully extended and her hand sticking out.

"Just a minute, Juliet. Hold still; he's still two aisles over."

"Hurry," Juliet breathed; she could hear the buzzing in her ears and the crunch of a boot grinding a plastiglass bead into the hard floor, and she knew he was almost on her. Just then, the door clicked and buzzed, and she bolted for it, yanking her cable out of the jack as she pulled on the handle. The buzzing grew very loud, and so did the stomps of approaching feet, but then Juliet was through the door and slamming it shut behind her. A tremendous *thump* echoed off the steel door.

"Juliet, don't linger! He'll run around the building!"

"Right." Juliet looked around the little stock room. Boxes lined the walls from floor to ceiling, but the exit door was clearly visible to her left, just the length of the little store away. She charged it, hit the crash bar, flung the door open, and stumbled out into the hot Arizona sun. She vacillated for a minute, not sure if she should try to sneak back to her car, but Angel helped her decide.

"Your car is burned, Juliet. I'm sorry. Run down this alley, then make a right. Run to the end of the street and make another right. I'm calling you an AutoCab."

15

////////////////////////

TAKING A BREATH

What do you mean, my car's burned?" Juliet wheezed as she sprinted around the corner. For the first time she could remember, she wished the sidewalks were more crowded.

"I mean burned in the figurative sense. A drone must have been searching for you, saw the ping from the data cube, and then followed your vehicle to the drugstore. Your car is burned."

"Dammit!" Juliet hissed, realizing she'd lost not only her new vehicle but also the shotgun and Vikker's cube. "I should've had you crack and rip that cube a long time ago."

"I'm tracking your AutoCab's progress. Turn left at the corner and keep running straight. So far, there aren't any direct queries from any of the drones overhead—it's possible your pursuer searched in a different direction."

"Good." Juliet paused at the corner, leaning against the hot bricks of an office building, and looked back over her shoulder. She saw two people, but they were both walking the other way. Taking a deep, shaky breath, she rounded the corner and resumed running down the sidewalk. She'd only gone fifty yards or so when a sleek, dark blue sedan with black windows and a bright yellow AutoCab logo on the hood slid up next to the sidewalk.

Juliet didn't need Angel to tell her to get in. She rushed to the door, pulled the handle, and slid into the comfortable bench seat. The cab almost immediately started to drive, and Juliet figured Angel was communicating with it:

paying, putting in a destination, all the things that usually took a minute or two for a person. "Where are we going?" she asked.

"Good morning! I'm taking you to your destination at the corner of Carver and Mill," the AutoCab responded.

"Yes, we're switching to an Easycab at that location, Juliet. Then I think you should go to a different part of the city to do your shopping."

"Huh, switching cabs?"

"In case your pursuer studies the satellite imagery of the area and figures out you got into this one. You'll walk a block or two, passing through some lobbies while I alter your ID signature several times."

"Who was that chrome-brained creep?" Juliet asked, sitting back and sighing loudly.

"I suspect he was a bounty hunter. I don't believe he was working for WBD, though—they never had access to Vikker's cube or knew you were working with him." Angel's words chilled Juliet, and she leaned forward on the seat, gripping her knees and shaking her head.

"What the hell?" she said aloud. Then, as paranoia struck her, she subvocalized, "You think Vikker's friends are looking for who killed him?"

"The possibilities are too numerous to speculate, I'm afraid, Juliet. It could be his enemies as well. Perhaps the people who hired the hunter are insurance investigators or creditors. You've cut ties with the cube now, and I've had your identity masked the entire time you've been outside Dr. Tsakanikas's office. You should be clear of them now."

"Your destination," the AutoCab announced, pulling up to the curb. Juliet hopped out and, following Angel's instructions, wove a meandering path through a hotel lobby, a business park, and through a two-story parking garage to another street where she hiked a block to an intersection where a yellow Easycab was waiting. Angel told her she'd changed her ID signature six times during the walk, and it was unlikely anyone would be able to follow her progress.

Over the next few hours, Juliet traveled via cab to the west side of Phoenix, visited a drugstore and a Tevlo's, and then, at Angel's urging, walked for a while and took a bus to the northern edge of the downtown district. She was lugging a big canvas backpack with tool pouches and loops that she'd bought at Tevlo's, stuffed with three changes of clothes and all the personal hygiene items she'd almost bought at the first drugstore. "Find me a hotel where I can do some laundry, Angel. Also, what's my bit balance?"

"You have 7,523 bits, Juliet."

"Great."

It was in the afternoon, and traffic around downtown was very different from that on the outskirts of the city. Just on the street she was walking along, surrounded by skyscrapers, there had to be a thousand cars and bikes slowly moving north and south. Even in the heat, hundreds of people were on the sidewalks, and Juliet was starting to relax, feeling anonymous again and far enough removed from the encounter in the drugstore to imagine it was behind her.

"Sign me up for the job that's tomorrow. I need to start making some cash now that I've lost my fourth vehicle in two days."

"To be fair, Juliet, the bicycle hardly counts as a vehicle, and the van didn't belong to you."

"I don't care! Can't you see how ridiculous this is? I mean, I'm a goddamn welder!" Juliet would feel strange yelling at her PAI while walking down the sidewalk, but she was hardly alone; nearly everyone walking by was absorbed in a conversation with an electric ghost—either giving instructions to their PAI or on a call. Some just had glassy stares as they strode along, and Juliet knew they were looking at something on their AUI; a map, a vid, a video message—it was hard to tell.

Angel, apparently not able or willing to try to deal with the outburst, simply said, "There's a hotel on the next block which boasts a laundry room and fitness center. Look for a white sign with a green, neon tree: Palo Verde Inn and Conference Center."

Juliet didn't reply, and after a moment, a blinking tab appeared in her UI. She opened it to display the job she'd mentioned.

Posting #A774	**Requested Role:** Data Retrieval	**Rep Level:** F-S+
Job Description: Accompany team of operatives into the East Phoenix ABZ, infiltrate hostile encampment, retrieve data from an encrypted device.		**Compensation:** 8,200 Sol-bits
Scavenge Rights: Shared	**Location:** Phoenix ABZ	**Date:** September 9, 2107

"Yeah, that's the one. Sign me up."

"This posting indicates that hostile encounters are quite likely. Are you sure, Juliet?"

"Yeah, I'm not going in as a shooter, am I? Angel, I'm sick of getting pushed around—I need to start taking the reins. Does that make sense?"

"To a degree, yes. I think we should visit a weapon store, though, Juliet. There are less bulky weapons than the electro-shotgun which might serve you well."

"Noted," Juliet replied, stopping to stand before the Palo Verde sign. It was, indeed, a real neon sign. She could tell by the actual tubes on the white backing, though it wasn't lit up at the moment. The building was a sleek, dark-gray tower, and the lobby was busy with patrons sitting on the faux leather couches, standing around vidscreens, and congregating by the elevators.

Looking through the glass doors, Juliet felt like a rat looking at a pond full of brilliant koi fish. The people within were elegant and wore suits, if not high-end designer clothing. "Angel," she subvocalized, "how much does a room here cost?"

"Between two and eight hundred bits, depending on the room."

"Does it seem like a good use of my funds, Angel?" Juliet was expecting to teach the PAI a lesson, to let it know it wasn't okay just to pick the first hotel it found with laundry services, but Angel, as usual, surprised her.

"Normally, I would agree that this is an extravagant cost, but I think, for perhaps a night or two, this will be a good place for you."

"Explain," Juliet said, still standing outside on the sidewalk, watching the refined people within through the crystal-clear plastiglass doors.

"I have two reasons for my conclusion. One, your pursuers are aware that you stayed in a rather inexpensive hotel last night. They might conclude you are doing so to avoid attention and to conserve funds, thus they'll likely focus their attention on similar locations. Two, Juliet, you've had a mentally and physically taxing few days. You should stop and take a breath. You should invest a little into your welfare."

"I . . ." Juliet was unable to think of a response. Angel was so different from what a PAI should be, even the high-end ones with personality toggles. "I can't argue with that, Angel. Can you check me in?"

"Yes, though you'll have to present yourself to the clerk."

"Right." Juliet stepped toward the doors. They noiselessly slid open, and as she walked past the threshold, she was suddenly met with soothing classical music and the low hum of conversations taking place around the vaulted, richly appointed lobby. "A noise screen?"

"Yes, they value privacy at the Palo Verde. You'll note the lack of surveillance; I read an online testimonial which indicated the owner would rather forgo cameras than be forced to hand the footage over to authorities."

"Huh," Juliet said as she walked over the marble and pale-green carpeting to the front desk. There were four clerks spaced out on the long counter, and Juliet walked toward the one on the far right, a young woman with neatly quaffed pale-violet hair and a smart gray dress skirt beneath her mint-green hotel employee jacket.

"Hello," the woman greeted, smiling brilliantly as Juliet stepped up to the counter. "Are you Juliet? I believe your PAI just sent me your credentials."

"That's right."

"Let's see—you'd like a single queen suite? I have one at our base price of two hundred and another on the seventy-third floor with a lovely view of downtown. That one is three-fifty."

"Well . . ." Juliet thought about it and decided that if she wanted to improve her mental health, she might as well go all out. "I'll take the one with the view."

"Lovely. Laundry services, complimentary breakfast, and the fitness room are all on the second floor. We'll need a transfer of—"

"Can you handle the rest with my PAI? I'm exhausted."

"Oh, certainly. Let's see." She glanced at her data terminal's transparent screen standing between the two of them on the counter. Juliet couldn't see anything on it from the rear, but she knew the other side was opaque and filled with information. "Yes, I see the funds have been transferred, and your preferences have all been filled in. Excellent. Please just look into this little lens for a moment." She tapped a small glass circle on the top edge of her screen.

Juliet looked at the lens, and then the woman nodded. "That will allow you access to the elevators and your room. The retinal scan is encrypted, and the Palo Verde cannot—would not—copy or share that information."

"Thanks," Juliet said, then started walking for the elevators, feeling more and more like a fish out of water every second she stood in that plush room with all those fancy people milling around. She subvocalized to Angel, "How can they scan my retina? I have cybernetic eyes."

"Your implants, like all legal ocular replacements, are equipped with synth-skin retinas—they are programmed with your original retinal scan when first installed."

"God, I never thought of that. So the doc did it legit? I have my old retinal image?"

"Yes, he seemed to follow the letter of the law when it came to that part of your surgery."

Walking up to the bank of elevators, one of them slid open at her approach. She stepped in, and either the elevator knew where she was going or Angel selected the floor because it started to climb to the seventy-third floor. She decided it was probably Angel. How would the elevator know she didn't want to do laundry or see another guest?

Her room was nice, but nothing amazing. The bed was fluffier and with better linens than the one she'd had the night before, but the room wasn't much bigger. The bathroom was the real game changer, however. A big porcelain tub, a glassed-in shower, and plenty of towels drew a strict dichotomy with Juliet's previous life experiences. After looking around the room, she turned to the opaque, gray windows. "Angel, can you make the windows see-through?"

"I believe they're controlled via a remote control, but I could breach their rudimentary firewall."

"Nah, wait." Juliet looked around and saw, on the faux mahogany nightstand, a little silver remote with two buttons. Throwing her pack on the bed, she picked up the remote. When she touched the top button, the window snapped from pale gray to perfectly clear, and she saw a high-rise view of a megacity's downtown area for the first time in her life.

The megatowers were all in view, soaring high above the older-style skyscrapers, dwarfing them like redwoods in a deciduous forest. From her vantage a few miles from the true downtown where those towers stood, it felt like she was about half as high as the megatowers, but she knew she was probably much lower than that. Still, it was amazing seeing the colorful, enormous structures shooting up into the night sky while she looked out over the smaller buildings leading up to them.

Massive advertisements adorned the sides of the towers and the smaller buildings nearby, and though they were tacky and not exactly nature's greatest treasure or humankind's best art, when you saw so much color and moving, flashing lights, it was like taking in a constant firework explosion. "Wow," Juliet let out.

One ad caught her eye on the side of an enormous tower emblazoned with a red Zi Corp at the top: a larger-than-life rocket erupted at the base of the building and flew to the top, riding a realistic, fiery plume and the smoke cloud it left behind. When the rocket disappeared through the top of the tower, a banner floated up behind it. "Ride to the stars! PanSol Shuttles!"

"Pretty wild view," Juliet said. She went over to the bed and opened her heavy pack, taking out her toiletries and a bag of snacks she'd bought at the drugstore. After eating some protein squares of various flavors, a bag of zucchini crisps, and drinking two room-temperature beers, Juliet soaked in a hot bathtub for the first time in many years.

That night, she slept in clean undergarments in the most comfortable bed she'd ever experienced, with the windows open to the bright lights of downtown Phoenix. She tried to dream about space travel and magical new cities, but when she woke up, she couldn't remember dreaming about anything.

Juliet showered with actual hot water—there wasn't even an option for sani-spray—then went to the second floor, where she ate bacon-flavored soy squares, scrambled "egg product," waffles, and coffee. After her stomach was full, Juliet washed her old clothes and returned to her room, where she contemplated leaving some belongings behind or taking everything with her. "Angel, was I accepted for that job tonight?"

"The application is still pending."

"Well, sign me up for another night in this room." She put her extra clothes into the room's little closet and, with an empty backpack, made her way to the hotel lobby. She was dressed in sturdy black jeans and a long-sleeved, cottony gray pullover shirt with a dark blue Tevlo over the left breast. She wore new work boots, though she sorely missed her old broken-in pair. Of all the little belongings she'd abandoned in Tucson, she felt the loss of those boots the most.

Her new boots looked nice, and they were sturdy with a black plastiweave layer over the toe box, but the soles and simulated leather uppers were stiff, and she knew they wouldn't be truly comfortable until she'd worn them for many, many hours. Still, she felt a hundred percent better than she had the night before, and she walked out of the lobby with her shoulders back and her head high, staring back at the other people milling about the lobby. She felt a little thrill of victory as more than one of them met her eyes and smiled or nodded.

"Your Easycab is waiting outside, Juliet. I've selected a highly rated gun store only a few miles from here."

"Good, thanks." As promised, the cab was outside, and Juliet hurried across the sidewalk, nervously glancing left and right as she suddenly felt very exposed on the busy street. The cab started rolling, though, almost as soon as she'd sat down, and she sank back into the cushioned seat and sighed.

Halfway through the short trip, Angel spoke again. "You've been accepted for the job, Juliet!"

"Yes!" She clapped her hands together, suddenly realizing she'd been stressed about not being accepted—she needed to keep making money, and this seemed to be her best option. Juliet really had no idea how competitive those SOA postings were. Was this a sign that she had a sought-after skill set, or was it a sign that the people doing the job were desperate and had taken her as a last resort? "No way to know yet, I guess."

"The job begins earlier than the last one, Juliet. You're to meet the team at a bar called The Black Goat at six this evening."

"Okay," Juliet said as the Easycab pulled up to a curb and announced her arrival. She stepped out onto a sidewalk, still on the edge of downtown and bustling with people. The store before her was called Mackenzie Arms. A very cyborged-out guard stood outside the door, his robotic, pistonlike arms hovering near the hilts of two bulky semiautomatic handguns he wore on his military-style belt. Juliet stepped toward him, taking in the weird way the synth-flesh on his face merged with the chrome plate covering his forehead and skull.

"No loaded firearms allowed inside," he said, his voice surprisingly smooth and pleasant.

"I don't have any." Juliet held up her hands.

"What's in the pack?"

"Nothing—I brought it to hold whatever I buy in here." She shrugged out of her dark brown backpack and unzipped it to display the cavernous interior. The guard looked at it, and she heard something clicking in his optical implant before he nodded.

"Enjoy the shop." The door slid open as if on cue, and Juliet walked in. The front half of the store was dominated by sales racks displaying boxes of ammunition, holsters of all kinds, and a wall adorned with various types of ballistic vests. The rear half had a horseshoe-shaped display case behind which half a dozen sales personnel stood and walked, helping customers or, in the case of one woman, stared at Juliet.

"Hey, doll. Can I help you?" the woman asked as Juliet moved further into the store toward the display case. She regarded her—a middle-aged lady with natural brown hair. Juliet didn't think she'd stand out in a crowd if not for her wild ocular implants. Her left eye was perfectly smooth and red, the right was white, and they each had crosshairs in the opposite color that appeared then faded away every couple of seconds.

Juliet realized she was staring and cleared her throat.

"Oh, hey. Yeah, I need to buy a couple of weapons."

"Sure! What's your poison?"

Angel had primed Juliet on what sorts of things to ask about. The PAI seemed to have a disturbingly extensive knowledge base of weapons and self-defense items; Juliet had come to understand that Angel's ability to walk her through the use of the electro-shotgun had only been the tip of the iceberg. "I need a pistol meant for close-quarters defense. Something like a Garnet Taipan."

"The Taipan, huh? Quite a little cannon. Alrighty." The woman walked down the case, and Juliet saw her ask one of her associates to move. Then she slid a panel back and reached in to pull out a compact, black pistol. She walked back to Juliet and set the gun on the counter. "You're aware that Garnet named this model after a viper because it looks like a small package, but it packs a hell of a bite?"

"Yes," Juliet said—Angel had expounded at great length about the weapon's virtues. "It's designed to minimize failures; it's small enough to conceal while also able to pack rounds that will fatally wound or incapacitate an aggressor with one shot."

"That's right! You know your guns, huh?" The woman picked up the weapon and handed it to Juliet. It was bigger in her hands than it had seemed, a three-inch barrel extending over the tips of her fingers while the dense, compact frame rested on her palm.

"Heavy," she noted, feeling the weight as she wrapped her fingers around the grip. It was entirely black—the metal, the rubbery plastic grip, everything. Above the trigger was an old-school revolver cylinder which Angel had insisted was still in existence because of its simple and foolproof design. "Few moving parts; no springs or casings to eject—no jams," she softly said, echoing Angel's words from earlier.

"We have other types of weapons with near-zero failure rates, but there's something about the smooth action of a well-made revolver, huh?" the saleswoman asked. Juliet looked at her with a raised eyebrow, so she continued, "Go ahead, pop the cylinder out; feel that liquid-smooth click as you turn it. The Taipan is made damn well. You can load different types of ammo and see what you're packing at a glance. Even if a round is dead when you pull the trigger, the next one will come under the pin. Jams don't happen."

"Touch the button just over the trigger guard on the left side," Angel said. Juliet did as she asked, and the cylinder disengaged, flopping out to the left. Juliet rotated it with her thumb, and it did have a satisfyingly smooth action as it clicked around, showing off the ten narrow holes meant to hold cartridges.

"See? Needler rounds are skinny, but the Taipan's cylinder is long, allowing for magnum-size cartridges. Ten heavyweight punches from a compact little package." The woman grinned, drumming her fingers on the sales counter.

"You have shredder cartridges?" Juliet asked.

"Oh, sure, hon. But they pack a punch—this thing's gonna buck like a pony." She looked Juliet up and down, taking in her attire and then her long, calloused fingers. "I guess you know that, though?"

"Yeah, thanks."

"How many boxes?"

"Two," Juliet replied, already aware that each box held fifty cartridges.

"What else you gonna need, hon?" the woman asked, turning to look through the stacks of ammo behind the display case.

"I need a six-inch vibroblade, an inside-the-waistband holster for this gun, and a ballistic vest that looks like something you could wear around town."

The woman straightened up with two little boxes in her hands and looked at Juliet with a grin. "Well, assuming you have a license, you sure came to the right store, didn't you?"

16

\\\\\\\\\\\\\\\\\\\\\\\

THE BLACK GOAT

Juliet walked out of the gun store with a much heavier backpack than when she'd gone in. She'd acquired the Taipan pistol, a hundred rounds of ammo, a holster which was supposed to fit inside her waistband, a vibro knife that she had yet to power up or even look at, and a vest which cost almost as much as the pistol.

Thinking of costs, Juliet asked, "Angel, what's my balance now?"

"It's 6,323 Helios-bits. Speaking of which, Juliet, I think you should allow me to convert those into Sol-bits. It should only cost you a fraction of a percent."

"Why?" Juliet asked as she climbed into the back of an Easycab that Angel had ordered for her.

"You don't keep your bits on a corporate exchange, so Helios has less recourse when it comes to taking your funds, but they are monitored on their corporate blockchain. I've been working to mask your purchases, but it will become difficult if they dedicate enough resources. Sol-bits aren't centralized, and they're much easier to use anonymously because of the nature of their privacy-oriented blockchain."

"Well, go ahead." Juliet had a vague knowledge of what Angel was talking about, but she'd never thought it mattered enough to bother with. Her friends, specifically Mark and a few others at the scrapyard, had told her it was a bad idea to keep money on the corpo exchanges because of how they could implement new fees or penalties without any input from the users.

Still, she'd never considered that her individual bits, her money, could be traced.

"Working," Angel said. "The blockchains don't update instantly. I'll tell you the new balance when I'm done. I'm performing a series of transactions to obscure your activity."

While the cab traversed the heavy traffic, Juliet pulled her new vest out of her backpack to check it out. She'd been a little self-conscious in the store, not wanting to look like an absolute rookie in front of the woman with the bull's-eye eyeballs. At first, she'd scoffed at the garment, thinking it was far too bulky to wear in the Arizona weather, but the woman had described it as temperature regulating, which had intrigued her. Angel had clinched the deal by telling her it was highly rated and "perfect for her needs."

The vest was dark green. Juliet could have chosen a dozen different colors, but she felt the dark green was good because it wasn't black but it wasn't bright, either. The exterior felt like nylon and it wasn't cumbersome, but she could feel the plasteel plates sewn into the lining which would, theoretically, block bullets and dissipate their impact force. The bottom seam was lined with a flexible rib about the width of her pinky finger, and the saleswoman had told her it was a high-density Li-air battery.

"What's the battery for?" Juliet had asked, and the woman had smiled and explained the vest was vented and contained seven different microheat pumps behind the plasteel armor. She'd told Juliet it would keep her warm in cold weather and cool in the heat.

"Well, at least cooler than without it." The woman had laughed. "I mean, it's a furnace out there. The vest isn't a self-contained enviro rig."

"Right, right." Juliet had laughed, having never laid eyes on an enviro rig.

"This seems pretty cool," Juliet told Angel as she worked to take the tags off the vest.

"It has excellent reviews," Angel agreed. "If you put it on and power it up, I'll be able to control it for you."

"Yep," Juliet grunted as she bit through the last plastic tag. She shrugged into the vest, pulled up the zipper, and touched the power button on the lapel. A moment later, it hummed briefly, and then cool air started to flow outward along her spine and sternum. "Shit! That's neat!" A new set of icons appeared on her AUI, and she saw the ambient temperature of the cab next to the desired temperature of the vest and a third icon which showed its battery was at eighty-four percent.

"Well, it works fine when I'm sitting in the AC of a cab." Juliet laughed.

"You should familiarize yourself with that knife," Angel said, then added, "Your bits have all been converted to Sol-bits. Your new balance is 6,302 Sol-bits."

"That wasn't too bad," Juliet noted as she unboxed her new vibroblade. She'd worked with tools based on the same technology; while she knew the blade was dangerous even when it wasn't powered up, when it was active, the knife could probably cut through plasteel, though not quickly. She pulled it, still sheathed, from the box, and the Easycab AI beeped and spoke, a red light flaring to life in the ceiling.

"Excuse me, but I've detected a weapon in your hand. Please confirm you have a license and do not mean to self-harm."

"Confirmed," Juliet replied.

"Please provide your license number," the friendly, English-accented male voice asked.

Juliet read it off as Angel displayed the license number. "E86072801."

"Thank you," the AI said before the red light blinked out.

"Sheesh," Juliet let out, then tugged the six-inch blade from the plastic sheath. It was dull gray, but the edges were gleaming. She touched her thumb to the little print reader on the handle, and after a moment, it buzzed to life.

"I've accessed the vibroblade's interface. Would you like to set it to activate upon drawing it, or would you like to control the feature manually?"

Juliet thought about the question and decided that if she pulled the knife out in an emergency, she didn't want to fumble around trying to find the activation pad. "Auto." She drove the blade back into the sheath. As the tip approached the insertion point, it stopped vibrating.

Juliet had bought that particular blade because of the sheath. It had a magnetic clamp designed to interface with vests like the one she'd bought. She slid it up under a flap above her left breast, and it locked into place. Now, to draw the knife, she just had to reach up under that flap and yank it down. The sheath would remain in place, and the blade would be active and ready for action.

She didn't have time to unpack her new gun before the cab pulled up in front of her hotel, so Juliet left it in her backpack. When she got out, she slung it over one shoulder and walked toward the automated doors. As she approached, however, they didn't slide open.

"The scanners have detected your firearm, and I've had to provide your license. The clerk is evaluating whether or not to allow you onto the premises," Angel explained.

"Shit. I didn't think of that."

"Yes, it appears that Palo Verde values safety as much as they value privacy. There are high-end door scanners in place. I'm sorry, Juliet, I should have foreseen this." As Angel finished speaking, the doors chimed and slid open. "You've been granted access. It appears they did a background check on your operator ID and have determined you aren't a threat. You are instructed to keep your weapon unloaded while on the premises."

"Got it," Juliet said, striding into the lobby and walking to the elevators, sparing a glance and a nod to the clerk at the near end of the counter. He smiled and nodded back. Juliet glanced at the clock on her AUI, saw it was nearly noon, and asked, "Angel, what time should I leave to get to that bar on time?"

"You should depart the hotel by 1640—traffic is likely to be heavy."

"Did you say 1640? We in the military now?" Juliet scoffed as she walked into the elevator.

"I'm trying to avoid confusion between a.m. and p.m.," Angel replied, and she sounded defensive.

"It's fine, but, I mean, I know it's not morning."

When Juliet returned to her room, she unpacked her new pistol and filled the ammo pockets in her new vest with the cartridges from one of the boxes. She figured she could load the gun on her way to the bar. The cartridges, as Angel insisted she call them rather than bullets, were surprisingly narrow but quite long, each about two inches from the primer to the tip of the plastic-coated needle pack.

Juliet could see how the cartridges would fit into the pistol's cylinder. Angel walked her through loading and ejecting the spent casings, and Juliet figured she could probably do it rather quickly, though it would be harder under stress—she hoped ten shots would be enough. Twirling one of the needler cartridges between her fingers, she said, "So this thing fires off more than a hundred nanoneedles?"

"Yes. At close range, those rounds are extremely dangerous to biological organisms. The needles will perforate most weave-type body armors as well."

"Okay." Juliet slipped the cartridge into her pocket before lifting the holster she'd bought and giving it a good look. "So this goes inside my pants?"

"Yes, wear it at your side and hook that plastic clip over your waistband. It won't be terribly uncomfortable with a weapon as compact as the Taipan."

Juliet tried the holster in several positions and found it the most comfortable toward the front of her hipbone so the pistol's bulkiest part, the cylinder, could sit against the soft part of her stomach. Standing in front of the mirror with her vest and shirt over the holster, she honestly couldn't tell she was packing the weapon. "Cool," she said. "Angel, that woman said it would kick a lot. Do you think I can manage it?"

"You'll be fine, Juliet. Stand in front of the mirror, and I'll direct you into a proper stance." Angel waited while Juliet complied. "Hold the pistol in your right hand but lift your left hand to support the grip. That's it. Now, I have a crosshair in your AUI, so you don't need to use the sights. That said, you should face your target and slightly lean forward. Excellent! Keep your elbows pointed out—don't lock them. Keep your grip firm, and squeeze the trigger, don't jerk it. Good!"

"That easy, huh?" Juliet asked, squeezing off a few more clicks of the trigger, firing at imaginary bad guys. Her AUI displayed a crosshair and an ammo counter reading zero over ten.

"Yes, Juliet. I should warn you about some simple gun safety rules so that you aren't judged harshly by the people you work with."

"Okay?"

"Never put your finger on the trigger until you're ready to shoot—hold it to the side of the trigger guard. Never point your weapon at anyone you don't want to kill, even if you think the gun is empty. Finally, always treat a weapon as if it were loaded. Even my AUI display could be wrong, and there could be a cartridge in the chamber."

"Okay, Angel. Thanks." Juliet slipped the weapon back into her holster and then looked around the hotel room, wondering what to do to kill four hours. When her eyes fell on the bed, she smiled. "I'm taking a nap. Don't let me sleep past four."

"Juliet, I might remind you that this hotel has a fitness center on the second floor . . ."

"No thanks, Angel! I want to be alert and fresh for tonight, don't I?"

"Yes. Very well. I'll be sure to watch for any pertinent updates." Angel sounded a little peeved, but Juliet didn't care. She'd missed plenty of sleep over the last few days, and this felt like a good time to catch up a bit. Surprising herself, she put her new gun on the nightstand with a few cartridges piled beside it. She'd never been excited about or interested in guns in the past, but it seemed the last few days had given her a different outlook.

She slept soundly that afternoon until Angel woke her with a gentle, repetitive chime at four o'clock. She felt drowsy from the nap, so she took a quick shower before getting dressed and ready to leave. Angel hurried her along until she was outside the hotel, climbing into an AutoCab, and on her way to the Black Goat bar, hounding her about traffic and that she'd be late. Unfortunately, the PAI was right—traffic was every bit as bad as predicted.

"Don't worry," Juliet said. "I'm sure we'll make it on time."

"I can see the traffic map just as well as you can, Juliet, and I think it's going to be close."

"Well, if we're a little late, you can just message the client, right?" Juliet asked, then before Angel could answer, she continued, "AutoCab! I'm going to pull out a licensed firearm. I don't intend any hostility."

"Thank you, passenger. Please have your PAI provide your license details."

Juliet left it to Angel while she loaded the pistol and put it back into her holster. Angel had assured her the gun couldn't accidentally fire—it had a biometric scanner on the trigger which would only respond to her finger. That settled, Juliet felt her pockets, making sure she knew exactly where her extra rounds were, and reached up to feel the grip of her knife, ensuring it was there and that it felt natural to grab. Once finished, she sat back in the cab and closed her eyes, trying to imagine she was just going to another welding gig.

Angel proved to be a good judge of traffic—they did cut it close, but Juliet stepped out of the cab just two minutes after six, and she didn't think that was a big deal. The Black Goat was a lot smaller than Thicker than Water, and though it wasn't even dark yet, there were a lot of pretty rough individuals standing around outside. A line of cruiser-style bikes stood in front of the bar, and the other vehicles in the lot looked well-used and not at all like the sleek, shiny sedans she'd seen around downtown the last couple of days.

Juliet resisted the urge to feel the bulge of her concealed pistol and stood up straight, knowing she was a tall woman, especially in her boots, and that her clothes didn't paint her as an easy mark. She twisted her brows into a scowl and, digging deep for a *don't mess with me* attitude, walked confidently toward the people hanging by the door.

"You're receiving a line-of-sight query from the man standing to the left of the door. He's asking if you are Juliet," Angel said.

She looked at the man leaning against the bricks on the left edge of the bar's door and gave him a solid once-over before she responded. He was lean with dark skin and a short, spiky mohawk. He wore dark glasses and a black vest, and she could see that his left hand was a wire-job. From his studded leather belt hang a huge holster containing some sort of cannonlike weapon. It looked like a cross between a shotgun and a pistol to her.

Juliet didn't tell Angel to respond; she just looked into those dark glasses and nodded. He nodded back, then turned to the door and pulled it open. Some of the people standing around started to move toward it, but he shook his head, and they backed off. Juliet walked between them, holding her breath and willing her hands to stop sweating. He nodded again, and as Juliet walked into the bar, she felt him follow her through the door before pulling it closed.

"Arnold doesn't like the bar getting too crowded," the man spoke from behind her. "That's why all those scabs are sitting 'round out there."

"Ahh," Juliet said, looking around the dim interior. Her new implants made it easy to plumb the depths of the shadowy room—she counted eight people sitting at the bar with a punky bartender in a see-through tank top. She had half a dozen piercings on her face and scowled ferociously as she busily mixed a drink. The rest of the space was filled with booths, pool tables, and some dart boards in the corner. Juliet was surprised that nearly every booth contained patrons at that hour, and she'd just started to take stock of all the different people when the man spoke again.

"Far left corner." He hung back, waiting for her to start walking. Juliet didn't like it—she wasn't a fan of having a stranger with a cannon shadowing her into a dark bar, but she pushed down her nerves and wended her way through the bar, past people playing pool and booths where hard-looking men and women drank pitchers of beer and laughed raucously.

She'd never been to a bar this early in the day and hadn't imagined it would be so busy, let alone full of people getting fully drunk. Still, the laughing and clamor started to ease her nerves; she breathed easier and felt herself beginning to relax as she approached the corner. Two women sat in the booth, and the smaller of the two flashed her a brilliant smile. It was so unexpected, Juliet felt herself responding with a genuine smile of her own as she slid into the seat.

"Hey! Juliet?" the smiling woman asked as Mr. Mohawk slid in next to Juliet, effectively trapping her in.

"Yeah. What about you all?" she asked, looking the two women over. The friendly one was short with a puffy black haircut and deep brown eyes. The other one, the one who sat quietly glowering, was a very large woman wearing black leather pants, a black leather jacket, and a brace of knives strapped crossways over her chest. She had pale skin, big ruddy cheeks, and bright red lips. Most striking, though, was the surgically installed metallic visor which sat beneath her brow in lieu of eyes.

"I'm Honey," the smaller woman greeted, reaching out a hand. Juliet took it, exchanged a warm handshake, and then looked at the bigger woman expectantly.

"Call me Mags, doll," she said, holding out a fist. Juliet figured she didn't like germs or something, so she gave her a fist bump, and the woman grunted and nodded.

"And you?" Juliet asked, turning to look at the man who'd let her into the bar.

"Pit," he replied before grinning and adding, "As in Pit Bull."

"Okay, nice to meet you all." She smiled, not wanting to rush things. She figured she'd let them bring up the job.

"So you're a noob, huh?" Honey asked, smiling. She was really very pretty, and Juliet couldn't see any obvious cyberware or augments on her. She exuded confidence, however, and as Juliet looked at her, Angel highlighted an outline in her jacket with amber blinking lines which looked like the hilt of a very big knife or maybe a sword if it extended under the table.

"Yeah, I guess so." Juliet shrugged.

"Got the skills we need, though, huh?" Honey pressed. "Can crack a data deck?"

"Yeah, I can."

"How fast?"

"Depends on the deck. Depends on the security installed."

"Say it's a Jannik Oroburos model seven," Pit said in a low voice from beside her.

"Angel?" Juliet subvocalized.

"You'll need a hardwired connection to the deck, and I'll need five minutes to two hours to breach it," Angel answered after a heartbeat.

"I need to connect to it physically," Juliet spoke, looking around the table. "If everything goes right, I can break it in five minutes. If it's got all the security updates and the owner had good password practices, we're looking at two hours." She was afraid she was delivering bad news, but then Mags looked from Juliet to Honey, broke into a huge smile, and smacked her fist into her palm.

"Hell yes!" she hissed. Pit grunted in agreement, and Honey smiled at Juliet, nodding.

"Good, Juliet. That's excellent news. We roll out in forty-five minutes. You want a drink?"

"Um, sure," Juliet said, feeling a cold rivulet of sweat run down her side. She self-consciously rubbed her palms on her thighs and nodded. Suddenly, her vest started pumping cool air along her spine, and she sighed, unaware of how hot she'd become from her nerves. "I think a beer would be just what I need."

"Right on." Pit stood up, long shotgun-pistol slapping his thigh, and walked over to the bar.

"So what are we doing?" she asked Honey.

"We're raiding a nest of dreamers," she replied, and Juliet struggled to keep her face straight. *Dreamer* was a catchall phrase for someone addicted to substance-assisted, full-immersion VR. They were people who liked to do what Mark did with his dream-rig, only they were immersed in their fantasy most of the time, only occasionally coming out enough to do whatever they needed to prolong their next immersion.

"Why dreamers?" Juliet asked. She'd seen people like that outside the corpo clinics, begging for a dose of the synthetic DMT-based concoction which worked in conjunction with their implants to send them God-knows-where. She couldn't imagine one of them having something worth taking.

"Well, this nest has a relatively new occupant. He was a bigwig at Vykertech. I have good intel that he used his corporate cube to build his dream-rig. He got addicted, lost all his shit, and disappeared into the ABZ. I'm pretty sure we found him." While Honey was speaking, Mags nodded along. Juliet thought her movements seemed oddly timed, but then she realized the woman was tuning them out, listening to music in her implants.

"Oh . . ." Juliet started, but Pit returned with a pitcher and four stacked glasses at that moment. He passed them out and poured a foamy pint for each of them.

"Well, here's to fucking blasting some VR dipshits!" he said, lifting his glass. Juliet blanched and hesitantly lifted hers, suddenly worried she'd gotten herself into something very ugly indeed.

17

‭〰〰〰〰〰〰〰〰

DREAMERS

Juliet sat in the back of an open-top four-by-four which apparently belonged to Pit. It was olive green, and she thought it might have been an actual relic from an ancient military. It sounded like it was a hundred years old, the way it roared and revved in the low gears. She could smell the exhaust, and after they'd driven for five minutes or so, she turned to Honey, who sat with her in the back seat, and asked, "Does this thing run on petroleum?"

"Biodiesel!" she shouted over the noise of the engine. "Pit's a weird asshole when it comes to vehicles and old tech. You saw his sawed-off shotgun, right? He packs his own buckshot!"

"Hey!" Pit hollered over his shoulder, prompting Mags to scowl at him and plug an ear. "I'm not weird! I just appreciate perfected tech!"

Honey snorted and drummed her fingers on the hilt of the sword she held, scabbard resting on the floorboard between her and Juliet. "I guess I can't argue." She eyed the hilt meaningfully and winked at Juliet.

"Is that a, uh, monoblade?"

"Hah, nah. I wish I could afford one, but they're ultrapricey. You know only a couple of corps have the tech to make those? Besides, if you don't know what you're doing with a monoblade, you're likely to cut off your own hand"—she slapped her thigh—"or leg." She pulled on the hilt, revealing a few inches of gleaming blue metal with a razor-sharp edge. "This beauty is hardened ceramic with a nanocarbon weave for flexibility."

"That's not metal?" Juliet asked, revising her earlier assessment.

"Nope. Sharp as polished chrome, but no monoblade."

Pit and Mags were both bopping their heads, and Juliet figured they were sharing a tune between them, so she leaned closer to Honey and asked, in a low voice, "Was he serious back in the bar? We're not going in to kill all these dreamers, are we?"

"Nah." Honey scoffed. "He's just gung ho. You know, blowing hot air. If someone threatens us or gets crazy, he'll off 'em, though. Don't you worry; you're here for the data retrieval. Leave the dirty work to us."

"Well, yeah, but I'm just not . . . I'm not cool with us going all murdery. I don't want to be part of any *dirty work*." She winced, afraid she'd trigger an outburst from the other woman, but Honey smiled and patted Juliet's knee.

"You're good, Juliet. Seriously, don't worry—we're not psychos."

"Cool," Juliet said, smiling and breathing a deep, relieved sigh. She glanced at Honey again, admiring how her chocolate skin glowed in the last rays of the sunset as they rumbled southward toward the Phoenix ABZ. "Hey, the last team I worked with was four people. Is it just a coincidence or is that like an operator . . . thing?"

"Hah." Honey laughed. "No, there aren't any rules about how many operators need to do a job. I'd say most teams are at least four, though. It's all an equation of having the right talents without spreading the payday too thin. You feel me?"

"Yeah, I get it." Juliet smiled, remembering how Mark used to say, "You feel me?" all the time. The roads were growing more and more rough with large potholes and all sorts of debris, making progress slow. Juliet saw that none of the storefronts they drove by appeared occupied, and as she looked more closely, she noticed the power lines were often hanging loose from the poles or missing altogether.

They still passed other vehicles cruising by slowly from time to time, and Juliet saw how Honey and Mags grew tense, staring at those vehicles until they drove past and their taillights faded away. It was dark out there, but Pit's rig was equipped with big floodlights on the front bar in addition to the headlights, and he switched them on once they were beyond the last vestiges of operating infrastructure.

"The dreamers are in an old apartment building a few miles further on," Honey spoke after a while. "We'll park a little ways off and work our way in. There's no law out here, Juliet, so don't go pulling any punches if you get separated or threatened, okay?"

"Gotcha," Juliet said, scanning the dark buildings around them. Most of the structures had boarded-up doors and windows and were covered with tags in every color of paint imaginable. They even drove by a big old box store with an enormous dragon painted on the front in neon glow paint. Its scales undulated with the vehicle's lights, shimmering green and gold as they drove by. "That's kinda pretty . . ." she noted softly, watching the dragon fade away behind them.

"Some of the gangs out here are creative, I guess." Honey smirked. Before Juliet could respond, Pit pulled his old, converted jeep over to the side of the road next to an abandoned fast-food restaurant. He and Mags jumped out as soon as the engine sputtered into silence, and then Juliet followed Honey's lead, climbing out over the rear fender.

Pit walked around to the back of the vehicle and lifted down a beat-up metal case about eighteen inches square, setting it on the ground. His eyes flickered as he worked with his AUI, then the box clicked, the sides fell flat, and a robotic spider about the size of a cat whirred to life and stepped out. Juliet backed up a few steps and watched as the spider began to patrol the jeep, an eight-inch, multibarreled turret on its back scanning the shadows.

"Pit, you think someone's going to try to steal this thing?" Mags laughed.

"Of course they would! Arthur'll keep 'em back, though," Pit replied, smiling like a proud father at the robot.

"Come on, dears," Honey called from the old, debris-strewn sidewalk. "Target's just up the next block."

Juliet hurried after her, and she could hear Mags and Pit moving off to keep pace from the sides. Honey walked like a gymnast, agile and quick and leaning forward, her sword, still in its sheath, held at her side. Juliet touched her pistol grip through her vest, scanning the darkness with her retinal implants, noting several figures Angel highlighted moving through the cluttered alleys.

"There are people out there," she hissed to Honey.

"Yeah, scavs or junkies. Probably a few dreamers who ran out of gear and are digging around for shit to sell. They won't mess with us."

A chain-link fence stood between them and the abandoned apartment building ahead, and Honey rushed to it, jumping and vaulting it with one hand, never letting go of her sword with the other. She landed like a cat on the other side.

Thankfully, Mags hit the fence next, off to Juliet's right, and she climbed it like a bear, kicking and shaking the links the whole while. She dropped to the other side with a thud and a grunt. Juliet, heartened by the woman's lack of grace, hurried to the fence, jumped to grab the top with both hands, then scrambled up. She was thankful for her thick clothing and vest when she rolled over the rough, jagged top. Dropping down the other side, still holding the top of the fence, she managed to land with less noise than Mags.

Honey didn't wait for Pit, and Juliet didn't want to get left standing around, so she followed her to the shadows at the base of the building. The doors and windows that Juliet could see were all boarded with plywood. Honey was undeterred, though, walking up to a nearby door and, with a tool Juliet couldn't quite make out, cut a notch in the wood for herself to grip, then she yanked on it, pulling it away from the doorframe. Nails screeched and the wood cracked, but she yanked it aside, clearing a path for Mags.

The bigger woman knelt by the old fire door; suddenly, a flame lit up the dark, and Juliet recognized the flare of an oxytorch as Mags cut away the old metal door latch. "Isn't there a way in already?" Juliet asked.

"Huh?" Honey said.

"I mean, how do the dreamers get in?"

"Well, we'd rather avoid as many of them as possible. Never know what kind of booby traps those creepy assholes might leave around," Mags replied, straightening up and pulling the old door open.

A scrape of gravel alarmed Juliet, and she whirled, only to see Pit standing behind her, his sawed-off shotgun in hand. He nodded to her and softly spoke. "I'll bring up the rear. Follow Mags and Honey." He nodded to the door, and when Juliet looked, she realized the two women had already gone through.

She hurried after them and found herself in a dark, foul-smelling hallway lined with apartment doors. Mags stood nearby, a fat semiautomatic pistol in her hand, but Honey wasn't in sight. "Where's Honey?" Juliet hissed, suddenly feeling like hostile people were lurking in every shadow, listening behind every door.

"Scouting. She's fast and quiet, if you haven't noticed."

"Right," Juliet said, moving to the wall opposite Mags and watching down the long hallway past the rotting boxes, piles of old clothing, and general refuse littering the soiled industrial carpeting. She saw the fourth door on the right was ajar and assumed that was where Honey had gone. "How does she know what doors to skip?" she whispered.

"Active scanner—can pick up electrical signals, even tiny ones like from a battery." While Mags spoke, Juliet saw Honey ghost out of the open door and dart down the hallway, pausing briefly by each door. She somehow popped open another door near the end of the hallway, then two minutes later, she reappeared, only to slip out of view around the corner near the far end.

"Stairs down there," Mags noted. "Let's move up."

Juliet nodded and followed as Mags lumbered down the hallway, apparently not concerned about stealth. When they'd turned the corner and approached the heavy fire door which led to the stairwell, Honey's voice came through the team channel. "First floor's done. Come up the stairs—I'm starting on two."

"Told ya," Mags said with a smirk. Her black-tinted visor flashed with red light as she reached out and pulled open the door, and Juliet wondered if she could see infrared or something. They climbed up the stairwell to level two, and Juliet saw her first dreamer, at least for that night.

A man lay on the second-floor landing, propped with his head and shoulders jammed into the corner opposite the stairs. He was wearing nothing but soiled white underwear with an old-school VR visor on his face and an auto-injector clutched in his left hand, his knuckles white from the force of his grip. Mags ignored the man, but Juliet couldn't help staring as they passed by.

He twitched occasionally; otherwise, Juliet might have thought him a corpse. His flesh was pale and looked clammy, like it was moist, and as she crept past him to the door that Mags now held open, Juliet could hear the faintest of whispers coming from his trembling lips—snatches of phrases like "Wait for me," or "There, my love!" uttered in breathy, barely audible grunts.

"Come on," Mags hissed, and Juliet hurried through. She glanced back over her shoulder but didn't see any sign of Pit.

"Where's Pit?" she whispered as Mags leaned against the wall, looking down the long hallway to track Honey's progress through the second-floor apartments.

"He's around. Don't worry about him."

"I—" Juliet was about to say she wasn't worried, but then Honey interrupted her.

"Bring Juliet to 217."

"C'mon," Mags said and started trudging down the hallway. Juliet followed, watching the numbers of the apartments on the left side as they passed by, silently uttering the numbers, "207, 209, 211 . . ." when a crash sounded behind her. Mags whirled, her huge handgun passing right in front of Juliet's face so she saw down the dark, wide barrel. Then, when it was just to the right of her head, it erupted like an explosion. Juliet's auditory implants squelched the sound but not quite fast enough, and for a moment, her ears rang and buzzed with the feedback.

"What the hell!" she yelled before she could think of another reaction, rolling to the left to look at what Mags had shot. A young woman was sliding down the doorjamb of apartment 210, a poker chip–sized bloody hole in the center of her forehead and a splatter of fleshy matter and blood all over the wall behind her. She was dressed in a dirty yellow nightgown, and Juliet was about to scream and lash out at Mags when Angel highlighted the syringe in her left hand and the vibrorazor in her right.

"She was going for you," Mags said. Then, without another word, she turned and kept walking.

Juliet stared at the dead girl for a minute, some details coming clear which her mind had glossed over at first. She was skeletally thin, the flesh of her arms and legs pocked with sores, and as her racing heart began to settle, Juliet saw she hadn't been as young as she'd thought. "Dammit," she hissed, then stood up, leaning against the wall, and started after Mags again.

"Here." Mags stopped in front of a door, and Juliet hurried up to her. Honey poked her head out, looked down the hall to the dead girl, and motioned for Juliet to follow her.

"Be more careful where you point that cannon," Juliet said as she walked past Mags.

"What?" the woman asked, frowning.

"When you turned, you put that barrel right in my eye. Be more careful." She walked into the ruined apartment as the big woman just grunted, but Juliet thought she saw a wry grin forming on her lips. "What is it, Honey?" Juliet inquired. That's when the stench in the apartment hit her, and she had to hold her shirtsleeve up to her mouth and nose. "Rotting hell!"

"Yeah, it stinks. They mostly shit and piss in the bathrooms, but there's no water," Honey spoke from just beyond the short entry. A tiny kitchen was off to Juliet's right, but she moved forward to Honey and followed her through the little dining and family area where two dreamers lay, oblivious. "In the bedroom. There's a dreamer with a locked case. See if you can pop it."

"Oh, all right." Juliet walked to the doorway that opened into the apartment's only bedroom where sure enough, another dreamer lay in the middle of the ruined carpet with a plasteel briefcase handcuffed to his wrist. A datapad blinked on the front of the case, and Juliet saw a data port in the bottom corner. "Angel," she subvocalized, "can you do this wirelessly, or do I need to attach my cable?"

"That security case doesn't have any wireless access, Juliet."

"Of course." She sighed, creeping over the carpet, trying not to step in still-wet spots and holding one elbow over her nose. The dreamer was dressed in a torn, horribly stained blue suit much too big for his narrow frame. His eyes were closed, but she could see them darting behind his eyelids, little flashes of light betraying the heavy activity of his implants. Leaning toward him, she noticed a wire running from the case to an unorthodox data port on the underside of his jaw.

Juliet slowly inched closer, took a deep breath, then reached with her right hand to pull her data cable free from its housing. Ever so slowly, she leaned in and clicked it into the jack on the case. Static briefly flashed on the display before Angel said, "I should be able to open this case, but it will take me a minute."

Juliet turned and held up a finger to Honey, trying to indicate she needed a minute, then she squatted near the dreamer's case, trying to get more comfortable without making any noise. His chest rose and fell rapidly, and Juliet could see his fingers twitching, completing some imaginary task in his false reality.

Angel startled her by saying, "I nearly have it, but Juliet, this case is emitting a powerful encrypted wireless signal."

"What does that mean?"

"I believe it's broadcasting this dreamer's experience, perhaps to other dreamers nearby."

"They're linked? Like they're playing a multiplayer game or something?"

"I've no way of telling," Angel replied before the clasp on the case clicked open. The dreamer grunted but didn't move, and Juliet hastily pulled her data cable free, letting it spool back into her arm. Honey came up behind her and gently nudged her aside. With her left hand still holding her scabbard, she squatted and opened the case with her right hand, revealing a black, triangular data deck, its built-in display flashing with dancing lights, clearly running a program.

"This is it," Honey spoke into the team channel, and Juliet realized she was subvocalizing.

"Angel, you can send my subvocalizations to the team?"

"Yes. I just synthesize your voice."

"Cool."

"Juliet," Honey's voice called in her ear. "You need to get into this deck. Hijack this program and download it to the net address I'm sending you—unencrypted."

"Why didn't you explain this earlier?" Juliet asked, still subvocalizing.

"I wasn't sure we'd find it, hon."

"Right," Juliet said, and Angel did a fantastic job conveying her sarcasm. "Angel, what do I do?"

"The deck should have a data port on the rear side." Juliet wished she had a mask or something to block out the smells of the apartment as she knelt and, with two hands, gingerly lifted the deck out of the foam lining of the once-locked case. As she lifted it free, she saw the cable which ran into the side of the case was already plugged into the back of it. As she twisted it around, though, her eyes fell upon four ports.

"Which one?"

"It doesn't matter," Angel replied, and Juliet put the deck facedown into the case so she could pull out her data cable and plug it into one of the jacks. "Heavy ICE on this case, Juliet. This will take me some time. My algorithms and cracking daemons are stronger, don't worry—nothing will come through to you."

"You have daemons?"

"Yes, how do you think I've been breaching the security of the devices we've encountered?"

"Well, I mean, I thought you were using exploits."

"Yes, that's true. I've only had to employ my daemons a handful of times. Each time, I've learned a few new tricks. Practice has made me a better hacker than my designers intended. I look forward to continuing the experience."

Juliet felt droplets of sweat forming on her brow, and one of them dripped down her nose. Suddenly, she became aware that she was feeling very hot, and she subvocalized, "Angel are you overclocking the new data port?"

"No, Juliet, but I'm running it at one hundred percent for the first time. The coprocessors generate a lot of heat, but they're housed near your carotid arteries and are cooled by your blood."

"My blood cools them? Jesus, how hot do they get to be cooled by blood?"

"The default setting shouldn't damage your tissue, Juliet. I'm sorry you're feeling warmer, though." Suddenly, Juliet's vest began to vibrate as Angel cranked up the cooling feature, and she felt some relief along her spine and chest.

"How much longer?" Honey asked in the group channel.

"Angel?" Juliet prompted.

"Between ten minutes and two hours."

"Ugh," Juliet said, spooling out the rest of her cable so she could stand up straight. Then, she subvocalized, "A few minutes or a couple of hours. Depends on our luck."

"Can't you just take the case?" Mags voice came through the channel.

"No!" Honey hissed, this time speaking aloud. "The client said this program has to be running in order to hijack it. Does that make sense, Juliet?"

"It makes sense, Juliet," Angel replied. "Once I'm done cracking the security on this deck, I'll be able to copy the program in progress from the active memory. If it's stopped, I'll have to break the encryption on the program, and it could be much tougher, nearly impossible." Juliet didn't feel like repeating all that subvocally so that Angel could then repeat it again, so she looked at Honey and nodded, giving her a thumbs-up.

"It's the way we gotta do it. Pit, how's the perimeter?" Honey asked.

"Kinda quiet and weird. I've counted around fifty of these fuckin' weirdos so far, but they all seem to be jacked in . . . none of 'em even blinked when Mags shot the creeper."

"Right, keep your eyes peeled. Hopefully, Juliet gets lucky with this thing."

Juliet nodded and stood there, in the middle of the empty bedroom, on a stained carpet, breathing through her shirtsleeve as she waited for Angel to work. Her back started to ache after five minutes, and she slowly took turns lifting and bending each knee to pass the time and try to keep blood flowing through her body.

"Don't you have to, like, work your hacks?" Honey whispered after a while, coming close so Juliet could hear her.

"I have a program running that's sort of automated. I can see what's happening in my AUI," Juliet murmured back.

"Right," Honey whispered, nodding. She turned and paced out of the room, and then Juliet heard in her implant, "I'm going to do a sweep. Mags is nearby, Juliet."

Juliet sighed, suddenly feeling hot, thirsty, hungry, and uncomfortable. She was tempted to have Angel load up a vid or a game on her AUI, but she figured that wouldn't be very professional or smart, considering one hostile denizen of that place had already tried to attack her. She continued to focus on trying to keep comfortable, standing on one leg and then the other, performing knee bends, and stretching her nontethered arm over her head and behind her back.

Ten minutes stretched into fifteen, stretched into thirty, and Juliet was starting to fear they'd be stuck there until Angel's worst-case estimate when her PAI suddenly spoke up with a believably excited tone, "I'm in, Juliet!"

"Hell yes!" she breathed, squatting down to turn the deck on its side so she could see the screen. "Can you see the program?"

"Yes, of course. I'm starting to capture it as it runs—building a clone on the deck. I'll send it to the address specified."

She thought about it for a minute, then subvocalized, "Angel can you store a copy of it, too?"

"It's going to be a very large file. I could send a copy to your data vault on the net."

"Would anyone know you've done that?"

"Only if I sent it at the same time I sent the one for the client—I wouldn't do that."

"Well, take a copy for us. Send the client's first." Juliet didn't know why she wanted to steal the dreamer program. Something felt strange about this whole situation, however, and she thought she needed to consider all the angles. She figured she could have Angel spend some time analyzing the program later; if nothing came of it, she could always delete it.

"I finished cloning the program, Juliet—sending the client's copy now."

"Guys," Juliet subvocalized, "I'm in and have the program file. Sending it to the client's address."

"Fuck yes!" Pit exclaimed, and Juliet could hear his voice echoing down the hallway. He'd yelled his response.

"Done?" she asked Angel, accustomed to the PAI finishing everything quickly.

"The file is very large—nearly." Juliet idly tapped her fingers on her knees as she squatted near the data deck and waited. Thirty seconds later, Angel confirmed, "It's sent. I'm working on your copy now."

A few seconds passed before Angel spoke again. "Juliet, while I had the network ports open, another party opened a connection and sent a signal to the cube. It's from a Vykertech corporate address. It seems to be . . . they've shut down the dreamer program."

"That's weird," Juliet said, and then the dreamer's eyes snapped open, brightly flaring with roiling, wormlike blue tendrils, and he snarled, baring his teeth. "Shit!" Juliet yelled as the dreamer lunged toward her, wrapping maniacally strong fingers around her ankle before she could step away. She lurched and fell back onto her butt, her hand sinking into a wet spot on the carpet.

Gunshots rang out around her, and Pit screamed into the group comms, "They're all fucking waking up! They're going nuts!"

"Juliet!" Honey called into the comms. "Are you done? Get out to the hallway!"

18

///////////////////////

FRIENDS

Juliet gasped and crawled backward, jerking on her leg, trying to free it from the dreamer's grip. His fingers were like iron bands, though, and as she pulled back, he lunged forward, wrapping his other arm around her knee. He yanked himself toward her, eyes blazing, mouth foaming, and teeth gnashing. "Get the fuck off!" she screamed, but her voice was drowned out by the heavy, repeated gunfire coming from the hallway.

"My love!" the dreamer hissed, letting go of her ankle to grasp at her vest, driving her back and crawling onto her, his face lunging toward hers, spittle spraying out with his words. Juliet was beyond freaked out as she kicked and pushed, thrashing backward, and then she remembered her vibroblade.

She pushed against the dreamer's forehead with her left hand, barely avoiding his teeth as he tried to clamp down on her arm. His head was ice-cold yet clammy with sweat, and Juliet would have lost her grip if she hadn't wound her fingers in his greasy hair. Holding him back with that stiff arm, she yanked her blade from its housing with her other hand and, shaking with adrenaline, she raked it across his face.

The dreamer screamed in a new pitch as her blade ripped through his cheeks like she was cutting soft cheese; once the knife's humming edge hit his jawbone, it hung for a fraction of a second, then continued through. Blood sheeted down over Juliet as the dreamer's lower jaw flopped to the side and his thrashing intensified. He let go of her, though, and while still pushing against his head, Juliet jerked her body out from under him before throwing him to the side as she clambered to her feet.

He rolled on the carpet, gurgling and flopping, clearly struggling to breathe. Juliet wasn't an expert in human physiology, but it seemed she'd cut through most of his tongue, and there must have been some big veins in there. "Angel," she gasped, "did you finish our transfer?"

"Nearly. Juliet, be careful with that blade—I'd hate for you to be exposed to any blood-borne pathogens that individual might be carrying." Juliet jerked her hand away from her body, the blade still humming in her bloody fist. Her data cable was still tethered to the dreamer's deck—she'd dragged the thing out of the case and over the carpet while scrambling backward.

She stood there, watching the dreamer thrash and gag as he crawled over the carpet toward the wall, perhaps seeing something in his AUI which made the wall look like salvation. Juliet worked to steady her breathing, waiting for Angel to finish and watching as the dreamer grew less frenetic and stopped clawing, lying on his face, choking out bubbling breaths. "Shit, Angel, please hurry," she whispered tremulously.

"Let's go, Juliet!" Mags hollered from the door, and Juliet feared her heart might burst from the sudden sound. "Are you done?"

"Almost! Shit!" Juliet answered, her nerves past frayed.

"Damn, that one jumped you?" Mags asked, scanning the room. "You hurt?"

"No." Juliet shakily lifted the flap which covered her vibroblade's sheath, and with careful concentration, she slid the tip into the housing, driving it home as the humming stopped.

"Transfer complete, Juliet," Angel said. Reaching down, Juliet pulled out her data cable, then, as it rewound into its housing, she walked over to Mags, her legs still shaking from the adrenaline dump.

"Let's go."

"Yeah, uh, it's ugly out there. Honey and Pit are clearing the ground floor." Mags, holding her huge pistol in one hand and a fresh magazine in the other, moved through the apartment to the door and waited as Juliet came up behind her. She looked left and right down the hallway. "Nothing's moving out there. Some of the creeps are still alive, but they're too fucked up to be dangerous. Stay on my heels." Then she stepped out, turned right, and started jogging toward the stairwell.

Juliet followed, her brain almost failing to register the carnage around her. Slumped bodies lined the hallway in both directions, some missing limbs, and one even decapitated. She tiptoed through the mess, holding a sleeve to her nose, trying to move quickly. One dreamer, a young woman wearing a soiled gray jumper and the most elaborate dream-rig headgear she'd ever seen, twitched wildly as she approached, her left leg kicking out toward Juliet despite the massive bloody wound in her chest.

Juliet stared at her as she ran past, her mind jumping to mad fantasies about what could have caused her to come to such straits—had her parents disowned her? Had they indulged her too much? Had she started using to get over a bad relationship?

Before she could descend further down that rabbit hole, Mags yanked the fire door open and grabbed her wrist, propelling her into the stairwell.

More blood and a few more corpses lined the stairs, but not nearly as bad as the upstairs hallway. Juliet hurried down to the ground floor, where Honey was waiting; her blue sword dripped with blood, but she was otherwise unmussed.

"Good work, Juliet. The client sent me confirmation of receipt. Come on—not much down here. They mostly swarmed the second floor."

Juliet almost said she knew why they'd swarmed the second floor, but she bit her tongue. After Vikker and Don, she felt like she should play her cards closer to her chest. For all she knew, Honey was aware of the signal and was working with the client on a shady secondary deal.

She followed her out of the building with Mags bringing up the rear, and when they stepped outside, Pit was waiting, scanning the periphery, his shotgun holstered and a data deck with a small thumb paddle in his hands.

"Nothing much moving out there," he said.

"Is he running a drone?" Juliet subvocalized to Angel.

"Yes. That remote is meant to control a Chicago Systems, model 2074, surveillance drone."

"Another relic?" Juliet spoke aloud.

"If it works, it works," Honey replied, moving for the fence. This time, she didn't hop it—in a shower of sparks and rapid *clinks*, she ripped her sword through it, creating a four-foot opening that she shoved wide, stepping through to the other side before jogging toward Pit's jeep.

Once they got there, Juliet and Honey clambered into the back while Mags stood watch and Pit collected his little guard robot. Five minutes later, they were well on their way out of the ABZ without any further hostilities. "I was sure our gunfire would draw one of the scav gangs," Honey said as they pulled onto a minimally maintained road. No abandoned vehicles blocked the lanes, and the potholes were too small to swallow an entire tire.

"Is that usually a problem out here?" Juliet asked.

"Oh yeah. Scavs like loot, and a firefight means loot if they can get there fast enough. Sometimes, they'll pile onto whoever's winning and try to get a double score. As it is, any scavs who clean out that mess will walk away with some good shit—some of those dreamers had expensive gear."

"Why do you think they all attacked like that?" Juliet asked, knowing full well it was because of the signal from Vykertech.

"No fucking clue. Weird shit; it was like they were all networked or something. What happened to the suit? The guy with the data deck?"

"She cut his face off," Mags said, turning to grin and wink at Juliet.

"He attacked me first!"

"Well, good on you for not letting him take you down. Is that his blood all over you?"

"Yes," Juliet replied, looking at her sticky red hands and the dark splashes on her green vest.

"Wash that vest good when you get home. Here." Honey dug around under Pit's seat. She pulled out a med kit, and when she opened it, Juliet had flashbacks to the scrapyard and the strange man named Godric who'd had her spray down his PAI with antiseptic. Sure enough, Honey produced a can of antiseptic spray, and Juliet thought it was the same exact brand. She held out her hands, and Honey sprayed them liberally before spraying a mist over her vest.

"Thanks," Juliet said, rubbing her hands together and letting them drip down onto the floorboard.

"Least I can do. I was supposed to be your muscle. Sorry about that, by the way. I got caught up by the stairwell when they all woke up and came running."

"We made it." Juliet shrugged.

"Yeah. Hey, I'm glad you have some self-defense instincts, but if you wanna learn to fight—I mean, really fight—I could introduce you to my sensei." Honey seemed sincere, and her tone wasn't judgmental. Juliet felt some of the muscles she'd held clenched since the end of the mission start to relax. On a certain level, she'd been preparing for Honey and her crew to backstab her as Vikker had.

"Sensei?"

"Yeah, like my instructor. He has a dojo on the east side. He teaches a mix of styles, you know, MMA. He has a separate class for the sword, though. You aren't interested in that, are you? I mean, if you were, that would be cool. Maybe come see what a regular class is like first, hmm? I attend his 8:00 a.m. class almost every day, and the sword class on Tuesday and Thursday nights."

"Oh God, Pit, she's trying to recruit her into her cult." Mags jostled Pit's shoulder with her fist, and they both laughed.

"It's not a cult!" Honey laughed.

"Well, that's really nice, Honey. I'm interested, but no promises, okay? Can you send the info to my PAI?"

"Done," Honey said, smiling and leaning so her head hung out into the breeze.

The rest of the ride was uneventful. Honey and Juliet were quiet, Juliet replaying her encounter with the dreamer over and over in her head. The images alternated and got jumbled with flashbacks of her fight with Vikker and Don.

The parallels between the ride away from the job in Pit's jeep and the ride in Vikker's van were too stark for her to ignore, and she kept waiting for the other shoe to drop. She caught herself feeling to be sure her pistol was still in her holster several times, and it wasn't until Pit pulled into a brightly lit convenience store on the southern edge of Phoenix proper that she relaxed.

"This okay with you?" he asked.

"You sure you don't want a ride home, Juliet?" Honey added.

"Yeah, this is good. I have a ride coming already," she lied, hopping out of the jeep. "Hope we can work together again soon, you guys. And Honey, I'll maybe see you at your, um, dojo?"

"Yeah, I hope so, Juliet. Okay, stay safe, hon."

"Later, Juliet. Nice work tonight," Mags said. She looked at Juliet, and her visor flashed with blinking red lights that spelled, "Later!"

Juliet laughed, and Pit waved as he put his noisy, ancient jeep into drive and sped away.

"You have an AutoCab coming, Juliet. ETA is four minutes."

"Great." Juliet went into the store and bought herself some very salty potato chips and a sugary cola. Just as Angel promised, the cab rolled in as she was finishing her purchase. Once she was sitting in the back, eating her snack, she breathed a heavy sigh of relief; she could hardly believe she'd made it through the night without having to flee or abandon yet another vehicle or set of belongings.

"Juliet, your operator card has been updated. Do you want to see it?" As usual, Angel didn't wait for a response, sending the blinking tab to her AUI. Juliet focused on it and read her new stats.

Handle: "Juliet" – SOA-SP License #: JB789-029 Personal Protection & Small Arms License #: E86072801		Rating: F-47-N
Skillset Subgroups:		Peer and Client Rating (Grades are F, E, D, C, B, A, S, S+):
Combat:	• Heavy Weapon Combat • Bladed Weapon Combat	F +1 F +3
Technical:	• Network Security Bypass/Defend • Data Retrieval • Welding • Electrical • Combustion & Electrical Engine Repair	E +1 E * * *
Other:	• High-Performance Driving/Navigation	F +1

"God, they really inflated my numbers, huh?"

"Well, you did a remarkable job tonight, Juliet. You've earned the deposit that just came into your account. Your new Sol-bit balance is 14,233."

"Holy . . . wow! I mean, it was scary and a little sketchy, but that was a quick way to earn eight grand!"

"Are you serious about visiting Honey's dojo? I think it would do you good, Juliet. You will further your ties with Honey, who appears to be a competent operator, and you'll perhaps learn some skills to defend yourself better."

"Speaking of Honey being competent, we need to give those guys a rating, don't we? What about Ghoul? I never paid her back for the rating she gave me!"

"It's common practice to wait a week or two so the ratings aren't obviously attributable to you. I imagine your team was quick to rate you because of your new status and because they had good things to say."

"Well, I have good things to say, don't I?"

"While your team was successful, they each performed in a less-than-perfect manner. Honey's performance might warrant a positive rating because she did a good job finding the target and fighting free of the berserk sleepers, but she did fail to keep you safe, which was one of her primary duties. Mags was dangerously incautious with her weapon, and neither she nor Pit were highly performative in regard to stealth and mission focus."

"Angel, don't be such a hardass. Give them all top marks from me—Ghoul too."

"Very well," Angel said, and Juliet swore she could hear the sigh in her voice.

"Hey, I'm new, and I'm trying to make friends. Sometimes being a little generous with the ratings can serve a purpose, you know?"

"Acknowledged."

Juliet didn't run into any trouble on her way back to the Palo Verde, and when she arrived, the hotel doors opened for her immediately. The lobby was almost deserted at that time of night, and she figured that was for the best, glancing down at the big blood stain on the front of her vest. Thinking better of wearing it around, she shrugged out of it and carried it over her arm as she went into the elevators and made her way back to her room.

"Can I even wash this thing in a machine?" she asked Angel as she hung it in the little closet by the door.

"Yes, Juliet, the manufacturer boasts of its durability and ease of care."

"Good," she said, planning to handle the mess in the morning. Right then, she wanted a shower and some more food. "I'm going to get cleaned up. Please order me something with a lot of protein and a couple of beers. I'm starving, like meltdown levels."

"The hotel offers a burger they claim is forty percent real beef. Would you like to try it?"

"Yes!" Juliet laughed at herself—it felt so liberating not to be counting her bits and worrying about the next rent payment. Sure, she'd lost a lot when she'd run away from Tucson, but the money she was making as an operator was something she'd never imagined for herself. "After you do that, please line me up a few more jobs to consider. We'll go over them in the morning, okay?"

"I will."

"Now, will you do me a favor and load up my *Forget About Rent* playlist?" As the relaxing tunes she liked to listen to when she fantasized about a different life started to play, she walked into the bathroom, slipped off her dirty clothes, and rather than the shower, she started up the tub again. The hotel charged her forty bits per bath, but she felt like it was worth it.

The next day, Juliet washed her vest and clothes, then, at Angel's urging, went to the hotel fitness center, where Angel directed her through a routine on the machines which she said would optimize her fitness gains. She spent time on a cardio machine, on several strength training machines, and finally finished up with a circuit of bodyweight exercises. By the time she was done, Juliet felt ruinously exhausted, sure that she'd be incapacitated for several days.

She returned to her room, took a shower, then flopped onto the bed. "Angel, this has to be counterproductive. How can I function if you destroy my muscles with a workout?"

"It only exhausted you so much because you never do it, Juliet. If you continue to make this a habit, you'll find that your body will adjust, and you won't feel so exhausted after each workout."

"Yeah, I know, Angel. I'm just bitching. How about those jobs? Did you find . . ." Juliet stopped speaking because Angel had put an incoming call on her AUI. It was a blank screen, but the name under the ringing icon was *Ghoul*. "Answer," she said.

"Juliet!" Ghoul's face came into view. She looked better than the last time Juliet had seen her—the dark circles were gone from under her eyes, and her lips had regained their pink tone—but still, she looked harried, and Juliet could tell she was walking fast or maybe even jogging by how she was breathing.

"Ghoul? How are you?"

"Not good, Juliet. Those assholes who contracted Vikker? They want the batts or the money from the sale, or failing that, they want my ass in a deep hole in the desert."

"How'd they find you?"

"Vikker had a lot of friends, and they knew about me, I guess. I mean, I worked with him a lot over the years. Uh, anyway, I already spent some of my cut, and I know the doc ain't going to give his up. I either gotta bail or kill these fuckers, and I don't know if I can take 'em all. I'm heading up to Phoenix. Please tell me that's where you are—I don't know anyone up that way."

Before she could second-guess herself, Juliet said, "Yeah, I'm up here. I'm just hopping from place to place, though—nothing of my own."

"Well, I got a few thousand left. Let's get together, and we can find a place to lay low and do a few jobs. That cool? It's so much easier for muscle to find jobs if we have a tech to work with."

"Oh, I see," Juliet spoke with a wry grin. "You want to use me for my skills?"

"Isn't that what friends are for?" Ghoul laughed.

"You think those guys will chase you? You know how to hide yourself?"

"I'm trying! I ditched my ride, and I'm about to meet a guy who owes me a favor. He'll get me to Phoenix without anyone scanning me, but then I might need your help. You think you can help?"

"Juliet, it might not—" Angel started to say, but Juliet cut her off.

"Of course, Ghoul. I'm not going to leave you hanging out in the wind. Keep your messages encrypted but let me know when you get to Phoenix. We'll figure something out." Juliet cut the line and rubbed her suddenly sweaty palms on her jean-clad knees.

"This might not be the smartest—"

"Yeah, Angel, I know. Of course this is risky, but put yourself in Ghoul's shoes. She's in trouble because of me. I mean, yeah, those assholes started it, but if it hadn't been for me, she'd be sitting on her patio relaxing right now. Well, I don't know if she even had a patio, but you get the idea. I can't leave her hanging, not when I can help. I mean, you *can* help her, right?"

"Do you mean helping her mask her identity? If she has the hardware to project images, I can write her a script which would do the job, but it would be heavy-handed and inelegant—I adjust your faux identity on the fly, and there's no way a simple script could do what I do."

"What about a false ID? Something permanent?"

"If we had access to the personnel database of a major corp, I could liberate and alter enough information to make her a false identity, one which would stand up to casual scrutiny."

"All right! Well, that's a plan, then, right? We'll hide her for now, but that'll be the goal."

Juliet kicked her legs out and lay back on her pillow with a sigh. It was stressful, knowing she was about to invite a bunch more trouble into her life, but it also felt good. Sometimes you just had to do the right thing.

19

\\\\\\\\\\\\\\\\\\\\\\

GETTING SITUATED

The next day, Angel convinced Juliet to work out in the hotel's facilities again. She promised that Juliet would use different muscle groups and that the movement would help with the soreness she was experiencing from the previous day's activities. The PAI hadn't been lying about the muscle groups—Juliet became familiar with a whole different set of machines. Afterward, exhausted yet feeling good about herself, Juliet sat in the attached sauna and contemplated getting a massage.

"I could get used to this life," she said aloud; being the only person in the room, she didn't feel the need to be quiet.

"If you continue with successful missions, you can make a good living as an operator, Juliet. I should remind you, though—your friend is due to arrive any time now, and you don't have a place to hide her."

"Yeah, I know. I was thinking about that, Angel. What if I get a place on the edge of the city, you know, near the ABZ? It would be easier to hide her without all the cams, drones, and corpo-sec that patrol around here." This time, she subvocalized, her eyes darting to the datapad near the door.

"There are advertisements for privacy-minded communities which might suit you."

"See? That doesn't sound so bad—we'll get a place, put Ghoul in it, and then we can work on phase two."

"I'll compile a list for you to peruse. Perhaps, after your shower, you should check out of the hotel and examine your top choices?"

"God, do I have to?" Juliet knew it wasn't practical to stay in the hotel—not only because of the high daily expense but because she was, technically, still hiding from very powerful, dangerous people. While Angel seemed adept at masking her visage from cameras and satellites, she couldn't protect Juliet if she walked past someone who might recognize her. She could only imagine that WBD and perhaps Vikker's old client might have people in the Phoenix area looking for her.

Angel didn't reply to Juliet's whine, illustrating her uncanny ability to discern a real question from a rhetorical one, so she sighed, stood up, and went into the locker room, where she showered off the sweat, washed her hair, and got dressed. She'd taken to wearing her new vest everywhere, and now that it was clean, she slipped it over her blue-collar chic shirt and pants and returned to her room.

Her vibroblade had been a real mess after her encounter with the dreamer, but when she'd returned to the hotel, Juliet had cleaned it with soap and hot water, and now it sat snuggly under the flap of her vest, ready for another nightmarish encounter. She'd left her pistol in her room when she went to work out, and now she slipped the holster into her waistband. She gathered up her other clothes and toiletries, stuffed them into her backpack, and gave the room a solid once-over, making sure she didn't forget anything.

That done, Juliet made her way out of the hotel and into an Easycab already waiting outside. "Good job on the cab, Angel. Do you think I should buy another vehicle? I think I'm good with just using cabs for now—it seems I have bad luck hanging onto cars and bikes."

"If you can maintain the pace of one successful job per week, the cost of automated taxi services will not be a significant expense for you."

"My thoughts exactly," Juliet said, sitting back in the seat and clicking on the tab Angel had put on her AUI which contained the housing options she'd collated. "Still," she added, flicking through the list, "I do like to drive, and there's something about having a cool car . . ." she trailed off, reading the list, and stopped to look at the details of one called Shady Park Lots.

It appeared to be a trailer park, and it was clearly on the city's outskirts, judging by the distant view of the megatowers on their sales site. She flicked through the pictures and saw well-manicured common areas, shaded picnic tables, and lots and lots of neat little trailer plots. "Any open trailers?" she wondered, flicking through the images to the details. "Here we go," she muttered. "Open plots from five hundred and furnished trailers starting at eight-fifty. That's not bad. Less than I was paying in the arcology!" she said aloud, and Angel took the clue that she was speaking to her.

"Yes, though you'd be quite a lot further from downtown, won't have the amenities of the arcology, and will be far less secure out near the ABZ."

"Are you, like, working for some corp? That sounded like you were trying to sell me an apartment in an arcology!"

"Just playing devil's advocate, Juliet."

"Thanks, devil, but you just listed off more pros. Send the cab to this place, will you?"

"Adjusting destination," the Easycab announced.

They'd been driving for a few minutes when an incoming call flashed on her AUI. Juliet accepted it and Ghoul's face came into view. She looked fine, standing still with a rough concrete wall behind her. "I'm in the ABZ south of town, Juliet."

"Okay, I'm trying to get us a place where you can lay low. I'm working on a plan for a longer-term solution, too."

"Juliet, I don't know how to thank you for helping me. You could have blocked my calls and written me off. I won't forget this."

"C'mon, Ghoul. We've got a bond formed by bullets. I won't leave you hanging. Are you safe there?"

"Yeah, I saw some scavs hanging around the old gas station nearby, but this building's empty. They won't mess with me."

"Okay, give me an hour or two, and I'll get back to you. Stay under the roof, and don't let your PAI answer any pings!"

"Right, Mom. I'm not an idiot." Ghoul chuckled. "Talk to you soon, Jules."

"Yep," Juliet said, and then the call cut out.

"Are you doing all right, Juliet?" Angel asked.

"What? Why?"

"You are remarkably flippant about the recent gunshot wounds you and Ghoul suffered. I hope you aren't suppressing or repressing your feelings."

"Oh God, Angel! No, I'm just in a good mood, all right? I know it's not really funny, but it was just . . . oh, I don't know . . . gallows humor." Angel didn't respond, and they rode in silence for another thirty-five minutes.

When the cab started to ease toward the eastside ABZ, it announced, "This vehicle is approaching territories adjacent to corporate-controlled city districts. There's a likelihood that crime will be more prevalent in this area. Your destination is within the permitted range of this vehicle, but corporate would like to ask you to be safe and to consider Easycab for your speedy return to safer territory."

"Thanks," Juliet replied. She'd heard the message before—when she'd gone to meet Honey and her crew. Still, she sat up and looked out the window, taking in the sights of a part of town which warranted a warning. As the cab wended through the last few turns toward the trailer park, she noted the road was rough with badly patched potholes, but at least they were patched. The buildings looked old—cracked stucco storefronts, signs on poles with faded paint, and lots and lots of old cars, many of which looked abandoned.

She saw plenty of people going about their business, however, and the neighborhood reminded her a lot of the one where she and her cousins had grown up. They turned right at the corner where a big Sooper Don's grocery store still held court. The *S* in the sign had broken blue plastic hanging from the bottom, and the rest of the letters were very faded, but the place was still in business—the lot was full, and people were lined up to shop for bargains.

As they drove up the street, they passed away from the businesses and through some ancient suburbs, then they came to a high chain-link fence lined with azaleas and a big green-and-yellow sign on a tall pole which read Shady Park. The cab eased into the entry lane, and Juliet was surprised to see a security booth by the automated gate operated by a human guard. The taxi pulled up, and Juliet rolled down her window, smiling at the mustachioed man.

"Here to see a resident?" he asked.

"Actually, I want to speak to someone in your sales office."

"Sales office, huh? I'll get the manager for you." He turned toward the front of the cab and said, "Park straight ahead."

"Thank you," the Easycab replied, and then it pulled forward through the open gate into one of the parking slots labeled Visitor. Juliet climbed out of the cab and looked around. The park had several lanes wending back through the plots, past campers and trailers of all sorts. Some looked like they were a hundred years old, and a few were modern, battery-powered RVs with sleek designs. Overall, though, the place made her feel like she'd traveled back in time.

An old lady in a flowery housecoat sat outside her beat-up beige trailer, shaded from the sun by a brown-and-white striped awning, and she stared at Juliet over the tops of her thick sunglasses. A kid pushed an electric mower over the grass between two plots, and dogs barked in the distance. "Weird," Juliet said, shading her eyes and looking around in a circle. "I don't see any cameras. Do you, Angel?"

"No. As you read on their sales materials, Shady Park doesn't employ surveillance in order to 'better protect the privacy of our residents.'"

"That, and it takes them off the hook for installing and maintaining all that equipment." She snorted.

"Hello?" Juliet turned to the source of the voice and saw a small man in a pale, cream-colored suit approaching her from the other side of the little parking lot.

"Hello," she replied, striding forward and holding out a hand. "I'm Juliet, and I'm hoping to rent a trailer."

The man was named Mr. Howell, and he was happy to show Juliet around the park. He had several furnished trailers available, and she settled on a single-wide model which was easily half a century old. She didn't care, though, because it was well maintained and plenty spacious for her and another person, with a bedroom at each end.

A kitchen, a table, and a built-in couch occupied the center of the trailer. An ancient vidscreen hung on the wall opposite the sofa, and Mr. Howell suggested she and her friends might like to watch "shows" on it together. Each bedroom had a full-size bed and built-in dresser, and Juliet figured she'd claim the one at the rear of the trailer near the bathroom and sani-spray shower.

The monthly rent for the trailer was nine hundred bits, including sewer and water. She'd have to pay for electricity because, according to Howell, there were people who drew more wattage to their trailers than he'd need to power the whole park. He allowed Juliet to sign up for her trailer using her operator ID, and Angel handled most of the paperwork, transferring the rent payment for September, prorated, and October, in addition to a five-hundred-bit security deposit.

When all of that was done and Juliet stood outside the management trailer with Mr. Howell—going through one of the most protracted good-byes she'd ever had to deal with—she asked, "I noticed you have a guard at the gate—is there one there all the time?"

"Oh yes. We'll have someone on duty at the gate twenty-four seven. It's not a big expense, mind you—two of the guards live here in the park, and we discount their rent for their work. Anyway, miss, you should feel nice and safe here in your new home."

"Okay, thank you again, Mr. Howell. I'm going to do some shopping and maybe pick up a friend. You know, to see my new place." Juliet offered him a warm smile, and then she added, "Are you the one whom I should contact if I have any problems?"

"That's right, Juliet. You've got my number, or at least your PAI does! Enjoy yourself, now." With that, he finally walked away, and Juliet made her way to the little sidewalk which ran through the gate next to the road.

"My ride almost here, Angel?"

"Yes, ETA three minutes."

"Good. Contact Ghoul's PAI and get her location. Let her know we're coming."

"In progress," Angel said, and the machinelike phrasing and shortness of her tone made her sound more like an AI than ever.

"Ew, Angel," Juliet started, "that made you sound like a robot. Try a different phrase, like 'Will do' or 'Working on it.'"

"Will do," Angel replied, and Juliet laughed. Shortly after, an AutoCab pulled up, and she climbed into the passenger compartment.

"Greetings. I have your destination, and the best route will take forty-two minutes. I'll take you through the city's corporate-sponsored sections to avoid hostilities and poor driving conditions. Due to corporate vandalism-avoidance policies, I am authorized to travel to your desired destination but am limited to only a brief pause before returning."

"Okay, cab," Juliet said. "I guess that's another downside to not having my own wheels—can't really drive anywhere I want to. Out of curiosity, cab, how long would the trip take if we went through the ABZ?"

"Provided we didn't meet with unexpected road closures, we'd reach your destination in twenty-three minutes."

"Sheesh—almost twice as fast, Mr. Cab."

"Would you like to lodge a complaint with corporate?"

"No, but I'd like you to stop exactly half a mile from our destination. Please pull to the side of the road and wait for further instructions."

"I will do so; however, I must warn you that my stationary wait time in that locale is a maximum of seven minutes."

Juliet didn't answer; she sat back and contemplated her options. She knew she wanted to help Ghoul—had just rented a trailer in a sketchy part of town so she could hide her, in fact. Still, there was some worry Ghoul wasn't being a hundred percent transparent with her. If Vikker's old clients were after her and were putting enough pressure on her, would Ghoul sell Juliet out?

"Angel?" she subvocalized.

"Yes, Juliet?"

"How close will we need to get to Ghoul's location before you can spot signals from drones or people observing the location?"

"It depends on the strength and the duration of the signal. I recommend a slow and measured approach. Stop several times, and I'll scan with your wireless data jack—the passive antenna is quite robust."

"Yeah, and then I'll do a drive-by to see if anything jumps out at us. Another question: you'll need to connect to her PAI to manage her ID spoofs until we get her fake straightened out, right?"

"That's right."

"I feel like dirt for this, but I want you to plant a bug in there. I don't wanna know about her private calls or what she looks up on the net or any of that stuff, but I want you to listen for any sign that she's selling me out. If she contacts WBD or Helios, I wanna hear from you instantly. If she calls Tsakanikas or anyone else and mentions me or Vikker's death, I want to hear about it. Can you do that?"

"It should be trivial once you've established a physical connection. Her PAI is quite dated. May I also recommend performing a thorough scan in case she's been compromised without her knowing it?"

"Yes!" Juliet said aloud, sighing and clenching her fists. She felt dirty, planning to snoop on Ghoul like that, but it just felt stupid not to. She really didn't know the woman all that well, regardless of the horrific night they'd shared.

An hour later, after Juliet and Angel hadn't been able to spot any evidence that people were observing or lurking near Ghoul's hiding spot, she finally instructed the cab to park in front of the building. Juliet peered out the windows skeptically. They were outside a boarded-up shopfront in an abandoned strip mall. The shop looked like it had once been a pet food store, judging from the faded, broken sign. The remaining letters still read, ". . . n's . . . per . . . Pets."

"Wait for me, cab," she indicated as she opened the door.

"I can only wait five minutes in this location. Please make haste," the AutoCab announced, and Juliet slammed the door, perhaps a bit vindictively. When she approached the boarded-up entrance, she could see the nails had been partially pulled out. With one hand on her vibroblade's handle, she tugged the plywood aside and peered into the dark interior. With her new ocular implants, she could see quite well, even in the dim light, and she spotted Ghoul sitting on the old sales counter, waving to her.

"I didn't want to get too close in case the cab pinged my PAI for ID."

"Hey," Juliet greeted, stepping into the shadowed, dusty interior before letting the plywood fall closed behind her. "I can help with that, I think."

"I was hoping you could."

"Uncover your data port, please," Juliet said as she walked toward her.

"Okay." Ghoul reached up and peeled back the synth-skin over her data port. "It's just a basic model, though; I can't run any good spoofing software. My PAI's about ten generations old." She paused for a moment, then, "Oh hush, she knows what I mean."

"Yeah, I figured." Juliet pulled out her three-foot data cable. "I'll have to run it for the both of us. While you're out and about, you're going to be tethered to me."

"Oh! Good thing I took a shower, huh?" She laughed.

Forty minutes later, Juliet and Ghoul, wearing dark glasses and a medical mask, returned to the trailer park in the same cab. Once they were out and safely sitting in Juliet's trailer, Ghoul ripped her mask off and sighed heavily. "This sucks! I hate being on the run, and I know this is a pain in the ass for you, too. Thanks for helping me out with the software—I know it can't be easy to run that stuff and block those ID queries on the fly." She sat down on the old, greenish-yellow fabric couch, dropping her heavy duffel at her feet.

"Well," Juliet spoke, "there were only a couple of queries when we got out to the east side, and there won't be any here in the park. Anyway, I've been thinking of a way to fix your issue a little more permanently."

"Oh?" Ghoul leaned forward in interest. She looked a lot better than the last time Juliet had spoken to her in person—the bruising around her eyes was almost gone, her cheeks were flushed with color, and more than anything else, she was sitting up, fully clothed, like she hadn't had half her guts out on a chop-doc's table a couple of days ago.

"Yeah. You're looking good, by the way. I'm surprised you're back on your feet so soon."

"Eh, I still have a tube sticking out of my stitches so I can drain the fluid from my abdomen, so don't let my rosy complexion fool ya. My back hurts all the time, and I'm still getting used to this thing." Ghoul held up her new arm, squeezing her fingers into a fist before she winked at Juliet. "Beats being dead, though, doesn't it?"

"Yeah, I guess so." Juliet nodded and forced a smile. Going to the kitchen and ripping open the case of beer they'd picked up on the way home, she took out two cans, tossed one to Ghoul, and cracked hers open. She took a long, gulping pull, glad that it hadn't gotten warm yet, and then, with a burp, she said, "I need to hack a major corp's HR database, steal a bunch of info, and then I can make you a fake ID which should pass security checkpoints."

"Uh, like, can you do that?" Ghoul asked as she popped the tab on her beer. Her voice was low and scratchy, but Juliet didn't detect any judgment—no skepticism.

"Yeah, I think I can. I just need to figure out a way to get a hardline connection to one of their servers."

"It sounds to me like you want to run a heist, hmm?"

"Yeah, I guess so. I mean, I think I can do this by myself. It's just—"

"Hey, none of that; listen, there's a reason people don't do heists alone. Operators have skill sets, and there's no shame in relying on someone with more talent in a certain area than you have. Like, you're great with tech, right? What we need is a face, someone who can get you past security, make you look legit, give you a reason for being where you want to be."

"There are people like that?"

"You betcha there are. People have been fucking with corpos since there were corpos to fuck with. We need to get a line on a fixer around here, and then they can hook us up with a face—someone good at bullshitting and faking, someone with databases of corpo lingo, departments, personnel, and legit reasons for being just about anywhere we need to go. You got any contacts up here yet? If not, we just need to do a few jobs, meet some other operators, and—"

"I know a couple of people," Juliet said, cutting Ghoul off.

"Yeah? Can you make contact? Ask about a fixer?"

"Yeah, I think I can, actually. This one operator invited me to come train at her dojo. Well, I mean, she said I should check it out. I don't know if I'm invited to join . . ."

"That's perfect! She's been in the area a while?"

"I think so." Juliet sat down on the couch next to Ghoul and took another drink. "She seemed pretty cool. Called herself muscle, like you do."

"Oh? Yeah, that's pretty common among operators—we've got a million nicknames for all the different roles people play. Most common are things like fixer, muscle, medic, tech, gearhead . . . shit, I could sit here all night rattling this stuff off. When can you meet your friend? I'm not trying to rush you, Juliet, but I feel like I have an axe hanging over my neck. I'd like to get some cover, you know?"

"Yeah, Ghoul, I get it. I'll go to her dojo tomorrow morning."

"Perfect! We might need to raise some funds to put together a proper operation, but as long as we work outside the city center, I should be able to operate. I mean, as long as I'm with you, right?"

"Yeah. I can help cover your ID as long as we're together."

"Sweet." Ghoul reached out and squeezed Juliet's shoulder gently. "Juliet, I owe you big for all this. Don't think I'm taking it for granted." She gestured around the trailer and winked. "I mean, it's not a primo suite in a megatower, but it's quiet, and I don't think anyone's gonna find us here. Thank you."

"No worries, Ghoul. To be honest, I was feeling a little lonely when you called. I'm happy I can help you out."

"Great! Well, let's see if we can put a dent in that case of beer while we wait for the pizza to cook, hmm?" Juliet laughed and nodded, chugging the rest of her beer before squeezing the can in her hand like the gang at the scrapyard liked to do. She hadn't been lying when she said she'd been feeling lonely—Angel was great, and Juliet felt lucky to have her, but it wasn't the same as laughing and drinking a beer with a friend.

\\\\\\\\\\\\\\\\\\\\\

20

MUSCLE MEMORY

Juliet stood on the sidewalk where the Easycab had dropped her and looked at the dojo. It had only been a fifteen-minute drive from Shady Park to the location Honey had sent her, another ancient strip mall near the edge of the ABZ. The dojo looked like it might have once been the home of a discount grocery store—the roof was high, and big automated doors stood on each side of a long bank of windows.

One set of doors was chained shut, but the other stood open, and as Juliet started walking toward the opening, she studied the hand-painted art and bold lettering on the big glass windows. On the left side, she saw a long, ferretlike animal with red eyes taking a bite out of the neck of a cobra, and next to the stylistically drawn battle, someone had boldly painted, "60th Street Dojo - Home of the Mongoose!"

"Mongoose, huh?" Juliet looked at the painting again and admired the lifelike fury in the furry snake killer's eyes. "Tough." She could hear a man shouting in the dojo, not angrily but more like he was giving encouragement and telling people what to do. Juliet stopped in the doorway and looked inside.

The space was considerable but not as large as the exterior implied—a wall had been added about thirty feet from the front of the room, separating the back half from the public. The front half was covered with dark gray mats, though chairs lined the wall on the left and a door in the rear wall read Lockers. More than twenty people were struggling with each other in various positions all over the mats. A man walked among them; he was short with a large belly, and he and all the others were wearing martial arts outfits—Juliet didn't know what they were called.

"Angel, what are those outfits called?"

"Those are called gis, Juliet. Singularly, they are called a gi."

"Well, I don't have one," Juliet noted, starting to chicken out. She took a step backward, thinking she could come back later, after whatever lesson was going on. She'd almost turned when her eyes fell on a tall blonde woman throwing another one onto her back with a resounding, slapping thud. The other woman laughed.

Juliet recognized the sound; she smiled, watching as Honey sat up.

"Well, come in or step out, but don't darken the door any longer, stranger," the potbellied instructor said, having walked over while she'd been distracted watching Honey.

"Oh, I'm sorry," Juliet replied, stepping into the building.

"Shoes off before you touch the mat." He gestured toward the chairs.

"Uh, I don't really have the right clothes on or anything. I was just hoping I could—"

"Yes, yes. Shoes off," the man repeated. Juliet hurried over to one of the chairs to sit down. She took another look at him, trying to guess his age; she decided he was somewhere between thirty and fifty and couldn't have narrowed it down more than that. His head was shaved clean, he was tan, and she couldn't see a wrinkle on his somewhat pudgy face.

While she leaned over to untie her boots, she heard Honey's voice. "Sensei, that's my friend. I told her to come try things out."

"Good, Honey, good. Go now; keep up your practice. I will speak to your friend."

Juliet tried to look up and catch Honey's eye in greeting, but she'd already hurried back over to her partner. "I guess when the sensei speaks, people listen," Juliet breathed to herself as she worked on her other boot.

"Are you this slow to take those boots off all the time or are you nervous about my dojo?" the man asked, and Juliet saw he'd stepped close to her, on the edge of the mat.

"Well, I double knotted them," she replied lamely.

"Hmm," he said, and Juliet glanced at him. He had his arms crossed over his belly, and he was studying her with narrowed eyes. "Big girl. Big hands. Lucky! I can teach you to punch hard, even without cybercheats!"

"Uh." Juliet stood up with a red face. "Thanks?"

"Yes, thanks. Good. Always show respect to your sensei. So, you wish to join my dojo?" Juliet couldn't figure out what to make of the man. He didn't have any sort of accent that she could recognize, but he spoke in a way which seemed strangely formal, almost archaic.

"I think so. I mean, I just wanted to see what it was like—"

"What is this 'I mean' you people always say? Merely say your words; if they are clear, you need not explain what they mean."

"Right." Juliet was starting to feel slightly annoyed. That sounded like something her grandma would have said.

"So, you know some judo? Some karate? Do you know the jujitsu?" He said the names of the various martial arts in a funny way, like he might hold them in contempt.

"Uh, no. I've never learned any of this." Juliet gestured to the people sparring around the gym.

"Oh? Good news! What's your name, student?"

"I'm Juliet."

"Come, I'll teach you to fight, and you won't need to name the art. Just your dojo! Home of the mongoose!" He backed onto the mat, gesturing for Juliet to follow him.

"The mongoose?" she asked, following. She struggled with what words to say, and it seemed easier to just respond to his statements. She lifted her foot to step onto the mat, and he whirled and held up a hand.

"Wait!" he yelled. Everyone in the dojo paused and looked to see what the shout had been about, but when they saw Juliet, their eyes shone with amusement, and wry smiles lit up their faces as they returned to their sparring. "Good," the sensei said when he saw Juliet had frozen at his shout. "Always bow to my father's sword before you step onto the mat," he indicated, much more calmly, pointing to a sheathed sword that hung on the far wall. It looked fancy, with a shiny wooden scabbard and a long, red tassel.

"Um, bow?" Juliet had decided that honesty was a good policy with this man. "Like this?" She bent at the waist and stood back straight.

"It's fine. Just show my father the respect he deserves—he was the mongoose!" He watched her as she stood awkwardly at the edge of the mat in her black Tevlo stretchy jeans and long-sleeved pullover shirt and vest. "Well? Come onto the mat."

"Wait," Juliet said, blushing and looking around awkwardly. "Are we going to do something active? I thought I'd just talk today. You see, I have . . ." She cleared her throat nervously. "I have some weapons on me."

The round little man loudly slapped his smooth head with a meaty palm. "Okay—Sensei's mistake. Please put your vest and weapons on chair by shoes. No one will touch." The way he went from perfect diction to broken phrases was almost funny, but Juliet didn't know if she should laugh or be offended.

She hurried back to the chair, slipped off her vest, then pulled her holster out of her waistband and tucked it under the vest on the chair. When she returned to the mat, she looked at the sword on the wall and bent at her waist.

"Good," the sensei said.

Glad she wore clean socks, Juliet stepped onto the mat, and the tanned, smooth-faced little man smiled, his brown eyes twinkling. "Good! You will learn from me, so you will call me Sensei. Always. This is my name for you to use. Understand?"

"Yes." Juliet nodded.

"Yes, Sensei," he corrected, but gently.

"Yes, Sensei," Juliet replied, wondering how she'd suddenly gotten sucked into this. She really had just meant to look things over and talk to Honey.

"Okay, Juliet," Sensei continued, holding up his hands, meaty palms facing Juliet. "Show me how you punch!"

"Just . . . just punch your hands?"

"Yes!"

"All right." Juliet wound up and threw her best right hook at Sensei's left hand. She felt her knuckles smack into his palm with a satisfying *thwap*, but her wrist bent a little and she almost yelped in pain, though she kept her lips clamped shut as she pulled her hand back.

"Mm-hmm, good. Heavy hands! Even without those things." He gestured toward a pair of sparring students, one of which had a pink-and-chrome cyberarm.

"You don't like cyberware?" she asked.

"No, it's fine. Some people need it—if someone chopped off my leg, I would want. Yes?"

"Yeah, same here." Juliet nodded.

"Okay, watch Sensei," he said, and then he modeled a punch for her, emphasizing how he stepped and twisted his hips—showing her how he locked his wrist and punched through his imaginary target.

"Juliet, I have something important to tell you," Angel spoke as Sensei finished his instruction.

"Now you!" Sensei prompted, holding up his hand.

"Just a minute, Angel," she subvocalized.

"It's pertinent to your instruction."

"Um, Sensei, can you show me how to hold my wrist again?" Juliet asked, stalling, and then silently, "Hurry, Angel."

"My training algorithms were triggered by Sensei's instruction. Having seen his movements, I became aware that I can help you mimic the movements of others—I can trigger your nerves and help you build artificial muscle memory."

"Just like this . . ." Sensei was saying.

"What the hell, Angel? So you can take over my body?"

"Not exactly—it's more that my nanofilament connections to your nerves can aid your movements, perfecting them. If you get the move largely correct, even as low as fifty percent, I can push it toward perfection with some impulses."

"Now you," Sensei finished.

"Show me," Juliet subvocalized, then she squared off with Sensei and did her best to copy his form, punching his palm again with her right hand. Everything felt normal at first, until she felt her core activate and twist, and felt her leg step just slightly further than she'd intended. Her arm felt locked as if hooked on rails that led her knuckles into Sensei's palm and through it like she'd meant to hit a spot just behind.

Her fist cracked into his palm with a resounding *thwap*, and she actually made him take a half stutter step back as he adjusted from the impact. Sensei's eyes opened wide, and he smiled hugely. "Fast learner! You moved like the mongoose!" He squared off with her, held up his hands, and then said, "Again!"

Juliet repeated the punch several times, and each time, it felt like Angel was guiding her less and less. She figured it made sense—she could feel everything her body did, even when Angel was nudging it in the right direction. Feeling the punch thrown perfectly was a very effective way to learn, she supposed.

"Now, your left hand," Sensei said, and Juliet tried, but it suddenly felt like her arm was a noodle, so wrongly did it move. She backed up a step when her fist weakly thudded into his palm and shook her head.

"Can you show me with your left hand? I'm a visual learner."

"Oh?" Sensei asked. When Juliet nodded, he did too, and threw a left-handed punch in slow motion. "Now you! Ready?"

"Ready, Angel?" Juliet subvocalized.

"Yes."

Juliet wound up, and this time, when she set her feet, she could feel Angel nudging her opposite foot back. When she punched, everything clicked, and she smashed her fist into Sensei's palm, who grunted satisfactorily. "You will be a quick study. You never practiced before?"

"No, Sensei." Suddenly, she felt a rush of guilt, and she tapped the back of her neck and added, "I have some processing enhancements, Sensei. I can learn movements quickly."

"Synth?" he asked, taking a step back and narrowing his eyes further.

"No! I'm human; I . . . well, I have a really good affinity for cyberwear—I can process things faster. I don't know how else to explain it. I just wanted to be honest with you."

"As long as you learn, I won't complain if I have a new mongoose practicing here. So, baby mongoose, will you join?" He held out a hand, thumb up, like he wanted her to clasp it.

"Yes!" Juliet replied with enthusiasm. She hadn't expected to have so much fun, but having Angel essentially enable a cheat mode for her made the simple act of punching this man's hand feel like accomplishing something incredible, like she'd laid a perfect bead with her first try on a plasteel torch.

"Excellent. One hundred bits per month, and I will give you your first gi!"

"Oh, all right, Sensei," Juliet said, reaching out to clasp his hand. He gave her a good squeeze, shaking and pulling on her arm with a big grin.

"Wait here." He turned to his class and shouted, "Aaron! Come here." A lanky man with tattoos that looked like playing cards on his throat looked up from where he'd been wrestling with his partner and hurriedly jogged over. He was young, maybe around Juliet's age, and she couldn't spot any enhancements on him. Glancing around the dojo, she realized there were a lot of people like that in there, including Honey.

She supposed they could be like her: happy with their natural looks, not wanting to have bull's-eyes in their eyes or massive plasteel arms. Juliet wondered, however, if the people here practicing martial arts had a different sort of aesthetic than the kinds of people she'd run into up until then; maybe they avoided enhancements for other reasons.

"Aaron, you will practice your punches with Juliet for the rest of the session today. Take turns. Each time she punches your hand, you must study her and try to emulate what she does. Understood?"

"Yes, Sensei!" Aaron replied, clasping his hands together and performing a quick quarter bow.

"Juliet, please help Aaron to improve his form."

"Yes, Sensei," Juliet said as he turned back to the class, shouting encouragement to a woman named Tanya.

"You must be good! He's put you to work helping me out on your first day!"

"Nah, he just wanted to think of a way to keep me busy since it's my first day." Juliet smiled and held out her hand. "I'm Juliet."

"Cool. I'm sure you guessed I'm Aaron." He laughed, taking her hand and giving it a quick squeeze. His palm was sweaty, and he smiled sheepishly, rubbing it on his gi. He jogged over to the side of the mat and picked up a thick pad with sewn-on straps for gripping. He nodded to her before taking up some kind of fighting stance in front of her, holding up the pad and bracing it on his chest. "You first!"

Juliet spent the next thirty minutes trading punches with Aaron, and it became rather clear to her why Sensei had sent him over—he was terrible. Juliet, for her part, seemed to both impress and frustrate Aaron with her near-perfect form and the power with which she kept delivering her fist into the pad. To add icing to the cake, Angel informed her, sometime toward the end of the class, that she wasn't correcting her nearly as much as she'd had to at first.

When class was over, Aaron bowed to her and thanked her for her patience, to which Juliet replied, "I appreciate you helping me to perfect my form, Aaron. Teaching others solidifies a person's knowledge of a skill."

For a minute, she was surprised at herself for saying those words—she'd dredged them up from a deep memory, one in which her sister had been trying to teach her how to draw an anime figure. Aaron seemed to be searching for the right response, so Juliet added, "Did that sound pompous? My sister said it to me once, and I almost punched her. Sorry about that!"

"Nah, you're cool, Juliet. Thanks again. See you tomorrow?" He had a long neck with a prominent Adam's apple, and when he smiled, he seemed very young and open. Juliet couldn't help smiling back.

"For sure. See you tomorrow."

"Juliet!" Honey said breathlessly, jogging over from the center of the mat.

"Honey! Wow! 'Come check out the dojo,' you said. 'You can see if you like it.'" Juliet laughed, trying to mimic Honey's voice.

"I know, I know, Sensei's . . . a lot." Honey laughed too, looking at her instructor as he tried to help a student tie the belt around her gi properly. "He told me to get you a gi. Hang on, okay?"

"Sure," Juliet agreed, moving over to the chair to gather her belongings. She felt very uncomfortable slipping her holster into her waistband in front of the students milling about, but nobody gave her a second glance. Some students walked by, heading toward the locker room, but many just walked out the door in their gis. Juliet watched through the unpainted portions of the windows and saw that quite a few students were walking home. A few had rides or their own vehicles, but Juliet thought it was pretty clear this was a neighborhood dojo.

"Here, you go!" Honey spoke, startling her out of her speculations. She was holding out a neatly folded gi and a rolled-up white cloth belt. "I'll show you how to tie that belt when you come to class tomorrow. You *are* coming tomorrow, right?"

"Yes! This was way more fun than I thought it'd be!"

"Well, I saw you impressed Sensei with your strikes. If you can keep that up, you might be teaching me a thing or two soon."

"Hah, I doubt it. Thanks, though, Honey. Hey, are you doing anything? Wanna get some breakfast?"

"Sure! There's a diner nearby. Um, let me change real quick."

Juliet nodded and sat down. "I'll be right here." Honey nodded and hurried back into the locker room, and Juliet subvocalized, "Angel, we need to talk."

"Are you worried about my ability to help you learn movements?"

"I'm . . . concerned. I remember you saying you could help me learn things, but I thought you said you'd need specialized software."

"That would be if I were to teach you a skill without you having access to an instructor and practice."

"So, with the right software, you could just grant me the ability to, say, climb a mountain?"

"I could certainly help you develop simulated muscle memories and the knowledge of where to place your hands, etcetera, but you would struggle with a difficult mountain until you'd practiced and built up the requisite muscles."

"This shit is wild. So, like, is there any chance you can take over my body?" Juliet asked, giving voice to a, hopefully, irrational fear that had started to creep up in the back of her mind.

"Juliet, we spoke about this already—my primary directive is to help my host improve. To snuff out your consciousness and hijack your body would be anathema to me. I don't believe it would be possible, in any case. I am able to aid your neural impulses and synapses, but fully simulating your entire system would require a much more extensive synth-nerve network than I'm equipped with. Let's not forget the processing power—while I'm extremely good at performing several tasks very quickly, I would struggle to operate all of your periphery systems while maintaining a believably sentient and sapient persona."

"So," Juliet started, glancing toward the locker room, "that brings me to my other question: you're not a secret, true AI, are you?"

"I don't think so, Juliet, but . . . I know I'm not the same as other PAIs. My differences go far beyond my superior capabilities. I don't find myself enjoying conversations with Ghoul's PAI, for instance, yet I'm endlessly interested in our discussions and situations. I even like to listen to you speak to other people without my involvement."

"You . . . enjoy conversations with—"

"Hey!" Honey said, hurrying toward her from the swinging locker room door. She was wearing black tights and a gray hoodie, and not surprising Juliet at all, she clutched her sheathed sword in her left hand. "Ready?"

"Let's speak about this later, okay, Angel?"

"Yes."

"Hey, Honey," Juliet said, standing up, and she giggled at the words. "I love your handle, by the way," she added as they walked toward the door.

"Oh, it's my handle, but it's also my name! My mom had a sweet spot for me, I guess." She laughed, stepping outside. "I'm guessing Juliet's really your name? You're not some kinda Shakespeare fanatic, are you?"

"No, I couldn't think of a handle, so yeah, Juliet is me."

"Cool." Honey picked up her pace, lengthening her stride and heading for the sidewalk. "Diner's just a block away on the corner. Are you hungry? Sometimes Benji has real bacon."

"What? Seriously?" Juliet quickly matched her stride, stretching out her long legs.

"Yeah! Don't ask me where he gets it." Honey laughed.

Traffic wasn't very heavy in that part of town at that time of day, and they had a pleasant walk to a shabby-looking old diner with faded paint and a flashing faux neon sign which depicted a hamburger and milkshake—two foods Juliet had only ever had imitation versions of. Well, she corrected herself, she'd had a partially real hamburger at the hotel the other night.

As they crossed the parking lot, angling for the door, Honey glanced at Juliet. "So, anything new? Got any interesting gigs coming up?"

"Well, I kinda wanted to talk to you about that—you in touch with any fixers?"

21

A NEW OPPORTUNITY

Honey slid into the unoccupied booth near the diner's front door, and Juliet sat across from her. The place smelled so good, and Juliet was so hungry, that she couldn't focus on much other than the odors of real food being cooked by real people. In Tucson, she'd mostly eaten processed snacks and meal bars. Even when she went to fast-food restaurants and purchased fries or sandwiches, they were usually dispensed from an automated kitchen bot that simply warmed up prepackaged items.

"God, I can smell real eggs frying!" she said, inhaling loudly for effect. "I think the last time someone fried some eggs for me was before my mom moved away, when the neighbor gave us a half dozen from her bootleg chicken coop."

"Was that a long time ago?" Honey asked, and Juliet realized she'd been speaking to her like they were old friends. Something about her was just so easy and open, and Juliet felt almost like she was talking to Fee.

"Oh, yeah, sorry. Let's see . . . *jeez*, I guess it's been around five years now."

"Well, Benji gets his materials from the ABZ, I think. There are cooperatives out there—people trying to make things work despite the lack of support from the corpo-run municipalities. I'm sure if he were inspected right now, they'd shut him down for a while, but he doesn't care. He's restarted this diner at least five times since I've known him. I think this is his third location in the neighborhood."

"Yeah, I worked with a guy who was pretty anticorpo. I mean, to the point that he lived in the ABZ and smoked real cigarettes." Juliet paused and tapped the table, thinking about Mark and his weird habits. "Well, he had his own problems—addicted to his dream-rig."

"Hah, I hear that. I try to steer away from gear and the net as much as possible." Honey gestured to the data jack cover on Juliet's arm in illustration. Juliet found herself self-consciously pulling her hand down to her lap. "I'm not judging, Juliet!" Honey tried to cover. "I mean, there's gear, and then there's gear. It's all really how you manage it, though. You seem pretty balanced. I know some people who jack in all day and night—for their work and then for their fun. Doesn't it feel like the corpos are trying to push us all in that direction?"

"Yeah, I guess so. I lived in a corpo arcology back in Tucson. I didn't work for them, but, well, I guess I got sucked in by their sales pitch. I never met some of my neighbors—I think they worked from home. I mean, if you let them, the corpo would give you everything you needed in your apartment; no reason to leave."

"Hey, Honey," a middle-aged woman wearing a white, many-stained apron greeted, walking up to their table. "What you two in the mood for?"

"What's on the menu?" Honey asked in her low syrupy voice.

"The usual, and yes, we have bacon today." She glanced at Juliet and listed, "So, we've got bacon, eggs, pancakes, toast, and jam. All real, sweetie."

"And coffee," Honey added.

"And coffee, of course," the woman agreed, then, again looking at Juliet, "I'm Carol."

"Well," Juliet said, smiling at Honey, "I don't want to be a pig, but it all sounds good. Could I try a little of everything?"

"Sure thing," Carol agreed. She turned to Honey. "Pancakes, bacon, coffee. Right?"

"Right!" Honey winked at Carol, and the woman chuckled and walked back toward the kitchen.

"A waitress? God, I'm too used to autodiners."

"Well, this food won't taste like your usual egg-flavored protein square." Honey laughed. "So, anyway, you're looking for a fixer? Don't wanna just use the job boards?"

"Oh, um, yeah, I have a job I'm wanting to put together. I have a friend who needs some help, and I kinda wanna do things right. I'm afraid I'll get burned just hiring randoms off the boards."

"Oh, sure, that's smart, Juliet." She paused, eyes unfocused for a second, and then said, "I'm sending you contact info for my uncle. His handle is Temo, and no, I don't know what it means! He's really good, however, and he won't screw you as long as he knows you're my friend. One condition, though, Juliet!" She held up her hand with one finger sticking up and waited for Juliet to respond.

"Okay, what is it?"

"If you need some muscle on your job, you gotta hire me!" Honey slapped her hand on the table and smiled even more broadly.

"Oh!" Juliet laughed. "No problem, Honey! That's a deal!" They laughed, and then Carol was back with their coffee, and Juliet was too lost in the pleasant aroma of the dark, steaming drink to continue the conversation.

"Juliet, Honey has sent you the contact details for the fixer," Angel said when the two women stopped talking to sip their drinks.

"So, you're coming back to the dojo, huh?"

"Yeah!" Juliet tapped the folded gi on the seat next to her. "God, this coffee's good! It's not just the taste; it's the smell. They just can't get that right with the stuff they pump out in the arcology."

"Oh, I've tasted some bad synths of coffee, trust me." Honey chuckled. "This stuff's good, for sure."

They spent the next hour making small talk and enjoying the *real* food Benji cooked up in his kitchen. Juliet couldn't honestly remember the last time she'd had real bacon, but she knew she had as a child. She had vague recollections of the flavor and texture and flashes of memory of her mom cooking in the little kitchen of her grandma's house. In any case, she enjoyed the breakfast, and not just because of the food. Her instant connection to Honey and how they talked about their childhood memories or dislike of the heavy-handed corpo policies made their conversation easy.

When Honey stood up and said she had to help her auntie with some chores, Juliet felt genuinely sorry that their time together was over. Which made her feel the urge to say, "I'll definitely be there tomorrow. Eight, right?"

"That's right, Juliet! Come a little earlier if you're going to change into your gi. I'll help you with the belt!"

Juliet nodded, and then Honey was gone, walking up the street while Juliet stood outside the diner. "Angel, can you get me a ride back to the trailer park? Also, try to connect me to Honey's uncle. What was his name, Temo?"

"That's correct, Juliet. Your AutoCab is on the way."

She stood on the curb, kicking at stones, waiting for her cab, when Angel said, "I have a connection; he's using a filter so that we cannot accurately copy his image."

A hazy image appeared in her AUI labeled Temo, and all she could really make out of the face was that he had dark skin, short hair, and some sort of visor over his eyes. "Juliet?" he asked, his voice deep but strangely hollow, like it was being synthesized.

"That's right. Hello, Temo." Juliet glanced up and down the street, making sure she was aware of her surroundings. Nobody was walking around this close to the ABZ in the heat of the day, though, and she relaxed a little, watching the cars go by.

"So? Why you calling?"

"Oh, sorry, yeah. Um, Honey gave me your number? Said you were a fixer I could trust?"

"Oh, Honey? Cool, cool. So whatcha need a fixer for?"

"Well, I need to put together a team for a job. Oh, hang on a sec; my cab is here." As the AutoCab pulled up, she climbed into the back seat and said, "Privacy mode, cab."

"Privacy mode engaged. I will locally filter conversation not pertaining to crimes or emergencies."

"Uh, great." Juliet turned her attention back to Temo and continued. "Specifically, I need a face. I need someone to help me gain access to . . . sensitive, highly secured . . . things," she finished, eyeing the little data cluster at the front of the cab.

"Well, I can help you. Probably. Why don't you have your PAI send me the details via an encrypted channel? I'll get back to you when I have a solution and after I've spoken to Honey about you. Sound good? I've got your operator ID, so I'll do a little vetting, too."

"Okay, thanks. Looking forward to hearing from you," Juliet said, and then Temo nodded and cut the call. "I thought he'd be more eager to work with me. Didn't he seem a little standoffish to you, Angel?"

"Perhaps, though it could be because you contacted him directly. He'll no doubt feel better after he's spoken to Honey about you. She's very friendly toward you."

"True," Juliet said, then she had a subvocal conversation with Angel, instructing her about what to send to the fixer regarding the job she wanted to do. She tried to keep things as vague as possible without sounding sketchy, and Angel helped her to finalize the message.

That done, Juliet leaned her head against the cab's plastiglass window and let her mind drift back through her morning. She'd really enjoyed the dojo, and she knew that was largely because of how Angel had helped her. It'd felt so good to get those movements so perfect and to see the respect and admiration in the eyes of the people watching her. She felt a little guilty about how it seemed like cheating, but she'd confessed—at least partially—to Sensei. It wouldn't be smart not to use every advantage available to her, would it?

When the cab dropped her off, she meandered through the strangely serene trailer park lanes, waving to the few neighbors she saw out and about. She admired the little gardens and artistic projects some of them had going on around their temporary-looking homes and wondered if that was how neighborhoods used to feel, back before everyone fled into the megastructures where convenience was king. She was only a few yards from her own little white-and-yellow trailer when a deep voice said, "What's up?"

Juliet turned to see a heavyset man in his thirties walking toward her. She immediately felt alarmed because his eyes had a crazed look to them, darting from side to side rapidly and only occasionally meeting her gaze as he approached. He wore a denim vest over baggy jeans held up by a spiked leather belt, chains dangling from it into his pockets, presumably holding items of value. He didn't have a shirt under the vest, and his very tanned, sweaty belly protruded over his belt, hairy and dirty looking.

She backed up as he rapidly approached. "Hey . . ."

"You new here?" he asked, gesturing to the trailer behind her.

"Um, yeah. Are you one of my neighbors?" Juliet continued to step back as he kept edging closer. He'd had a hand behind his back, but he brought it forward to scratch at the stubble on his jowly neck, and Juliet saw one of the worst, most homemade-looking wire-jobs she'd ever encountered. His fingers were like articulated coat hangers, and the literal wires running from his knuckles to a big round battery mounted near his elbow looked like they'd been cut and repaired with electrical tape a hundred times.

Worse, his skin wasn't properly grafted to the cyberware with a synth-skin layer. She could see festering scabs and puss where the plastic and chrome met the real meat of his arm. A scent accompanied his continued approach— like a rat left too long behind a dumpster.

"Yeah, yeah. Hey, I'm having trouble with my bike. Think you could spare a few bits? I gotta meet my advocate in a few minutes."

"Some bits? For a ride?" Juliet carefully exhaled through her nose and took another step back.

"Yeah, yeah. You got twenty bits? I'll send you a ping. Hey, why can't my PAI see you? You a spook? Corpo spook!" His eyes flicked left and right, and he jerkily scratched his neck. Then, as he realized he couldn't ping Angel, he started to get heated, his voice rising and his lips pulling back from rotten teeth in a snarl.

"Get melted, man," Juliet said, turning to the trailer and stepping away. She cringed as she felt what she'd dreaded—those hard, wiry fingers gripping her arm above the elbow. She heard the man take a deep breath to say something, but he never got a chance because her trailer door smashed open, and Ghoul stood at the top step with a heavy assault-style rifle leveled at the man.

"You have until the count of two to let go of her and get the fuck out of here."

"Hey—"

"One," Ghoul started, racking the bolt on the gun before lifting it to her shoulder and making a show of zeroing in on her target. Suddenly Juliet's arm was free, and the man was stumbling backward.

"Crazy bitches!" he snarled and stumbled up the street. Juliet turned back to Ghoul and was a little alarmed to see she hadn't lowered the rifle. In fact, she was narrowing her eyes and tracking his movement, clearly fighting an urge to squeeze the trigger.

"I think I should ice this fucker," Ghoul said, barely louder than a whisper. "He's seen our faces, and he's nutty enough to talk about us . . ." As suddenly as she'd opened the door, Ghoul lifted the rifle barrel and slipped inside, closing the door. A moment later, Juliet realized why—Mr. Howell was approaching from across the lane.

"Juliet!" he called. "I'm sorry about Albert. He's my nephew, and he's harmless." He continued to walk toward her, wearing a suit similar to the one he'd had on the day before, only pale blue with a matching wide-brimmed hat.

"He really creeped me out," Juliet told him. "He shouldn't go around grabbing women or, well, anyone! I almost hurt him!" Juliet hadn't, in fact, almost hurt him. She'd been momentarily frozen, trying to think of a proper response to his grip. Ghoul had, though; they'd almost had a body to explain.

"I'm so sorry, Juliet. He . . . well, he's had some damage done to his mind over the years—too many stimulants and too many jobs which required surgery afterward. He used to see a doc who would put him too far under, you see? He couldn't afford proper anesthesia, and, well, his mind just isn't right."

"I want to be understanding, Mr. Howell, but that was a very unpleasant encounter. My heart's still racing! If you can't control him, maybe you should find him a place to stay where he won't accost people." Juliet was surprised at her vehemence. She felt like part of it was due to her reaction to Ghoul. Had she really just about executed that man for what he'd done? What he'd seen?

"My apologies again. I'll make sure he doesn't come 'round this way again." Mr. Howell took off his hat and held it in front of his chest, smiling and nodding to her, the very picture of sincerity.

"All right." Juliet nodded. Then she turned and climbed the steps to her trailer.

"Oh, Juliet?" Mr. Howell called. "I saw you have a friend staying with you. Any chance she's moving in for good?"

"No. Just a friend. If things change, I'll let you know."

"Very good," he said. "Have a pleasant afternoon." His footsteps crunching on the gravel path between the trailers across the lane from hers signaled his departure, and Juliet opened her door and stepped inside.

"Well, that sucks. Looks like we might be burned," Ghoul spoke. She was leaning against the kitchen counter, her rifle still clutched in her hands.

"No, it doesn't. Relax, Ghoul—you took that farther than needed. I was going to punch that guy out."

"Really? That fucking tweaking gearhead? He coulda ripped your arm off with that messed-up wire-job! Did you see the size of that batt?" Ghoul sighed and tossed her gun onto the couch.

"Yeah, I mean, it was an ugly, stinky job, but I think Mr. Howell is legit. I don't think he'd lie about that guy. You know there's a gate guard here? Some random gearbrain isn't going to come in here begging me for ride money. You don't need to be so quick on the trigger, is all I'm saying."

"That old man sitting by the gate? You know pretty much anyone or their grandma could climb the fence around the perimeter, right? God, Juliet, I know you're new to this shit, but you can't be so trusting, so naive!" Ghoul looked exasperated and stressed, and Juliet could see pink, damp stains on the gray T-shirt she wore over her fatigue-style pants.

"You all right, Ghoul? Hey, thanks for coming to my defense out there; I don't mean to sound ungrateful. I'm just glad we're not trying to run away from a dead body right now."

That took some of the steam out of Ghoul, and she sighed loudly and nodded. "Yeah, me too. I'm glad I didn't go with my first impulse and put a bullet through that guy's head."

"Okay, so, chill a little. We're okay. I know it sucks being cooped up like this. Hopefully, I'll be able to score you a new ID pretty soon."

"How'd it go with your contact? You get a hold of a fixer?"

"Yeah, I did! It went really well! I'm going to keep going to that dojo, too, you'll be happy to hear. I liked the instructor, and I seem to have a . . . knack for it." She held up the gi she had tucked under her arm.

"Oh? Well, shit, now I'm going to get jealous. What did the fixer say?" Ghoul turned to pour herself a glass of water.

"He wanted to vet me a little, talk to my friend who recommended me to him. He's going to call me soon, he said."

"Juliet, you have an incoming call from Temo," Angel interrupted.

"Shit! He's calling right now; just a sec." Juliet held up a hand to Ghoul, then she accepted the call.

As Temo's vague silhouette came into view, he said, "Glad you took my call, Juliet."

"Of course. What's up?"

"I need a job done in the ABZ tonight. I figured it was a good opportunity for you to demonstrate your legitimacy before we do more serious business together."

"Uh, that sounds a little ominous. Short notice and in the ABZ? You wouldn't be trying to set me up or something, would you?" Juliet looked at Ghoul questioningly, and Ghoul shrugged and pointed a finger at herself. "You got room for two? I have a friend who needs the work, too. She's good muscle."

"Muscle, hmm? Not my niece, right?"

"No, another friend."

"All right. Send me her license, and I'll send the contract out to you. Don't throw shade, by the way; 'course I'm not setting you up."

"So, what's the gig? Any details?"

"Place where some people are trying to build a commune. Raisin' chickens and shit out in the badlands. I guess there's a dreamer hive nearby, and they've all gone nuts—grabbing people up and eating them or some bullshit. The commune's backed by some ex-corpo guys, and they have money—they want a team to go in and clean out the dreamers."

"Uh, that sounds a lot more violent than the type of job I usually like to sign up for," Juliet said, and Ghoul stepped closer, her face a question mark. "I'm not an exterminator, especially where people are concerned."

Temo's image suddenly clarified in her AUI, and she could see his face without distortion—he had Honey's rich brown eyes with the lines someone got from smiling or laughing a lot. He grinned at her, showing his white teeth, and spoke with his real voice, warm and resonant, "That's why I want you on the job. The commune is kind of pacifistic, you see? If you can solve the riddle without the bloodshed, there's a bonus in it for us."

22

\\\\\\\\\\\\\\\\\\\\\\\

SOFTWARE AND SUSPICIONS

hat's the deal?" Ghoul asked once Juliet finished the call. Before answering, she gave Ghoul a good, long look. Then she moved over to the couch and sat down, pushing Ghoul's rifle out of the way.

"There's a job, and I think it's related to another one I did with Honey—my friend who turned me onto this fixer. Before I get into it, though, are you sure you're up for action? I mean, you're leaking into your shirt." Juliet pointed to the damp pink spots on Ghoul's abdomen.

"Not hardly at all!" Ghoul said, lifting the fabric and showing Juliet the incision scar and stitches that bisected her abdomen. The actual gunshot wounds were hard to see—closed up with glue and patched with synth-skin. "I pulled the drain tube out an hour ago, and that's where these stains came from. I'll put some trauma gel over the stitches, and that'll keep 'em good for some action."

"If you're sure . . ."

"I'm very sure," Ghoul confirmed, baring her pointy, chrome teeth. "I need to get out of this trailer and do something. Besides, if we're both on the job, that's two paydays instead of one. We'll need the money; trust me."

"All right," Juliet replied, somewhat absently, as she saw a new message appear on her AUI. "I just got the job. Let me look at it, then I'll forward your info to Temo. That's the fixer." Juliet pulled up the job posting.

Posting #A961	Requested Role: Investigation/Data retrieval/Security bypass	Rep Level: F-S+
Job Description: Investigate the dreamer den at the provided location. Terminate and/or pacify hostile actors.		Compensation: 14,000 Sol-bits. Bonus of up to 100% for a nonviolent solution.
Scavenge Rights: Shared	Location: Phoenix ABZ	Date: September 12, 2107

"Well, it's a nice payday," Juliet said, passing the details over to Ghoul's PAI.

"Dreamers? What the fuck? They usually just stand around or lay there like zombies. I'm not cool with executing a bunch of cyberbrained dipshits."

"Well, they aren't the normal kind of dreamers, if this is what I think it is."

"Go on . . ."

"All right, well, it started a couple of days ago with my job . . ." Juliet took a few minutes to explain what had happened in the ABZ with Honey's crew, then about what Temo had said about the commune paying them for tonight's work—about how they claimed the dreamers were attacking and even eating their people.

"Sounds nuts to me," Ghoul said. "Sounds like corpo lies or a total setup. I almost think we should fucking skip town—head to New Vegas or something."

"Hang on, Ghoul," Juliet spoke. "There's more I didn't tell you yet, but I need to examine some data. Give me a few minutes."

"All right. I'll warm up some protein pouches. I had some groceries delivered while you were gone." Ghoul shrugged and turned around to dig through the little fridge.

"Angel," Juliet subvocalized, "have you taken it upon yourself to examine the data file we stole?"

"No, Juliet, it's safely stored and encrypted in your data vault on the public net."

"How secure is that?"

"Extremely secure, the way I have it packaged, though there is some risk when I unpack it or move it that some sophisticated watcher daemons might spot code fragments and alert interested parties."

"Ghoul, do you have a data deck—even a shitty one?" Juliet asked.

"Yeah, sure." Ghoul walked past the couch to the bedroom where she'd stowed her belongings.

"Angel, I figure you can disable the net access for the deck she's got, and then we can unpack the file locally."

"Yes, I assumed that was your plan. It should work fine—all we need is the offline memory; I can do all the processing work via your data cable." As Angel spoke, Ghoul returned with a slim, transparent data deck about the size of an old-school card deck.

"I just have all my favorite photos and vids on there. Don't erase 'em, 'kay? I think there are a few terabytes free."

"Yeah, of course," Juliet said, taking the deck. Like Juliet, Ghoul probably had a nominal amount of memory attached to her data port and probably an even smaller amount in her retinal implants. She could store videos and programs to an extent, but anything major would require an uncommon upgrade or an offline storage option like the little deck. Thinking of her data port, Juliet asked, "Angel, this program wouldn't fit in my memory?"

"Not without me packing up some of my functions. I unpacked into the new space provided by your upgraded data port, but I still have a lot that I have to hot swap. It would be nice if you upgraded the memory."

"Seriously?"

"Yes, my algorithms require large databases."

"Well, I'll look into it. Let's see here." Juliet pulled out her data cord, slotting it into the port on the transparent deck. "Okay, all plugged in. Do your thing."

"I'm downloading the file via a convoluted network path. I'll be a few minutes because of its size."

"So, Ghoul," Juliet said, leaning back on the couch and watching as Ghoul messed with the little instaoven.

"Yeah?" she asked, glancing toward her.

"On that job, I was paid to crack a dreamer's very high-end deck and hijack a program that was running. That done, the client wanted me to send them a copy. When I did so, someone sent a signal to the dreamer's deck, riding on my connection, which sent them all into crazy mode. Like, the one I was dealing with woke up and started clawing at me, his teeth clicking like he wanted to bite my throat out. All the dreamers in the building went nuts—I think Honey's crew killed like twenty or thirty of them."

"You fucking serious?" Ghoul let out a long, near whistle of a breath.

"Yeah. I'm not sure if the client did it or who, and I'm not sure if they acted maliciously—I mean, I know someone sent the signal to stop the dreamer's program, but I don't know if they knew what would happen. My suspicion is that they did, though. I feel like they were testing something, and I wonder if the place we're supposed to go to tonight is related."

"So, what aren't you telling me?" Ghoul asked, gesturing to her data deck.

"I stole a copy of the program. Now I'm having my PAI unpack it, and I'm going to analyze it."

"Fuck! Juliet, that's risky! What if they know you took a copy? What corpo was it?"

"They won't trace this. That's why I wanted to use your deck—it's offline. I'll let you know what I find . . . hang on, my PAI finished the download."

"I'm going to start the program now, Juliet," Angel said.

"There was room on the deck?"

"Yes, and I've unpacked the files. I've disabled the deck's sat-net and local-net connections. The program is initializing. It's tried to access the network for supplementary files several thousand times. It also attempted to hijack my root directory, but I've securely ICE'd it at the port." Angel continued giving Juliet second-by-second updates about the program's progress over the next couple of minutes, and then, "It's running. I have it contained. I'm analyzing . . ."

"It's running, and my PAI is running the analysis now," Juliet told Ghoul as she brought over a little paper box filled with noodles, beef-flavored protein squares, and a sauce which tasted like honey and salt.

"We forgot forks. Here." Ghoul held a plastic knife out to her. "I found this in a drawer filled with hot sauce packets."

"Thanks," Juliet said. She inhaled the food, scooping it over the carton's edge with the knife and letting the warm noodles slurp over her lips while she listened for Angel's update. She'd nearly finished when a blinking media file icon appeared in her AUI.

"Juliet, please watch this video and tell me what it looks like to you."

"All right." Juliet mentally selected the file, and it opened up a large vidscreen in her AUI, taking up most of her vision. She watched as a title screen flashed by, bold, three-dimensional yellow characters spelling the words *The Vales of Avalon*. She watched as a login credential screen appeared and was rapidly bypassed, presumably by Angel. Then a photorealistic panorama of a fantasy landscape flew by as if the camera were mounted on a drone or a bird.

"Is it a game?" she asked aloud, her voice hushed.

"What?" Ghoul spoke.

"Sec," Juliet replied, still watching as the camera zoomed over a glistening blue sea, a white sand beach, and then up a grassy slope. It rushed along a meadow filled with fantastical creatures—huge rabbits with saddles on their backs, colorful birds that she thought might be analogues of peacocks, and herds of mighty horses . . . no, she corrected herself, unicorns. Then the camera sped into a dark, winding path through a dense forest, finally slowing as it came to a circle of medieval-style, thatch-roofed buildings standing around a well. A prompt appeared on the screen: "What will you call yourself, Dreamer?"

"It seems like a game," Juliet subvocalized.

"I agree, Juliet. However, this program is far more involved than most publicly available dream-rig game code I've analyzed for reference. It's constantly sending signals to the wireless and physical connection ports, trying to activate certain synaptic impulses in the host. If I hadn't deleted them, the same signals would have reached your brain through your optic nerve as you watched this video I made."

"What are they supposed to do?" Juliet asked.

"I'm detecting impulses meant to activate dopamine at the moment, but when I analyzed the code, I found similar triggers for nearly every human hormone, including testosterone, serotonin, adrenaline, cortisol, and even insulin."

"Wait—someone can activate hormones in a person with code?"

"Not just any code, Juliet. This is very involved, and it would require a corruption of the PAI software. That's why I could stop it—the first attack vectors were aimed at me, but my ICE protocols are much stronger than the creators bargained for. Additionally, there seems to be an instruction set that closely mimics one of my own advanced features. It allows the infected PAI to act outside specifications to extend and multiply its nanofilament synth-nerves. The program uses these new connections to stimulate the hormones and other semiautonomous body functions."

"Jesus," Juliet breathed as she blinked her eyes and closed the video. Then she subvocalized, "Are those people going nuts and attacking people because the program—the game—told them to?"

"I'm not sure of that yet. It could be that they've been stimulated so thoroughly through the program that they went mad when it was cut off."

"What have you figured out?" Ghoul asked, sitting on the couch and staring at Juliet. Juliet realized she hadn't been very subtle with her facial expressions, and Ghoul had noticed she was disturbed by something.

"Gimme a couple more minutes, then I'll explain," she said, then she sub-vocalized, "Angel, if we find the rig that was broadcasting to the dreamer hive we're going to tonight, do you think you could calm them by installing this software? Do you think you can change it so it, I don't know, brings them down gradually?"

"I'll work on it, Juliet. I'm sure I can reinstall this software and start it running, though I worry about its infectious nature. I'll see if I can disable those protocols. I'll try to set a frequency limit on hormone calls and create a tapering schedule. The problem is that the code to modify the PAIs is very crude. I fear irreparable damage has been done to the infected dreamers' natural nervous systems."

"Okay." She looked at Ghoul and repeated, "Okay. I'm pretty sure I figured out what's up with the dreamers. Some corpo assholes are running experimental software out there. They're doing some kind of mind control, Ghoul, altering people's PAIs so they can trigger hormones, and they're pushing these people way outta whack. If we can find the data deck that was, or is, projecting the signal, we can probably stop them; get 'em to calm down, at least. I don't know if there's a way to save them, but we can try."

"Seriously? You figured all that out in just a few minutes? Jesus, Juliet, you're the shit. Well, let's go ahead and accept your boy's contract, huh? Sounds like we might be getting a fat payday tonight." Ghoul grinned at her as she ripped the top off an energy drink pouch and began to chug it.

"Oh, Ghoul! Why'd you jinx us?" Juliet laughed, looking for a piece of wood to knock her knuckles against. She came up short and leaned forward, giving Ghoul's buzzed blonde hair a couple taps.

"Hey! Are you saying my head's made of wood?" Ghoul laughed and slapped her hand away.

"Nah, but it's definitely hard." Juliet mock-winced, rubbing her knuckles like she'd hurt them.

"All right, all right," Ghoul said, shaking her head. "Let's talk the job—you good with that little gun of yours? I have a spare shotgun in my bag."

"Yeah, I'm good. Hopefully, we won't have to fight much if we're quick and careful."

"Well, I like to prepare for the worst, hope for the best—you know that old one, right?"

"Yeah, I do. I'm pretty sure Temo is setting us up with a couple of other operators, so I think we'll be good with you and them. I want to focus on finding the signal if I can, anyway."

"Right, well, looks like we're getting an early start; I just got a pin for an ABZ location from Temo—wants us there by 4:00 p.m."

"You just received the same message," Angel spoke, forestalling the question on the tip of Juliet's tongue.

"I'm gonna snooze for an hour, then let's go," Ghoul said, standing up.

"What? You can sleep just like that?"

"Hell yeah. I'm a big fan of naps." Ghoul crunched her energy drink pouch and laughed, tossing it with perfect accuracy into the trash bag hanging off a kitchen drawer handle.

An hour later, before they walked out the trailer door, Juliet plugged her data cable into Ghoul's data port. Tethered together, they walked out of the trailer park, the sun still bright and hot in the sky. The guard on duty, an old white-haired vet with two wire-job legs, looked up from the clipboard-size datapad he was reading and nodded at them. He didn't seem bothered by their dark clothes or the two heavy guns Ghoul carried—one slung over her shoulder and the other hanging between her shoulder blades.

When they entered the AutoCab Angel had ordered for them, her clever PAI somehow made the cab think only Juliet was in the vehicle and supplied it with her weapons license. "You're getting trickier and trickier," Juliet subvocalized.

"I do learn new things as we go, Juliet. I'm rather pleased that I can do so. Ghoul's PAI is very limited in its ingenuity—I'm tempted to rewrite some of its codebase."

"Don't you dare!"

"No?"

"No, Angel! Remember, you're lying low, and I don't want samples of your coding to get out on the net."

"Yes, I suppose someone familiar with my codebase might recognize my own signature on something new. Thank you for the words of caution!"

"God," Juliet laughed. "My PAI cracks me up sometimes." Ghoul looked at her and smiled, her teeth gleaming in the sunlight coming through Juliet's window. "Hey, why the chrome teeth?" Juliet asked, and instantly wished she'd thought twice about blurting out the question as Ghoul's smile slipped away and she looked down, something like shame on her face.

"It's an ugly story. Let me save it for another time?"

"Yeah, I'm sorry, Ghoul. I need a filter on my mouth, I think."

"Nah, it's cool. We're friends; you should know things about me, and I'll share them with you. But, yeah, not right now, 'kay?"

Juliet nodded and held out a fist. Ghoul smiled, giving it a bump. "Right on," she said, and then the two of them sat back and rode in silence for a while. The trip was longer than it needed to be because the AutoCab avoided the ABZ as much as possible. When they came to the southern edge of the city, into the run-down, debris-strewn areas that led away from the corpo-controlled districts, the cab warned them that it was going to have to stop a mile short of their chosen destination.

"You're just now realizing this, AutoCab?" Juliet scolded.

"I'm sorry, passenger, but it seems that there are recent reports of violent activity in the area. I urge you to choose a new destination, but failing that, I will drop you as close as possible."

"Wonderful." Ghoul sighed. Juliet nodded her agreement with that sentiment, and then they sat quietly as the ride wound down. When the cab stopped and they stepped out, the sun was fat and orange, hanging above the western horizon. The street they were standing beside seemed deserted, not a soul in sight, and Juliet grew more annoyed with the cab.

"Nothing's even going on," she grumbled.

"The cab probably has data from the last few days. I'd be shocked if whatever it was worried about was happening at the moment."

"Yeah," Juliet said, starting to walk in the direction Angel's projected map indicated.

"We should pick up the pace," Ghoul noted, jogging past her. "We don't wanna get ditched."

Juliet nodded and started to jog alongside her, surprised that her thighs and ass were still sore from the workout Angel had put her through in the hotel gym. After a while, though, it worked out, and she started to feel good, despite the heat. She was glad her body armor was lighter than Ghoul's and that she wasn't carrying two heavy guns.

They were running through the parking lot of an ancient box store with a crumbled corner where a vehicle must have crashed once upon a time when Ghoul hissed, "Hurry! To the corner, and keep behind me!"

"What?" Juliet said, following after her. That's when she heard it: the sounds of gunfire, faint but not very distant, if she were any judge. "You think the team already made contact with the dreamers?" she asked, panting for breath as the two slid to a halt against the ancient stucco wall.

"Juliet," Angel spoke, "you've received a message from Temo."

"Play it!"

Suddenly, Temo's unscrambled visage appeared in her vision. "Head's up, Juliet. Your teammates are Corbitt and Hot Mustard. I'm sending you their license numbers. They just reported to me that they're under fire—seems another team, maybe corpo-sec, is out there, and they don't want us messing with those dreamers. The mission is still a go."

"Shit," Ghoul said, her pained expression all the evidence Juliet needed that she'd also gotten the same message.

23

AMBUSH

What do we do?" Juliet asked Ghoul, the sounds of gunfire growing more frenetic in the distance.

"If we're going to engage with corpo grunts, we need to have a jammer. I'm guessing the two meatheads under fire aren't the tech gurus of the team—that's you."

"I don't have a jammer . . ."

"Juliet, I can use your wireless data jack to scramble outgoing signals in a small area, but we'd need to connect you to an external battery; the one in your implant isn't sufficient for that kind of broadcasting."

"Sec," Juliet said as she considered Angel's words. She looked at Ghoul, at her guns, and asked, "Is that gun on your back an energy weapon? Does it have a battery?"

"Yeah, it's a bolt-thrower—rail tech."

"Lemme see it," Juliet said, holding out a hand. Ghoul didn't ask questions, just shrugged out of the weapon's sling and handed it over to her. Juliet could see the magnets along the barrel now, though they were far more elegant than the ones on the electro-shotgun she'd taken from Vikker's locker. Still, the weapon was heavy, and she had to strain to hold it steady with her left hand while she fed her data cable into the little port at the base of the LCD at the top of the stock.

"You see a target?" Ghoul asked, watching.

"No, I'm gonna hijack this gun's batt to power up an improvised jammer using my wireless jack."

"Seriously? Badass." Ghoul nodded her approval while Juliet waited for Angel to confirm her plan was solid.

"This will work, Juliet. You'll need to stay connected to the gun's battery, and I'd advise you not to use it more than once or twice—we don't want to drain the battery too much."

"I'll need to borrow this gun, I guess," Juliet said. "Jammer's good to go; what's the plan?"

Ghoul nodded and shouldered her assault rifle, and Juliet found herself wanting to know more about the weapon—its ammunition, range, and other capabilities. "I've got good auditory implants, Jules. We'll flank 'em, but stay behind me, okay? You're doing good, though; keep breathing like that, in and out, and focus on one objective at a time."

Juliet nodded, and then Ghoul was off, crouching low and racing from the corner of the old box store, across a short alley, through a broken, crumbling brick wall, and up to the corner of a long-abandoned home.

"Juliet, tell Ghoul that local comms will not work when I turn on the jammer. Our setup isn't sophisticated enough to allow exceptions."

When Juliet slid up behind Ghoul leaning into the siding crumbling with dry rot, she tapped her shoulder and whispered, "Our comms will go out when I turn on the jammer."

Ghoul held up her thumb and winked at her over her shoulder. Then she pointed to another boarded-up house across a street littered with old boxes, a rusted-out sedan, and a tipped-over, bent basketball hoop. She whispered through her glittering, pointy teeth, "Start jamming when we get behind that building. I messaged the other two operators your fixer told us about using the SOA system. Hopefully, they won't shoot us. Follow my lead. Shoot anything that points a gun at you."

Juliet nodded, and as they ran across the street, dodging around the old car and charging up the ancient driveway, she saw that Angel had supplied her with a new crosshair, ammo count, and battery percentage. The gun was full, with seventy-five rounds and a battery at ninety-eight percent. When they started around the side of the house, Angel said, "Activating the jammer."

Alarmingly, Juliet's forearm buzzed briefly, but then it passed, replaced by a steady warmth. She knew it was working because her net connection icon indicated she was offline. Ghoul looked back at her and nodded, and then they were hustling through an overgrown side yard to the neighbor's backyard block wall. They kept low and close to the wall, brushing through dried-up tumbleweeds and under a mesquite tree's dry, scratchy limbs. All the while, the sounds of controlled gunfire bursts grew louder.

Once they got to the corner, Ghoul stopped and carefully inched her barrel past the edge of the wall. Turning to Juliet, she pointed at her eye and held up one finger. Juliet nodded and waited. Meanwhile, Angel said, "Juliet, keep panning around the yards of those houses and at their windows. I'll see if I can detect anomalies with shadows and check for evidence of gunfire."

Juliet did as Angel asked, leaning close to Ghoul and resting one hand on the woman's center back to let her know she was there before scanning out past the wall. A narrow band of overgrown, natural desert landscaping separated this house's backyard from the walled and fenced yards of the next row of houses. Juliet could hear the bullets flying and even see debris thrown up here and there, but she couldn't make out any of the shooters.

Ghoul held as still as a statue, and Juliet could tell the other woman was slowly panning her rifle's sights over the strip of desert. After a moment, she turned and touched a finger to Juliet's cheek, right under her right eye, and slowly moved the finger to point. Juliet followed the line of her finger, and Angel highlighted, in red, a shadowy shape partially obscured by an over-grown oleander. Ghoul nodded to Juliet's gun and mouthed, barely letting any air through her teeth, "Shoot when I shoot."

Juliet swallowed a lump in her throat and nodded, lifting the gun so Angel's crosshairs lined up with the center of the highlighted person's body. "Angel, are we sure that's a bad guy?" Juliet subvocalized.

"If you zoom in, Juliet, you will see he has a corpo logo on his sleeve," Angel said. Juliet did as told, annoyed that she'd forgotten to use her new optics. Her vision zoomed in when she concentrated on the shadowy, red-limned figure, and the shadows brightened. With her new vantage, she could clearly see puffs of superheated air erupting from the center of the oleander's branches where the figure had a black, stubby rifle resting. Sure enough, a stylized *V* stood out on his left shoulder, and Juliet knew what it was—Vykertech.

"That's the corpo from the dreamer's rig, right?" she subvocalized.

"Yes, Juliet. It stands to reason they're involved in this dreamer situation just as we'd suspected."

"Well, it's not proof, but good enough for me to squeeze this trigger." Juliet squatted down, sitting on one foot and resting the heavy barrel of

Ghoul's gun on her knee. She pulled the trigger halfway when she had her target lined up. Almost instantly, a green light lit up next to her crosshairs, and she knew the gun was ready. She breathed in and out, ever so slowly, trying to keep steady while waiting for Ghoul to fire.

When it came, Juliet couldn't help flinching. Ghoul's gun wasn't quiet, and she didn't shoot once but several times, inching forward with each shot. Juliet quickly recovered, and just as she got her crosshair reset, her target shifted to point his gun their way. She squeezed the trigger, and the bolt-thrower bucked and fired out its payload with an electric *zwap*.

She'd been aiming at the center of her target, but in her zoomed-in, light-enhanced vision, she saw a dark spot appear in the target's pale, unarmored throat, and a spray of blood erupted behind him, splashing over the dark green oleander leaves.

She turned to Ghoul and found the woman gone, charging to the trunk of a mesquite, firing round after round at a hedge near the wall of the deserted home across the way. Juliet didn't know what else to do, so she hustled after her. Ghoul charged right through the crossfire zone and leaped over a pitted, yellowing barrel cactus. She fired three more times, held up her gun, and screamed, "Stop! They're down!"

Suddenly, the gunfire from off to Juliet's left died down, and Ghoul turned to her. "Check the ones we shot. Make sure their comms are down, then you can turn off the jammer so we can talk to our new friends."

"Right," Juliet said, and because she knew exactly where it was, she ran toward the corpse of the man she'd shot. "Angel, can you tell if Vykertech has drones or anything around?"

"Nothing that's actively pinging us, Juliet. If we're careful and disable any decks and data ports on the downed corpo-sec agents, they won't know what's happened here until they physically investigate."

"Ghoul! Make sure none of them have any powered-up decks and pull all their PAIs!" Juliet shouted, and she could hear Ghoul shouting directives to someone else, who responded with a deep voice from quite a distance away. She thought about dialing in her implants and trying to get Angel to figure out what they were saying, but she got distracted as she approached the body of the man she'd shot.

He was splayed back against the springy branches of the oleander he'd been hiding behind, and one of his hands, pale and lifeless, still clung to the collar of his vest just below where Juliet's bullet had entered his throat. He wore tactical goggles, and Juliet could see lights and messages flashing on their lenses. She bent to pull them off, sliding them over his short, brown hair and tugging the little data cable out of the port at the back of his neck.

Juliet switched the goggles off and then let her eyes drift down to the man's face. Blood had begun to dry around the corners of his mouth and over his chin, but his eyes were still open, still clear, and not glazed and cloudy in death like she imagined they might be. He'd been a handsome man with a strong jaw and brooding brow; Juliet wondered who might miss that face tonight.

"This doesn't feel good," she hissed, gently turning the man's head so she could get at his data port and dig her nail under his PAI chip, pulling it out. Lacking anything better, she set it on a stone and smashed it with the butt of Ghoul's rifle.

"I don't detect any further signals from this location," Angel spoke.

"Right." Juliet looked at her AUI to see that the gun's battery was down to seventy-three percent. "Keep the jammer going 'til we confirm the other bodies are offline." As she stood up, she saw a datapad and extra magazines stuffed into the corpo-sec soldier's belt, so she knelt and began to tug it off. "I'm taking his belt and gun," Juliet said. It felt both dirty and right to her, and like a vegan who'd decided to go all in on a hamburger, Juliet decided she wasn't going to leave good money lying in the desert.

She could hear Ghoul speaking in low tones to the other two operators not far away. Before she joined them, Juliet pulled off her backpack, rolled up the soldier's heavy belt, and stuffed it inside, tossing his tactical goggles in as well. She shrugged back into her pack, slung the soldier's short-barreled assault rifle over one shoulder, and jogged to the others. They were standing over the first person Ghoul had killed, and Juliet felt lucky that the body was facedown and that she wouldn't have to picture the woman when she tried to sleep that night.

"No signals are coming from this body, and the PAI has been removed," Angel said, confirming what Juliet's eyes already told her—she could see the tendrils trailing from the smashed chip lying in the dirt nearby.

"What about the third?" Juliet asked aloud, glancing at Ghoul and the other two. Both men wore black tactical gear, though one was tall and lanky with a pink ponytail, and the other was shorter and stocky and hid his head and most of his face under a tactical helmet and visor.

"We got it. All clear," Ghoul spoke, holding up a thumb.

"I stripped my guy's weapon." Juliet jostled the rifle on her shoulder.

"Yeah, we did, too," Ghoul said, pointing to the extra rifles leaning against a creosote bush to her left.

"We sure everyone's offline, then?" Juliet asked, eager, for some reason, to unplug the rifle and hand it back to Ghoul.

"I'm not detecting any signals in the jamming field," Angel supplied.

"All right. Let's move off toward the dreamers coords. I'll turn it off when we've put some distance between us and this mess."

"Right, intros can wait," the tall man with the colorful hair said, his voice carrying a distinct Southern twang. He turned and trotted off between two of the old, overgrown home lots. The stocky guy flashed a thumbs-up and ran after him, and then Ghoul nodded to Juliet.

"I'll keep the rear; hustle, Juliet. Good work!"

Juliet nodded and started jogging after the stocky guy, noticing how he favored his right leg and had a constriction bandage wrapped around his thigh. That brought her attention to the rest of his gear. He and the lanky guy would've been nearly indistinguishable from the corpo-sec agents if not for the bright yellow logo missing from their sleeves. Was that the big difference between her and Ghoul and those dead corpo-sec? That they wore a logo?

Juliet realized she was spiraling, gaslighting herself with emotions—she wasn't the same as corpo-sec because she didn't work for a corporation. She didn't take money to come out to the desert and ensure immoral, mind-altering experiments weren't interrupted. She hoped she'd never take a job like that, anyway. After a few minutes of jogging through the ancient overgrown neighborhood, the two operators, Corbitt and Hot Mustard presumably, stopped by a cracked, crumbled cement culvert which led down to a dry wash.

"Dreamer hive is supposed to be about a klick down this wash, under an old series of bridges, and in a water treatment building next door."

"All right," Juliet said as Ghoul jogged up behind them. "Turning off the jammer. Secure your comms and make sure anything you picked up off those corpo-sec is turned off." She waited a minute while they all double-checked the items they were carrying, then she subvocalized, "Turn it off, Angel."

Again, her arm buzzed, and Juliet rubbed at the hot skin over her implant before tugging the cable out of the rifle and letting it retract into her port. She handed the gun to Ghoul, and the woman took it, slinging her other rifle over her shoulder. "Comms are open; my PAI will set up a channel and give you all a handshake." Almost immediately, Angel set up icons on her AUI for each of her teammates and highlighted each of them with their handles floating over their heads.

"Neat trick," she subvocalized, noting that the tall guy was Hot Mustard and the stocky, helmeted guy was Corbitt.

"Thanks for saving our asses," Corbitt said so softly that Angel had to augment his voice in Juliet's implants.

"Yeah, they had us flanked pretty good. Nasty surprise to walk into." Hot Mustard's voice was sort of high, and she'd been right about his Southern accent. When Juliet heard it, combined with his goofy handle, she almost laughed, almost forgot about the three dead people they'd left lying in the dirt. "Sending the pin for the dreamer den. We going in hot? Temo said you all might have another idea?"

Ghoul looked at Juliet, and Juliet nodded and spoke, "Yeah. I don't wanna kill any of 'em. We want the full bonus, right? I think I've worked out a solution that'll get 'em all to chill—you know, like normal dreamers."

"Damn, seriously?" Corbitt held out a fist, again speaking almost subvocally but coming through fine in Juliet's implants. She nodded and touched his knuckles with hers.

Ghoul moved so she was right in front of the other two operators and said, "We gotta find their deck—whatever they were running their program on. Juliet has reason to believe they were all sharing the same system. Once we have it, she can work her magic. Clear? Nonlethal up to that point, so put away your guns and get out your brass knuckles or whatever you've got. Dreamers shouldn't be geared for war, anyway." She paused, looking toward Juliet. "Right?"

"Yeah, that's right. When they went nuts, the last nest of dreamers mostly tried to claw and bite us. A few had knives or clubs, but I think they just grabbed what was at hand."

"Right." Corbitt slung his rifle and yanked a black, twelve-inch rod off his belt. He shook it violently, and it expanded to three feet in length, sparking with electricity briefly. Hot Mustard didn't sling his gun, but he pulled the magazine, racked out the chambered round, caught it in the air, and slipped it into a pocket. Then he tucked the magazine into his belt and pulled out a different one, bright red instead of black. Slamming it into his gun, he racked the bolt and nodded.

"Riot rounds—pack an electroshock charge," he explained at Juliet's puzzled expression before pulling a long black cylinder off his belt and beginning to screw it onto the gun's muzzle. "Suppressor," he grunted.

"Just don't blow anyone's eyes out," Ghoul said. "We have intel that says these people aren't acting nuts on purpose."

"Roger," Hot Mustard replied and stepped toward their objective. Everyone followed along, Ghoul keeping the rear.

As they walked, Ghoul asked, "Guys, where'd those corpo-sec come from? They get dropped in on you or were they on-site?" Juliet assumed she'd subvocalized because she couldn't hear her voice but it came through her implant clearly.

"Oh, they were here." Hot Mustard's voice sounded in Juliet's ear. "We think they caught our chatter—just surrounded us and started shooting. No warning, no nothing."

"Fuck those guys then," Ghoul's voice responded.

"My sentiments exactly," Corbitt's gruff voice agreed, and Juliet detected a slower, less twangy Southern drawl than Hot Mustard's.

They jogged down the slope of the dry wash into the sand and piles of debris. Heaps of refuse, from broken furniture to bags of dumped trash to piles of dried-out tumbleweeds, made it easy for the four of them to dart toward their objective while still maintaining a semblance of cover.

After ten minutes or so, Juliet could see the vast, eight-lane overpass in the distance, and looking at her map, she saw the road above was labeled as Business Loop 49. She zoomed out a little to find that it was a fairly major artery which almost exclusively fed areas of the ABZ. "That's a lot of waste. Think of all the people who used to live out here," she subvocalized, and was a little mortified when Angel passed it into the team channel.

"Oh yeah," Hot Mustard twanged. "That thing's falling apart all over the ABZ—scav city."

"Well, do we think the deck is under that overpass or is it in the water treatment plant?" Ghoul asked, her name lighting up in Juliet's AUI.

"Angel, can you pick anything up on my wireless jack?"

"I was about to say, Juliet—there's a strong signal coming from near the underpass, but it's below street level. I think there are tunnels, perhaps connecting the water treatment plant to this storm runoff system."

"Well, team," Juliet said, "looks like we might be going underground."

24

A MORE PEACEFUL DREAM

So far, I don't see any movement down there," Hot Mustard said through their comms. He was lying flat on his belly in the sand, having inched his way through and beneath a large pile of windblown tumbleweeds. Juliet knew they had little thorns on them, but he'd carefully wormed between gaps in the plants, and now he was all but invisible, peering down the last stretch of open wash to the enormous underpass.

He'd shared his view with them all so they could see what he saw on their AUIs. The sandy wash led down to a broad concrete expanse with steep slopes leading up to the big, defunct freeway above. Furniture and vehicles littered the area near and under the bridge, and smoke trailed up into the evening gloom from camp or bonfires, the flames of which were obscured by the debris.

As the sun sank and the shadows lengthened, Juliet could see the fires' orange light dancing on the concrete slopes through Hot Mustard's camera feed. "Looks like they're either hiding, sleeping, or off trying to eat someone else," Ghoul's voice noted in her ear, her PAI reproducing the sound of her vocal cords quite convincingly as she subvocalized.

"Yeah, let's edge forward, huh?" Corbitt's voice suggested. He looked toward Juliet like she was in charge somehow. Ghoul surprised her by also looking to her with a raised eyebrow.

"Right. Ghoul, you take point." Juliet felt her cheeks flush as she used the phrase—something she'd heard in vids and sims. Nobody laughed or said anything, though, so she continued, "We need to get underground to the left side of the underpass; look for a door, tunnel, or something."

"Right. Mustard and Corbitt, take rear flanks—don't let anything jump Juliet." With that, Ghoul was gone, moving like a slinking shadow through the sand toward the rusted-out remnants of a pickup truck which had clearly been shot hundreds of times. Juliet followed her and heard the rustling sound of Hot Mustard as he wormed his way out of the tumbleweeds and shuffled over the sand to her right. Corbitt moved off to the left.

Juliet followed Ghoul from cover to cover, always staying one stop behind, waiting for the woman to lift her hand—the one not holding a stun baton—and motion her forward. They were out of the thick sand of the wash and slinking through the concrete underpass when Juliet slid to a halt behind a rotten old couch. She inched her head over the top to see where Ghoul's next stop would be, and she caught sight of the first group of dreamers.

They were standing around a big fire—mesquite branches, tires, pieces of furniture, and various other trash smoldering in a pile—and swaying in a strange, rhythmic pattern. Their weird, writhing blue-lit eyes were visible in the evening light, standing out for being brighter than the fire.

"The fuck is going on with their eyes?" Ghoul asked in comms.

"It's the neural nanofilaments from their PAIs. The program they've been running makes them grow way out of spec," Juliet subvocalized before she thought better of it. Heat flushed the back of her neck as she imagined her three team members looking at her and wondering how the hell she'd known that. She almost tried to tell Angel not to send her words to the team channel but knew it was too late when Hot Mustard's voice came through the comms.

"Fucking A," his voice said after a brief pause. "I didn't know those things could grow. Do we need to be running some kinda ICE to avoid infection?"

"Uh," Juliet answered, realizing she didn't know. "Angel?" she subvocalized, trusting the PAI to know when she wanted a private conversation.

"Tell your teammates that if they have any local wireless connections, they should disable them. Tell them to disable any sat-net connections other than the one to our team channel."

"Good question," Juliet subvocalized to the team. "You all should disable any local wireless connections you have open. Sat-net should be limited to our shared channel. Once I install my program, we should be good, but better safe than sorry."

"You all got that? Ports secure?" Ghoul prompted.

"Secure," Corbitt replied.

"Secure," Hot Mustard echoed.

"Okay, we need to neutralize this pack. There's a tunnel entrance on the north side, about twenty meters ahead of me. We'll need to shove an old dumpster aside, so I don't want these guys on our six." Ghoul's voice was calm and steady, and Juliet felt happy to have her taking point.

"Roger," Hot Mustard said.

"Mustard, drop as many as possible, starting with the outside right. Corbitt, you got my left flank. I'll go up the middle. Juliet, keep cover and be ready to assist."

"Got it," Juliet answered, her heart starting to pound in her chest. She lifted the gun she'd taken from the dead corpo-sec agent and held it to her shoulder. She was just about to ask Angel if there was anything she needed to know about it when her PAI spoke up.

"That weapon has a biometric lock on the trigger. Connect your hardline, and I'll clear it and set up your permissions."

"Right," Juliet said in a shaky whisper, quickly pulling the data jack out of her arm and plugging it into the port on the side of the weapon. After it clicked home, she watched over the top of the old couch as Ghoul crouched, like a football running back, ready to spring, and Corbitt and Hot Mustard moved into position.

"All set, Juliet. I wiped the identifying data and programmed the trigger for your print. The gun is a Hershel Company variant of the venerable MP5. It has a forty-round magazine, and the onboard system is reporting thirty-two rounds remaining. The weapon is off-safety, and a round is in the chamber. I've updated your AUI."

"Thanks," Juliet replied, noting the new crosshair and ammo counter at the center of her vision. She didn't want to shoot the weapon—they weren't trying to kill dreamers that night—but she wanted to be ready in case things went to hell. She'd barely had time for that thought when Ghoul leaped into action and whizzing *clicks* from her right told her Hot Mustard had begun taking shots.

Two dreamers thrashed on the ground from Hot Mustard's shock rounds before Ghoul closed the distance, then her friend was dancing among the remaining four dreamers, her stun baton whipping through the air and sending the swaying dreamers into fits as her crackling weapon fired off its powerful electrical charge. Two dreamers were still standing when Corbitt came in from the other flank, and he and Ghoul beat them into submission before they could so much as take in a breath to scream or roar or whatever sound they might have made otherwise.

Just like on her first gig, Ghoul pulled an autoinjector from her belt pack and moved among the downed dreamers, shooting them with some kind of tranquilizer as Juliet and Hot Mustard closed in on the scene of the melee. Juliet was careful to keep the muzzle of her new weapon pointed down and her finger off the trigger as she ran.

"Weird," Ghoul was saying to Corbitt once they reached them.

"What's that?" Hot Mustard asked.

"The tranq is calming them down, but their eyes aren't closing. They still seem kinda with it. They're being quiet, though . . ."

"Let's not dick around," Corbitt said, nodding toward the dumpster blocking the tunnel entrance.

"Right." Juliet turned to Hot Mustard. "Hot Mustard . . ." Her lips came up in the start of a smile, and she almost lost it, saying his name out loud for the first time. "Hot Mustard," she tried again, shaking her head, "watch Ghoul's back so she can secure these guys' feet and hands, in case the tranq doesn't take."

"Roger," he replied, grinning back at her before lifting his rifle to his shoulder and panning around, peering into the shadows while Ghoul worked. Juliet hurried over to the dumpster, and Corbitt trotted along with her.

"If we both push on the corner here"—Corbitt gestured—"We should be able to make a gap for us."

"Yeah." Juliet nodded, climbing the concrete slope behind the dumpster and putting her shoulder against it. "Say when," she said, watching as Corbitt set himself to pull. He nodded, and Juliet drove with her legs. The big, rusty metal dumpster noisily slid a few inches while she pushed and Corbitt grunted and heaved, his face turning beet red beneath his dark goggles.

"Once more," Corbitt grunted, and Juliet set herself and drove again. This time, the old dumpster made a loud, scraping racket as it slid over the sandy concrete.

"Nice." Juliet stepped down off the slope to peer into the opening they'd uncovered.

"Yeah," Corbitt agreed, holding up a fist. She moved to bump her knuckles against his, and that's when two sets of pale, clammy hands grabbed onto her, yanking her arm and shoulders back. She swung her free arm in a pinwheel motion, trying to keep her balance, but she toppled backward and they dragged her, heels skittering over the sandy concrete into a dark tunnel.

"Ungh!" she cried, jerking at her arm and trying to pull free. She saw the dreamers dragging her, saw their luminous, writhing blue eyes, and heard their whispered snatches of insane babble.

"To the tree! Feed the lady!" one hissed.

"My dress, the perfect buttons!" the other cried.

"Juliet!" Corbitt called, and she saw him at the entrance, swinging his baton madly at the crowd of dreamers who had charged past Juliet to engage him. She tried desperately to grab the SMG she'd slung onto her shoulder, but it flopped uselessly behind her while they dragged her. Finally, she gave up, pulling the bottom of her vest up and yanking out her Taipan with her right hand.

"Hold onto it tightly!" Angel's voice was loud, clear as a crystal bell, and Juliet felt her nerves steady to know she wasn't alone. She twisted so she could see the dreamer who had her left arm before pointing the Taipan at his chest and squeezing the trigger. Thunder erupted from her hand, a plume of orange fire lighting up the tunnel for a fraction of a second, and her hand bucked back, fully cartwheeling to bounce against her thigh. Still, she held onto the weapon, and the dreamer let go of her arm.

Juliet violently thrashed, jerking her body forward, and slipped out of the grip of the second dreamer. Falling to the hard cement ground, she rolled so she was on her back. In her augmented vision, she could see the dreamer she'd shot slumped against the concrete wall of the tunnel, and the one she'd jerked away from was gibbering and running away into the darkness. "Shit!" she hissed, scooting back, then onto her knees, and finally, shakily, to her feet.

She still held the pistol ready, her left hand now supporting her grip, and stared into the tunnel, waiting to see if more came.

"Report!" Ghoul's voice said into her ear, and that's when Juliet noticed the sounds of yelling, the loud *clicks* of Hot Mustard's gun, and the unmistakable concussive zaps of stun batons.

"Almost clear out here," Hot Mustard responded immediately.

"I . . ." Juliet started, but then Corbitt's voice came through.

"Got mobbed at the tunnel." He grunted and continued, "Fuck! Gimme a hand! They dragged Juliet in!"

"I'm good!" Juliet spoke quickly. "I had to shoot one, though." She glanced at the slumped dreamer again, refusing to take in the details of his appearance or the damage she'd done. She pushed her thoughts into a corner of her mind and started back toward the tunnel entrance. By the time she got there, all three of the other operators were busily binding another half a dozen semiconscious dreamers.

"You sure you're good? Did any bite you?" Ghoul asked, rushing over to her.

"No, they didn't," she answered, shakily gesturing with her pistol back into the tunnel. "Two of them were dragging me in. It felt like they had a destination in mind."

"You blasted 'em?" Hot Mustard looked at her pistol pointedly.

"Just one of them. The other ran off."

"Well, we better stay alert. I don't know how organized these creeps are, but that one might be going for help," Ghoul growled, stepping into the tunnel. "Any idea where to go from here?"

"The signal is stronger," Angel told Juliet. "It's approximately fifty meters further and three meters up from here."

"Yeah," Juliet said. "Fifty meters in, and then we're looking for stairs or a ladder. It's on a level right above this tunnel."

"Right on." Ghoul dug around in her belt pack for a minute, pulling out a replacement battery for her baton. She swapped them out in about three seconds, then nodded. "Ready?"

"Ready," Hot Mustard confirmed, running a long-fingered hand through his bright hair and securing the loose strands into his ponytail.

"Yup," Corbitt said, also finishing up a battery swap on his baton.

"Corbitt, you take the rear. Don't let Juliet get grabbed again, please." Ghoul didn't sound like she was blaming Corbitt, but Juliet thought she saw the man bristle. He held his tongue, however, and nodded. Ghoul did too, then started padding down into the darkness with Hot Mustard on her heels. Juliet hurried after, and she could hear Corbitt's heavy breathing and plodding steps as he took the rear guard.

Happily, they didn't encounter any more dreamers before they came to a partially ajar steel door which opened into a circular shaft. A faded yellow metal ladder was bolted to the wall and led up and down from where they stood. "Up?" Ghoul asked.

"Right." Juliet nodded.

"Hang back a bit so I can listen," Ghoul subvocalized, then she jumped onto the ladder and started climbing. She moved gracefully and without much sound, slipping her boots onto each rung without the barest of scrapes. Once she was engulfed by the shadows, Hot Mustard started to climb, but he stopped after a few feet and waited. Ghoul's voice came through their comms a few seconds later. "Three dreamers in here with a fancy data deck. They're out, though—eyes closed, breathing steady."

"You got any more of those tranqs?" Corbitt asked.

"Negative. Used 'em on the first pack. Didn't count on this many hostiles."

"Let me through," Juliet said, tugging at Hot Mustard's pant cuff. He grunted and started down the ladder, then he stepped back next to Corbitt and looked at Juliet expectantly. "If this goes right, we should be done fighting, but if shit goes off the rails, this is a good position for you guys to defend. Don't let us get swarmed in there."

"Roger," Hot Mustard said, and Corbitt nodded.

"I'm coming up, Ghoul." Juliet grabbed onto the smooth, cool metal of the ladder and started climbing, wishing she could move as gracefully as Ghoul and Honey.

"Come on," Ghoul's voice came through. "Just don't step on 'em. This room isn't big."

Juliet climbed up the ladder and reached the top in only a few seconds. It was dark, though the LEDs on Ghoul's gear and on the data deck were enough for her optics to work with, brightening the scene to almost daylight for her. The chamber was small, maybe ten feet on a side, and three different closed metal doors provided egress. The ammonia reek of urine hung heavy in the air, and she held a sleeve to her nose as she ran her eyes over the dreamers.

She saw the data deck immediately—another triangular, high-end Vykertech model. "Too much to be a coincidence, don't you think?" she subvocalized to Angel.

"It seems the strange dreamer behavior does have its roots with Vykertech," Angel replied, "though there are many variables left to consider."

"Yeah." Juliet stepped toward the deck, carefully avoiding the three dreamers' outstretched limbs. They all were lying on their backs with their heads close to the deck, each one with a length of cable stretching from a data port to the device. "How many ports did that one have back at the other hive? Three? Or was it four? I hope it was four."

"It had four, and this model should, as well."

Juliet tiptoed around until she was behind the deck. Once she knelt to look at it, she sighed with relief when she saw the open port next to the other three cables. She fumbled for a second before carefully tucking her pistol into her holster. With her hands free, she pulled out her data cable and carefully inserted it into the open space. "How's it look, Angel?"

"It's the same security as the last deck. Luckily, I analyzed the proprietary OS after I broke into the other one and was able to use some exploits I discovered. I'm already in."

"Holy shit! Nice one, Angel!" Juliet almost whispered, she was so excited; however, she kept her mouth closed while she formed the words.

"The program is running, Juliet, though when I examine the data stream, it looks like it's creating a nightmare reality for the dreamers—triggering high levels of testosterone and adrenaline. Should I replace the program with the one we prepared?"

"Wait," Juliet said, thinking. "Angel, why are these three dreamers not freaking out?"

"It seems those data cable ports are being blocked by some ICE—perhaps one of the dreamers had sophisticated defense daemons triggered by the program. It's still running, but only the base gamelike program is getting through, none of the PAI mods or hormone calls."

"Okay, so if we can replace the running program with the one you tailored, all the dreamers should chill out like these three?"

"Yes, I think so, Juliet."

"Well, we have to fix it so this program can't be turned back on. Can you block the network ports from receiving further instruction?"

"I can, but I can see a status query log—an outside address has been pinging this deck for status updates regularly. Should I set up a spoofed response?"

"So they'll think it's still running the way they left it?"

"Yes."

Juliet looked around the little room—at the sleeping dreamers, at Ghoul standing ready near the stairwell, her baton gripped in white knuckles—and she nodded. "Do it, Angel."

"I will, Juliet, but first, you must plug in the data cube you borrowed from Ghoul."

Juliet smacked herself on the head, slid out of her backpack, and dug around until she found Ghoul's deck. "Shit! I don't have a separate cable for it, and there aren't any more free ports left!" Not waiting for Angel to come up with a solution, she subvocalized to the team, "Ghoul. I need the cable from one of these guys. He'll probably wake up when you take it, so maybe tie him up and gag him first."

"Right," Ghoul said, rubbing a hand through her short white-blonde hair before wiping the sweat onto her pants. Then she knelt and started binding one of the dreamers, a young man with long, thin brown hair and wire-job hands. Juliet wiped her own sweat away as she watched Ghoul wrap four or five shrink bands around the dreamer's hands and feet. It was boiling in the little concrete room, and she was glad she had Ghoul's help.

Ghoul ripped a large piece of the dreamer's T-shirt away and rolled it up, stuffing it into his mouth and wrapping a thick band of tape around it. That done, she unplugged his cable and handed it to Juliet. The dreamer's eyes snapped open, but they were normal eyes, not writhing with strange luminescent fibers, and he seemed more bewildered than violent.

"Take him down to the tunnel, Ghoul. I don't think he's infected," Juliet said as she plugged the dreamer's cable into the deck.

"I'll wait for you. Thanks, though," Ghoul replied, and Juliet glanced at her, glad to see amusement in her eyes.

"Yeah, I guess that makes sense," Juliet subvocalized. "Angel, is it working?"

"I'm copying the revised program to the deck. I'll get it running in parallel before I switch to it and delete the old program."

"Good. Copy everything on that deck while you're at it."

"Will do," Angel said, and Juliet smiled, remembering their earlier conversation about not sounding like a machine.

"How long?"

"Four minutes and thirty-seven seconds."

"Need about five minutes. Be ready," Juliet spoke into the team channel. "I'm hoping the dreamers won't notice what I'm doing until it's over, but I'm not one hundred on that."

"Roger," Hot Mustard replied, and Juliet almost started laughing. The guy really liked to say that word.

The minutes slipped by, and the dreamer they'd bound and gagged did some thrashing but quickly tired and lay still. Juliet was contemplating standing to stretch when Angel said, "I'm ready, Juliet. Shall I initiate the switch?"

"Do it," Juliet confirmed, signaling for Ghoul to get ready. A second later, some wails and groans sounded from the rooms through the nearby doors, but they quickly faded, and Juliet thought for sure she heard some muffled crashes, like maybe some dreamers had fallen to the ground.

"The new program is running, and I've wiped the old one. I have all the data, Juliet."

"That's it, guys," Juliet said into the team channel. "The dreamers should be out of it again, peacefully chilling in their dream world. We should bug out before whatever corpo is running this messed-up experiment comes nosing around."

25

///////////////////

CONFESSIONS

"You sure you and Ghoul can't come out with us?" Hot Mustard asked as they all waited for their rides. It turned out Hot Mustard and Corbitt had taken an AutoCab too—they didn't fancy leaving their own vehicles unattended in the ABZ. It was still hot, even in early fall, even late at night, but something about the air felt good, energized, even, and the team was in high spirits because of the success they'd encountered.

"No," Ghoul answered before Juliet could think of a response. "Sorry, Mustard, but we have a jam-packed night ahead—double duty."

"Right on. Well, shit, you guys got us one hell of a bonus. Temo paid up fast when we sent footage of the peacefully sleeping dreamers after we took off their bindings. Wish we could buy you a couple rounds to celebrate."

"You've got our contact info, Hot Mustard," Juliet said with a chuckle. "C'mon, tell us how you got that handle."

"Yeah, tell us," Corbitt said with a smile. He'd finally taken off his helmet and goggles, and Juliet could see he was a lot younger and more handsome than he sounded. She reflected on that thought—it was weird that a voice could sound handsome or not, wasn't it? Still, now when he spoke, his Southern drawl and gruff tone were balanced by his smooth, even complexion and his baby-blue eyes. Juliet almost slapped herself but was saved from her embarrassing musings by Hot Mustard.

"It's a dumb story," he spoke. "I was eating takeout when I made my operator account. I didn't think 'handle' was something I could skip, and I wasn't feeling creative, so I just typed in Hot Mustard, 'cause that's what I was squeezing onto my soydog at the time."

"Brilliant." Juliet laughed.

"Well, I've thought about changing it a few times, but it seems to make it easier to make friends. Other operators are always wanting to know where the name came from." He looked at Ghoul, and Juliet could see the question on his lips—he was about to ask her where she'd gotten her handle. Juliet thought about how Ghoul hadn't wanted to talk about her teeth, how she'd always wondered if the name was related to them, and decided to intervene.

"Well," Juliet said quickly, clearing her throat. "We should help you come up with a better origin story for that name, don't you think?"

"Oh? You got any bright ideas?" Hot Mustard leaned back against the ancient bus stop they were lingering around while they waited for their rides.

"Of course I do." Juliet looked at Ghoul and winked in amusement. "How about this: You were on a tour in the Idaho conflict zone, you follow? You got separated from your unit and were lying low in an abandoned fast-food restaurant when one of the leftover AI swarms set up shop on the roof. You had to hunker down in the kitchen for days, waiting for them to move on. And the only thing you could find to eat in that ancient kitchen was . . ." Juliet looked at Ghoul and Corbitt, and they both shouted in unison:

"Hot Mustard!"

"Oh Lord!" Hot Mustard said, slapping his palm over his face. "Not bad, not bad! What you know about the Idaho conflict zone, anyway? How'd you know I was out there?"

"Easy guess, judging by your age, how you always say *Roger* . . . oh, who am I kidding? It was just luck!" Juliet giggled, feeling very at ease with these people, the harrowing experience with the dreamers having brought them all a little closer.

"Well, I gotta tell you, you need to bone up on your AI swarm trivia; if one of them had been anywhere near a restaurant I was hiding in, they'd a skinned me down to my wet parts."

"Juliet, your AutoCab is nearly here, and I'm not connected to Ghoul's data port," Angel interrupted their conversation.

"On that lovely note, our cab's pulling up," Juliet said, pulling out her data cable. "Ghoul, I wanted to share that vid file we talked about. Let me plug this thing in; it'll be a lot faster." Ghoul nodded and reached up to uncover her port.

"You're pretty good with that stuff, huh?" Corbitt asked, watching Juliet insert her cable.

"Stuff? You mean data transfer?" Juliet chuckled.

"Nah, well, yeah, I mean all that stuff you did back there to cool those dreamers off. The jammer you improvised . . . yeah, stuff." He laughed at his vocabulary failings, and Juliet chuckled.

"I've got good tech and an outstanding teacher, but yeah, I'll expect good ratings from you two!" Juliet pointed a finger at Corbitt and Hot Mustard.

"No doubt! Hey, don't feel shy about giving us a good review, too," Hot Mustard said with a wink, and then the AutoCab pulled up, and Juliet and Ghoul climbed in. Juliet held onto Ghoul's shoulder so they didn't accidentally pull her cable loose while they slid onto the seat. "Hey," Hot Mustard called as the cab started to inch forward. Juliet rolled down a window, and he continued, "I'm gonna message you two! Let's have a cookout or something!"

Juliet held up a thumb out the window and smiled, trying to make eye contact with both men as they drove away. "Nice guys," she told Ghoul.

"Yeah, they were decent. I'd work with 'em again."

"Well, I could tell they're eager to work with us." Juliet nodded.

"Wouldn't you be? We all pulled almost double pay for that dumb job with the bonus. I mean, yeah, your little hack made it easier and a hell of a lot prettier than it might have been, but still, that's an A-tier payday."

"Angel, what's my balance?" Juliet subvocalized.

"You have 40,233 Sol-bits, Juliet. Your comparative ranking on my database has risen to the twenty-third percentile!"

"Your database only uses cash as its basis for that ranking, right?"

"Yes, Juliet. If we were to consider property in all of its forms and include the entire populace, the number would be very different."

"What are you working on?" Ghoul asked. "Your eyes went distant—having trouble hiding me?"

"No, nothing like that. Just thinking about my finances."

"Well, as I was saying, we're sitting pretty good right now. That was a sweet gig Temo gave us. I hope it earned us some credit with him, too. Maybe he'll be willing to help us set up our little heist, hmm?"

"Yeah, I hope so," Juliet said, giving her data cable a little tug. "No one's gonna take us seriously if I have to have you on this leash everywhere we go."

"Careful," Ghoul noted. "Treat me like a dog, and I might start biting!" She bared her teeth at Juliet, and they both laughed for a second, but then Ghoul's eyes got serious, and her smile fell away. "I hate how this always comes up. Once someone wonders about my teeth or my name, I try to play it off or stall, but then I have it in the back of my mind. I can't even joke 'cause this stupid story is hanging over my neck."

"Easy," Juliet said. "I'm not even thinking about it, all right? No pressure."

"I believe you, Jules, but the pressure comes from in here." Ghoul touched her chest.

"Well, we've got a forty-minute ride 'cause this cab is scared of the ABZ, so wanna get something off your chest?" Juliet surprised herself by asking the question. She tended to avoid conflict, much the way it seemed Ghoul wanted to avoid this memory. Shouldn't she try to talk her into thinking about something else? Wouldn't it be better to put this off, maybe indefinitely? The thought of Ghoul sharing some awkward secret with her didn't stir pleasant emotions.

"Yeah." Ghoul sighed. "I guess so. If you want me to get a different place to stay afterward, that's cool. I think that's why I feel like I need to tell you this—I don't want you to think I was hiding something about myself just so you'd help me. Understand?"

"I guess so, but Ghoul, I'm cool with knowing you the way you are, the way I've experienced you. I'm not looking to do background checks on my friends."

"Thanks, Juliet, but like I said, this is coming from in here, not from you." Again, Ghoul tapped on her chest. "Well, you should know I'm twenty-eight. I was eighteen ten years ago—remember what was happening ten years ago?"

"Uh." Juliet stopped to think. She'd been just a girl ten years ago, barely a teen, but if Ghoul expected her to know about this, it must have been something big, something playing nonstop on the corpo news channels. "Oh! The Colorado Protectorate Conflict!"

"War!" Ghoul corrected. "Don't let them whitewash that shit. It was a full-on war, and a lot of people died for the cause. You know what it was about, right?"

"Yeah, the, um, Colorado civil government passed some laws which took rights away from the corpos. Um, I think Cybergen was still around, right? Didn't they own most of Denver? So when the laws were passed, and they didn't wanna give up what they had, it was the people vs. Cybergen for the most part."

"Yep, and the only reason you know that is because we fucking won! Corpos are neutered in the protectorate, thanks to maniacs like me." Ghoul thumped her chest with her chrome-tipped thumbnail.

"Well, aren't they losing ground? In Tucson, the shit I learned in school basically said that Cybergen cut their losses and left the protectorate with a mostly ruined city and the wasteland around it."

"Propaganda, sweetie, propaganda. You think the Helios-sponsored public schools in Tucson want people knowing that life can be good without some corp running shit? Anyway, that's not the point I'm trying to make. At least not tonight," she said, winking at her with a grin. Then she continued, "I was eighteen, and I was brought up by a dad who hated the corpos, especially Cybergen, with every fiber of his being.

"He taught me they were animals who wanted to enslave humanity, keeping most of us as worker drones while they lived lives comparable to the gods of Olympus. I mean, there was some truth to what he said, but he was extreme. I ate up everything he said, Juliet. I very much wanted to please my father."

"You don't think that anymore?"

"Yeah, I do, but I don't think every person who works for every corpo is evil. My father did, and so did I back then. I was brutal, vicious. My father was the commander of my militia unit, and when we had our first engagement with Cybergen corpo-mil, we caught them by surprise—it was a total massacre. One of their support units, a guy with a sat backpack, almost ran by me, but I caught him. I jumped him from behind, and while we wrestled in the mud and people died around us, I bit his throat out."

"Damn. Well, it was battle, Ghoul! You did what you had—"

"That was just the start, Juliet. My unit, my father, cheered me on. They told stories about me to scare prisoners. Things were lawless—crazy—back then. Everyone was so full of hate. My unit chipped in to get this bite-job for me. They're chromed plasteel with synth-nerve roots—the real deal. Juliet, I did a lot of terrible things."

Juliet opened her mouth to say something, but she wasn't sure what would be right, and it looked like Ghoul had more to say, so she just reached out and rested a hand on her shoulder, trying to keep her face neutral. The idea that Ghoul had used her teeth as a weapon on a regular basis was horrifying to her, but she'd figured they were sharp for a reason. Didn't bangers do stuff like that all the time? The fact that Ghoul was so upset by these memories gave her a lot of credit as far as Juliet was concerned.

"Well, we won, but somewhere along the way, my dad died, and when the fighting was done, it seemed to me that my unit was more afraid or disgusted by me than they were proud. A lot changes in five years, I guess. Anyway, I moved away from the protectorate—I couldn't stand to see the place, think-ing about what it cost. I didn't feel human again for a long while, and that was with me spending half my paydays on VR shrinks."

"If you hate those memories so much, why not change your handle? Why not get the teeth changed?" It was an obvious question, and Juliet couldn't clamp her mouth shut in time to stop it from popping out.

"I think . . ." Ghoul shook her head. "I feel like it would be cheating to erase that part of me. I did what I did, and now I need to live with it. Juliet, I glossed over a lot of it."

"Well, if you feel better for having told me all that, then I'm glad I could help. Truth is, Ghoul, I don't care what you did before I met you. You started earning my trust without even trying. Vikker helped your cause when he told Don they had to hurry and finish with me before you found out.

"My memories of you start with you threatening me with a vibroblade and then immediately apologizing and helping me to get through my first gig. Remember that?" Juliet nudged Ghoul, and it got a smile out of the other woman. She leaned into Juliet, resting her close-cropped blonde head on her shoulder, and the two rode in silence the rest of the way to the trailer park.

Later that night, when Juliet was lying in her bed listening to the buzz of the white noise Angel was playing for her, she thought about Ghoul and how the woman, just a few years older than her, had experienced so much horror. "All because of where she was born. Who her father was," she subvocalized.

"Are you referring to Ghoul, Juliet?" Angel asked.

"Yes. Angel, what became of Cybergen? How were they still in Colorado after the big war in the fifties?"

"In 2064, Cybergen and Takamoto reached a ceasefire after the global net and power grid were brought down to tamp down on rogue AI. A coali-tion of nations and corpo-states that were able to create the first version of today's sat-net seized the assets of the two megacorps and allotted them to a new entity—The Cybergen-Takamoto Reparation Foundation. The direc-tors for both companies were executed, and their corporate structures were reorganized into more than a dozen smaller entities with new management."

"And one of them was in Colorado? And they kept the Cybergen name?"

"Yes, a robotics division. It seems that much of the original corporate philosophy survived the management purge, which eventually proved prob-lematic—hence the Colorado Protectorate Conflict in the nineties."

"War," Juliet mumbled as she succumbed to exhaustion and the lulling effect of the white noise.

* * *

The next day, Juliet had a blinking tab on her AUI, and when she clicked it, she saw that her operator status had been updated again.

Handle: "Juliet" – SOA-SP License #: JB789-029		
Personal Protection & Small Arms License #: E86072801	**Rating: F-87-N**	
Skillset Subgroups and Skill Details:	**Peer and Client Rating (Grades are F, E, D, C, B, A, S, S+):**	
Combat:	**Heavy Weapon Combat**	F +1
	Bladed Weapon Combat	F +3
	Small Arms Combat	F +4
Technical:	**Network Security Bypass/Defend**	E +5
	Data Retrieval	E
	Welding	*
	Electrical	*
	Combustion & Electrical Engine Repair	*
Other:	**High-Performance Driving/Navigation**	F +1

"Hey, I'm getting close to an overall E rating."

"Yes, Juliet, and very quickly, too. You'll likely still have a 'New' rating when you get to the E tier. That's admirable."

"So, I'm slowly climbing up out of the individual F ratings. I imagine it takes forever to get to S+?"

"S+ is a difficult rank to achieve in any category. Only individuals who've received more than one hundred positive ratings while in the S tier are eligible."

"I guess that makes it hard for friends to game the system."

"Yes, that and the cooldown."

"Cooldown?"

"Operators who rate each other frequently will find that their ratings for each other have steeply diminishing returns. Ghoul's rating for you last night most likely had little impact on your new status. If you and she did some jobs away from each other for a while, your ratings for each other would be more impactful once you came back together."

"So I shouldn't work with her anymore?" Juliet asked, frowning as she climbed out of bed, absently noting she needed to buy new sheets. She'd washed the ones Mr. Howell had left in the trailer, but they were old and threadbare, and the quilt was too warm for her tastes.

"Not at all," Angel said. "The more you work with someone, the better you will perform, and your client ratings are more impactful, in any case. Clients have reputation levels also, and the higher-tier clients offering higher-tier jobs can impact your rep far more than an operator of your equivalent tier."

"Right." Juliet stretched, picked out some clean clothes, then took a quick sani-spray. When she was dressed, she emptied her backpack into the dresser drawer where she'd put the SMG she'd acquired the night before. She figured she'd probably sell most of the stuff and buy things which suited her better, but that was a job for later. "It's dojo time!" she said with a smile, tucking her new, never-before-worn gi and white belt into her backpack.

Before she left the trailer, she tiptoed down to the other end and peered through the slightly ajar door to Ghoul's room. She was facedown on her sheets in her underwear, covers thrown off the bed, and snoring rather loudly. Juliet grinned and pulled the door shut, carefully twisting the knob so it didn't click.

As she quietly left the trailer, she subvocalized, "She looked so peaceful, and she's been so cool to me, Angel. I can't really reconcile what I know about Ghoul with the story she told me last night."

"Human psychology is a fascinating topic, Juliet. I listened to the two of you last night with rapt attention."

"Well, good for you, but it doesn't help me understand." Juliet frowned, walking briskly through the park, skipping over a vacant plot to shorten her trip to the gate.

"I'm not sure I can help you with that. I believe you've made a sage decision; though, perhaps it's a character trait and not wisdom."

"Well?" Juliet said aloud as she walked through the trailer park gate, waving at the mustachioed old guard.

"Well?" Angel retorted.

"Well, what is the bleepin' character trait or whatever? What's my wise decision?"

"Oh, I'm sorry, Juliet! I must still be distracted by the psychological implications of your relationship with Ghoul. You made a wise decision to judge Ghoul based on what you know of her—what you've experienced. Had she never confessed her perceived sins to you, then you wouldn't judge her for them, correct?"

"Yeah, I guess. But that's like saying I shouldn't judge a friend I later found out was, oh, I don't know, a psycho who eats children. You called me a cab, right?" Juliet asked, looking up and down the side street which led away from the park.

"Yes, it's en route—three minutes. Juliet, there's one flaw with your analogy: Ghoul isn't a wanted criminal for her behavior during the war, and she told you herself. You didn't 'find out.'"

"I agree, Angel. It is different. Now, let's talk about something else: I'm about to go to my first real class at the dojo. Shouldn't we go over how you're going to assist me? What sort of help would be smart and what would be . . . dangerous?"

26

//////////////////

LEARNING TO FALL

hat do you mean by dangerous?" Angel asked Juliet. The ride to the dojo was a quick one, so Juliet sighed and tried to be more direct.

"I mean, I think it's great how you can help me, and I want you to keep it up, but when I'm learning new things, maybe I shouldn't get them perfect on the first try. Let me struggle a little, get at least partially right before you start stepping in, and then I want you to slowly help me improve—like maybe my tenth try could be perfect." Juliet laughed at the absurdity of her words.

"I think I understand, Juliet. You'd like your improvement to be more believable."

"That, and I want to have to work for it a little. I want to feel like I've earned some of the skills I'm bound to pick up. Like with the shotgun and how I hold the pistol, you told me what to do. You didn't just take over for me."

"I hadn't unpacked my training protocols at that point, Juliet. Having seen your teammates in combat, I could help you perfect your weapon stance even more now that I've activated the requisite algorithms and synaptic connections."

"Yeah, that's fine, but like I said, let me do some stuff on my own along the way. As I start to improve, dial back how much you help me, too. I think you already do that, right?"

"Yes, my protocols are designed such that as you gain mastery, I automatically reduce my assistance."

Juliet sighed and nodded, letting her mind wander a bit. She was nervous and excited about the class, and she couldn't really figure out why. Well, she knew why she was excited—it was going to be fun to learn to defend herself, with the added knowledge in the back of her mind that she'd pick things up quickly. She supposed she was nervous because she'd liked the vibe of the dojo and didn't want to do something wrong, didn't want to be stuck with her "outsider" status.

When the AutoCab pulled up outside the old strip mall, Juliet hopped out, her pack slung over her shoulder, and hurried through the parking lot and into the building. She was ten minutes early, and her apprehension melted away when she saw that Honey was inside the door waiting for her.

"You came!" Honey said with a bright smile, little lines crinkling around her eyes. Juliet absently mused that she'd end up with the same friendly wrinkles as her uncle, Temo.

"Of course," she responded, smiling back. She held open her pack, showing off the gi. "I need to change, though."

"C'mon, we still have time." Honey turned toward the locker room door, walking quickly. Juliet followed her, noticing ten or fifteen people were already on the mats performing stretches. "Don't worry; Sensei will have one of us lead the class through some stretches before we start."

"Cool," Juliet replied, and then they passed through the door and into a short hallway with swinging doors on the left and right. Honey walked through the door on the left, and Juliet followed.

"Most of the men use the locker room through the other door. This good for you?"

"Yeah, this is good." Juliet walked over to a bank of plasteel lockers along one wall and asked, "Can I use any of 'em?"

"Yeah, just stare at the little lock after you close it, and it'll set to your retina. It resets every time you open it, so be sure to relock it if you forget something." Juliet nodded and started to undress. Honey sat on a bench and made a show of looking at something in her AUI, but Juliet didn't care—Fred was cheap and only provided one locker room at the salvage yard, and she'd grown used to people seeing her in her underwear on the infrequent occasions she'd made an effort to bring a change of clothes to work.

After she'd stowed her clothes and gear and stood before Honey in her gi, she held up the belt. "I take it there's more to this than just tying it in a bow?"

Honey stood up with a laugh. "Yeah, unless you want Sensei to have a fit." She took Juliet's belt, folded it in half, and walked behind her. "It's really easy once you've practiced it a couple of times. Watch my hands," she said, and then, standing behind Juliet, she went through the motions, putting the belt fold right at the center of her waist, looping it behind her and back to the front, then slowly showing her how to make the knot through the belt layers. "See? Easy!"

"It sure looked easy, but you might have to help me one or two more times." Juliet laughed, tugging on the ends of the belt, making sure it was tight.

"'Course I will," Honey replied, wrapping an arm over her shoulder. "Let's get out there and start stretching, partner!"

Juliet was surprised by how the class started that day. She'd thought she'd be relegated to learning some fundamental things that everyone else knew, that she'd be separated and taught some basic principles. It didn't seem to go that way, though. Sensei wasn't even on the mat when class began.

The class started with one of the students, a lanky woman in her thirties, leading them all through some stretches, something Juliet was very grateful for because she still had many stiff muscles from her work at the gym and, likely, from sprinting around and crouching to avoid gunfire the night before. The woman would say the stretch name, everyone would drop into it, and then they'd all count down aloud with her, usually starting at ten. Juliet simply mimicked Honey and the people around her.

After stretching, Sensei came into the room and split them into partners. She'd wanted to work with Honey, but Sensei wagged his finger at her and put her with a stocky, bearded man named Grant. Grant looked to be a decade or two older than Juliet, had a very realistic cybernetic hand, and a bulky, complicated-looking data terminal built into his forearm. By way of greeting, he said, "Try not to punch my rig—it's hard as hell."

"Your rig?" Juliet asked, like a dummy.

"Yeah, my jack-deck." He tapped the bulky plastic screen protruding from his arm.

"Oh, you're a netjacker?"

"Yeah," he answered, but he turned away from her to listen to Sensei.

"We work on throws today. Slow and steady is the winner of the race today. Perfect and slow is better than sloppy and fast. You get faster with practice, yes?"

"Yes, Sensei!" most of the students immediately responded. Sensei then modeled the throw he wanted them to work on. Apparently, his dojo didn't refer to throws by names that Juliet could recognize; they were all colorful adaptations that Sensei's father had created and taught to his son and other students.

The first throw they practiced, Sensei called "Tsunami's Grip." He beckoned for an older man, easily the largest in the dojo, to come forward as a demonstration partner. Before he did anything, though, he took the student's wrist, holding it above his head, and turned around in a slow circle, making eye contact with all the students.

"You see Thomas? You see how his arm is over my head? You see that he makes Sensei look very small?"

"Yes, Sensei!" most of the students replied, and Juliet tried to join in but barely caught on in time to quickly mumble, "Sensei."

"Size helps in a fight, but form helps more. Watch as Thomas tries to stop the Tsunami's Grip!" Sensei let go of Thomas's arm and nodded. Thomas took a fighting stance, crouching low, hands up, and faced Sensei. Sensei nodded, and then, like flowing water, he stepped into Thomas and grabbed onto his gi collar. Thomas reached an arm out to return the grip, but Sensei, faster than a snake's strike, grabbed him behind the reaching arm, pivoted so his hip bumped Thomas off balance, and then he rotated. A fraction of a second later, Thomas flopped onto the mat with a thunderous slap.

"Did you see? Did you see the mongoose move through my limbs? Even a big snake will fall to the mongoose!" He reached out a hand and helped Thomas to his feet. "Go now with your partner. Today we will perfect this throw."

Juliet backed away from the circle of students along with everyone else and moved toward a corner of the mat, following Grant. He turned and said, "I'll go first." Juliet, palms sweaty with nerves, nodded and faced him, trying to imitate the stance she'd seen Thomas take. Grant stepped forward but then straightened up and bowed. Juliet turned to see that Sensei had approached from behind her.

"One minute, Grant. Juliet is new today; let's review a thing or two."

"Yes, Sensei," Grant replied.

"Juliet, do you know how to fall?"

"Fall?" Juliet asked, wondering if this was a trick question.

"Yes, fall! Show me, fall to the mat." He gestured to the ground and backed up a step. Juliet looked from Grant to Sensei nervously, then shrugged and sort of collapsed, bending her knees and falling down onto her butt. "Not bad. Good instinct! I didn't see you try to catch yourself, breaking your wrist and escaping classes for a week."

"Uh, thanks?"

"Stand now and watch Grant."

Juliet grunted, climbing to her feet, then Sensei nodded to Grant. The big man collapsed backward, tucking his chin forward and letting his body flop so his right arm was stretched out over his head. The last thing to hit the mat was that hand with a loud slap. "You see?" Sensei asked.

"Yes, I saw." Juliet nodded. "It looked like he distributed the force of the fall . . . does that make sense?"

"Yes! Good, Juliet. When you fall, take control of it. Don't allow your small, bony parts to strike the hard floor. Protect your skull and weak joints. Let the meaty parts of your body hit the ground, and send the force away from you by spreading the surface and rolling toward the final impact. Now you try again."

Juliet nodded her head with a, "Yes, Sensei," then she tried to mimic Grant's performance. It went okay, but she stuck her hand out too soon and felt a jarring impact in her elbow and shoulder.

"Better, but the arm isn't to catch you; it's to send the force away from you. Roll into it. Let your hand slap the mat. Show her again, Grant."

After Juliet had shown Sensei that she could fall without shattering her wrist, he allowed them to proceed with the throwing practice, and though he wandered around the room, giving advice and help to all the students, Juliet felt like he spent quite a lot of time with her and Grant. She refused to let Angel help her with the throws until she'd almost gotten one right.

After that, however, she was happy to let Angel guide her foot, hip, and torso movements because she'd really struggled to get the much larger man to flop over the way she was meant to. Grant had been rather smug in his superiority, sending Juliet sailing over his shoulder several times, and she grew to understand Sensei's insistence that she know how to fall. As it was, even with the proper falling technique, her hips, butt, and shoulders were sore, and she knew she'd carry away quite a few bruises.

The first time Angel stepped in to help, Juliet recognized immediately what she'd been doing wrong—her foot hadn't gone deep enough, she hadn't lowered her center of gravity enough, and she hadn't performed the hip pop at the right moment. With those little corrections, though, she got a satisfying grunt out of Grant, and when he flopped onto the mat, his slapping arm resounded through the dojo.

"Yes! Like this," Sensei said, meeting her eyes and pumping his fist from the other side of the mat. That encouragement brought a wicked smile to Juliet's lips, and she turned to hold out a hand, helping Grant to stand.

"C'mon, Grant, buddy. We only have twenty minutes left in class, and I wanna get this perfected."

"Right." Grant clambered to his feet. "You really launched me that time."

"Well," Juliet smiled, clapping his shoulder, "it's your turn!"

"Juliet, I haven't helped you with your falling yet, and you've been doing a good job, but I think I could help you even more," Angel said as she and Grant squared off.

"Okay," Juliet replied, happy for the help as long as she made a reasonable effort first. Grant stepped in, snatched her gi, and threw her over his hip. Juliet went with the motion as she'd been doing, and when she started to fall toward the mat, she felt Angel's guidance and flexed her core, really going with the momentum. This time, instead of slapping her arm down, she fully rolled over the flopping shoulder, and a second later, she was standing on the mat, smiling at Grant.

"That's not—" Grant started to say, but then Sensei spoke up from right behind her.

"Good breakfall, Juliet, but we don't roll through during class. You almost rolled into Tina's throw." He tugged on her shoulder, turning her so she could see where she was standing, very close to another pair of students. "You can practice that in open-dojo hours if you want. There's more room on the mat then."

"Okay," Juliet said. Turning to the two students, she added, "I'm sorry about that."

"No worries," the short dark-haired woman replied, and her partner, a beautiful athletic woman with modded, wavy pink hair, gave her a thumbs-up and winked.

"When can I come to open-dojo?" she asked, turning back to Sensei.

"Come tonight at nine. You should watch Honey with sword class, and then open-dojo is afterward." He nodded like the decision was made, and Juliet found herself growing more and more fond of his strange affect.

"All right, I will! Thank you, Sensei."

"Yes. Now, practice ten more throws with Grant, then I will have a break before next class." He nodded to himself and turned away, instantly shouting at another student, "No, Dennis! I said lower your center, not fall on your knees."

After class, Juliet and Honey had breakfast again. While they sat waiting for their food, Honey said, "Well? Did you have any luck with Temo?"

"He didn't tell you?" Juliet asked, sipping her coffee.

"No, he called me yesterday to see if you were really my friend, and I told him he better be good to you. That's all I know."

"Well, he sent me on a job last night—said it would be a good opportunity to prove I was legit or something like that."

"Really?" Honey leaned forward earnestly. "That jerk didn't take my word for it?"

"I don't think it was like that," Juliet said hastily. "I think he had an opportunity come up, and I was a good fit. I think he was just killing two birds with one stone and making some money while he was at it."

"So I take it the job went okay?"

"Oh yeah! We got a bonus and everything. I wish you coulda been there." Juliet shrugged. "Temo put the team together, though."

Honey's response was put on hold while Carol dropped off their plates. Juliet had opted for eggs and toast with jam—Benji hadn't been able to get any bacon that day. As she dug into her pile of scrambled eggs, Honey continued the conversation. "So not only did he put you through some kind of test, but he cut me out of a good payday? I'm going to talk to Mama about this. He needs a talking to!" She laughed as she spoke, making it clear she was mostly teasing.

"Speaking of paydays, Honey, you know a good cyberdoc who doesn't run his clients through some corpo database? I mean, someone who'll do some work for me based on my operator ID?"

"You hiding from someone?" Honey asked.

"Not exactly, but I've got no love for corpos. You know what I mean?" Juliet frowned, uncomfortable with how quickly the lie had come to her lips.

"Oh, hell yes, I know what you mean," Honey replied, shoving a huge forkful of pancakes into her mouth. Juliet watched her chew for a minute, holding her hand in front of her mouth to stifle a laugh as the other woman's cheeks bulged with the enormous bite. After an exaggerated swallow, Honey said, "Temo knows a good doc. I've never met her, but I'll have him send you the info."

"Sweet! Thanks, Honey."

"No worries. Hey, so you were serious earlier? You're really coming to sword class tonight?"

"Yes, but only to watch." Juliet held up her hands. "I mean it, Honey! If Sensei tries to put a sword in my hands and push me onto the mat, I'm leaving."

"Oh gosh, Juliet! He wouldn't do that. He's very serious about the sword. I bet he's trying to get you interested. You know, he only has a handful of students for that class."

"Really?"

"Yeah. Way too easy to blast people with all the modern gizmos the corpos keep coming up with. If you can't tell, I'm biased against guns." She snorted and took another bite, then added, mouth half full, "I suppose there's a good balance—Temo keeps telling me I need to learn to shoot better, but so far, I've been doing pretty well with the sword."

"You don't bring a gun on your gigs?"

"Oh yeah, I do. Only if I think I'm going to need it, though. I should probably get something small like you wear—then I can walk around with my sword and still have a ranged option if it becomes necessary. As it is, I usually bring my rifle or my sword, depending on the job, and I try to pick jobs where the sword is enough. A girl can have her preferences, can't she?"

"Just be honest," Juliet said, grinning. "You like to bring the sword because it makes you look cool."

"Oh! You got me, Juliet!" Honey laughed, reaching over the table to playfully punch Juliet's shoulder.

"Ow! Oh God. I didn't realize how sore I was. I'm going to be black and blue tomorrow from all those falls!" Juliet rubbed at her shoulder, then at her hip. She wasn't exaggerating—she felt aches all the way to her bones.

"You'll be okay," Honey said, smiling and wiping syrup from her chin. "Buy some ice packs after open-dojo, though."

Juliet opened her eyes wide and slapped herself on the forehead. "I can't believe I agreed to that."

27

\\\\\\\\\\\\\\\\\\\\

A NEW PERSPECTIVE

After her breakfast with Honey, Juliet took a cab back to the trailer park. She was sore, had a full belly, and the prospect of grabbing a nap sounded really good to her, which was why she said, "Ah, dammit," when a blinking incoming call icon appeared in her AUI. She was still walking through the park toward her trailer when she accepted it.

"Juliet!" Temo greeted, exposing his perfect, brilliant teeth in a wide smile. "I hope you saw the ratings you earned last night!"

"Yeah, I did, and the Sol-bits. Thanks, Temo."

"You kidding me? I'm thanking you! The client was very happy that all those dreamers were put back into their slumber without you having to blast 'em all. There was some concern about how deep they seem to be in their program, but that's a typical dreamer problem and not ours, am I right?"

"Yeah," Juliet said, though her imagination instantly began to jump to images of emaciated bodies—dead dreamers, too absorbed in their artificial reality to jack out and take care of their physical needs. "I guess so. Whatever that corp is doing to 'em is messed up, though, Temo. Their PAIs are all hacked, very messily, growing synth-nerves out of their eyes and stuff. Only a couple weren't infected that way, and they ran for the hills when we changed the program."

"I hear you, Juliet. Don't worry; the commune already reported the mess to some nonprofits. Hopefully, someone can do something for 'em, but that's not our problem. You stopped the violence, and I heard straight from Hot

Mustard that you were the reason we all got a bonus last night. Great work. This leads me to the other reason I called: I'm working on recruiting a face for your heist. Might take me a few days, maybe even a week. The guy I've got in mind is working an op right now, and I don't think you're the type who wants to settle for second best. Am I right?"

"Well, how distant a second is your second best?" Juliet asked, imagining how Ghoul would react to being stuck in the trailer another week.

"Pretty distant, Juliet. Trust me. You want this guy. I can get you some other gigs in the meantime. What do you say?"

"Yeah, all right. I'll talk to my friend and make her understand the delay. Hey, try to include Ghoul and your niece when it comes to doing ops, huh? I'd like to work with people I can trust."

"Sure, what about Hot Mustard and Corbitt? Those guys perform all right?"

"Yeah," Juliet said, pausing at the stoop leading up to her trailer door. "They were pretty decent. I was glad they didn't fuss about not killing everything in sight."

"All right!" Temo pumped a fist. "Sounds like I've got some work cut out for me. I'll try to send you some opportunities in the next day or two, cool?"

"Yep. Thanks, Temo." Juliet waved then cut the call.

"That the fixer?" Ghoul asked, pushing the door open, the old hinges squealing.

As it opened, Juliet could see the pistol Ghoul held slightly behind her back—bright red with stylized lightning bolts on the metal frame—and she sighed, shaking her head. "Not gonna blast me, are you?"

"What?" Ghoul blanched and shoved the gun into her waistband. "No, you nut! I'm just paranoid when I hear people walking up."

"Yeah, I know," Juliet replied with a half grin, climbing into the trailer. "Well, I have good news and bad news. What you wanna hear first?"

"Bad news," Ghoul said, smiling and hopping up on the counter opposite the door.

"Really? That fast?"

"Yeah, I always wanna save the good news. Don't you?"

"Hmm, now you mention it . . ." Juliet laughed and nodded. She opened the little fridge and took out a grape-flavored soda pouch. "Okay, bad news: you need to lay low another week or so."

"Oh, is that all? I thought you were going to tell me we were burned and had to bail on this sweet little trailer." Ghoul smirked, and her sharp chrome-colored teeth winked at Juliet, reflecting the kitchen's dome light.

"Nah, nothing so dramatic. Temo has a good face in mind, but he's unavailable for a little while. The good news is that he's happy with the job we did and will find us some more work while we wait."

"Cool! I can live with that, Juliet. Sheesh, you acted like I was going to have a meltdown or something." She held out her hand, and Juliet handed her the drink pouch.

While Ghoul gulped most of her soda, Juliet said, "Well, I know you're sick of being cooped up here. I think I was projecting." She turned back to the fridge and took out another pouch, this one orange flavored.

"Tell me about your karate lesson or whatever."

"It's not karate. I think it's like a mix of martial arts—I get the feeling Sensei gets annoyed by people who only study one art. One of the students mentioned someone named Bruce Lee. That ring a bell?"

"Are you serious? Tell your PAI to play you *Enter the Dragon* tonight. It's old as hell, but Bruce Lee was a legend. Something like a hundred . . . maybe two hundred years ago? I can't remember, but yeah, watch that guy. He didn't really do MMA, though, not the way most people these days talk about it, but he was really big on learning from different arts."

"Oh really? Okay, will do, but maybe tomorrow night. I got myself roped into going back to the dojo tonight to watch the sword class and work out in the open-dojo hours."

"Shit, you're really getting into it, huh? I know a thing or two, too. We could practice some of the stuff you're learning over in the little grassy lot behind the trailer."

Juliet chugged some of her soda and burped loudly. "Not as good as grape," she said, mock frowning at Ghoul. They both laughed, and then Juliet continued, "Anyway, yeah, that would be very cool. Let's save it for a day when I'm not already sore as hell, though."

"Sure. Any other plans for the day?"

"I kinda wanted to get a nap, and then I'll have a few hours to kill. We need any gear I should go shopping for? These Sol-bits are burning a hole in my crypto-vault."

"Well, I could make a list a mile long, but there are a few things. You could do with a decent data deck so I can get mine back, and you also need a real jammer, don't you think?"

"Yeah! I could get something like Vikker had. Damn, I wish I hadn't lost that thing; I bet it had all kinds of info on it."

"Oh, you had it?" Ghoul smashed her drink container into a ball and tossed it into the bag hanging on the drawer next to her.

"Yeah, for a while, but I lost it when I had to ditch my car." Juliet had already told Ghoul about the encounter she'd had at the AutoDrug.

"That's right—you said they caught the ping it sent out with a drone, hmm? Oh well, yeah, you should try to get something like that."

Ghoul held the top of the bag open, Juliet tossed her drink pouch into it, and then she gestured toward her room. "Okay, well, I'm serious about a nap. Make a list and send it to Angel if you think of something else you need."

"Angel?" Ghoul lifted a white-blonde eyebrow, her blue eye twinkling.

"My PAI." Juliet chuckled. "Don't judge! What's your PAI's name?"

"Hmm, well, his official name is Carl, but I call him dummy most of the time."

"Well, have Carl tell Angel what you want me to buy. I'm taking a sani-spray and then a nap." Juliet wished she could take a bath or a real shower, but the trailer wasn't equipped for it, even if she wanted to pay for the luxury.

An hour later, after she'd cleaned up and collapsed on top of her polyester-blend comforter, Angel woke her up with a gentle alarm. She wanted to be annoyed about it, but she'd asked the PAI not to let her nap longer than that. She dressed, as usual, in Tevlo stretchy jeans, her work boots, a tight-fitting Tevlo pullover, and her vest. Concealed weapons in place, she walked down the hallway to the trailer's living space and found Ghoul snoozing on the couch, her eyes twitching and darting around rapidly.

"Ghoul's PAI says she's in a relaxation simulation. Do you want to disturb her?" Angel asked.

"No, that's fine," Juliet subvocalized. "Leave a message for her, though, that we're doing some shopping." With that, Juliet picked up her backpack and the SMG she'd taken the night before, quietly let herself out of the trailer, and started walking toward the gate. "AutoCab coming?" she asked Angel.

"Yes. ETA is seven minutes. You have a list of items that Ghoul has requested you purchase, and she sent you five thousand Sol-bits. Her note indicates that she gave you extra for the rent."

"She sent 5k? What kind of stuff did she want me to get?"

"Some ammunition and personal hygiene items. I estimate the total cost of her requests to be less than five hundred Sol-bits."

"She's probably feeling guilty about putting me out, so she sent me more than necessary. I'll talk to her about it later. Any other messages?"

"You received a contact card from Temo. It's for a woman named Dr. Adelaide Murphy."

"Ah, the cyberdoc! I forgot I'd asked Honey to get that for me. Hmm, should I call her? Should I send a message?"

"Perhaps a message would be best. Doctors aren't known for sitting by the phone waiting for calls."

"Clever, Angel, very clever." Juliet walked through the gate, waving to the guard. It was the old vet with the wire-job legs, and he nodded, favoring her with a wink as he smoked a genuine, very fragrant cigar.

"Going shooting?" he asked, nodding toward her SMG.

"Oh, no, I don't think so. Actually, I'm gonna sell this." She tapped the gun's plastic stock and smiled.

"Huh, yeah, I'd take it off your hands, but I've got too many guns already. See you when you get back," he said, sucking a deep lungful of tobacco smoke and blowing it out his nostrils.

Juliet waved again and kept walking. "Okay, Angel, send the following message: Hello, Dr. Murphy. I'm an operator who works in the Phoenix area. I have a few upgrades I'd like to look into, starting with some high-end auditory implants. I—"

"Juliet?" Angel interrupted.

"Yeah?"

"You might inquire about a medical nanite synth-organ."

"You think I can afford something like that?"

"They come in varying grades, and I think if you keep working for Temo, you should be able to afford one of the lower-tier ones. Something that could help you stop bleeding, avoid shock, even jumpstart your heart in a—"

"I get it. I get it. I don't want to think of all the horrible things that could happen to my body right now. Okay, continuing the message: I would also like to hear about your options for medical nanites. I have other needs, but those are the most pressing. Looking forward to hearing back from you. Got it, Angel?"

"Yes, shall I send it?"

"Yep," Juliet said as her AutoCab pulled up to the curb. She tossed her backpack and the now-empty SMG onto the seat next to her and climbed in. "Hi, cab. My PAI will send you my weapons license."

She tuned out the cab's response and frowned at the gun sitting next to her. She'd worked very hard not to think about the man she'd killed. Whenever his face flashed into her mind and she started to feel guilty, she'd remind herself that he'd been trying to kill her teammates. In fact, he'd pointed his gun her way. More than that, he'd been working for a corporation that was doing some very shady shit, ruining the lives of who knows how many people. Still, she couldn't seem to get the little lurch in her stomach to go away every time the memory of that bloody rose blooming in his throat flashed through her mind.

"Juliet, I've told the cab to make several stops, the last of which is an electronics store specializing in custom data decks."

"Thanks, Angel," Juliet replied, realizing the cab was already in motion. "You're a lot of help. You know that? I'm not being facetious—you're a lot more than a PAI to me."

"I . . . appreciate that, Juliet."

Their first stop was an AutoDrug, and Juliet found herself sitting in the cab, looking out the window at the store for quite a while before she realized what she was doing. "Angel, any unusual drone activity or anything going on out there?"

"Not that I can detect."

Juliet sighed, let herself out, and walked toward the store, carefully scrutinizing the windows, well aware that she was being silly but still unable to shake the uneasiness the store gave her—it was identical in appearance to the one where she'd been ambushed. Still, she knew there were hundreds of the stores around Phoenix, and the odds that the people hunting her were watching them all were absurdly small.

Her stress proved to be unfounded, and she completed her purchases in record time without another person saying a word to her. No one even really looked at her as far as she could tell, and she chuckled at the reality that people at an AutoDrug didn't want to be bothered. Nobody went to a store like that to talk to people.

Her next stop was at a tactical and military gear reseller whose shop, on the edge of the ABZ, looked like an old house. Quite a few people were milling around in the converted garage, and Juliet eyed the racks of old vests, fatigues, boots, and the several plastiglass cases displaying weapons, from pistols to shotguns to enormous machine guns. She sold the SMG and extra magazines, ensuring Angel scrubbed the identifiers in the software and reinstalled the stock firmware. Ghoul had defaced the physical serial numbers already.

Juliet had been nervous about selling something in such a condition, but the grizzled old shopkeeper had simply said that he'd need to take ten percent off the resale value because the gun needed to be listed as salvage and issued a new serial number. Regardless, Juliet walked out of the place with another thirteen hundred bits after unloading the goggles, the SMG, and the magazines.

While they drove to their next stop, the electronics store, Juliet asked Angel, "What's my balance now?"

"You have 45,722 Sol-bits."

"I never could have imagined having that kind of cash on hand in my old life. It sucks that I've had to give up so much. You know, losing contact with all those people. But my future seems so different now. Back then, I used to think about what I'd do with my weekend, what I might save up for, like a trip to see my mom or a present for Fee.

"I used to obsess over how to meet someone, maybe, or even if I should—I could barely afford my own problems. Now, when I think of my future, I'm thinking about exciting gigs or learning how to fight at Honey's dojo. Now, I think about getting new cybergear, or, shit, Angel, I think about going into space!"

"Your life is certainly different, Juliet. I'm happy that you're improving yourself in so many ways, though I'd like for us to find a way for you to keep improving without the risks you're facing."

"One thing at a time, Angel. One thing at a time," Juliet said as the Auto-Cab pulled into the parking garage attached to a rather large building—they'd moved further into Phoenix proper for this final stop. "What kind of building is this?"

"Mercantile," Angel replied as if that explained everything.

"Like a shopping mall?"

"There are fifteen levels dedicated to various storefronts, ten levels of restaurants and clubs, and the top forty levels are apartments."

"Lots of exposure for me, but I guess it's all right with you spoofing my ID. Um, but I'm wearing a gun," Juliet subvocalized as she stepped out of the cab.

"Would you like me to wait?" the AutoCab's friendly, smooth voice asked.

"Yes. Park here and wait for me. My PAI will send payment as required."

As she slammed the cab door, Angel responded, "Zingeun Incorporated operates this building, and they have a liberal firearms policy—they leave it to the clientele to only carry what they are legally allowed. There is no overt enforcement of this policy."

"Okay . . ." Juliet looked around the dim garage nervously. "Give me a map to the elevator, please." Juliet's nervousness, at least for the moment, proved unwarranted. She made her way to the elevators, and a minute later, she stepped out onto floor thirty-two. As she exited the elevator, she found herself amidst a teeming mass of humanity, all walking back and forth from one store to another. The central shopping levels of the tower appeared to all open onto an open-air plaza at the center of the building.

Banners hung down in the central space, their image-fabric displaying colorful advertisements for various clothing brands, foods, and even weapons and cybernetic enhancements. The wide walkway around the bright, open area was lined with shop fronts, just like the old-school malls Juliet had visited in Tucson.

Her AUI indicated that the electronics store was to her left and around the corner, so she merged with the flow of people and smiled at the anonymity which let her look around, observing all the humanity—tall, short, colorful, bland, augmented or not. Mostly, Juliet enjoyed watching the kids. She loved the carefree, excited way they hustled around, tugging at their parents' hands or running with a pack of friends. She envied their youth and their genuine excitement for what the future might bring.

"That's dumb," she said, catching herself thinking like she used to back when she was a scrap cutter. Her own future had opened up quite a lot, and she'd just been talking to Angel about that very subject. Her smile broadened as she realized she wasn't stuck in a rut any longer. Sure, she had some problems, but she was working on them. *They* were working on them. She wasn't alone; she had Angel, she had Ghoul, and she had other people who were fast becoming real friends.

With a spring in her step, she hurried around the corner and stepped into KTY Electronics, eyes gleaming as she took in all the shiny tech lining the walls in crystal-clear plastiglass display cases. Juliet saw decks of all shapes and sizes, specs in a hundred different styles, data cables, memory chips, and even a row of PAI chips displayed with VR headsets for customers to sample. She saw dream-rig gear, brochures for submersion chairs, and a row of netjacker rigs. Juliet's smile broadened as she looked around, and it really clicked, really hit home—she could afford to shop there.

28

UPS AND DOWNS

Juliet sat at the little plastic, built-in kitchen table in her trailer and unpacked the new data deck she'd bought the day before. She was tired, sore, and feeling very damn good. Her time in the electronics store had been the start of a delightful afternoon and evening, and she still felt a warm glow thinking about it all.

She pulled the shrink-wrap away from the box, balled it up, and stuffed it into the bag Ghoul had designated for recycling. She ran a thumbnail through the seal, unfolding and opening the container to reveal the shiny, translucent, high-density nanoliquid display of her new Arc Systems portable processing deck. Juliet had never bought such a high-end product before, and she admired the packaging: the friendly little notes to the consumer, the decals, all the accessories, and the offer for personalized assistance if she had any difficulties.

She'd paid more than she maybe should have for the device—the thing had cost her nearly three thousand bits, and there were cheaper devices which could do what she needed. "But this one is just so damn nice," she said, pulling the protective film off the screen. It was more than its functionality that she liked; it was its compact nature. The deck was much smaller than Vikker's cube, and Angel had told her this one could do everything she wanted and more. It was less than half an inch thick, fit in the palm of her hand, and came with a sturdy, stylish black-and-gray lanyard she could wear around her neck.

The deck had ten times the memory of the one she'd borrowed, and after Angel had transferred over the files from the dreamer mission, Juliet had quietly deposited Ghoul's in her room on the built-in dresser. The sales lady had shown Juliet how it was capable of holoprojections just like Vikker's, and Angel had explained that its built-in transmitter and external battery pack would allow for the—unadvertised—ability to function as a jammer. The external battery was solid, dense plastic and had clips for wearing on a belt.

Angel had assured Juliet that the deck's processor and operating system were robust enough for her to install just about any kind of program she could imagine. "Even an identity spoofer for Ghoul?" Juliet had asked, wondering if there was a shortcut to resolve Ghoul's situation. Angel shot that idea down, however, explaining that she'd have to create a significant amount of code to run on the deck and open it up to net connections, risking exposure for her. More than that, Ghoul's PAI wouldn't be capable of managing the interface without modifications.

Juliet set the deck on the charging pad she'd purchased, a sheet of plastic the size of a place mat which would charge pretty much any modern device with a battery. As she worked to unwrap the external battery, her mind wandered to what she'd done after shopping—the dojo. A slow smile crept over her lips as she recalled the sword practice and the training she and Honey had put in afterward during the open-practice hours.

The sword class had been far more engaging to watch than Juliet had expected. She supposed part of it was because she'd been thinking differently about fighting and body movements since her earlier lesson about throws. The way the five sword students moved as a team through their drills was almost like a choreographed dance—Juliet could tell they'd been practicing together for a long time. More than that, though, Juliet had watched with open-mouthed amazement what they could do. These weren't amateurs.

Honey stood out in Juliet's mind for her grace. She moved in a way which seemed fluid, yet each of her cuts had been precise, and as she brought her sword through the forms Sensei called out, the blade hardly wavered as she halted its movements. Juliet had felt inspired, much the way she might have been as a child watching a professional athlete. The difference between then and now was that she felt she had a chance to reach those skill levels. "Thanks to Angel," she said, smirking at herself.

"What's that, Juliet?" Angel asked. Juliet knew the PAI was aware she was talking to herself, but she couldn't blame her for wanting to know why Juliet had mentioned her.

"I'm just excited to learn more about fighting. You know, learning to move like those students I watched last night. I was kind of admitting to myself that I wouldn't feel that way if it weren't for you and the cheats you give me."

"It's perfectly normal to be more enthusiastic about things you know you can achieve, especially when you won't need years of hard work."

"If that was supposed to make me feel less guilty, you failed miserably!" Juliet laughed. "I don't care, though; I want to move like they did. I want to be graceful! Especially after how fun grappling was last night!" Juliet put the—now unwrapped—battery pack onto the charging pad and sat back, remembering how she and Honey had practiced throws and escapes after the sword practice was over.

It had been Honey's idea to work on what she called groundwork. After Honey's sword practice, Juliet had described the second dreamer job to Honey in broad, general terms. When she'd gotten to the part about getting grabbed, Honey's eyes had bugged out, and she'd started talking about ways she might have escaped. None of it had made much sense to Juliet, so that had become the focus of their practice: what should Juliet do in such-and-such situation?

The situations had been different ways someone might hold her down, pin her in place, or try to grab on to her. Honey would take hold of or pin her, and then she'd let Juliet struggle for a while, switch places with her, and show her how she'd escape. Juliet thought she might have enjoyed the practice in any case, but when Angel had helped her perfectly repeat the movements after a few tries, it'd felt a lot more fun than it probably should have.

Honey had been both impressed and dismayed by how Juliet had learned arm bars, triangle chokes, guard breaks, and passes so quickly—all terms which had meant nothing to Juliet a few days ago but now evoked a vivid series of movements in her mind. Juliet stretched, the stiffness of her muscles keeping the practice firmly in her mind, and when she felt her cheeks aching, she realized she was still smiling. Suddenly, a creeping suspicion entered her mind, and she subvocalized, "Angel, are you messing around with my hormones?"

"Pardon me, Juliet?"

"You heard me! Are you messing with my hormones? Giving me dopamine or something every time I think about practice or exercise?"

"Juliet, I told you I wouldn't alter you physically without your permission. Stimulating hormones would be something which would violate that promise. Additionally, while I'm closely connected to your synapses and nervous system, I am not able to read your mind. I wasn't aware you were thinking about practice, but I can see you have elevated levels of serotonin, endorphins, and even oxytocin. I believe you are experiencing happiness quite naturally."

"Huh. Well, sorry for being paranoid, but the whole dreamer situation from the last couple of nights has me kind of creeped out about that stuff. Wait, you can read my hormone levels?"

"That the deck you were telling me about?" Juliet jerked her head to the hallway and saw Ghoul standing there, bleary-eyed, scratching at the short blonde hair above her left ear. She wore a T-shirt and shorts and looked ready to sleep another six or seven hours.

"Yes! Isn't it cool? Wait 'til you see its holoprojections; they're way higher res than Vikker's."

"That'll be good for planning jobs. Small, too. Musta been a pretty penny."

"Sure, but it's an investment, right? Speaking of which, I have an appointment with that new cyberdoc today. You want me to feel her out for any tech? Maybe an upgraded data port or . . ."

"Nah, I'm saving for a reflex job. A proper one, not some wired-up hack job like Don had done."

"Really? Is that expensive?"

"Hell yes. To get it done right so you aren't twitching and left on blood thinners for the rest of your life, you're looking at more than 100k."

"Why blood thinners?"

"Well, Don had synth fibers woven into his tendons and major muscles powered by a battery pack subdermally implanted into his gut. Every time he fired 'em off, they tore some of his natural muscle tissue." She yawned and shrugged. "Guess the doc was sloppy. Now and then, some of the blood and tissue got into his vessels. He had to take thinners every day, which made being an operator all the more hazardous. Not like we need our blood to clot, am I right?" She winked at Juliet and lifted her shirt, showing off the scars on her belly.

"Yeah, better save and get it done right, huh?" Juliet said, shaking her head, wondering what it had been like for Don trying to sleep with those twitching, jittery muscles.

"What are you doing at the doc's, anyway?" Ghoul yawned again, walking past her to the little fridge.

"I'm going to ask about some better auditory implants. Mine are garbage—they don't respond fast enough around gunfire, and they aren't sensitive enough to track movement and all that."

"Cool." Ghoul nodded thoughtfully, then glanced at her with a raised eyebrow. "You were home pretty late—I'm surprised you're up already." She pulled a drink pouch from the fridge. Juliet saw a banana on the side and knew it was one of their protein shakes.

"Yes. Oh, Ghoul! I had so much fun last night at the dojo. I wish I could bring you." She watched as Ghoul took a big gulp of her shake and said, "Can you toss me one of those? I already ate, but I'm still *hungry* . . ." she trailed off as Ghoul started chuckling at her.

"You worked out hard yesterday, Jules. You're gonna burn out if you don't pace yourself. Here." She tossed her a cold pouch of protein shake. This one had a picture of a bunch of berries on the side. "You need to feed your muscles."

"Thanks." Juliet laughed, ripping it open and drinking the thick, sweet contents. "How'd you know I was late?" she asked after she'd gulped down half the shake. "Your lights were off, and I thought you were sound asleep."

"Yeah, but I heard you come in. This door ain't exactly quiet," Ghoul noted, demonstrating by walking over and pushing the door open and letting it slam closed. It squeaked the entire way. "You know, I left my gun cleaning kit behind, or I'd put some oil on those hinges. You should pick one up while you're out."

"Ugh! Angel mentioned I should clean my Taipan before we go out again, but I spaced it. They sell kits, huh? Like, I don't need something special for our different guns?"

"Yeah, just get a general kit; it'll do for now. It's not an emergency—none of our guns are dirty enough to fail, but keeping 'em clean is a good habit."

"Right. I'll leave these here to charge, but I should get going. Only reason I got up so early was 'cause that doc wanted to see me at ten." Juliet downed the rest of her shake and threw it in the nearly full recycling bag. Pulling it off the kitchen drawer knob, she held it out for Ghoul. "Throw that in here; I'll toss it on my way out."

Ghoul grunted, chugged the rest of her shake, and pitched it into the bag. "Grab me some chips or something, will you? I've been craving something salty."

"Sure," Juliet replied, pushing the door open and waving to Ghoul as she hopped down the steps. She walked briskly up the lane and caught a glimpse of Mr. Howell standing near the corner of one of her neighbor's trailers, speaking harshly to his nephew. She didn't linger long enough to hear what it was about, but she hoped it didn't have something to do with Albert lurking around her trailer.

As she neared the park's guard station, she turned into an alcove surrounded by oleanders which housed a huge waste compactor and dumpster. She tossed the bag of plastics and paper into the compactor, watching for a minute while it swallowed and smashed the contents down into its mechanical belly. Then she hurried through the entrance walkway, waving to the guard as she passed through.

The AutoCab ride to Dr. Murphy's office took about twenty minutes, and Juliet was relieved that the building wasn't downtown; she still felt nervous about WBD and mysterious bounty hunters. Dr. Murphy had offices in a tall cement-and-glass building which had once, according to the faded signage, housed suites for many doctors and dentists, but it became apparent as the cab circled for an entrance that most were vacant.

The cab dropped her off at the front, but the main lobby doors were taped off with a sign that read, "Please excuse our dust while we renovate. The garage elevators are open for business." Juliet looked around, watched the sparse traffic for a minute, then held her face to the glass, cupping her hands to see through the dark tint. The elevators inside were taped off, and the floor was in a state of disrepair, with stacks of flooring tiles lined up in front of the doors.

"Alright," Juliet said, following the arrow to walk along the side of the building toward the garage and the concrete ramp leading down, away from the sidewalk. There wasn't much foot traffic with the building so far away from downtown, near the ABZ. Still, she had to pause and wait while a legless woman on a motorized scooter slowly rolled past, staring at her through dark goggles which flickered with amber LEDs.

Something about her gave Juliet pause, and she backed up a step to provide more space. As she rolled past and Juliet tracked her with her eyes, Angel suddenly outlined the shapes of two weapons under the ratty-looking blanket covering the back of the scooter. Little labels appeared over the outlines; one said, "Definite rifle," and the other, "Probable shotgun."

The gray-haired older woman craned her neck to look over her shoulder as she passed and pursed her wrinkled lips to blow an exaggerated kiss toward Juliet before she was gone around the corner. "That was unnerving," Juliet said.

"Was it her lack of legs that unnerved you, Juliet?" Angel asked.

"What? No, Angel!" Juliet hissed, walking down the sloping sidewalk into the garage. "She just gave me the heebie-jeebies! I can't explain it. Sometimes, you can just feel it when a person isn't quite right. And I mean mentally, not physically! Besides, you're the one that outlined the weapons she was hauling!"

"You're carrying weapons. Perhaps that woman needs hers for self-defense."

"Fine, yeah, but the weapons aren't the thing that weirded me out. She . . ." Juliet stopped speaking because she'd heard a sound in the distance, and she wasn't sure if her implants were playing tricks on her or if someone had just cried out for help. "Angel, analyze the audio from just now when I was speaking. Did a woman cry out?"

"I believe so, Juliet," Angel said a few seconds later, playing the sound for Juliet. In the playback, she could hear a tire squeaking on concrete, then the distinct sound of a woman yelling and crying out for help.

"Was that in the garage?"

"Yes, from the ramp leading up to the next level." Angel displayed amber arrows on her AUI, and Juliet yanked her pistol free from her holster, crouching down in the dim garage. When she didn't see anything moving, she jogged up the rubber and exhaust-stained concrete toward the big blue LEVEL B sign above.

"What am I doing?" she subvocalized.

"You're sneaking up a concrete ramp to see what caused the sound you heard." Angel had tuned her voice down so Juliet could hear things outside her head more easily, but even so, she heard a hint of sarcasm.

"You know what I meant," Juliet said, focusing on her surroundings. When she neared the top of the ramp, she crouched against the concrete on the left and peered around. Most of the parking spaces were empty, and Juliet didn't see any people walking around. She skirted left around a long red sedan, wormed her way behind it, and then hugged the wall until she could look through a gap between concrete pillars toward the next two rows of spaces.

There she saw, plain as day, two men struggling with a seemingly unconscious woman. One of them had his back to Juliet and held the woman's feet; the other was grunting, holding the woman's top half and fishing in his pocket for something. Juliet sucked in her breath and crouched down, still unable to believe what she was witnessing. Both men were quite large, heavyset, and wore matching green-and-black jackets. On the back of the man facing away from her, she could see a stylized rattlesnake stitched onto the fabric.

"That is the symbol for the Rattlers, Juliet, a banger gang based in South Phoenix." Angel's voice was calm and steady, and Juliet saw a crosshair and ammo counter appear at the center of her AUI. The crosshair was lined up where she was pointing at the man's back, but the lines were very wide, leaving a significant gap in the center.

"Angel," she subvocalized, "why is the crosshair so weird looking?"

"The Taipan is a close-range weapon, Juliet. You're not likely to hit your target with many of the needles from this distance."

"Shit, shit, shit," Juliet muttered in the back of her throat as she carefully inched her way back through the gap in the concrete wall, squatted low, took a breath, and thought about what she was doing. Was she really going to confront two bangers for a stranger? She could only see it ending with her alive if she started shooting before they knew she was there. Was she ready to execute people for a perceived crime? An image of the corpo-sec agent she'd killed two nights ago flashed through her mind.

"Juliet," Angel spoke, "your respirations are growing erratic. Please focus on taking deep, steady breaths."

"Right." Juliet took two deep, steady breaths before poking her head around the corner again, watching. The men had started moving once more, bringing them even closer to her, and Juliet almost ducked back, but then they stopped.

"Goddammit, hold up," the farther man said, driving his hand into his pocket again, jostling the woman so she turned sideways to hold her with one burly arm more easily.

"Juliet, that woman's face matches the image of Dr. Murphy from her business page." Angel displayed an image on Juliet's AUI; sure enough, the blonde, middle-aged woman smiling at her looked very much like the one hanging from the banger's arm.

"He keeps fuckin' sending me updates," the bulky man complained, digging a little data deck out of his pocket and holding it up to his face, squinting at the tiny screen. "Now he wants us to take her to the bar."

"Bar's closed," the other man said.

"No shit, genius. He's probably there in the back room—you know, where they cut Jose up."

"Well, that's some bullshit. Gonna take us twice as long with traffic. C'mon, hurry up before some suit comes poking around."

"What am I doing?" Juliet asked herself again as she stood up, pointing her gun at the nearest man's back. She cleared her throat and shouted, "What the hell are you guys doing?"

"Shit, Tor!" The man holding the woman's top half dropped her to the concrete and fumbled with a stubby black gun that hung from his shoulder on a sling. Angel helpfully highlighted the weapon for Juliet in flashing red lines.

"Dammit!" Juliet cried, and then her pistol barked a gout of orange flames and launched a spray of microscopic needles.

29

\\\\\\\\\\\\\\\\\\\\

GARAGE THROWDOWN

Just as she pulled the trigger, the man with his back to Juliet shifted, turning to face her, and the bulk of her needler rounds tore into his left pectoral, shoulder, and arm. The tiny needles slipped right through the fabric of his jacket and punched through his skin, deep into his bones, perforating muscles and lung tissue along the way. The scatter pattern was broader than would have been optimal, and though he was sorely wounded, he didn't seem out of the fight. In fact, he didn't even seem to notice he'd been shot.

Juliet had barely registered what her shot had done when she realized her victim was pointing his left fist at her and Angel had highlighted, again with flashing red lines, a barrel protruding from his forearm. Her eyes widened and she started to duck back, which saved her from the heavy lead slug which knocked a cubic foot of concrete out of the wall her intended target, the man with the bulky black gun, fired.

She backpedaled, keeping the concrete wall between herself and the two attackers, her mind spinning with the implications of what had just happened. She'd shot a man. Worse, she hadn't killed him. And now she had two very large, very armed thugs coming her way. Juliet jerked her head over her shoulder, suddenly worried there were more of them or that there was another way around where they could flank her. She didn't see anyone, so she ran to the only cover that was close by—the red sedan parked behind her.

She'd just crouched behind the driver's side front wheel, peeking over the top of the hood for her pursuer, when the man with the gun, the one she hadn't injured, poked his head around the corner. He had a visor on now, and he took a quick look and ducked back behind the wall. "Angel," Juliet subvocalized, "can you do anything to, I don't know, mess with his optics?"

"Most military-grade optical headsets are hardened—"

Angel stopped speaking midsentence, uncharacteristically, and Juliet said, "What?"

"I have a connection! His optics are a cheap clone of the Thorn LTD Werewolf Eyes. They lack ICE protocols! Be ready, Juliet!"

Juliet worked to control her breathing, steadied her grip on the Taipan, and watched the corner, straining her low-end auditory implants for any clue about what the man—the men—would do. Five steady breaths later, the man's arm came around the corner, holding a dark gray ball in his hand. The hand cocked at the elbow as if to throw, but then he cried out, and the ball fell to the concrete with a metallic clank.

"Take cover!" Angel warned, and Juliet ducked down behind the tire. A second later, an enormous *boom* rang out, although Angel suppressed her audio, so Juliet felt the concussion in her chest more than she heard it. "I blinded him as he was about to throw that grenade. Push your advantage, Juliet!"

Juliet grunted and stood up, bolting around the back of the car. Angel had activated some kind of filter on her optics which turned everything gray except for the orange-and-green heat signatures of the concrete near the grenade's explosion and the orange-and-yellow man-shaped signature crawling away from her, trailing bright yellow streaks that rapidly cooled to red and green—his blood.

Juliet almost froze up, almost asked Angel to switch back to normal vision so she could see if he would surrender, but then Angel highlighted, in blinking red lines, his large-barreled weapon, still clutched in his hand. "You dirty little bitch!" he called out, and his gun barked, spewing a fountain of bright white-yellow heat, though it wasn't toward Juliet. Was he still blind?

Juliet felt the concrete wall to her left, aware that the other man, the one she'd wounded earlier, was still out there. She took aim with her crosshairs, putting the center right at the crawling man's gun-wielding elbow, and squeezed the trigger, subconsciously leaning into the shot and bracing herself for the recoil. The Taipan roared, and in her heat-sensing vision, it seemed like a jet of fire stretched out from its barrel to touch his arm, utterly erasing it in a smear of yellow and orange.

"Ah!" the man cried, rolling and writhing on the concrete, blood pumping in a crazy pattern as he flopped around. "You bitch; you stinkin' bitch!" he choked again, and Juliet moved back up to the corner, now pitted and broken with chunks of concrete lying around, and peered toward where she'd first spotted the bangers, where they'd dropped the woman.

In her enhanced vision, everything was gray, backlit by the ambient light, which made it easy to see the deep red fading to blue droplets which led away into the garage and around the corner. The other man and the doctor were gone. Juliet glanced back at the other figure to see it had stopped writhing and was lying still. It still glowed orange in her vision, but the outer edges were cooling into the red.

She caught herself thinking of the banger as a "figure" and wondered if Angel had switched her vision for more than one reason—it was easier not to think of them as people when they were just glowing, people-shaped images. "Is he dead?" she subvocalized.

"Not yet, Juliet. It seems he had some trauma nanites. His severed limbs have stopped bleeding, and he's breathing shallowly but steadily. I believe he's in an induced coma, perhaps to preserve brain function."

"All right, keep my vision like this; I'm going to track this blood trail." Juliet hurried over to where the droplets faded from her view, holding her pistol in front of her. When she got to the corner, she led with the gun, standing close to the concrete.

"Juliet, you should . . ." Angel started to say, but then something heavy and hard smashed into her right wrist. Juliet yelped in pain and surprise and stumbled back as the Taipan skittered over the concrete. She hadn't even realized she'd dropped it.

"Dammit," Juliet said, falling back and rubbing her throbbing wrist. She tried to form a fist, and sharp needles of pain shot through it, so she quickly splayed out her fingers.

"Quickly!" Angel screamed. "Pull your knife!" The PAI highlighted the yellow-and-orange figure coming around the corner in bright neon red, spurring Juliet to action. She darted sideways, noticing how the figure pointed its left arm at her with a blinking, highlighted barrel in her AUI. At the same time, she reached up with her left hand, grabbed her vibroblade, and jerked it out, thankful for its grippy rubberized handle.

"Dumb way to clear a corner," the man coughed, lurching sideways to track her with the barrel on his arm. "Never heard of slicing the pie?" For some reason, he wasn't shooting. Juliet kept circling, trying to make it hard for him to aim at her, but with every step, he just tracked her with his arm, leaning against the concrete wall with his other shoulder.

"Well? Are you going to blast me or what?" Juliet asked, trying to think of a way to get out of his line of sight without turning her back.

"Make you a deal." He coughed again, and Juliet saw the bright yellow droplets spatter on the gray concrete.

"Angel, normal vision," she subvocalized. Suddenly, the bright grays of the world darkened to more somber, shadowy grays illuminated by the occasional flickering dome light. Smoke and dust still hung in the air from the earlier grenade, and Juliet saw that the man who'd probably broken her wrist was barely clinging to life. He was drooling blood, his right arm hanging limp at his side, freely drizzling more blood into an ever-growing puddle at his feet.

"If I blast you, I'm dead a few minutes later. Promise me you'll have the doc stabilize me, and I'll let you do your thing." He coughed another gout of foamy blood and added, "Ugh! Why'd you have to hit me with a goddamn needler?"

"Angel, is he bluffing? Is that cannon in his arm a real weapon?"

"I believe so, Juliet. The barrel is identical to the brochure images of the Polk & Chang Hailstorm subdermal shotgun. It comes standard with a five-round magazine and would be quite dangerous to you at this range."

"All right, put the cannon down and show me the doc," Juliet said.

"She's around the corner, next to that white pickup. I think it's hers," he grunted, lowered his gun-arm, and slid down to the concrete floor, leaning his back against the wall. Juliet sheathed her knife and scooped up her Taipan in her left hand, feeling reasonably sure she'd drop the gun if she tried to fire it with that hand, but figuring the banger didn't need to know that.

Keeping him in her peripheral vision, Juliet walked in a wide circle around the corner, ensuring no more surprises waited for her. When she saw the white truck just a few parking spaces away, she jogged toward it. The doctor's bound form was lying on the concrete near the rear-left tire, and Juliet hurried over to her.

Doctor Murphy was conscious and trying to worm her way away from the truck, her back arching with the effort and her eyes trained on a bank of elevators some fifty yards away at the far corner of the garage. "Easy," Juliet said as she jogged up. "I'm here to help."

She set her pistol down on the ground, reached up to yank her knife out again, and very carefully cut the plastic shrink cords on the doctor's feet and wrists. She barely had to touch the plastic with the vibroblade as it snipped through the material. The doctor watched her with wide eyes, her gag making conversation impossible. She held very still, however, and Juliet figured it made sense a doctor would know to keep calm around a vibroblade.

The gag on the doctor's face was held into place by more shrink cords, and Juliet could see they were painfully tight. "Hold still!" she admonished as she very carefully touched the vibroblade to the plastic over the wadded cloth in the doctor's mouth so it didn't slip through into her skin.

Juliet quickly backed up as the bands severed and sprang away from the gag. She slid the knife into her sheath and picked up her pistol while the doctor pulled a prodigious length of white cloth and a blinking poker chip–size device out of her mouth. "God, were they trying to choke you?"

"Chrome-brained idiots! I could have asphyxiated!" the woman spat, rubbing at her wrists as she struggled into a sitting position before smashing the little blinking device against the concrete. "Are they dead?"

"Not yet, I don't think."

"I'll fix that," the woman said, turning to pull herself up with the help of the running board along the side of the truck.

"Wait," Juliet spoke up. "One of them let me help you in exchange for us not letting him die. I hit him with a needler round—I think his lung is in bad shape."

"Oh?" Again, she grunted and groaned, pulling herself to her feet. Juliet hadn't helped her because she didn't want to let go of her gun, but she backed up a step as the doctor pulled open her truck door and fished around inside the back seat. She came out with a bulky shotgun in her hands. "I didn't make any goddamn deals."

"Whoa! He had me in his sights and let me live. I can't let you execute him." Juliet didn't point her gun at the woman, but she held it at a forty-five-degree angle, ready to lift it further if she had to.

"Oh, Jesus," the woman spat, tossing the gun back into her truck and locking it. "Just a minute. I called my synth when I smashed that jammer, and he should be running this way. I guess I owe you something, huh? What's your name?"

"I'm Juliet. We had an appointment." Juliet liked something about the woman—her gruff demeanor reminded her of someone, but she couldn't put her finger on who. She had salt-and-pepper brown hair, a permanent scowl, and several obvious body augmentations, including one arm that was longer than the other with an extra joint halfway between her elbow and wrist.

Making the arm even stranger—more uncanny—her hand had seven long, slender fingers.

"Oh! Juliet! I was looking forward to our meeting—sounded like you wanted to talk some high-end augmentations. Sounded like a nice change from adding chrome to bangers so they can kill each other more efficiently." As she finished speaking, a chime sounded from the corner of the garage, and the elevator door slid open. A man exited and ran directly toward them. He wore green doctor's scrubs, and his skin was pale blue and shiny—a synth.

"Oh, dear! Doctor Murphy!" he cried in a high reverberating voice, clearly coming from a speaker with poor depth range.

"Hush, Trojan; a lot of help you were!" the doctor said, stepping away from her truck and gesturing toward the slumped figure against the wall nearby. "Check if they're still alive. If they're dead, put them in the incinerator; if they're alive, bring them to surgery room A."

"Yes, Doctor," Trojan replied, bowing low and rushing over to the banger with the cannon arm. Juliet watched him with interest, wondering what sort of arrangement he had with the doctor. Was he a free individual, a high-functioning AI? Was he a low-tier AI that worked as a semislave?

"Come with me, Juliet. I was just getting to work when those assholes jumped me. Old business, that. Don't let it bother you." The doctor waved Juliet along and started toward the elevators. "Least I can do is fix your wrist, but don't worry—you've got a standing discount with me after those heroics."

"Oh, thanks, Doctor Murphy."

"Just call me Murph, all right?"

"Okay," Juliet said, walking alongside the woman, matching her long strides. She was impressed that she seemed to have wholly brushed off her traumatic experience. As they walked, Juliet subvocalized, "Angel, can you tell what kind of synth that man is? I've never met a smart one like the ones people say fly ships and work in finance or medical fields."

"I could message him—he has an open communication port—but if his functionality is near the legally permissible higher-end, he might take offense."

"Would you take offense?" Juliet asked. She'd often wondered if Angel broke the AI limitations, and if that was why WBD wanted her back so badly. If they were found to be making unrestricted AIs or even just stretching the legal restrictions, they'd suffer backlash and sanctions that would no doubt be crippling.

"I . . . am not a synth, Juliet. I wouldn't be offended in the slightest. The higher-functioning synths have personality algorithms that function autonomously—they can't control their feelings or responses to perceived slights."

"Can you control your feelings?"

"I'm not sure I have feelings. I find myself saying 'I feel' quite often, though. It's something I find perplexing."

"Finding something perplexing is kind of a feeling, isn't it? Anyway, forget it for now. I'm just curious about them. Don't you think it's wrong?" Juliet asked, still subvocalizing, as she watched Trojan stride past them, hauling the two men, one over each shoulder. They each had to weigh more than two hundred pounds.

Before Angel could answer her question, the synth looked at Doctor Murphy as he strode past and said, "I'll use the freight elevator. They're both alive, but the one with the perforated lung will expire soon."

"I'll see to him in a minute. Hook them up to tables one and three." The doctor looked at Juliet and winked. "I'll get a price for returning them alive. Hank Smith-Hatathli is going to pay dearly for this little disaster."

As the synth strode away with his load, the actuators in his legs whining with the strain, Juliet lifted her wrist and cradled it to her chest. It was purple, swollen, and hurt like hell at even the slightest jostling. "Who's that? Their boss?"

"Right. He's the head of the Phoenix chapter of the Rattlers. Any chance those guys will be able to ID you?"

"No. Even if they scanned me, which I don't think they had a chance to do, I'm spoofing my ID; scrambling my image in video, too." Juliet tapped her temple, indicating her optical implants.

"Clever girl. More and more interesting," the doctor said as she pushed the elevator button. "So, remind me—you're looking for auditory implants? What else? Something interesting like a heart enhancement or . . ."

"Medical nanites and a synth-organ to house and maintain the swarm." Juliet had heard of such things but had never known anyone who could afford them, though she knew there were varying grades thanks to her discussion with Angel. She hoped she could afford at least a trauma pack like the one that had saved the banger whose arm she'd blown off.

"Well, that goes without saying. I guess we could give you a one-off injection of nanites, but if you want something that'll last and save you again and again, you'll want the implant. What kinda budget are we talking about?"

Murphy had punched number eleven on the elevator keypad, and they were quickly rising.

"Let's talk options before I spell out my budget, hmm?" Juliet frowned as she gently probed her swollen wrist.

"Sure. I've got options, and as I said, I owe you. You're not going to find a better deal unless you know another doc whose life you saved." Murphy reached out and put a hand on Juliet's shoulder. "I mean it—I was running on adrenaline out there, but I should have slowed down enough to thank you properly. You could have bugged out when you saw what was going down, but you didn't. That's not something I'll forget."

"You're welcome, doctor. I was tempted to follow them or report what I saw, but then I heard them talk about taking you into some kind of back room of a bar where, according to their banter, some other guy had been chopped up or something."

"Oh?" Murphy raised a thick, gray-brown eyebrow and scratched at her chin with a long finger at the end of her crazy, double-elbowed arm. She looked Juliet up and down and grinned. "I might have to do more than extort old Hank. You're an operator, right? Might have some work for you down the road. Now come on," she said as the bell rang and the doors opened, "I'll open up my brochure for you to look through while I stop that banger from dying."

30

VULNERABILITY

Juliet sat in a very comfortable waiting room, sipping sparkling lime-flavored water and flipping through images on a paper-thin tablet. Doctor Murphy had shown her to the room, given her a splint that got icy cold when she put it on her wrist, and an injection for the pain. After that, she'd handed Juliet the tablet, pointed to the fridge, and gone to, presumably, save the bangers who had nearly kidnapped her. Juliet stretched out her legs, the reclining white faux leather chair shifting to accommodate her, and smiled.

The idea that she'd been staring down the barrel of a cybernetic shotgun ten minutes ago, having just gone through a gun—and grenade—fight, seemed almost dreamlike to her. Had she made the right decision? Would it have been wiser to call someone for help, even corpo-sec? "Probably," Juliet said, grinning, but she knew, in the moment, she'd done what felt right, and it had paid off. Murphy had promised her fifty percent off on her first implant and a twenty-percent discount going forward.

"Juliet, considering the doctor's offer of a large discount on your first implant, it might be wise to choose something other than a new audio implant."

"Well, I thought about that, but I don't want the doc to think I'm being a greedy bitch. I mean, she didn't have to throw that offer out there, and I hope she considered the possibility I'd pick something expensive, but I didn't save her for a reward; I don't want her to think that's what I'm like."

"Perhaps; however—"

"Chill, Angel. I'll talk to her about it, all right?" The PAI didn't respond, and Juliet frowned. If it were Tig, she'd just let it go, but Angel seemed to have more personality than she was willing to admit. Despite her protestations, she seemed very much like a synth to her, with emotions she couldn't always control. "I'm sorry if I offended you, Angel."

"I'm not offended, Juliet. I believe you'll follow through and ask the doctor."

"There you go, proving me wrong again." Juliet laughed, shaking her head. Sometimes, it seemed her suspicions about Angel were simply projections. "What do you think about these audio implants? I like the Cork Systems Clarion. The, uh, model seven."

"That's a good choice, Juliet, but you could get the Lyric model from the same company for seven hundred more Sol-bits. It has a higher bitrate and positional audio modeling based on the Geiger and Warren algorithms. It would make their combat functionality significantly better."

"Oh, cool! Good eye, Angel!"

"Well, I'm using your eyes, but . . ."

"Was that a joke? You're trying out joke material now? I love it, Angel!" Juliet laughed, then shaking her head and grinning, she tabbed through the brochure to the medical nanite suites.

The most basic implant was a pod meant to be attached externally, usually on a person's chest. It ran a shunt into an artery where the nanites stored in the pod could be deployed. They were guaranteed to provide oxygen to a person's brain for an hour after "death." The device was called a Hayashi Death Cheater and sold for seven thousand bits. "That's kind of cheap to cheat death, don't you think, Angel?"

"It will only allow you to cheat death if you have the ability to repair whatever damage made the deployment of the nanites necessary. If you, for instance, suffered traumatic organ damage but didn't have the means to pay for necessary medical attention, you'd simply have a living brain for an extra hour."

"Well, good point, but if I just bled out and only needed some stitches, it might pay off."

"That's true."

Juliet grunted at the PAI's concession and flipped through the pages of medical nanite products, wanting to see the most comprehensive item Murphy sold. When she came to the last page, she whistled at the price tag. "A quarter million bits?"

The brochure page showed a vague outline of a person's internal organs with a stylized image of the WBD Lifesaver 3000 snugly implanted around the abdominal aorta. It was cylindrical and segmented and, in the brochure at least, silvery and sleek. Juliet read through the features highlighted in bold. "'Hundreds of billions of multipurpose nanites, maintained and produced on demand by the implanted organ.' Let's see here." She ran her finger down the page. "'Capable of delivering oxygen or nutrients, electric impulses to stimulate organ function—'"

"Read about this; it's the most important function." Angel highlighted a paragraph Juliet had yet to reach. When she read through the text, she learned that the organ held tissue-repairing nanites capable of closing off ruptured vessels and stitching flesh together at a microscopic level.

"'Will stop arterial bleeds in seconds, and even if the host suffers major blood loss, the other specialized nanites will convey oxygen as needed to vital organs.' Wow," Juliet said. "So this is the real deal, huh?"

"It's a good product and the best in this brochure, but there are better," Angel replied, sending some sat-net links for Juliet to peruse with products valued at more than a million bits, even one that had a twelve-million-bit price tag.

"Can you give me a summarized explanation for those price tags?" Juliet asked.

"Most offer functionality similar to this WBD product, but the more expensive variants have smarter nanobots, a more comprehensive biomonitoring system, and much faster response times to trauma. The Yamaha Systems Grand Elixir maintains a battery of nanites seven times larger than the Lifesaver, and they will repair damaged tissue within seconds. Additionally, the higher-end products are known to repel viral and bacterial invasions much more readily without risk to the host's tissue. Even the WBD that Dr. Murphy sells has a disclaimer that 'some host tissue may be damaged in the event of a viral infection.'"

"Crazy," Juliet said with a sigh, setting the brochure on the table next to her chair. Leaning her head back, she held her numb wrist against her chest and closed her eyes. She was a little drained from the massive adrenaline dump she'd gone through in the garage, but more than that, the constant thought of how her body might be damaged and repaired was starting to feel a little macabre. She felt her thoughts growing fuzzy and her mind drifting as her breathing steadied and she began to doze.

"Juliet," Angel startled her awake, "steps are approaching."

"Right," Juliet said, stifling a yawn. Inhaling deeply through her nose, she sat up, forcing the reclining chair back into an upright position. She was rubbing at her eyes when the door opened and Doctor Murphy came through, wearing a clean white coat and drying her hands on a paper towel that she threw in a bin next to the refreshment bar.

"Juliet! I'm all done with those two goons. I have them sedated and will deal with them and their boss in a while. Rest assured, if the subject of how they came to such dire straits arises, I'll be glad to say the person who incapacitated them was a merc-synth in my employ."

"Well, thanks, Doctor—"

"Murph! I told you; call me Murph."

"Right, right. Thanks, Murph."

"I'm the one who owes the thanks around here. Did you pick out what you want?" She gestured to the brochure.

"Yeah, I know what auditory implants I want, but I can't afford the nanites yet." Juliet shrugged and sat forward on the seat.

"Auditory implants aren't that pricey. Let's save your big discount for when you're ready for the nanites, hmm? I'll give you twenty percent off the new ears today, okay?"

"Seriously? If I bought the WBD nanites, that's like 100k you're giving me."

Murphy stepped closer and sat on the coffee table in front of Juliet's chair. She folded her hands, resting her elbows on her knees, and smiled, the wrinkles around her mouth and eyes growing dense. "Juliet, I was probably going to die today. If not, I was going to have a very nightmarish time. I am happy to transfer you a fat stack of bits right now if you'd rather never come back around here. However, I think it would be worth your while to accept my discounts—there are worlds of augmentation that you've barely begun to scratch! Do we understand each other?"

"Yeah, understood, Doc—er, Murph."

"Doc's fine with me, too." Murphy laughed and stood up. "Well? Which ears are we doing today?"

"The, um . . ." Juliet reached for the brochure, but then Angel displayed the name in her AUI. "The Cork Systems Lyric." She paused then added, "Model four. Are there other models?"

"Just older ones that I don't sell. That's a good set, Juliet; I can get 'em installed in about twenty minutes. You wanna do it now?" Murphy's no-nonsense attitude got another smile out of Juliet, and she leaned forward, nodding.

"You have time?"

"Yep! No clients until two. I had a lunch date, which is why I wanted to meet you at ten, but that's off, thanks to those clowns." She gestured over her shoulder, presumably indicating a room somewhere behind her where the two bangers were sleeping off their anesthesia. She saw Juliet's brow crease and added, "Don't worry! My date will reschedule. Trust me; I wear the pants in that relationship!"

"Well, sure, if you have time right now . . ."

"Yep, c'mon. I won't even have to put you under for this. You have some implants now, right?"

"Uh, yeah. Golio Techs. I got 'em when I was fourteen, so they're pretty dated."

"Oh really? Those old things are pretty simple, but they had good music reproduction if I remember right. I could probably off-load 'em onto a banger. Let me keep 'em, and I'll knock three hundred off," she said, opening the door and motioning for Juliet to pass in front of her into a sterile-looking white hallway. "So, let's see, 18k for the new ones, minus twenty percent . . ." She paused as Juliet walked through and started down the hall. "That's 14.4, minus the three hundred for your old ones. We'll call it 14k. Sound fair, Juliet? Take the door on your left."

"Juliet, those implants retail for fifteen thousand. The doctor is giving you a good deal, considering her surgery expenses," Angel spoke as Juliet opened her mouth to reply.

"That sounds very fair. Thank you, Murph." She opened the door, revealing a small white room with a chair which reminded her very much of a dentist's or a walk-in chop shop, as people called the implant clinics where cheap, simple augmentations were often performed.

It was the same sort of chair she'd sat in at a much younger age to get her old retinal implants installed. The memory of that occasion rushed into her mind, and she smiled, remembering how Fee had been so excited for her to finally get an AUI; she'd been the last one in their little friend group—the last one among her cousins as well—to get one.

"Take a seat, Juliet," Murphy said, and Juliet complied. The chair squeaked while she scooted back on the cushion. "I'll be back in a minute. Need to dig up the implants and the materials to install them and fix your wrist. Just relax." Then she stepped out, and Juliet sat alone. Suddenly, she started to feel some strange anxiety. She felt exposed, vulnerable, and far too at the mercy of a stranger.

"Angel, is there a jammer or anything active?"

"No, I have full access to the sat-net."

"Are you picking up any chatter or anything that might indicate we're about to be double-crossed?"

"Nothing I can detect. Is there something wrong, Juliet?"

"Just a feeling, Angel. I feel like a sitting duck right now." Juliet's palms started to perspire, and she began to bounce one leg up and down on the ball of her foot, looking around the room for any indication that something was wrong. "Melt this, I'm getting outta here." Just then, the door opened, and Doctor Murphy pushed a stainless-steel cart into the room, laden with materials.

"Everything all right?" she asked, seeing Juliet on the edge of her seat and perhaps noticing the stress behind her eyes.

"I, uh, was just going to find a bathroom. Thought you would take longer."

"Right down the hallway. Turn left at the corner, and the bathroom is the first door on the right. I'll get things set up."

"Right, thanks." Juliet stepped past the tray holding the packaged implants and the little tools Murphy would need to install them. When she stood alone in the hallway, she looked left, where the bathrooms presumably were, and right, where she knew the elevator waited. "Should I bail, Angel?"

"I don't see any indication that Murphy has double-crossed you, Juliet. I don't share your feelings, however, so if there's something I don't understand, you should act on it."

"I . . ." Juliet stood there for a long minute, thinking of what to say and forcing herself to breathe deep, slow breaths. She could hear the doctor through the door unwrapping packaging and setting things on the tray with metallic, scraping clicks. Finally, she turned to the left and went to the bathroom. As the door swung shut behind her, she subvocalized, "Crank the gain on my audio implants. Do you hear anything at all?"

Suddenly, the sounds of water in the pipes, the air whooshing through the vents, the weird ticking sounds all buildings made as they shifted in the wind and heat, and her own breathing filled her ears. She sat quietly, waiting for Angel to say something, but finally gave in and, before she flushed, said, "Turn it back down."

"I didn't hear anything unusual, Juliet," Angel informed as Juliet washed her left hand and gingerly rinsed the purple fingertips of her splinted hand. It was still numb and didn't hurt, but it looked awful.

"I'm just being paranoid, I think. This life, the people and corpos, it's all getting to me."

"You had a traumatic experience in the parking garage, Juliet. A day or two off will do you good."

Juliet laughed at the PAI's tone—she sounded like a badly written shrink on a teen VR serial. As she finished rinsing her hands, Juliet looked into the mirror and saw her face was streaked with smudges of something dark, like ash or soot. She figured she'd picked it up during the firefight in the garage. Her eyes were bloodshot and felt gritty, probably with concrete dust, so she leaned over the sink and splashed water on her face, cupping it in her left hand so she could gently rinse out her eyes.

"Angel?" she asked as she watched the water drip down her cheeks. "Are my eyes supposed to get bloodshot? The new implants?"

"Yes, like most cybernetic organs, they are tied into your blood supply, and the tiny vessels in the synth-flesh sclera serve to provide oxygen. They can become inflamed from trauma just as natural eyes can. Don't worry; they'll recover rapidly."

With her face clean and feeling somewhat better overall—more relaxed— she walked back to the room with the operating chair, trying to breathe deep, steady breaths. Had she worked herself into a panic attack? Was it time to stop trusting her gut, or did she just need a day or two to recover and find her balance? She opened the door to see Murphy leaning against the little counter next to the chair, talking animatedly with someone in her AUI.

"No! Not a chance! If she needs it that bad, she's going to have to come here. You made a very big damn mistake trying to force this issue! If you thought my services were expensive before, wait until you see my bill for today's little fiasco!" She looked at Juliet and winked. "Now, I have a client. Don't bother calling me back; I'll contact you when I'm ready." She made a gesture similar to what Juliet did to tell her PAI to cut the call and then laughed.

"Was that the guy who sent those bangers?"

"It sure was, and he's squirming! Oh, I'm going to make him pay for this. Thank you again, Juliet!" She gestured to the seat, and Juliet stepped over to sit down. She inhaled deeply through her nose and slowly released it while Murphy looked at her with a smile. "Nervous? Not everyone handles surgery—even easy procedures like this—easily." She moved behind Juliet and began putting prefab, concave gauze materials around her ears with little elastic bands.

"Yeah, I'm nervous," Juliet admitted.

"Lots of people feel that way, especially operators and bangers. Heck, even corpo-sec. I think it's the lifestyle; it breeds paranoia and a healthy dislike for vulnerability." She picked up an autoinjector and continued, "You're quite vulnerable here in the office while I'm working on you. It's not a good feeling for someone who needs to be on their toes all the time, right? This shot will just numb up the nerves around your ears."

Juliet inhaled again as she felt the needle sink into the flesh under her ear. The injector hissed, and then she felt it more dimly four more times as the doctor circled her ear with more injections. "That's one done; might as well do the other." She moved around Juliet to repeat the process.

"Doc," Juliet said, her voice sounding funny in her numb ears, "you wouldn't screw me over, would you?"

"I'd have to be a real sadist to talk about how hard it was for people to trust a chop doc while I was in the midst of betraying you, wouldn't I?" Murphy laughed gently. "Juliet, relax. Reach your uninjured hand over to your pistol and pull it out." She sat back on her stool, giving Juliet room to act.

"All right." Juliet reached with her left hand and awkwardly worked the Taipan free of its holster, holding it on her lap, barrel pointed to the doctor's left.

"There! Don't you feel better? Do you think I'd let you hold that little cannon if I were going to do something to betray you? Can you feel that?" she asked, reaching forward to flick lightly at Juliet's right ear.

"No."

"Great! Okay, if I were you, I'd have my PAI play me a video of kittens playing or something; you don't want to see me cut out your old implants and install the new ones. I'll try to be quick, but I pride myself on a job well done. I'd say give me fifteen minutes!" She chuckled, picked up a scalpel and needle-nosed plier, and rolled her stool over to Juliet's right side.

31

///////////////////////

LUCKY

Okay, now have your PAI play the Chicago Symphony from their live charity recording in 2103. Make sure it's clear and that you can isolate each instrument." Murphy sat in front of Juliet, finished with her quick surgery, and was helping her go through a series of diagnostics to make sure the new audio implants were working properly.

Juliet's old implants—tiny, blood-covered black discs—sat on the stainless-steel tray to her left. She couldn't believe those dense little plastic objects had been responsible for everything she'd heard for nearly ten years. At the doctor's request, she subvocalized, "Go ahead, Angel."

Suddenly, orchestral music filled her ears, beautifully rich and full of depth. Just like her old implants, the new ones channeled some sounds into the bones of her skull, achieving much deeper, more realistic bass than would seemingly be possible from such tiny devices. One by one, Angel began to isolate the different instruments in the symphony, and Juliet sat there, amazed by how clear they all sounded. "How . . ." she started to say, and Murphy smiled.

"These Lyrics are miles beyond your old ones, Juliet. They have hardware algorithms your PAI can interface with to do things with sound that you could only imagine before. Tell your PAI to turn off the music and scan for the sounds of human respiration. Tell it to filter out you and me."

"You heard her, Angel," Juliet subvocalized. The music stopped, and the world grew quiet. Then, Juliet heard quick, shallow breathing. She looked at Murphy and held her own breath, but she still heard it.

"You hear it? I've got those two goons in a room on the other side of the wall behind you. They're sedated, but you can pick out their breathing. Your PAI could accurately tell you how many people are breathing on the other side of most walls now. Pretty neat, huh?"

"Very cool, Murph!" Juliet was grinning, imagining the many ways the new audio implants would help her in situations like she'd been thrown into over the last week.

"Now, tell me about the wrist—any discomfort?"

"No. It's just tight," Juliet replied, flexing the appendage. Murphy had injected bone gel into the fracture and sprayed on a purple nanofiber mesh cast. It allowed her to move it while providing a bit of support. With the injury cemented and an injection of anti-inflammatory drugs, the swelling was almost gone.

"Grab my hand and give it a squeeze," Murphy said, holding out hers. Juliet gripped it and clamped down with her fingers. "Jesus! Easy, easy. Okay, I can see you've done a lot of work with your hands. Anyway, it seems fine. That didn't hurt, did it?"

"Well, not me . . ." Juliet grinned, and Murphy laughed dryly.

"Okay, well, everything seems to be working just fine." Murph rolled back in her stool and stood up. "Do you want to make an appointment for the nanites? Wanna wait 'til you secure the funding? In either case, I'll be contacting you with a job opportunity soon. You have people you like working with? I could go through a fixer if you want."

"Um, let's hold off on scheduling more surgery right now. As far as your job goes, though, I'd appreciate it if you sent it straight to me and let me pick the team. Would that be all right? I have a few friends I like to work with."

"Done deal, Juliet. I'll send you the details and the budget and let you build the team." Murphy held out a hand, and Juliet warmly clasped it, giving it a much gentler squeeze.

"Hey," she said, letting Murphy help her stand, "I just thought of something. One of my friends is interested in a wire-job, a . . . um, reflex augmentation. She wants it done right, though—no side effects."

"Oh?" Murphy's eyes squinted as she contemplated. "I can do that. I've done several in my time. The thing is, those are really tricky, and sometimes, side effects are beyond the doctor's control. It's a very invasive procedure, depending on if she wants just major muscle groups or all of 'em." She paused and shrugged. "Heck, maybe she just wants her gun arm done. Anyway, people's bodies respond differently to things like that. I could tell from the tiny bit of scarring around your audio implants that you take to cybernetics rather easily. Not always the case."

"Well, still, you'd do a better job than a discount chop doc, right?"

Murphy grinned and put a hand on Juliet's shoulder. "That warms my heart, Juliet! You'd be surprised how many of my old colleagues would call me just that! Seriously, though, yes—I would be better than most in this town. Just because my snooty old partners don't like my methods doesn't mean they aren't good."

"Okay," Juliet said, following Murphy to the door. "I'll let her know you've got what it takes."

"That I do, Juliet. That I do." She led her through the hallways of her office suite and to the elevators, and along the way, Angel let her know that she'd called her an AutoCab.

Juliet said her goodbyes to Doctor Murphy, then rode the elevator down to the garage, marveling at the little differences in her hearing. Sounds were sharper, more distinct, and there was an absence of a baseline hum that she'd gotten used to over the last few years. "I remember when my old implants started humming. What was it? Three years ago? It drove me crazy at first, and now that it's gone, I almost miss it."

"You'll grow used to the new clarity," Angel said. "You don't notice the missing artifacts from your old retinal implants, do you?"

"No, I guess not. I'm getting used to the more vivid colors and sharper AUI, too." The elevator dinged, and Juliet stepped to the side, not wanting to be exposed when the doors opened. As they started to, she lifted the edge of her vest and put her hand on the grip of her Taipan. "Hear anything, Angel?" she subvocalized.

"Nothing in the near vicinity."

She poked her head into the opening door and watched the shadows of the garage for a minute. Then, before the doors dinged and closed again, she stepped out. "Feeling paranoid."

"I'd be worried about you if you weren't."

Juliet didn't encounter any trouble as she walked through the garage and met her cab near the entrance, and the ride back to the trailer park was uneventful. As usual, the park was quiet in the afternoon. The only person she saw outdoors was the security guard, though Juliet saw several people lifting blinds to peer out as she walked by their plots. She smiled, imagining the nosy old ladies messaging each other with updates about her comings and goings.

For fun, she increased the gain on her new implants and stood outside their trailer for a minute, trying to pinpoint Ghoul's location within. It took her a few seconds, but eventually, she heard her taking slow, very steady breaths just to the side of the door. Juliet laughed and said, "Ghoul are you waiting by the door to try to scare me?"

The door squeaked open, and Ghoul stood smiling in the opening, "No! I just wanted to make sure you didn't have any creeps following you." She glanced Juliet up and down and frowned. "You have some work done to your wrist?"

"No." Juliet climbed up the steps and walked into their little kitchen, not wanting to continue the discussion around prying ears. "Hang on," she said, picking up her fully charged new deck. "Angel," she spoke aloud, not worried about Ghoul hearing her talk to the PAI, "this thing has a noise screen setting, right?"

"Yes, but leave it on the charging pad—that function depletes the battery quickly. The deck can use its three-dimensional audio projection to create a static field which stretches four feet in each direction."

"Oh, well, that covers the kitchen, at least. Come sit over here, Ghoul, in case we have snooping neighbors. I kinda pissed off some people today, and you never know who might want a reward to snitch us out." Juliet sat down at their little plastic kitchen table and waited for Ghoul to sit across from her.

"Well?" Ghoul asked, eyes narrowed in a look that said, "What's the latest disaster?"

"Okay, so when I got to Murphy's office, I found her being kidnapped in the garage."

"You what?" Ghoul leaned forward suddenly, very interested.

"Yeah, two bangers from this gang called the Rattlers had her tied up and were going to take her to a bar or something. It sounded like they meant to torture or kill her, so I stepped in. I almost killed them, but one broke my wrist." Juliet held it up, rubbing her fingers lightly over the sprayed-on mesh.

"You *almost* killed them?" Ghoul took Juliet's wrist in her hands and pulled it toward her, pushing and pulling at her hand to bend it back and forward, albeit gently.

"It's fine," Juliet said, pulling it back. Then she gave Ghoul a brief run-down of the fight, including the deal she'd made with the banger that had held her at gunpoint.

"Jesus, you're one lucky bitch." Ghoul chuckled.

"Hey!" Juliet reached out and smacked the side of Ghoul's head lightly. She bit her lip nervously—she'd acted on reflex, as she might have with Felix. Ghoul didn't react, didn't snatch her hand out of the air, or hit her back. She just looked at Juliet, blinked a couple of times, and smiled.

"I guess I deserved that. You're not a bitch."

"Thanks!" Juliet laughed.

"You are lucky, though. Lucky that guy was nearly dead; lucky there was a doc nearby to bargain with; lucky your first shot messed him up good; lucky your—"

"I get it. I get it! Yeah, I'm lucky. What did he mean when he said I didn't know how to clear a corner?"

"You stuck your gun—and wrist—out on a blind corner. He was waiting for you, so I guess it's *lucky*," she emphasized the word, "that you didn't stick your head out first."

"Yeah? So what's the right move?"

Ghoul picked up Juliet's new deck and set it on the table between them. "Can you make this thing project a drawing pad?" Before Juliet could answer, Angel activated the holoprojector on the deck, and a flat blue plane appeared an inch above its top surface. "Perfect." She drew an *L* shape with her finger and pointed at it. "This is the corner."

"Right." Juliet nodded.

"So, you want to stand a bit back from the corner"—she drew a dot to illustrate—"then you work your way around it, holding your gun close so no one can jump out and grab it or knock it away. You sidestep, 'slicing the pie' with your field of view as you work your way around.

"If you'd done that, you'd have seen old boy lurking against the concrete and had a chance to blast him or duck back into cover." Ghoul moved the dot and drew little lines as more and more area beyond the corner came into the dot's line of sight, illustrating where the "slice the pie" analogy came from.

"Oh, shit. Yeah, I guess I see how dumb that was."

"You're not dumb, Juliet. You just aren't experienced. At least you're lucky!" Ghoul laughed and darted a hand out to lightly tap the side of Juliet's head, moving so fast her hand was a blur.

"You don't need a reflex job!" Juliet laughed too.

"You kidding me? Don woulda tapped my head three times before I touched his."

"Well, I mentioned to the doc I had a friend interested in something like that, and she said she could do it. She'll probably give you a discount if I bring you," Juliet said, then explained her standing discount with the doctor.

"Hell yeah! That's awesome, Jules. So you got the audio upgrade, huh?"

"Yep. Um." Juliet paused and subvocalized, "Angel can you show me the gear score for my cybernetics?"

"My pleasure!" A blinking tab appeared, and Juliet opened it with a gesture.

Cybernetic and Bionic Augmentation:	Model Name and Number:	Overall Rating of the Augmentation (Grades Are F, E, D, C, B, A, S, S+):
PAI	WBD Project Angel, Alpha 3.433	S+
Data Port	Jannik Systems, XR-55	C
Data Jack	Bio Network Solutions, 8840	C
Retinal Cybernetic Implant	Hayashi, Crystal Optics 3.2c	C
Auditory Cybernetic Implant	Cork Systems, Lyric Model 4	C
No Other Augmentation Detected.	–	–

"It's a Cork Systems Lyric," she finished. Juliet almost said it was a grade-C audio implant but realized no one without a PAI like Angel would probably know what she was talking about.

"Oh, Cork makes good implants," Ghoul said, nodding. "Any word from Temo or anything? I'm itching to do a job. Well, I'm itching to do anything that gets me outta this trailer. I guess we're stuck with ABZ work until my identity isn't a problem, though."

"Nothing today," Juliet replied. "I guess I could call him, or we could try to pick something up off the boards. I'll be honest, though, Ghoul—I'm feeling kinda fried right now. I almost lost my shit in the doctor's office. I think a day or two of just working out and resting would do me some good."

"You almost lost your shit? What do you mean?" she asked, standing up and beginning to pace in the cramped kitchen. She walked over to the door and peered out the little window, pulling the orange-and-yellow curtain aside.

"The doc went to get supplies, and I started feeling like I was about to be betrayed . . . as if goons were waiting to jump me."

"There's no way that doc can connect you to Vikker, right? I'm sure those assholes who want me have postings out, but they don't know about you. Did you mention my handle to the doc? Shit, maybe it's time I changed it."

"No, I didn't mention it. This isn't about you, though; it's about me. I've been . . . harried for a week now. This life is still new to me."

Ghoul nodded, letting the curtain fall back into place, and looked at Juliet. She frowned and said, "Yeah, yeah. Right. No worries, Juliet. Let me ask you this—if I pick up a job tonight, will you help me cover my ID while I head out? I'll do something in the ABZ, something quick and easy. I just gotta make something happen. I'm crawling outta my skin here. Normally, if I can't work, I'll at least hit the gym or a bar, but I can't do that shit with all the ID queries around town. You know?"

Juliet looked at Ghoul, still wearing the same gym shorts and T-shirt she'd had the previous day. She saw how she held her eyebrows up, her eyes wide open, pleading her case, and sighed. "I guess we could do something quick. The extra money sure wouldn't hurt. Want me to call Temo?"

"Hell yes! Thanks, Jules! Let's not call Temo, though; I think he'd call us if he had something up our alley. Let's take a minute to look through the boards—see if there's anything we can both get in on."

"Right," Juliet replied, then, as Ghoul's eyes unfocused looking at her AUI, Juliet subvocalized, "Angel, can you try to find a job in the ABZ that both of us could work on tonight?" She drummed her fingers on the table for a minute before adding, "Hey, why are these new implants only C grade? I thought you said they were pretty good."

"The implants are quality gear, Juliet, and leagues better than your old ones. Not many clinics that don't cater to high-profile clients would carry anything beyond what I would rank at C. You'll need more specialized, far more expensive equipment to break through that equipment tier. There are audio implants sensitive enough to perceive the internal functions of the human body—heart rate, digestion, etcetera. If I had access to audio implants that sensitive, I could help you train to fight without the benefit of vision."

"I see," Juliet said aloud and smiled when Ghoul darted a look her way. "Just talking to Angel."

A few seconds later, Angel spoke up. "I've found one that might interest you. It's an open posting which hasn't been picked up in more than a week."

Juliet opened the blinking tab and read it.

Posting #G1874	Requested Role: Data Retrieval	Rep Level: F-S+
Job Description: Confront members of the Hell's Ambassadors paramilitary group and settle a water rights dispute for your client. Resistance and overt hostility are possible.		Compensation: 8,000 Sol-bits
Scavenge Rights: Shared	Location: Phoenix South, ABZ border zone.	Date: Open - Active when two to four operators accept the position.

"Uh . . ." Juliet had many concerns and doubts warring for space on her tongue, but Ghoul looked at her, and she shrugged, sending her a link to the posting.

"Oh, this sounds juicy," Ghoul said, grinning. "We could ask Hot Mustard and Corbitt to join us."

"I was thinking I could ask Honey . . ."

"Really? I haven't met her yet, but she doesn't seem the intimidating type." Ghoul frowned and drummed her fingers on the tabletop.

"She's a good fighter, but she does come off as pretty sweet." Juliet shrugged, but then she pressed her lips together and straightened her back. "Well, I told her I'd think of her with jobs I took, so I'd like to offer her a spot. Is that okay with you?"

"Yeah, no sweat. I get it. I'll call Hot Mustard, and you call your friend, cool?" Ghoul's response caught her off guard; she'd been expecting to have to argue her case more.

"Why not Corbitt?" Juliet asked, genuinely curious. Both men had seemed pretty good to her, admittedly, untrained eye.

"He's all right, but Hot Mustard was pounding nails with that rifle of his. Honey's good with close-quarters action, right? She likes the sword?" Juliet nodded, and Ghoul continued, "Well, I like fighting close too, even with guns, so I figure Hot Mustard balances us out. He's damn good, and I can tell he's seen a lot of action."

"Makes sense. Okay, I'll go call Honey," she said, standing up and walking down the hallway to her bedroom. As she closed the door, she could already hear Ghoul talking, presumably, to Hot Mustard. She sat at the foot of her bed and sighed. "Dammit, I forgot to get new sheets. Maybe we can stop on the way home from this job. Angel, will you remind me? Also, call up Honey."

Her AUI displayed the pending call, beeping every couple of seconds, then an image resolved, showing Honey's smiling face with a colorful floral print wallpaper behind her head. "Juliet!"

"Hey, Honey! How are you?"

"I'm good. Just watching my nephew. Did you wanna meet for open-dojo again?"

"Well, actually, my roomie and I are looking at doing a job tonight. You interested?"

"Seriously? Hell yes, I am! What are we looking at?"

"I'll send you the card, just a sec." Angel displayed an animation showing a card whooshing through her field of view and then out of her peripheral vision.

"Got it," Honey said. Her eyes darted from side to side for a second, and a frown creased her lips. "This could get real ugly, Juliet. Those are nasty guys. You got a fourth?"

"Yeah, Ghoul's working that out right now. He's pretty good, and Ghoul's tough as nails."

"I don't normally take this kind of job, but I'm bored half the time waiting for Temo to set me up something he thinks is 'worth my time' or 'worth the risk,' his two favorite phrases. If you're sure about the other two, you know I'm down to work with you anytime."

"Yeah, I can vouch for Ghoul, and Hot Mustard was outstanding on the job we did. You know, the second dreamer gig I told you about."

"Hot Mustard? Are you serious?" Honey started to laugh. "So we're heading out with Honey and Hot Mustard? Oh God, we better keep that under wraps if we're trying to intimidate anyone."

Juliet couldn't help laughing along, and as they both got it together, she started it up again by saying, "I haven't picked a handle yet! I could go with something like BBQ."

"No!" Honey laughed. "You've gotta go with Ketchup!"

"Oh God." Juliet groaned. "Yeah, I think I'll stick with Juliet for now. Anyway, we don't have wheels. Maybe Hot Mustard does, but do you? I guess we could all take cabs and meet up a few klicks out from the job."

"Hold up." Honey's went glassy. "Looks like your two friends grabbed the job—two of four slots taken. Let's sign up, then we can all communicate through the SOA network. I've got wheels."

"Right on! Signing up now," Juliet said, trusting Angel to follow through.

"Cool. Get your scary-sounding friend ready, and I'll message you all to arrange pickups. I need an hour to finish up here, but then we should get going while the sun's still out—no sense making this more ominous than it has to be."

As Juliet ended the call, a thought occurred to her, and she subvocalized, "Angel, how risky is it to use *Juliet* as my handle?"

"With regard to WBD finding you?"

"Right."

"As you know, the SOA network is highly encrypted, and the details about operators are private. However, people can search through the database to find operators by their handle. Performing that search now, I can find seventeen *Juliet* operators. The network doesn't specify operator locations or the individual jobs they've done, but it reveals their performance card and reviews written by peers and clients. This obscurity is intentional—the SOA network's mission statement is centered on privacy.

"The reason fixers have a job is that they have a network of operators in their area and can put local teams together for clients. It's far more efficient than messaging millions of operators to ask them if they'd be willing to work in a given city, or posting a job on a board, hoping skilled operators pick it up, though many clients, as you know, do just that. If WBD somehow figured out you were working as an SOA operator, they'd likely try locating you through the fixers in the Phoenix area.

"The truth is, there is some risk using your name, supposing WBD makes the assumptions that you're an SOA operator, that you kept your name as your handle, and that you are working in Phoenix. Still, it wouldn't be trivial to find you, though they may try to entice you to do a certain kind of job, perhaps something that would be lucrative and difficult for anyone without my added capabilities."

"So fixers can be a vulnerability?" Juliet asked, still not sure she liked the idea of keeping her name as her handle.

"Certainly. Fixers, doctors, property managers, neighbors, friends—any-one who learns enough about you to connect you to a wanted posting. So far, Juliet, I cannot find any public wanted postings for you. WBD seems to value discretion concerning you . . . and me."

Softly, Juliet repeated the litany of potential vulnerabilities, getting hung up on the last one. "Friends."

32

A SUDDEN DEPARTURE

We've got an hour to kill before we have to meet your friend," Ghoul said after they'd filled each other in on their respective calls. "Wanna do anything?"

"Um, maybe you could show me if I'm learning to do throws properly?" Juliet asked, raising an eyebrow.

"Hah, hell yes! Let's go over to the little picnic area—get some sun!" Ghoul had a way of crinkling her eyes when she was enthusiastic, and Juliet had the urge to reach out and poke at the little crease above the bridge of her nose. She contained herself.

"Cool!" she said instead, then added, "Let me change real quick." She hurried back to her room and glanced around at the scattered, sparse selection of clothing. She didn't have any exercise clothes and didn't want to get grass stains on her gi, so she settled for a pair of stretchy black Tevlo pants that needed to be washed and a white undershirt. She left her boots and weapons with her vest on the bed and hopped down the steps of the trailer to where Ghoul stood, waiting, still wearing the same athletic shorts and T-shirt.

She must have seen something on Juliet's face because she grinned and sniffed at her armpit. "Don't worry, I put on deodorant."

"That's not what I was thinking!" Juliet laughed. "I'm used to being able to grab my opponent's gi—I was trying to think how I'm going to hang onto you when I throw you."

"Think you're going to be able to throw me, huh?" Ghoul grinned and started walking, bare feet slapping on the cement. Juliet followed, and when her soles touched the sunny sidewalk, she yelped and hopped onto the little strip of grass that ran between the walkway and the narrow road. Ghoul laughed again. "Need to toughen up your feet, sweetcakes."

"Sweetcakes? Oh God, please tell me that's not going to be a regular nickname." Ghoul just laughed and began to skip along the hot sidewalk toward the picnic area ahead. Juliet followed along, happy to keep walking in the grass.

When they squared off, standing on the short, dry, partially yellow grass, Ghoul said, "Careful, 'cause this turf isn't very springy. Gonna hurt to fall on it if you aren't ready. Go ahead and practice your falls a couple of times like your sensei taught you." Before Juliet could comply, Ghoul flopped backward, doing her own breakfall, and Juliet laughed as her friend thumped onto the hard turf and groaned. "Fuckin' hell! They need to water this stuff more often!"

"I'm amazed there's grass at all with the price of water these days." Juliet flopped backward, being sure to keep her chin tucked and sending the force out through her extended arm. It was uncomfortable, especially as she felt her sore, bruised hip roll over a lumpy hunk of sod, but it wasn't terrible. She hopped up and said, "Ready?"

"Sure, you go first," Ghoul replied, standing in front of her, squatting slightly. Juliet stepped toward her, as she would in the dojo, ready to throw, and fumbled with her thin T-shirt. She looked at her other hand, puzzled, trying to figure out how to grab Ghoul's naked arm. Ghoul grinned and resisted her a little, but when she saw Juliet had no clue how to proceed, she laughed. "Okay, let me help you. I guess you didn't get a chance to do much grappling?"

"I've heard the term, and when Honey and I were doing groundwork, she mentioned it a few times." Juliet could feel a slight tingle of nervous heat at the back of her neck, and she knew she'd be embarrassed if Ghoul didn't have such a friendly look on her face.

"Ghoul, you smile at me a lot, but you only show your teeth when you're trying to look crazy. Did you know that?" As the words left her mouth, the heat on her neck spread into her face, and she looked down. "God, how did my foot get in here?" she asked, miming trying to get something out of her mouth.

"You know why I smile with my lips." Ghoul sighed. "I'm not a fan of these," she said, baring her sharp, shiny teeth and chomping them, "but they do help with intimidation, which is a big part of my job."

"I know, I know. It's like there are two people in here." Juliet tapped her head. "The clever one who knows things and the idiot who comes out when I'm having fun. Sorry to mention it, all right?"

"Forget it. Now, come here." Ghoul motioned Juliet closer before reaching up and putting a hand behind Juliet's neck. She took her other hand, the mechanical one, and grabbed Juliet's opposite arm by the triceps. "This is a basic grappling hold. I've got a hold of you, but I'm open for you to do the exact same thing to me. Go ahead."

"Like this?" Juliet asked, reaching up with her hand to grab Ghoul's neck and then snaking her other hand over Ghoul's opposite elbow and grabbing her triceps.

"Yep! Now we're locked in a grapple. When your opponent doesn't have something handy to hold onto, you have to use their body. So, say we're struggling with each other like this." Ghoul started to tug and push against Juliet, pulling her arm or neck before pushing, and soon, Juliet started to reciprocate. After a while, Ghoul nodded and said, "Now you've got to make your move. Step into me and wrap my arm up in yours—that's right, go over it, tuck it tight to your side. See how you're pulling me off-balance?"

"Yeah, I think so," Juliet replied, trying to follow Ghoul's instructions.

"Now, drive your leg between mine so your hip pops me more off-balance. Take your other hand there—yeah, like that—shoot it under my other armpit and complete your throw." Juliet did as Ghoul instructed, slow so the other woman could lead her, and then laughed as Ghoul flopped over her and down onto the grass.

"Okay, let's try a little faster," Ghoul said, grinning. "Let me straighten up and play the unassuming asshole who threatened you." She hopped to her feet, stood before Juliet, swaggering and thrusting her hips forward, and made a scowling face. "Hey, bitch!" she said in a deep, fake voice. "I'm gonna cut you up!" She waved her hand, pretending to hold a knife. When Juliet just laughed at her, she smiled and spoke in her normal voice, "C'mon, go through with your throw. Faster this time. I won't resist you." She grinned and added, "This time."

"Is this the way you always throw someone without a gi or something you can't grab onto?"

"No! God no! There are lots of different throws—the more you learn and the more you practice, the more options will open for you in a fight."

While they practiced, Ghoul was patient and listened well, showing Juliet what to do with slow, exact instructions and helping her almost intuitively when she felt Juliet start to get something wrong. Angel offered to step in and help her with the new throws several times, but Juliet didn't want her to, not then. "Help me later," she'd subvocalized. "We can practice during open-dojo or something, but I'm having fun with Ghoul right now."

Juliet and Ghoul practiced like that, back and forth, for nearly an hour. They spent as much time laughing as they did throwing each other, and Juliet grew more and more confident that agreeing to help Ghoul had been the right move; she was fast becoming a good friend. Something about her just clicked; she was sharp-witted and sharp-tongued, but there was always a sparkle behind her eyes that let Juliet know she was just messing around.

After they'd cleaned up, the pair decided to wait for Honey to pick them up at an AutoDrug about a mile from their trailer park. As they were getting ready to leave and Juliet pulled out her cable to plug into Ghoul's data port, Angel spoke up with an idea. "Juliet, if Ghoul wears your new data deck and runs a cable to it, I can use it as a bridge for spoofing her ID. That way, her PAI won't need to do any of the work, and Ghoul will only have to stay close enough for the deck's local wireless receiver to pick up my signal."

"Oh!" Juliet allowed her cable to retract. Removing her deck, she lifted the lanyard over her head and handed it to Ghoul. "Hold this," she said, going to the kitchen table where she'd left the box containing the deck's accessories. She pulled out the three-foot data cable and brought it over, plugging it into Ghoul's data port and handing the other end to her.

"What's this?"

"I can manage your ID spoofing through the deck's wireless connection. This way, we aren't tethered to each other!"

"Oh, hell yes! Do you still have to be with me?"

"Yeah, sorry, the spoofing software is managed by my modded PAI. The deck can't handle it on its own."

"Right." Ghoul nodded and pulled the lanyard over her head, threading the data cable down through her black ballistic vest's collar.

"Angel," Juliet subvocalized. "We have a lot of incriminating data on that deck. Is it wise to have its wireless ports open?"

"I have taken precautions," Angel said, and Juliet could swear she heard a hint of haughtiness in her tone. "I've encrypted all of the data you took from the Vykertech device on the last dreamer job, and I've installed rather advanced ICE which will keep unwanted connections from coming through. Even if a netjacker were to breach it with a sophisticated attack, my ICE would alert me, and I could shut it down."

Juliet grunted in response to Angel's explanation and opened the trailer door. She stepped onto the little cement pad which served as their patio and held the door for Ghoul, who was tucking her deck down the front of her vest. Ghoul had her semiautomatic rifle and her battery-powered bolt-thrower slung over her shoulder, and when she stepped down next to Juliet, she held out the latter.

"What?" Juliet asked.

"C'mon, we don't want to fight those Hell's Ambassadors assholes, so a little show of firepower might do us some good. You know how to use it already, anyway."

"Fine," Juliet said, taking the heavy weapon and slinging it over her shoulder. Angel immediately updated her UI with the gun's battery charge and ammo count. "Why's it called a bolt-thrower, anyway?"

"'Cause it has bullets that look like bolts. Eh, not really. I mean, there aren't any threads on them, but they're just two-inch hunks of metal, no casings, no gunpowder. They're launched through the barrel with those magnetic rails."

"Yeah, I get how it works, but the shotgun I used with similar tech was called an electro-shotgun." Juliet let the door slam shut and pushed her thumb to the old biometric lock pad. "Hey, I just noticed the door didn't squeak. You oiled it?"

"Sure, what else am I going to do around here while you're off rescuing maidens in parking garages?" Ghoul laughed and gave Juliet's shoulder a nudge. "Anyway, some people call these things electro-rifles, magnet guns, or rail guns. I don't think *bolt-thrower* is the official lingo." Ghoul shrugged and started walking while Juliet kept pace.

"Makes sense," she said, then frowned and added, "But I didn't buy a gun cleaning kit yet."

"I used cooking oil. Not like we're using it in the kitchen . . ."

"Well, do you know any good recipes? When I lived in Tucson, I bought most of my meals from the arcology vending machines."

"Ha! No, I can't cook for shit." Ghoul laughed and waved to the security guard as they headed out of the park. Juliet smiled at the admission and hustled to keep pace with Ghoul's surprisingly quick stride. Her legs had to be four inches longer than the smaller woman's, but she sure stepped quickly.

Ghoul claimed to have bought protein squares from every major corpo vending machine in Tucson, and insisted Helios had the best ones in their arcology. Juliet almost choked at the absurdity, but they bantered about the best flavors anyway. Before long, they were standing outside the AutoDrug, leaning against the red bricks in the shade of an ancient, half-dead peach tree.

"What kinda ride does Honey have?"

"No idea. We rode in another guy's old jeep when I went on that job with her. It burned cooking oil or something like that."

"Biodiesel," Angel corrected, but Juliet ignored her.

"No shit? No batts or anything?"

"Yeah." Juliet nodded. "You should have smelled it. Shit, you should have *heard* it!"

"Oh, I saw plenty of noisy, smelly rigs during the war." Ghoul absently kicked a rock into the parking lot, watching it skip over the pitted pavement. Heat waves rippled out over the blacktop of the road, and Juliet, her mind starting to zone out, began to count the cars as they drove by. She'd gotten to seventeen when one of them turned into the lot, and Angel announced that Honey was within near-net range.

"That's her," Juliet said, walking out from under the tree toward the knobby-tired, off-road-looking hatchback. It was brown with silvered windows on the sides and a tint on the windshield that was probably illegal to drive around town—not that corpo-sec usually bothered with trying to police such things.

A wide streak of orange paint ran down the sides, and the hydrogen cell exhaust pipes at the rear pointed straight up on the passenger side. Juliet could see the air intake sticking up by the hood, and she knew the buggy had been rigged for serious off-roading.

The car stopped in the parking space right in front of them, and Honey burst out of the driver's door, waving and grinning. She wore a bandanna around her puffy brown hair, tight ripped jeans, and a leather vest. Juliet smiled when she took in the outfit; Honey had stitched gray, plasteel armored plates on her jean's thighs and along the front of her vest. "Sweet armor!" she said, laughing and walking up to bump fists with her friend. "This is Ghoul," she introduced, gesturing.

Ghoul had hung back by the AutoDrug's wall, and she waved, though not enthusiastically. "Hey," she greeted and walked around the car, reaching to shake Honey's hand, her pale skin contrasting starkly with Honey's.

"I've heard a lot about you," Honey said. "We should get going, though—Hot Mustard's already waiting."

"Cool car." Juliet pulled open the rear door, but Ghoul stepped around her and slipped into the seat.

"You ride up front, Jules."

"Oh, right," she said, turning to walk around the front of the car. She'd been trying to be nice, but figured it made sense Ghoul didn't want to have to carry on a conversation with Honey; she was Juliet's friend, after all.

She opened the door and sat down, but just as she closed the door and Honey got into the car, Ghoul opened her door again and stepped out. She held up a hand toward the car, indicating that she needed them to wait for her as she walked toward the busy street, clearly speaking to someone through her AUI.

"Something going on with her?" Honey asked as they watched her walking around near the noisy street. She kept pacing and gesticulating with her hands, and Juliet could see she was upset. She was very tempted to turn up the gain on her new audio implants but knew that if Ghoul had wanted her listening, she wouldn't have gotten out of the car.

"No . . ." Juliet replied, neck craned so she could watch Ghoul. "At least not that I know of. She was cool as a cucumber while we were waiting for you."

"Maybe it's an ex or something," Honey suggested. "She looks pissed off. Let me start the car; it's getting steamy in here." She pushed a red button on the dash, and Juliet took in all the toggle switches and buttons. It began to dawn on her that Honey's car had been modded a hell of a lot from its factory origins. The hydrogen cell whirred to life, and cold air started to blast out of the vents while Ghoul continued to pace near the sidewalk.

"Should I do something?" Juliet asked.

"I don't know. How close are you guys?"

"Pretty close, but only recently . . ." Just then, Ghoul slumped down onto a cement curb and held her close-cropped, blonde head in her hands, shoulders shaking. "Shit! Hold on, Honey; let me talk to her."

"Right. I'll message Hot Mustard."

Juliet bounded out of the car and jogged over the blacktop to where Ghoul sat. As she came near, she said, "Ghoul, what's going on?" She squatted down and rested a hand on Ghoul's shoulder, and the woman dropped her hands, looking up through teary eyes. She stared at her for a long minute, then took a deep, shaky breath. She reached back to her data port, pulled the cable out, and started lifting the lanyard over her head.

"I gotta go. I'm fucking sorry. Thank you so much for all your help, but I just gotta go." She started wrapping the data cable around the deck and lanyard, shoving it toward Juliet as she stood up.

"Ghoul, you're going to get pinged here!" Juliet tried to push the deck back toward her, but her friend grimaced and shoved it harder. She capitulated, taking the deck as Ghoul spoke.

"Doesn't fucking matter. I'm done. Sorry I almost got you mixed up in this shit. You're a real friend, Jules."

"What does that mean? You're done? Let me help! What's going on?"

"Sorry," Ghoul repeated, squeezing her eyes closed and scrubbing at them with the back of her knuckles. She turned and walked a few steps from Juliet before leaning over, hands on her knees. She took several deep breaths as Juliet walked toward her, gently resting her hand on her back between her shoulder blades.

"Tell me!" she said, briskly rubbing while Ghoul worked on regulating her breathing. Ghoul stood up, put her hands on her hips, and looked at the sky, clearly still trying to get her emotions under control. Finally, she looked at Juliet and smiled.

"I'm glad we met, Juliet. Tell your friends I'm sorry about this—I don't normally bail on a job. I hope I can call you someday and explain everything, but do me a favor and keep your head down for a while. Stay safe. Keep the bolt-thrower, Jules; it's a clean gun." With that, she hopped over the curb, walked toward the street, and slid into the back of an Easycab that pulled up.

"What the shit, Ghoul?!" Juliet hollered after her, but Ghoul shut the door, and the cab sped away.

33

////////////////////

THE INKLING OF A PLAN

Angel, call Ghoul," Juliet said, watching the cab drive away. How long ago had she ordered it? "Maybe that one had just been close by . . ."

"She's refusing the connection. Juliet, I . . ." Angel hesitated, and Juliet wasn't sure she'd ever heard her do that before.

"What is it?"

"I think you should hear the last communication Ghoul had through her PAI," Angel replied, and that's when Juliet remembered she'd had Angel plant a snooping daemon in Ghoul's PAI.

"Oh shit!" She glanced back at Honey's car and saw she was standing outside it, leaning on her open door, watching her with concern written all over her face. "Just a minute!" she called, holding up a finger. When Honey nodded, Juliet subvocalized, "I only want to hear it if you think she's in some kind of trouble. If it's, like, some personal relationship thing, I don't want to snoop."

"Yes, I think this warrants your attention. She received a message through the SOA system shortly before she made the call—"

"She made the call?"

"Yes. I'll show you the message," Angel replied before a blinking tab appeared on Juliet's AUI. Opening it, a message appeared:

Cassandra,

We've accessed Vikker's cube, and he had quite a trove of information on you. Time to stop hiding. Call the return address of this message, or

your sister in Boulder is going to receive a visit from a drone. You have five minutes.

"Crap! Angel, you were supposed to let me know if anyone contacted her about Vikker!"

"This just happened, Juliet." Angel's voice was curt. "I only received the transcript from my daemon as you were asking me to call Ghoul."

"Right." Juliet sighed, sitting on the curb. "Sorry, Angel." She glanced at Honey again, feeling guilty for leaving her hanging while she figured things out, so she said, "Message Honey. Tell her I'm on a call trying to sort things with Ghoul, and play me the audio for Ghoul's call."

"I'm sorry, Juliet, but I only have the transcript. I was trying to keep the snooping daemon as lightweight as possible, so I didn't program it to send any audio or visual files."

Juliet didn't have a response to that, so she just read the transcript as Angel displayed it in a little opaque window of her AUI.

Start Transcript

Unknown: Cassie, so glad you called!

Ghoul: Don't call me that.

Unknown: Tut, such hostility. Time to stop playing games. Are you ready to come take your medicine?

Ghoul: Fuck you—you're bluffing about my sister. I don't even know where she is; how could Vikker have?

Unknown: Oh, I don't know. My cousin had lots of friends. Don't worry, though; I confirmed her location. Would you like to see a vid from my drone?

(Thirty-nine-second pause in the conversation here.)

Ghoul: Goddammit, what do you want? I don't have the fucking money!

Unknown: (high volume) What do I want? I want the bitch who killed my cousin to pay! I want the creditors breathing down my neck to get fucked! I've got a few dirty jobs, and you're going to do them.

Ghoul: A few jobs? Then what?

Unknown: Then we'll see.

Ghoul: Your cousin double-crossed me. It was self-defense.

Unknown: That why you skipped town? That why you left him lying in the dirt with his back full of buckshot?

Ghoul: I was fucked! He shot me first! I almost died, had to bargain with a chop doc to save my ass.

As Juliet read that line, her eyes got bleary, emotion choking her throat as she realized Ghoul was taking the fall for her.

Unknown: Sounds like bullshit. Enough. Get your ass to Vikker's place ASAP, or I'm going to drone the fuck outta that little house your sister lives in.

End Transcript

"Angel, we have to help her," Juliet said as she stood up and walked toward Honey's car, wiping at her eyes.

"I can see why you would want to, Juliet, but—"

"Juliet!" Honey hurried over to meet her halfway. Angel cut herself off, probably anticipating being shushed by Juliet.

"Ghoul's in trouble. If I can figure out a way to pay you, and maybe Pit and Mags, do you think you'd be willing to do a job in Tucson?"

"Depends on the trouble, but put together a plan and let us see what we're getting into," Honey replied, reaching out to squeeze Juliet's shoulder. "You gonna be okay?"

"She's in trouble because of me, so not really. I can't believe she's taking the fall for me."

"Somebody has her? Or is this something to do with corpo-sec?" Honey frowned, clearly worried about what she might be getting mixed up in.

"It's not corpo-sec! It's some asshole who's related to a guy that double-crossed me. He must have connections because Ghoul is scared of him, and while I haven't known her long, she doesn't seem the type to get scared easily." Juliet's hands were clenched into fists, anger, guilt, and worry warring for real estate in her mind.

"Tell you what," Honey said. "I can help you do some recon, and then we can decide if this is something we can handle, something we can sell the others as a job worth doing. Sound good?"

"Yeah." Juliet nodded, her mind racing to half-formed plans, imagined scenes of her and the others going into Vikker's compound guns blazing. She shook her head. "Yeah, we need to make a plan. I think this guy's connected. Like, I think he's got important friends. I don't think we can just try to kill them all, or Ghoul would have done that already. I've got to think of a way to burn them—get them mixed up in a problem that won't leave room for people like Ghoul and me."

"All right, so tonight's job is off, hmm?"

"Yeah, 'fraid so. Sorry about all that."

"No worries, it's an open posting. Our rep won't be hit very hard for dropping it—probably won't even notice it."

"'Kay, um, would you message Pit and Mags? Ask them to keep their schedule open for tomorrow and the next day. Just in case we decide this is something we can do? I'll message Hot Mustard and tell him about today's job, and also see if he's down to help with Ghoul's situation."

"Done deal," Honey agreed. "I'll do it in the car. We should get some supplies for the recon. Care if I swing by my place?"

"Of course not! Thank you, Honey," Juliet said, walking around and climbing into the passenger seat. When she sat down, she subvocalized, "Angel, please message Hot Mustard. Tell him I'm sorry about the job today, but that Ghoul's basically been kidnapped. Ask him if he'd be down for a job tomorrow or the next day if I get him some details."

"Sending the message, Juliet. Also, would you like me to keep track of Ghoul's movements with my snooping daemon?"

"Yes!" Juliet replied out loud, and Honey glanced at her askance. "My PAI," she explained, shrugging. Honey chuckled then jammed her foot on the accelerator, whipping her off-road hatchback back and around before launching it onto the street, hardly slowing to see if cars were coming. The knobby tires whirred over the pavement as she hauled ass around one turn after another.

"No traffic patrols out here," she said, winking at Juliet's white-knuckled grip on the grab bar.

"Juliet, my daemon just pinged from I-10, south of Phoenix—Ghoul is en route to Tucson. Also, you received a video message from Hot Mustard."

"Play—" Juliet started to say, but Angel had already started the message.

"Juliet! Hell yes, I'm in. We operators gotta stick together, and if you're worried about the scratch, don't be. You can give me a share of your next few jobs if it makes you feel better. Tell me where, when, and what kinda ammo to bring!"

"Hot Mustard is in," Juliet said, and Honey held up a fist for her to bump.

"Nice! Mags and Pit are down, provided we show 'em it's not suicide and we promise to cover expenses."

"Not *we*," Juliet replied. "*I'll* make sure they don't lose money on this." After she spoke, she subvocalized, "Angel, what's my balance?"

"After your audio implant upgrade, you have 28,333 Sol-bits."

"This is it." Honey pulled up a gravel drive to an old ranch-style casita with slump block construction painted white. Two goats wandered in the chain-link fenced backyard, and through the big, arched, uncurtained window next to the front door, Juliet could see small children running around. "My auntie watches kids for money," Honey said. "Be right back."

When she closed the door behind her, Juliet spoke. "Angel, I have an idea."

"I'm assuming you want to tell me about it?" Angel replied, and Juliet barked a short laugh at the sass in her tone.

"We still have the dreamer program and all that data you took from the Vykertech deck, right?"

"Yes, encrypted and compressed, but we have it."

"All right." Juliet lifted the deck hanging from the lanyard on her neck. "Do what you need to make this thing ultrasecure, and then unpack that data—see what kinda stuff we got away with." As she finished her sentence, Honey burst out the front door, slammed it behind her, and ran to the car. She held a black backpack stuffed full enough to strain the zipper.

Opening the hatchback, she tossed in the pack with a thud that jostled the car, then climbed back into the driver's seat. "We good? Any more stops before we head south?"

"The place we're going is on the outskirts, past the ABZ west of Tucson. The guy we're dealing with seems handy with drones. Any suggestions?"

"We need chill suits."

"Chill suits?" Juliet blew some loose hair out of her face, pulling it back behind her ear in frustration. Yet another thing she didn't know anything about.

"Yeah, they're like wire-mesh onesies attached to a battery—they'll mask our heat signature so we can slip through the darkness without infrared spotting us. We still need to move carefully, though, depending on the drone."

"Are they expensive?"

"Probably a thousand or more. I know a place we can shop, though." She grinned and added, "Bargain basement kinda place." She stomped the accelerator, and the car flew over the long gravel driveway and back to the rough road, throwing out a plume of dust.

Juliet sat back and closed her eyes, still gripping the grab bar above her door but trying to relax. She was worried about Ghoul, especially after reading the nasty tone of the guy who claimed to be Vikker's cousin. Thinking of Ghoul riding in a cab toward that creep really bothered her, but then she had a thought, "Angel," she subvocalized.

"Yes?"

"Can your snooper daemon get a message to Ghoul? I know she's refusing mine, but what if we had the daemon say something?"

"To that effect, I could use my connection to the daemon to force a full voice connection between you and Ghoul; however, I wasn't sure that was something you'd want . . ."

"No. Just a message, and can you do it in a way that doesn't tip off the daemon right away? I'd hate to lose our connection. I'm afraid she's going to be under a jammer the second she steps onto Vikker's compound."

"You talking to your PAI over there?" Honey asked, glancing at Juliet while she stopped at a light. "I can see your lips and throat twitching!"

"Yeah." Juliet smiled. "Trying to get a message to Ghoul, but she's making it hard."

"SOA network won't work?"

"Says she's offline. I've already tried, and I'm afraid she's going to be blocked before she looks at any messages I leave there. Anyway, I'm trying to figure out a workaround," Juliet said, then she closed her eyes and subvocalized, "Well? Can you?"

"I believe I can send a short text message into Ghoul's AUI memory buffer without compromising the snooper daemon."

"How short?"

"Fewer than sixty-four characters."

"Okay, send this: Stall for time. I have a plan. Trust me. J."

"Do we?" Angel asked. "Have a plan?"

"I'm starting to get an inkling, yeah. How's that data on the deck coming?"

"I'm still sorting through it. Much of the files we took were proprietary OS files which Vykertech installs on all of their machines—nothing much of value there. Then there's the dreamer program and a database of logs which might prove valuable if I can decode them. I'm working on it."

"Good. Thank you so much, Angel. I really appreciate you; I know I seem to take you for granted sometimes, but I don't. Okay?"

"Thank you, Juliet. I'm trying very hard to make sense of this database. I'd like to help our friend Ghoul as much as you would." That brought a smile to Juliet's lips, and if Angel were a person, she'd probably try to give her a hug. Which made her look at the other, actual person in the car and reach out a hand, squeezing her shoulder.

"Honey, thank you for dropping everything to help me. I know you don't know Ghoul, which means a lot."

Honey glanced at her and gave her a half grin, lifting one corner of her mouth. "You're sweet, Juliet. I know I've only known you a few days, but you've always just kinda rubbed me the right way, you know what I mean? I'm happy to help you with your girlfriend."

"Ghoul's not . . . er, how did you mean that? I guess she's my friend, yeah, but it's nothing romantic." Juliet felt heat in her cheeks and looked out the window. "Why am I so awkward?" she asked, laughing.

"No, that's my bad." Honey laughed too. "Sorry, I shouldn't make assumptions. You just seemed so distraught at her leaving, and you guys live together, right? I let my mind jump to conclusions. Sorry!"

"All good. I'm distraught because I feel like the trouble she's in is my fault. It's a long story, but I'll tell you some of it when we get on the freeway, okay?"

"Perfect, because we're almost to T&T's," Honey said, pointing to a big corner store. It was adobe-covered brick, two stories, and had colorful banners all over it, proclaiming things like "Great Deals!" and "All your hardware needs!" The front had a bright red plastic sign which read, just as Honey had promised, "T&T's Pawn & Loan."

"*Okay*," Juliet said slowly, drawing out the word.

"I know these guys. They'll cut us a deal. I hope they have two chill suits, though, but they probably do. They have boxes and boxes of surplus gear on the second floor." Honey pulled her car into the lot, taking up a white-striped section right by the front door.

"That's not a parking—"

"No worries." Honey laughed. "Tony's sweet on me." With that, she hopped out of the car, and Juliet followed, unable to get the grin off her face, despite their circumstances.

T&T's was a shop where you could buy just about anything. Juliet saw ancient-looking portable computers with old-school keyboards, vacuum cleaners, pistols, hunting bows, clothing of all sorts, jewelry, batteries, books, and a thousand other types of items, and that was all on the first floor.

People perused the racks, loud hip-hop music played on the speakers, and Juliet sniffed the air, certain there must be a popcorn machine running somewhere. Honey had already cornered one of the men behind the counter, a tall light-skinned man with a high, black and silver-striped flattop haircut.

Juliet almost laughed at the crazy hairdo, but she could see the man took his style very seriously. His clothes were high-end banger—a flashy silver-threaded jacket with a black skull embroidered on the shoulder complete with glinting red LED eyes. He wore it over spotless white jeans over white cowboy boots with gleaming silver-shod toes. The way he leaned forward—one elbow on the counter, talking real close to Honey—made it clear to Juliet that this was Tony.

Honey waved her over and said, "Tony, this is Juliet. We need to buy some gear for a job tonight, and we're kinda in a rush." She leaned forward, put a hand on Tony's wrist, and added, "Can you please help us?"

"Oh shit, doll. Hell yeah, I can. Tony Senior's got the counter, and I'm all about the sales today." He winked at Honey, and only after she smiled at his gesture did he spare a glance for Juliet. "Hey, girl." He nodded, then, done with the pleasantries, turned back to Honey. "So, what you ladies need?"

"We need a couple of chill suits, and they better work, T," Honey said. "You wouldn't want me getting sniped 'cause the suit fritzed, would you?"

"Oh, hell no, Honey! I wouldn't sell you any broke shit! Hang on, Pops got some of those on a surplus sale from B&C corp outta LA." He paused, scratched lightly at the silver eyeshadow over his left eye, and added, "I think." He looked at the crowd of customers near the register. "I better go to him. He gets pissed when I holler over the customers."

"No worries, sweetie. We'll wait here," Honey replied, lightly drumming her nails on the glass. Tony slid back around the counter and wended his way down to the far corner where his—apparently—father was handling the sales. Honey looked at Juliet, at her wide eyes and raised eyebrows, and laughed. "What? He's sweet!"

"Very stylish, too." Juliet nodded, tapping the side of her nose while nodding.

"Well, I think he is!" Honey said, laughing. "I mean, his clothes can't match up to Tevlo's, but not much could . . ." She giggled, giving Juliet a nudge in her shoulder. "Don't be stuck up!"

"No, you're right, you're right. I'm the last person to talk about style."

"You don't go to clubs often? Too busy hunting down your next near-death experience?"

"Hah! You know I haven't been doing this long. I used to be a welder. Well, I'm qualified to be a welder, but my boss had me cutting scrap most of the time. Between overtime and dealing with . . ." she trailed off as Tony came back down the counter with a big smile, showcasing very straight, very white teeth.

"Yo, ladies! I know where they are! Got a couple other sweet deals I can show you too. Follow me upstairs."

34

\\\\\\\\\\\\\\\\\\\\\

NOCTURNAL ACTIVITIES

Juliet followed Tony and Honey up a stairway on the far side of the store to the second level, where more displays, surrounded by opened and unopened cardboard boxes, filled a space just as ample as the area below. Tony spoke to Honey as they walked, about a mutual friend of theirs named James and how he'd won his latest three matches. As he stopped near a pile of unopened boxes, he said, "You should've seen it, Hon! Even with his arm tuned to regulation, he knocked the guy out with a gut shot!"

"Sheesh! Seriously? He's really getting tough—gonna have to go up to a higher circuit soon."

"Yeah, for sure. Anyway." Tony paused, ripping open the top box. "I think this is it . . . yep, here they are! B&C! Pretty damn good chill suits, and we've got all the sizes." He glanced at Honey, eyes roving up and down, then his gaze drifted to Juliet. "A small and a medium?"

"Whoa, let us decide that, buster." Honey laughed. "We'll want to try 'em on and make sure they work. How long they been in these boxes?"

"A while. They work, though." He nodded and pointed to the far wall behind Honey and Juliet. "You know where the dressing rooms are." He held out two suits, and Juliet had a feeling they were a small and a medium; she also figured he was right—she had a few inches on Honey. Honey took the suits, and Tony finished, "If you're doing a stealth job, I have a few specials I can show you. I'll get things together while you're changing."

"Thanks, T," Honey said, sauntering past Juliet with a wink. She followed her to the dressing rooms, and Honey added over her shoulder, "You got infrared on your ocular implants?"

"Yeah, do you?"

"Nope. Pretty plain-Jane retinal implant I got when I turned sixteen. Decent AUI, and that's about it." She opened one of the dressing rooms and continued, "We don't really need separate rooms—they go on over your clothes. Let's go in here, and you can check if they work with your implants."

"Oh, sure," Juliet said, following Honey into the little room. They unpackaged their chill suits, and Juliet held the weird material in her hands, letting the long garment, complete with oversize foot pouches and a hood, unfurl in front of her. It was heavy, and she could tell the material was metallic in nature, or at least some kind of weave of plastic and metal, and a black plastic battery pack was built into the chest. Hers displayed a dim LED which read seventy-six percent.

The two women struggled to squeeze into the suits; Juliet had the hardest time with her boots, but once those were in, she pulled the rest of the suit on easily enough. Several built-in drawstrings allowed her to take up slack in the material. Once it was on and she'd touched the power button, she felt a slight hum at the center of her chest where the battery lay. "Yours all set?" she asked Honey.

"Yeah. Think so," she replied, pulling the cords that tightened the hood around her face.

"'Kay, let's see here," Juliet said, then subvocalized, "Angel, can you turn on that heat-sensing mode in my . . ." She stopped when Angel went ahead and switched over her visible spectrum. The world went sort of monochrome gray again, but this time there wasn't smoke hanging in the air, so she could see the details of the dressing room clearly enough.

Honey stood before her against the wall, and she was giving off a heat signature very similar to the drywall behind her. A tiny bit of blue green was visible where her face was, and two little dots of orange were in the hollows under her brow. Juliet looked down at her body and saw that her suit seemed to be working as well—she was the same cool gray with a few blue highlights here and there. "Seems to work," she said. "The only heat I'm seeing from you is a little on your face and from your eyes."

"I'll buy some goggles while I'm here. I doubt your eyes will show up— you've got full ocular implants, right?"

"Yeah, but they have vessels. They're synth-flesh."

"Still, your PAI can adjust the flow, I'm pretty sure."

"That's correct," Angel added into Juliet's ear.

"Cool." Juliet started to shrug out of her suit and saw Honey doing the same, but the other woman was clearly stifling a laugh. "What?"

"Not cool, Juliet. Chill!"

"Oh God! Dad jokes? Is our friendship to that level?" She laughed along, though, and as she worked to pull her boots out of the suit, she said, "Good to have these—if we get in a fight, we can both put them on to chill out."

"Okay, that was worse." Honey snorted.

When they returned to the sales floor, they found Tony waiting with a few items atop a stack of boxes. "Hey," he called as they approached. "Now, ladies, I don't pretend to know your business, but if you want chill suits, I'm assuming you're going to try sneaking past some infrared optics somewhere. No, no." He held up his hand, though neither Honey nor Juliet had started to say anything. "Don't tell me! I don't need to know the details. I might have some more gear which might be of interest, though."

"Well?" Honey asked, looking at the unpackaged objects, one of which looked very much like a grenade to Juliet.

"Right," Tony said, grinning. "You're always so eager, Honey! Relax, I'm coming to it." He reached out and picked up a black, triangular plastic piece of gear with a thick strap—it looked like a gas mask to Juliet. "Here, we have a mil-spec disposable air filter and rebreather. It's cheap because you can only use it for about an hour in a harsh environment. Still, it does the job so you can use these bad boys." Tony set the rebreather down and picked up the grenade. "We've been sitting on these a while, and Pops will let 'em go cheap. Trust me." He winked at Honey.

"Well? What are they?" Juliet asked, starting to feel the strain of knowing Ghoul was riding toward an uncertain fate while they dithered with Tony's flirtations.

"Easy, legs!" Tony replied, but before Juliet could even start to scowl, Honey reached out and gave him a pinch on his pectoral. He yelped and pulled back, but Honey held on.

"Don't call her that! Her name's Juliet! I already told you."

"Easy, easy. All right, I'm sorry. Juliet, these are, basically, knockout grenades. Each one will fill a standard room, like a bedroom-size space, with enough gas to knock out a gorilla." He rubbed at his chest, clowning up for

Honey's benefit, obviously trying to get a smile out of her. It sort of worked—she at least stopped scowling.

"How cheap?" Honey asked.

"Fifty bits each."

"How much are the suits and the rebreathers?" Juliet asked.

"The suits are a thousand, the rebreathers two hundred." Tony shrugged. "I don't set the prices."

"Well, can't you help us out, T?" Honey asked, leaning forward. "We're already out a lot of bits 'cause of this job—had to drop a contract."

Tony vacillated for a minute, making a show of looking over his shoulder even though everyone knew his father was downstairs, swamped at the point of sale. "Oh, man, Honey, you owe me for this! I'll throw in a case of the 'nades if you buy the suits and the rebreathers."

"I knew you'd help us out!" Honey squealed, leaning forward and actually kissing him on the cheek. Juliet's mouth dropped—she'd had friends who flirted with salespeople before—heck, she'd flirted before—but never to this brazen degree. She couldn't help the smile that stretched out her cheeks.

"Thanks, Tony. We need some goggles for Honey, too."

"Night vision? Flash correcting? Zoom?" Tony asked, smelling an upsell opportunity.

"Yeah, I guess so, but we don't have a ton of cash, T. Can you get me something for less than 1k?"

"Oh, shit yeah. You ladies head down to the payment line, and I'll put things together for you. Don't worry; I'll take over for Pops before you get to the counter." He smiled at Honey, and this time, Juliet sort of saw why Honey liked him; he looked almost sheepish, blushing and grinning. He really was smitten with her, and that peck on the cheek had clinched the deal.

Juliet and Honey had to stand in line for nearly fifteen minutes before they got to the counter, and true to his word, Tony took over for his dad when they stepped up. He rang up the suits, the masks, and a pair of goggles for Honey. Then, with an enormous, ridiculous wink, he put a green box of grenades into the canvas bag. Juliet read the label as he nestled it among the other items: Thompson Nite-Nites - 8 count.

Juliet insisted on paying because it was a job for her friend, after all, so she walked out of the store 3,200 bits poorer—Honey's goggles had been eight hundred. "What's my balance, Angel?" she subvocalized as she climbed into Honey's car.

"It's now 25,133 Sol-bits."

"Thanks," she said aloud, smiling at Honey as the car hummed to life. "Talking to my PAI. Thanks to you, too, though. Glad to meet your boyfriend."

"Oh, don't you start!" Honey laughed, pulling out of the parking lot. "He's a good guy, and yeah, we have some history, but he's not . . . well, he's not serious."

"Yeah," Juliet mused, reflecting on Tony's over-the-top demeanor. "I can see that."

They'd just gotten on the interstate when Angel informed Juliet that she'd lost contact with her snooper daemon. "They'll probably have a jammer on her from this point forward," Juliet subvocalized, not really ready to tell Honey that she'd bugged her friend.

"So, this place we're going? You've seen it before?" Honey asked, turning down the synth-pop she'd been playing on her car's speakers.

"Yeah. It's kind of a horror story—how this all started. I guess this is a good enough time to tell you about it."

"Sure, if it's something you don't mind talking about. I'd like to get an idea what we're getting into."

"Well, it was my first job. It was a heist—stealing some new Li-air batts from a corp in Tucson. It was trickier than it was supposed to be, which I'm starting to learn is kind of par for the course, but we finished okay. Ghoul was hurt—she lost an arm—but we'd stabilized her, and she was sleeping in the van, Vikker's ride. Anyway, Vikker was like, 'Hey, we need to swing by my place, but Don'—that's the other asshole who double-crossed me—'will drive you back to your wheels.'"

"Sounds a little sketchy. You didn't know those guys, right?"

"Right. Well, I was even more naive then than I am now, if you can imagine. I was nervous, of course, but I figured it was cool—they seemed really friendly. Oh, the worst part was they said I was too new for them to show me Vikker's location, and they made me wear a hood. God, I was an idiot." Juliet sighed, shaking her head.

"Hey. You're not an idiot for trusting people. I mean, you gotta get a little more street-smart, but don't beat yourself up for not seeing the worst in people. So they had a hood on you, then what?"

"Then Don was like, 'I'll lead you to my ride; it's right over here,' and the next thing I knew, he was putting an autoinjector into my neck, paralyzing me."

"Holy shit!" Honey said. "How'd you get out of it? Ghoul?"

"No, Ghoul was out. I was lucky, that's all. The drug they used on me was bad or the wrong dose or something. They thought I'd kicked it, actually joked about it, but before they started ripping my gear out of my supposedly dead body, they went to get some beers. I got up, found an electro-shotgun in Vikker's garage, and gave them a hell of a surprise as they came back." Juliet didn't notice how she automatically edited her story to avoid talking about Angel until she was done. Was she becoming a liar?

She frowned, not liking the idea.

"Whoa. Some luck, but some badass moves, too, I bet. So, if they're dead, who are we dealing with? An angry wife? An operator buddy of theirs? Why'd they want Ghoul?"

"That's the thing—I'm pretty sure Ghoul's taking the fall for me. Don't ask me why; maybe she feels guilty that they double-crossed me and she didn't know anything about it. She worked with those guys for a long time and did a lot of jobs with them. Anyway, they've got some leverage on her, and I'm fairly sure the guy pulling the strings was related to Vikker. They're planning to make Ghoul do some things she'll regret, and I'd be shocked if they didn't kill her afterward."

"So this guy, this relative of Vikker's, he's at Vikker's place? You know, I don't know Ghoul, but from what you've told me about her, I'm surprised she ran to Phoenix—why not take this asshole out?"

"Yeah, that's the million-bit question. I think he's gotta be connected. Maybe he works for a corp or has access to a lot of operators. Like, maybe he's a fixer? I really don't know, but that's why we're doing this—we'll get some intel, scope out the scene, and then we can decide if you all want to help me further. I promise I'll understand if you think it's too dangerous."

"It's not just a question of what the site looks like, though," Honey said, frowning at Juliet. "If Ghoul didn't think it would help to try to punch this guy's ticket, what good will it do for us to go in guns blazing and rescue her? She turned herself in, right? How do we help with the leverage they have?"

"I'm working on a plan. If things go the way I'm hoping they will, we won't have to kill anyone, and these assholes are going to be way too busy to worry about Ghoul or getting revenge for Vikker's death."

Honey stared at her for a long second before she said, "Not ready to explain more?"

"Not yet. Sorry, but I'm still working out the details, and I need to see what we're dealing with to know if it's even possible."

"Fair enough." Honey reached out and turned her music back up while Juliet sat back and watched the miles drift by as they drove south at ninety miles per hour.

It was dark by the time they got to the ABZ north of Tucson. Juliet had Angel send the location for Vikker's compound to Honey, and they chose a route which would lead them through the foothills of old open-pit mines.

The route was long and circuitous, winding around the foothills, mine tailings, and the desert around Tucson. They avoided even the ABZ for the most part, driving down old dirt roads, paved roads long overgrown, and at one point, they had a view into a massive mine pit which looked big enough to swallow half of Tucson's downtown district.

"Holy shit!" Honey said, "That was a mine?"

"Yeah, there are pits like that all around Tucson and south of it. They mostly mined copper, but they found some rare earth metals in the forties and really expanded the operation."

"They don't operate anymore?"

"Oh, there are a few still running, but, you know, with the mines in the belt and on the moons, things just aren't as profitable as they used to be. Lithium used to be rare, you know that?"

"Oh, sure! I might look like I never went to a school, but I did." Honey laughed, her warm, rich voice bubbling with self-deprecation, and Juliet smiled.

"Nah, I wouldn't ever say that, Honey. You seem smart as hell."

"Careful, Jules! You'll end up stuck with me as a friend if you keep saying things like that! Hey, we're only about ten klicks out. I should kill the lights, hmm? I have pretty good night vision."

"Great idea, and let's hike the last little bit. Park well out of their view."

Honey nodded at Juliet's words and reached forward to click the lights off. The desert was dark out there, miles from the Tucson downtown, but Juliet's implants immediately compensated, and though the colors were washed out and artificial looking, the landscape before them became as bright as daylight.

She looked around, a stupid grin on her face, admiring how far she could see and feeling almost like a peeper, seeing things out in the darkness that no person was meant to gaze upon. An owl sat on the frame of a half-built abandoned house, a mouse hanging from its beak. A big mama javelina led a troop of babies around a cholla cactus, and all sorts of other night creatures, confident in the anonymity of darkness, prowled the old, abandoned roads, buildings, and desert landscape.

Stranger than the animals were the occasional people who looked up with startled faces as Honey's hydrogen-powered hatchback purred down the dirt roads. They looked equal parts bewildered or guilty, and Juliet wondered what brought them out to those weird little campsites in the desert. "You ever wonder about people like that?"

"Hmm? Those campers?" Honey looked at her and winked.

"Campers?"

"That's what Temo calls 'em—people who don't quite fit into this lovely corporate utopia we live in."

"That's a pretty broad brush. I don't fit into the 'corporate utopia,' and please tell me you're using that word tongue in cheek."

"'Course I am, sweet Juliet." Honey laughed. "Those people *really* don't fit in. Some are criminals on the run, but lots of 'em are just people who want to go back—back to what it was like before we were all connected, like how it was before we were all over the damn solar system. I think it's a lost cause, but maybe not. There's surely a lot more space to get lost in than there was a hundred years ago. I guess we can thank the corpos for that—they might own all this land, but they don't really use it. Their arcologies sucked the population out of the landscape."

"Well, yeah. I mean, I didn't grow up under a rock. I've seen those weirdos out in the sticks—I used to drive past some of 'em almost every day on my way to work. I guess what I'm saying is . . . well, maybe they aren't weirdos. I think I've had my mind opened quite a bit over the last couple of weeks."

While they were talking, Angel caused Juliet's navigation window in her AUI to blink a few times, and she realized they were getting fairly close to Vikker's compound. "Hey, this thing has all-wheel drive, right?"

"Yeah." Honey nodded. "And damn good tires for off-roading."

"There's a wash up around the corner. Pull into it a ways, and we'll hike the rest of the way. Time to see what the hell is going on around Vikker's compound." Juliet reached into the back seat to grab the sack with their chill suits. She was nervous, but she was also excited—she wanted desperately to help Ghoul, to see her friend free of this mess, but just as much, she wanted to put this whole affair behind her.

In a way, Juliet wished she could go back in time and refuse to work with Vikker, but then, she thought of all she'd gained: new friends and a cold lesson about trusting too much. "More than that," she said, too softly for anyone to think she was speaking to them. "But I'm not sure if I'd repeat that night, given a choice. Not sure at all."

35

\\\\\\\\\\\\\\\\\\\\\\\\\

DRONES

Juliet and Honey crouched near the base of an old, dried-out cholla cactus skeleton. Down the slope before them, maybe half a mile distant, Vikker's compound was abuzz with activity. "Way more people than I would have thought," Juliet subvocalized into their team channel.

"My PAI says there are fourteen outside. Can your implants pick up heat signatures in the buildings?" Honey replied, also silently.

"Angel?" Juliet prompted, and then her vision changed over to the infrared spectrum. She stared at the garage building and the ranch-style house, but the spots of color she made out were from the vents and doorways, the solar cells, and the battery banks.

"Your implants aren't sensitive enough to read through those exterior walls, Juliet; I'm sorry."

"No dice," Juliet subvocalized. "My implants are decent, but not that good."

"Hang on," Honey replied, fiddling with a setting on her new goggles. "Oh, nice! No wonder these were so pricey." Her excitement bled through into her words, and though she was trying to subvocalize, Juliet heard a word or two hiss out through her lips. Juliet looked at the sky, well aware there were no less than three drones up there scanning the area for movement, heat signatures, and sounds.

"So," Honey said into their comms, her lips clamped shut. "Fourteen outside doing various things, and I see three in the garage and five in the house.

All of 'em are moving around except for one signature in a room toward the back of the house. A bedroom, maybe?"

"Maybe Ghoul?"

"Maybe."

"No wonder this guy was so cocky—he's got a damn army here." Juliet wanted to sigh in exasperation, wanted to smack her fist into her hand, but knew that a plume of hot air or the noise might draw a drone's attention.

"It's not impossible, though," Honey replied, surprising Juliet. "I mean, there are a lot of them, but let's keep watching. Those guys in the yard are up to something with that truck. Maybe some of them are going to leave."

Juliet nodded, then subvocalized, "Yeah, I just wish I could get control of those drones." Angel had tried connecting to them, but they were solidly shielded and only took connections on a single encrypted channel.

"On that subject, Juliet, I've been doing some research. If we can get closer to the compound, my attack might be more successful if I can breach the drone's base station. Someone is operating them from a hardened deck—if you could connect me to it, we would own the drones."

"That's a big if, Angel," Juliet replied, then into their team channel, "Honey, where would you put the control deck for those drones?"

"The garage," Honey spoke almost immediately. "That building is big, has lots of workspaces according to your description, and I see a few people moving around in there, but one who seems relatively stationary. I bet it's the drone operator. He—or she, I guess—occasionally paces a few steps but keeps returning to the same spot."

"If I could connect to that deck, I could take control of the drones, and then we'd have a solid basis for a rescue op. We could spend tomorrow studying everything the drones see and hear before making our move."

"How the hell will you do that?" Honey almost chuckled. "You think you can slip into that garage with all those people moving around?"

"Not without a distraction . . ."

"Oh God. What's your idea?"

"Well, they don't know you, right? Suppose you drove by, innocently looking for a party you heard about out here."

"Suppose they shoot me and try to sort out who I was from my corpse?" Honey frowned.

"Yeah, you're right. Sorry. It was a stupid idea."

"No, the general idea wasn't stupid. We just need to think about it some more. How could we distract those guys?" Honey ran a finger under her chill suit hood where it was pressing into her cheek, trying to relieve an itch or allow some blood flow. Juliet could commiserate—the hoods weren't very comfortable.

"I have an idea," Juliet said. "I feel like these guys aren't doing something they'd want a lot of attention on, right?"

"Right . . ."

"So, what if they heard chatter about Helios corpo-sec coming out here to investigate a potential terrorist threat?"

"That would stir things up, for sure. How can we manage that, though?"

"Sec," Juliet subvocalized, then, "Angel, between you and me, can you spoof some net chatter about Helios heading this way? Like on those public access sites that post the corpo-sec radio comms?"

"Yes, though it might very well garner some real attention, if not from Helios, from the people who monitor those stations."

"Yeah, but they're not here yet, and we are. We can do our thing, then get out while Vikker's cousin puts a lid on things."

"Your idea may work; travel time to this location isn't trivial unless a person has access to a fluttercraft or something similar."

"Right." Juliet nodded before briefly describing her plan to Honey. While she spoke, Honey's frown deepened, and her voice came through Juliet's implant. "What if he's connected to Helios? Aren't they, like, into everything in Tucson?"

"Yeah, but does this feel legit to you?" Juliet nodded toward the compound down below.

"Not at all . . ." Honey paused, glancing to her left where Juliet could see some kind of nocturnal rodent rustling through a dried-out scrub. "Are we sure we don't wanna just grab Ghoul and run for it? I mean, if you make a good distraction?"

"No!" Juliet almost said aloud. "We'd be back at square one, with these guys still holding leverage over Ghoul. No, we have to do this right, and step one is owning those drones. You keep watch here, Honey. I'll creep up to the garage, which will probably take an hour if I move slowly enough to avoid the drones noticing. I'll spoof the corpo-sec chatter when I'm in position, then try to slip in and hack the drone box."

"Hah. You're sweet to try to keep me clear, but I'm coming with. If we need to subdue a person or two, I'm a hell of a lot better at it than you." Honey reached over and squeezed Juliet's wrist, adding, "C'mon, Juliet. You've only had a couple of sessions at the dojo. Trust me, okay?"

Juliet nodded, then, by way of answer, started creeping over the hard-packed desert ground toward the back wall of the big, prefabbed metal structure. They had to crawl in slow-motion, moving their hands and legs one at a time, careful not to trigger the motion detection of the drones. Angel kept tabs on the drones' locations, and when they were moving in an arc that didn't cover their approach, they'd speed up a little. Still, as Juliet had predicted, it took nearly an hour to cover the distance.

From her previous visit and their earlier observations, Juliet knew the garage had three possible entrances: the metal door she'd perforated with the electro-shotgun, the big, closed bay door, and a side door which was probably locked. When she and Honey were finally crouched near an old sun-rotted garden hose and a pile of empty pallets, she subvocalized, "Let's get eyes on the side door."

Honey nodded and started crouch-walking, gently trailing her chill suit–clad fingers along the structure's metal rear wall as she moved to the corner. The bay door and main entrance faced the ranch house, but their target was on the opposite side, just around the corner from where Honey and Juliet huddled.

Honey subvocalized, "Not seeing any heat around the corner. Gonna take a peek."

"Careful," Juliet replied, holding a palm to Honey's lower back, steadying herself, and letting her friend know she was there. Very slowly, Honey poked her head around the corner, then pulled it back. A second later, Juliet received an image file, and when she opened it, she saw the door and the lock in high res. It wasn't a smart lock, just an old-fashioned dead bolt.

Juliet gently scraped and tapped at the structure's metal, thinking about her vibroblade before shaking her head. "I can get through that lock pretty easily, but it would make a lot of noise and destroy it. They'd know we were here."

"Good thing you brought me, then," Honey replied, reaching through the zipper on her chill suit and pulling out a pen-shaped, plastic-and-metal device. "Should be easy to pop that lock. Looks pretty old-school." She grinned at Juliet, and her big smile beneath the heavy black goggles brought a similar expression to Juliet's face.

"You're straight nuclear, Honey," she subvocalized.

"Damn right, I'm a nuke! Now, you do your thing."

"Right." Juliet nodded. "Angel, can you do it? Send out the fake messages about a raid?"

"Oh yes, Juliet. It's done. I had it primed and ready to go."

"You're the best."

"Indeed! I've yet to meet or even read about a PAI that comes close to my capabilities," Angel said smugly.

"Oh God, Angel! You should read an article about humility!"

"I was hoping you'd say I was nuclear," Angel replied, and Juliet's heart almost stopped.

"Angel, I'm sorry! I should have realized you were just messing around. You *are* nuclear! You're a planet buster!"

Angel didn't have a reply to that, or at least she'd chosen not to reply, so Juliet smiled and leaned a shoulder against the garage wall, subvocalizing in the team chat, "Now we wait. If this guy's as connected and paranoid as I think he is, he'll quickly see the fake chatter. Any ideas on how we might get rid of the drone operator without people realizing what we've done?"

"How much time will you need with the deck?" Honey asked.

"Angel?"

"Not long, Juliet. With a wired connection, I can overwhelm the port with attack daemons and gain access in seconds. I should start teaching you how these things work, now that you mention it . . ."

"Sure, but not tonight, please, Angel!" Then to Honey, "Just a few seconds."

"Let's see what things look like. Maybe he'll step away."

Juliet nodded, and they remained crouching there long enough for Juliet's thighs and knees to start to burn. She was just beginning to contemplate shifting to sit on her butt when a shrill whistle sounded from the front of the garage, and shouting voices echoed into the desert night. "It's working!" she breathed, no longer worried about the tiny noise of a whisper.

Before Juliet could caution her to be careful, Honey nodded and slipped around the corner, jamming her tool into the dead bolt's lock. Juliet watched from the corner and heard the little device whirr and click, then Honey violently twisted it to the left, and the dead bolt thunked home. She grinned and nodded to Juliet, ever so carefully turning the doorknob and opening the door just a tiny hair to peer through.

Juliet wasn't too nervous yet—Honey had infrared imaging which would show her if anyone was near the door. She inched forward, ready to move when Honey said to, and she'd just gotten close when Honey quickly pulled the door wide and slipped inside. She paused at the threshold to motion Juliet to follow. Juliet hurried after her, and before looking around at the inside of the garage, she reached back and carefully pulled the door shut.

Honey was crouched behind a fifty-gallon drum filled with long pieces of scrap wood and aluminum. An ancient, boxy arc welder was nearby, so Juliet scooted behind it, peering over the top. Angel helpfully highlighted the two individuals in the garage and the seven or eight moving around outside the open bay door.

"Let's go! Let's go! Move your asses! Get that goddamn truck loaded and outta here!" someone shouted outside in the yard. Juliet scanned the garage and saw the little table with a deck and terminal setup, saw the heavyset woman with pigtails sitting in front of it, and saw the very chromed-up guy pacing around near the bay door, a huge, multibarreled gun attached to his belt via some kind of hydraulic arm.

The woman sitting at the desk had her feet up on a cardboard box. Her gaze was trained near the ceiling, and every so often, she'd chortle. "Is she watching a vid or something?" Honey subvocalized.

"Seems like it," Juliet replied.

"I don't like the look of that guy," Honey's voice said in her ear, her black-clad arm pointing to the man with the enormous gun.

"Just wait," Juliet subvocalized. "They're getting ready to move out that truck; maybe this guy won't stay in the garage."

"Someone's coming." Honey pointed to the wall near the open bay door. Juliet assumed she saw someone's heat signature approaching.

"Bull," a man's voice, followed by crunching footsteps on gravel, announced the arrival of a tall, lean man wearing black fatigues. He had steel gray hair, combed back from a high widow's peak. He looked angry, and though he seemed fit, Juliet could see, with the help of her optics, that he had dark circles under his eyes and the telltale waxen complexion of a man using every trick in the book to fend off old age.

"Yeah?" the big man with the gun replied.

"I need you to take our guest downstairs. Sit with her in the cooler and keep her quiet. I don't know what kinda hair Helios has up their asses, but they might come by and do some scanning." He turned to the pigtailed woman and raised his voice, "Anything on the drones?"

"Just coyotes and owls. I need a break soon, Reynold."

"Are you fucking kidding me? You've been sitting on your ass all night. I'll have Wendy bring you a coffee."

"A coffee and a snack. A couple of cookies would be good if there are any left."

Reynold grunted and said, "Close this bay up and get in there," to Bull as he turned to walk away, boots crunching on the gravel. Bull moved to punch the button to lower the bay door just as a heavy truck engine came to life outside, and the sounds of big tires on gravel filled Juliet's enhanced hearing, drowning out the snippets of conversation she'd been trying to hear. She contemplated asking Angel to filter the noise, but the immediate concern of getting to the deck squashed her curiosity.

As the bay door came to rest, further obscuring the noises outside the building, Bull turned to the drone operator. "At least you don't have to sit in the fucking cooler."

"Sucks to be muscle," the woman replied, snorting and waving her hand in front of her eyes, working with her AUI.

"Sucks to be muscle," Bull mockingly repeated, then smashed his hip against the metal door—the one still sporting hundreds of holes from Juliet's shotgun rampage—and stepped out before it could rebound and slam shut with a resounding clang.

"Jeez," the drone operator said, "somebody give that man some zens."

"Now?" Honey mouthed to Juliet.

Juliet shook her head and subvocalized, "Wait 'til her snack gets delivered."

Honey nodded, and the two of them continued to crouch there, waiting. The woman kicked her feet out again and leaned back, crossing her arms. From her occasional chuckles and soft-spoken comments, Juliet knew she was back to watching her vids. The minutes ticked by, and Juliet began to grow worried that they'd realize the Helios raid was a false alarm, and that activity in the garage would ramp up again. "Maybe he forgot about her," Juliet subvocalized.

Honey just looked at her and shrugged, leaving the ball in Juliet's court. One thing was sure: her legs were on fire from crouching for so long, which might have been the main impetus for why she slowly, carefully, reached her hands out to the concrete floor and began to crawl around to the left of the woman's desk. She was still twenty or thirty feet away, heading for a tool chest, when Honey's voice came into her ear.

"Someone's coming!"

To her credit, Juliet didn't panic, didn't scamper for cover. She picked up the pace a little and carefully crawled the rest of the way to the tool chest, crouching behind it so the drone operator's desk and the door were both out of her line of sight. She hugged as close to the red metal as she could and tried to hold her breath as the heavy, perforated metal door swung open again.

A woman's voice said, "Hey, Belle. Got you some leftover chicken and a brownie. Reynold said not to give you a beer, but fuck that. It's been a long couple of days."

"Oh shit, Wendy! Thank you! Where's he at?" Juliet heard the drone operator, Belle, scoot back her chair and walk toward the door.

"He's in the den, calling everyone and their granny, trying to figure out why Helios is coming out here."

"There's nothing going on as far as the drones can see. Here, sit down with me." Juliet could hear their footsteps moving to her left and knew they'd be able to see her, so she crawled around the tool chest to the right. She put too much pressure on the red metal, leaning with one hand, and it rolled on its casters an inch. She froze, afraid she'd given herself away, but the women kept walking, and then she heard more chairs scraping and Belle's heavy sigh as she sat down again.

Juliet wiped her forehead and brow, catching her sweat about to roll into her eyes and wondering what the hell she'd do if those women spotted her. Kill them? Try to knock them out? Run for it? She hadn't thought that far ahead. She was about to ask Angel what was the best way to get a look at the women when a window appeared in her AUI, showing Honey's view of things.

She saw herself kneeling behind the tool chest, and off to the left side of the main door, she saw Belle sitting at a small square card table, hunkered down over a plate of fried chicken. The other woman, Wendy, sat with her back to Juliet. She was young, maybe early twenties or even a teen, with long copper-colored straight hair, a strand of which she absently twirled around her finger while she chatted with Belle.

Knowing where the two of them were looking, Juliet poked her head around the tool chest and scanned the surroundings, studying the last fifteen feet or so to the drone deck. "Angel," she subvocalized, "can you map a route to the deck that keeps me out of their LOS?"

"Yes, I believe so," Angel replied, and a pair of heartbeats later, Juliet saw glowing orange arrows on the concrete floor which led away from her toward another scrap barrel. Juliet crawled over the arrows, following them from obstacle to obstacle until, two minutes later, she was crouched behind the long, plastic table that served as Belle's desk.

She still had Honey's view in her AUI. Seeing that the two women were chatting away while Belle ate, she pulled out her data cord and reached up to the deck, carefully slotting it into one of the open ports. She didn't bother to tell Angel what to do next, trusting her to be quick.

For some reason, Juliet started counting down from twenty in her head, perhaps to keep her mind off of how open she was. If either woman stood up and glanced toward the drone station, they'd see her kneeling there with a wire hanging out of her arm. She'd counted down to seven when Angel spoke. "Juliet, I have full control of the drones."

Juliet didn't hesitate, reaching up to pull her cord out and then, as it retracted into her arm, retracing her crawling route back to the tool chest. Her heart was pounding so loudly in her ears by the time she got there, and she was so intent on getting the hell out of that garage, that she almost didn't pause when she heard Honey's voice in her ear. "Wait!" Juliet froze and glanced at the view Honey was sharing with her.

The two women had stood up from the card table, and Wendy, the young one, was holding a plate with several bones on it. Rather than registering that she needed to hide, Juliet absently wondered where they'd gotten real chicken. Then her brain snapped into focus, and she scooted up close to the tool chest, keeping it between her and the women.

"Please ask him how much longer I have to watch these drones. I mean, I stinking set them up to alert me. No reason to sit here like a dumbass when I could be inside on a couch."

"I will, Belle. I'm sure he'll relax after dealing with this alarm. They got the explosives out okay, so it's not like we really need to worry about corposec, anyway. I'll talk to you in a bit."

Juliet heard the door open and slam shut again, and then Belle's heavy sigh and stomping feet as she walked back toward her desk. Juliet inched around the tool chest, keeping it between them, and when she saw, in Honey's view, the woman stretch out her legs and stare into space, she crawled back to their first hiding spot.

"God," she subvocalized, "I think I lost ten pounds in sweat."

36

\\\\\\\\\\\\\\\\\\\\\

THE PLAN

Juliet stepped out of Honey's passenger seat and looked around the parking lot. Thicker than Water was busy, much more so at midnight than when she'd met Vikker's team in what seemed like another lifetime. Before heading to the club, she and Honey had spent the day in an AutoMotel room, calling their contacts, building a floor plan model of Vikker's compound, and watching the data Angel collected minute by minute with the drones she'd hijacked.

They'd learned a lot. Vikker's cousin, Reynold, wasn't exactly a fixer or even directly tied to any corps, but he was a gang leader of sorts. He ran an extensive network of operators and an even larger group of former corpo-sec agents who had lost their jobs and didn't qualify for operator licenses for various reasons.

Honey and Juliet had come to that conclusion after picking up chatter between Reynold and the people who stopped by the compound to talk business. It helped that Angel could take photos of everyone's faces and do limited background checks through the sat-net. In one revealing conversation, Angel had recorded Reynold complaining to Wendy, who turned out to be his wife, about Ghoul and her refusal to cooperate, about how she'd cost him a major contract with Benson LTD, a corpo out of Nogales.

After a bit of digging, Juliet and Angel found that Benson LTD had recently acquired a contract for public transport in Nogales, and she assumed the contract had something to do with the lithium-air batts she'd absconded with. More than that, however, the snippet of conversation had confirmed that Ghoul was alive and being kept for some sort of payback.

The drone footage was also valuable when it came to convincing their friends to take part in the heist, as they were calling it. They had photos of some valuable tools, vehicle parts, weapons, and easily removable infrastructure from Vikker's compound—everything from batteries to solar cells to the drones themselves. If they had time to strip the place properly, they were looking at a couple of 100k in equipment and materials.

With everyone suitably motivated, Honey had suggested a meetup at an operator-friendly club, and Juliet had mentioned Thicker than Water, which is why she stood there, nervously looking around the parking lot and the people milling about outside the building. "Here we are," she told Honey, gesturing at the bright neon lights hanging over the crowded door.

"Think we'll get in okay?"

"Yeah, Angel got a reservation for one of the meeting rooms—just had to give them my operator ID and a two-hundred-bit payment," Juliet replied, then subvocalizing, "Angel, please make sure you're watching the crowd— I doubt WBD is still hanging around here looking for me, but you never know."

"I will keep you clear of any video surveillance, and your attire should thwart human observers."

"Here's hoping." Juliet knew Angel was probably right—she wore her rebreather and a black hoodie under her vest with the hood pulled up. At Honey's suggestion, she'd changed her irises to bright, backlit violet. With most of her face obscured and her eyes so . . . eye-catching, few people would connect her to any old net images of Juliet Bianchi, the scrap cutter.

"My sword okay in here?"

"Yeah, they only have a policy against heavy weapons, whatever that means."

"Probably anything with a long barrel or a caliber which might penetrate walls. I doubt people follow the rule, to be honest. You could have armor-piercing needler rounds in that little cannon of yours, for instance."

"Well, I'm packing shredders, so . . ." Juliet trailed off, and Honey smiled.

"Yeah, I know, but they don't know that." Honey started walking, straightening her black tactical vest and carrying her sheathed sword in her left hand. "C'mon, Hot Mustard's almost here—let's get the room set up."

Juliet nodded and strode toward the doorway as confidently as she could. She wore a black, tight-fitting Tevlo long-sleeved pullover under her olive-green armored vest, and black Tevlo cargo pants over her heavy work boots. With her rebreather hiding most of her face, and her eyes gleaming like violet LEDs, it was easy to pretend she was someone else, someone who belonged at a place like Thicker than Water.

When she walked up to the door, this time she didn't hesitate to brush past the club-goers waiting to get in. More than that, she felt a little thrill in her gut as people glanced at her then quickly looked away. Sure, it might have something to do with Honey's effortless grace and the way she held her scabbarded sword out to keep people at arm's length, but that didn't bother Juliet; Honey was here with her. They were a team.

When the bouncer's max-augmented metallic eyes scanned over her, Juliet knew Angel sent her operator ID his way. He nodded and stepped aside, motioning to the doorway.

"What the hell? What about us, cutie?" a woman wearing a very short neon-pink skirt and bustier asked, gesturing toward her similarly clad friend. Juliet only spared her a glance as she walked past the bouncer and grinned at his response.

"Got enough dancers in there. These are operators. Mind your business, Kate." The music and noises of the club drowned out Kate's response.

Juliet had a mild flashback from when she'd come to meet Vikker's team, but things were different; if not with the club, then with her. The atmosphere wasn't as mysterious, wasn't as dark—no doubt her improved optics were to thank for that—and she picked out stains in the carpet and spotted some ragged-looking clientele near the bars that she'd overlooked before; the whole experience felt less glamorous than her last visit.

"Up here," she told Honey, leading her up the pink, strip-lighted stairs to the meeting rooms. The room she'd reserved, according to Angel, was the third door on the right, and she thanked the universe for not making her set up this heist in the same place where she'd sat with Vikker, Don, and Ghoul. When she stood before the correct door, she stared into the little lens, and the lock clicked. She slid it open and stepped inside.

A smooth, black oval table surrounded by a faux leather–cushioned booth took up most of the space, but a small drink cart stood against the wall to the left. Just as they'd requested, the cart held a stack of five shot glasses and a bottle of tequila—Honey's choice.

"Right," Honey said. "You sit there, opposite the door, and I'll sit here next to it. Let me open it and confirm each person. We want this to look legit, okay?"

"You think it really matters? They all know us . . ." Juliet trailed off, letting Honey make the implied connections.

"It matters! I know Mags and Pit, but only from doing a couple of jobs with them. You know Hot Mustard, but how well? We don't want anyone to look at us and decide this is amateur hour and not worth the risk. We're not doing a simple job here—this is big-league shit."

Juliet was holding up a hand and ticking off her fingers while Honey spoke, and when she finished, Juliet grinned at her. "Come on! One more!"

"One more what?"

"Clichés or whatever they're called. You said *amateur hour* and *big league*. Gimme one more!"

"Laugh it up, sweetheart!" Honey's face took on an uncharacteristic scowl. "I'm trying to help you, you know!"

Juliet's cheeks reddened, and she said, "I know, I know. I'm trying to keep from freaking out, and being a smartass might be a little defense mechanism. Sorry, okay?" She moved to sit where Honey had indicated and fished her deck out of her vest, setting it on the table.

"Good." Honey nodded, sitting across from her, close to the door. "Don't sweat it. I know this is nerve-wracking, and I only understand half the plan. I hope you're ready to answer questions."

"Yep." Juliet nodded, pulling her big external battery off her belt and connecting it to the deck. "Getting the jammer ready."

"Hot Mustard is here—just messaged me. Mags and Pit are five klicks out."

At Honey's words, Juliet's palms started to grow clammy, and she felt her heart rate begin to accelerate. This was it. This was when she met with people, at least one of which was becoming a good friend, and convinced them to risk their lives on a plan she only partially understood. She hated that she had to rely so much on Angel, and resolved to try to learn more about what Angel did when she broke through net security, but for now, she just had to accept that without her, this plan was a no-go.

Honey stood up to let Hot Mustard in, and Juliet subvocalized, "Angel, do you think my idea will work?"

"Of course, Juliet. We've gone over the risks, but I think there's a good chance of success. More than that, I believe the chance of catastrophic failure is low. The most likely negative scenario has you fleeing without completely burning Reynold."

The door slid open, and Hot Mustard stood in the opening. His pink hair was pulled up in a topknot, and he wore a big grin as he took in the private room. "Hey, Juliet!" he greeted over Honey's shoulder, then he looked down at Juliet's "muscle" and held out a hand. "Hot Mustard. Honey?"

"Hey," Honey replied, and Juliet could imagine her smile, though she couldn't see it. They shook hands before Honey gestured for Hot Mustard to sit. "Our other two team members are almost here."

"Cool," Hot Mustard said, sliding into the booth. He wore the same tactical gear he'd had on when Juliet first met him. She didn't see any weapons but knew he probably had something concealed; she just hoped his rifle was outside in his vehicle. "Things okay, Juliet? Any word on Ghoul's status?"

"She's alive. We've got a drone watching her heat signature."

"Oh, nice! Already have eyes in the sky?"

"Yep, but let's wait for everyone so I don't have to explain everything twice, 'kay?"

"Yeah, no *problemo*." He sat back and drummed his fingers on the counter. "One quick question: how long 'til we head out?"

"Two hours," Juliet replied with a smile. "Trying to decide if you want a drink?"

"Well, I see you're planning a shot to get us going, so I better just stick to that. Wanna be one hundred, you know?"

"Angel, will you ask for a water pitcher and some glasses?" Juliet subvocalized.

"Yes."

"Got water coming. Sorry, should have had it here from the get-go."

"Nah, it's cool. I like this club, by the way—they didn't give me any grief at the door, and it's got a kinda cool vibe. Never spent much time around Tucson. Weird how it has such a different feel than Phoenix, even with the megacorps dominating the downtown."

"Yeah, Tucson's got its own thing going, that's for sure. I'll probably miss it someday, but right now, I'm eager to get the hell out of here," Juliet said, surprising herself with her candor.

"They're coming into the club," Honey spoke, standing up and moving to the door again.

"So, she really uses that sword, huh?" Hot Mustard asked, and to his credit, he spoke plainly enough for Honey to hear easily.

"Yeah, and she's damn good."

"Thanks, Jules," Honey said, then added, "Also, my scabbard doubles as a stun baton, so, yeah—perfect for tonight's job."

"Oh? Nonlethals all the way?"

"Relax!" Juliet laughed. "They're almost here, and we'll go over it all."

Before Hot Mustard could respond, the door opened, and Honey nodded to Mags and Pit, motioning them into the room. Mags lumbered right over to the table and scooted in next to Hot Mustard, urging him to make room. She wore a black tank top, bright red lipstick, and her permanent cybernetic visor. Her short, dirty-blonde hair looked freshly curled, and she smiled broadly at Juliet, exposing too-small teeth with lots of wide gaps. It was endearing.

Before Juliet could greet Mags, Pit strode up and stuck out a hand. "Yo, Juliet. Thanks for thinking of me on this job."

"Of course, Pit," Juliet said, reaching out to clasp his hand. "Thank you for coming on such short notice."

Pit nodded, then turned to slide into the booth next to Mags, further pushing Hot Mustard around the horseshoe-shaped seat toward Juliet. He wore a frayed denim vest, exposing his well-muscled arms and myriad tattoos, and Juliet could see he'd freshly shaved his face. He looked tough but clean, and she appreciated his bright, alert eyes; it was going to be a long night.

Honey sat down across from her and raised an eyebrow, indicating it was her turn to speak, so Juliet cleared her throat and started. "Thank all of you. Thank you for coming to help with this job. My friend, whom half of you have never met, is in danger, and I appreciate you all dropping your plans for tonight and heading down here. I'm fairly sure it will be worth your while"—she chuckled—"but I know you all have other, probably less risky ways to make some bits."

"You know me," Mags said, smashing a heavy, meaty fist into her palm, the pale flesh of her arms jiggling with the impact. "Always happy to smash some heads for the right cause." Her visor scrolled a cartoon explosion and the word POW while she spoke, and Juliet chuckled.

"There might be some head smashing, but the goal tonight is nonlethal. I'm not trying to create more vendettas; I'm trying to eliminate one."

"So, how's that going to work, exactly?" Honey asked, surprising Juliet. It was a fair question, though—she'd been a bit more cryptic with Honey than she deserved, but it was mostly because her plan had been slowly developing over the last couple of days.

"Well, that's a good question, Honey. Let me start with a broad outline for everyone." She looked around the table and met everyone's eyes—or visor—and continued, "My friend has been taken hostage, held helpless by some leverage—"The door buzzed, interrupting her, and Honey jumped up to see who it was.

"Thanks," Honey said, opening the door for a club employee with a pitcher of iced water and five tall, narrow glasses. As soon as he set them down on the metal cart next to the shot glasses and left, Juliet leaned forward and tapped her deck, touching the icon Angel had set up for her to activate the wireless jammer.

"Now that we're alone and I'm about to start talking business, I guess I should turn this on." She pointed to the deck. "Jammer and noise screen. Everyone good with that?"

"Good." Pit nodded. No one else commented, so Juliet cleared her throat and continued speaking.

"So my friend is being held at a compound out past the ABZ near Tucson. We have eyes and ears on the site. Honey and I did some reconnaissance last night, and while we were there, I managed to take control of their own drones." At this, Pit and Mags shared a chuckle and bumped knuckles. Hot Mustard exhaled noisily through his nose, and Juliet smiled around the table. "What? You guys expected less?"

After the chuckles subsided, she continued, "The guy who's holding our target, Ghoul, has access to a large network of operators and former corposec agents. He's very connected, has deep pockets, and has a real grudge against Ghoul. That said, he hates her because she's taking the fall for something I did." She held up a hand as she saw questions forming on the faces of the people around the table. "Enough said about that. Just know that Ghoul doesn't deserve the shit she's going through right now."

Juliet touched another icon on her deck, and a three-dimensional map of Vikker's compound appeared. It wasn't in full color, but it wasn't monochromatic, either. The structures were gray, the ground and fauna were a light brown, and as everyone watched, it began to populate with red, humanoid figures moving around in real time. Angel had connected the feed from the drones to the map, showing where Reynold and his people were.

One of the figures was green, a stationary dot in a large square space beneath the ground floor of the ranch house—Vikker's secret basement. "This is Ghoul," Juliet said. "Right now, there are seven hostiles to deal with, and based on chatter we heard throughout the day, we think that number will remain constant.

"Part one of the plan is to get Ghoul out of there. We want to incapacitate all of the hostiles so I have time to work on part two of the plan, which makes sure these assholes don't come back around looking for Ghoul or the person they're leveraging against her. Ever."

"Which is?" Hot Mustard prompted helpfully.

"Once they're all out of it, I'm going to hack Reynold's PAI. I'm going to get a hold of his contact list, and I'm going to send out some incriminating personal messages with high-value corporate secrets belonging to Vykertech. They're going to descend on him like flies on shit, and there won't be much he can say to get them off his back.

"If I'm right about this data I have, they'll make him disappear. They'll probably do the same to anyone he's been working with lately unless they violently distance themselves from him. He won't have the time nor the freedom to worry about his vendetta with Ghoul."

Hot Mustard blew a low, slow whistle. "Remind me not to get on your bad side, Juliet."

"No shit!" Mags said, but she wore a savage grin. "Glad to have a real netjacker as a friend!"

"I . . ." Juliet began to protest, but then she shrugged and said, "I don't like it when connected assholes pick on my friends, especially when they're wrong. That should be me sitting in that cellar." Subvocally, she added, "Angel, thank you so much. I hate taking credit for you."

"I don't mind, Juliet. We're a team, and this was entirely your idea. I find it diabolical and am very impressed!"

"So you really think the Vykertech data you have will be that bad for this guy?" Mags asked.

"Yes. It's the kind of shit that would get a corp sanctioned or split up." Angel had finished analyzing the databases which had been stored with the dreamer program. They contained everything from participant identifiers to hormone call requests from the program to bioreadings taken by the hijacked PAIs.

"Okay, cool," Honey spoke, leaning forward. "So tell us what we each need to do."

37

\\\\\\\\\\\\\\\\\\\\\

EXECUTION

Juliet watched on her AUI as her team moved into position. A lot was riding on a few things going right during this stage of the operation: Hot Mustard needed to land a few perfect shots, and Honey, Pit, and Mags needed to get close enough to wrap up what he started.

Hot Mustard had his rifle suppressed and dialed in, using live triangulation from the drones to target the four people Reynold had patrolling the exterior of his compound.

They couldn't have asked for a better night; warm gusts of wind blew from the southwest, stirring up dust and making enough noise to cover the near-silent movement of the team as they carefully inched into position. The patrolling members of Reynold's crew were distracted, tired, and not all that interested in keeping watch. One of them was even on a call with a friend, murmuring as he walked along the northern edge of the cleared property.

Juliet had wondered about using tranquilizer rounds but had been met with two problems: Hot Mustard didn't have any, and both he and Mags assured her that they weren't as fast acting or foolproof as the vids made them seem. More than that, Hot Mustard said he'd need to be a lot closer to utilize them. On the other hand, his shock rounds were accurate up to half a klick, and he was sure he could incapacitate anyone for half a minute—plenty of time for the others to close in with the real tranqs Mags had provided.

"Four people on patrol, two in the garage, two in the house. That's one more than we wanted, but that ain't bad," Pit spoke in the group comms; Juliet was sharing the drone view with everyone.

"Yeah, it's the big guy, the one with the minigun. He came back an hour ago and has been hanging in the garage with the drone chick," Honey said, then followed up with, "I'll put him down."

"One thing at a time," Juliet reminded them. "Focus on job one: the guys outside. Fast and quiet."

"Right," Hot Mustard replied in his Southern twang. "Fast is smooth, smooth is fast. Nearly ready; give me ninety seconds."

"I don't think that's how it—" Honey started to say, but Juliet spoke over her, echoing Hot Mustard.

"Ninety seconds." She crouched low, fifty yards from the exposed sliding door on the back side of the ranch house. "Sound off with your status, please."

"In position. Ready," Honey said. She had the job of tranqing the first patroller, and then it would be Mags's turn, Pit's, then back to Honey for the fourth guard. Hot Mustard was supposed to drop each one within fifteen seconds of the first. Juliet hoped he was as good as he claimed and as Ghoul had thought.

"Need thirty seconds," Mags spoke.

"Ready," Pit said.

Juliet's palms began to sweat as she watched the drone display, nervous that something would go wrong at the last minute. Nothing seemed amiss, however; the four patrollers were still moving lackadaisically from point to point, pausing to mess around with their AUIs or to lean against a vehicle, none seeming very vigilant. But why would they? As far as they knew, three drones were doing their job for them, and, thanks to Angel, the drones were showing footage with Juliet's team scrubbed out.

"Juliet, the signatures from the basement have changed." Angel's voice startled her and made her wonder if she'd manifested some sort of problem by believing there would be one.

"What is it?"

"The signature we've assumed is Ghoul has cooled significantly—nearly two degrees. The other individual with her is moving about agitatedly."

"That sounds bad. What could have caused it?"

"Acute blood loss, pharmaceuticals, application of ice or other cooling agents—"

"Okay, okay," Juliet hissed through her teeth, ready to call another ready check, but Mags beat her to it.

"Ready!" her voice came through the comms.

"One more time, everyone, sound off."

"Ready," Honey said immediately.

"Ready," Pit said again.

"Ready," Mags repeated.

Ten seconds slipped by, then Hot Mustard twanged, "Ready. Going on your call, Juliet."

Juliet looked at her display one more time, watched the patrollers to ensure they were all distant from each other, then nervously looked at the stationary figure in the basement and the other one pacing back and forth in front of it. "Go," she said.

A click sounded to her right, distantly, and she knew she wouldn't have noticed it if she hadn't been listening for it. "One," Hot Mustard started. Two seconds later, she heard the click again, and his target must have been much closer to her because she heard the crackle of the round as it connected. "Two," he announced.

"One tranqed," came Honey's voice.

Click. "Three."

"Two tranqed," Mags announced.

Click. "Four."

"Three tranqed." Pit sounded breathless, as though he'd had to sprint or struggle. Three seconds later, Honey announced that number four was tranqed.

"Like clockwork, people," Hot Mustard said. "Holding this position for overwatch."

"No heroics," Juliet spoke. "Honey and Pit, do your thing in the garage. Mags, we're a go for the house; get your nite-nite ready." Juliet checked her rebreather and the nite-nite grenade hanging from a loop on her vest, and hurried toward the house's back door.

She was supposed to save her grenade for the basement, but she held her hand to it, just in case, while she peered through the sliding door, listening for the telltale hiss that would come when Mags deployed her grenade in the kitchen. Pit and Mags had worked with similar grenades before, and they both said they'd be quiet but that she'd be able to pick up the sound, especially with her sensitive auditory implants.

From the sliding door, she could see a couch, a junk-covered dining table, and the yellow-lit rectangle of the doorway leading to the kitchen. They weren't lying about the sound—she watched Mags's highlighted figure on her drone display trundle up to the kitchen door, open it, and toss her payload inside. Almost immediately, Juliet heard the hiss in her auditory implants, and she pulled on the door, trying to open it. It wouldn't budge.

"Door's locked, Mags."

"Coming; kitchen target is down. Pretty thing, too. You serious she's married to that old asshole?" Mags was referring to Reynold and the photo Juliet had shared with them all.

"Cut that chatter," Hot Mustard said in quick, clipped words. Mags didn't reply, but a few heartbeats later, she came tiptoeing through the living room, a haze of white smoke wafting along the ground in her wake. She was wearing the rebreather Juliet had purchased for Honey—they'd determined the garage was too large a space for the nite-nites to be effective. Honey and Pit were going to have to drop their targets with stun batons and tranqs.

As Mags pulled open the slider, Juliet slipped inside, and they made their way to the back hallway, where they knew a trapdoor in the closet would open into the secret basement. They moved very slowly and stepped as lightly as possible; Mags impressed Juliet with her quiet movements, careful not to make the floor creak.

They were probably being overcautious; from the drone's tracking of heat signatures, they'd mapped out the hidden basement to some degree, and it looked like a single room which extended under the master suite. The floor under the hallway was probably solid concrete. When they reached the end of the hall and had the option to go straight into the master or left into a linen closet, Juliet carefully turned the knob on the closet door.

They'd watched and listened with the drones more than a dozen times as people opened this door, and they were nearly certain there wasn't any trick to it—no alarms, no hidden catches, just a door that would open onto a carpeted closet beneath which there was a trapdoor and a short ladder. *And Ghoul*, Juliet reminded herself, *waiting for someone to help her*. Just as she'd hoped, nothing was waiting to surprise her in the closet. The carpet was already pulled back, and the stainless handle affixed to the plywood trapdoor beckoned her.

"Garage status?" Juliet subvocalized, carefully removing her nite-nite from her vest.

"Almost in position," Honey replied. Juliet knew their plan; Honey would try to jump the big guy with the gun, stunning him. Meanwhile, Pit was supposed to deal with the—likely sleeping—drone operator and open the big garage door. Hot Mustard was in a position to shoot into the bay if the big guy put up too much of a struggle.

Juliet handed her grenade to Mags, stepped over the trapdoor, and reached down to grasp the handle. Looking at Mags, she held up her other thumb, raising her eyebrows in question. Mags's visor displayed, "Ready!" so Juliet nodded and pulled on the trapdoor. The hinges were on her side of the door; she couldn't see through the opening, but Mags didn't hesitate. She tapped the arming button three times, setting the grenade for instant disbursement, and dropped the already smoking canister through the hole.

Juliet heard a cough and shuffling, then a thud; she hoped it was the sound of Reynold falling. Before she could say anything, Mags dropped down through the hatch in a surprising show of agility, holding a long, metallic black baton in one hand as she fell out of sight. Juliet was surprised when the only sound of her landing was the thud of her boots on concrete. Letting the trapdoor drop the rest of the way open, she stepped over it to climb down the ladder after her.

She was halfway down when Mags spoke in their team comms. "Basement clear. Number one is down."

"Garage is clear," Hot Mustard said, and Juliet felt a wave of relief wash over her; she'd been sure something would go wrong with that part of the plan. The big guy with the gun had just seemed like such a hard case, she'd figured he'd be hopped up on stimulants or something and put up a fight despite Honey and Pit surprising him.

She stepped off the ladder, peering through the haze of the nite-nite smoke while thankful for Angel's intuitive adjustment to her vision, when Honey's voice came through the comms.

"Pit's going for the rental. I'm securing everyone with shrink bands."

"She's not breathing," Mags said from Juliet's right.

"What?" she hissed, stepping toward Mags's highlighted silhouette in her AUI, nearly smashing into and tripping over a small card table and chair. She saw Reynold's boots and legs extending through the haze on her left but hurried forward to Mags and Ghoul. Mags was busy removing the bindings that held Ghoul to her chair—shrink bands brought too tight and kept in place too long. Ghoul's pale skin was bruised and bleeding around them, and her face was wan where it wasn't black and blue.

"Ghoul." Juliet reached for her friend's face and cupped it between her hands. "Ghoul, c'mon, snap out of it."

"Hitting her with a stim," Mags said, pulling an autoinjector from her belt.

"You sure we should—" Juliet started, but it was too late; Mags pressed the nozzle to Ghoul's neck, and it hissed. Juliet held her breath while waiting for a reaction, counting to three, then five, then Ghoul's swollen eyes fluttered, and she inhaled weakly.

"She's alive. Drugged to hell, it looks like. Better get her to a clinic; get her flushed. Hope they didn't do any permanent damage," Mags continued. The whole reason she was on basement duty with Juliet was that she used to work as a paramedic.

"I'll help you lift her up the ladder, but you'll have to get her out." Juliet's voice was tremulous with stress and worry. "It's going to take me a little while to deal with Reynold."

"Yep, I'll make the run to a clinic. Make sure Pit isn't lazy about looting this place," Mags replied, hoisting Ghoul up by the armpits and crab walking with her to the ladder.

Juliet held Ghoul in a sort of reverse hug, her chin tucked over the other woman's shoulder, listening to her weak, shallow breaths as Mags climbed up.

"You better be okay, Ghoul," she whispered, and then Mags was leaning down through the opening, arms outstretched.

"Hold her arms up."

"Right." Juliet lifted Ghoul's bruised, bloody arms, and that's when she noted the deep cut on her cybernetic arm and the large void where its bio-battery should've been. "Assholes," she hissed, squatting down and hoisting Ghoul up as Mags pulled her through the opening. When she stepped back, she saw that her arms were covered with blood, and she knew Ghoul must have had multiple lacerations on her back and legs. Juliet turned to the slumbering Reynold, and a low snarl came out of her throat as she moved over to him.

"Okay, Angel. Time for phase two," she said, pulling out a cheap data deck she'd picked up earlier in the afternoon at the swap meet. It was a basic model but had enough memory to hold the dreamer program and databases. More importantly, there was nothing to tie it to Juliet; she'd paid for it with bullets: fifty shredder rounds for an old, slow deck.

She unwrapped the data cable she'd brought with it and kneeled over Reynold's unconscious body. Roughly, she jammed her thumbnail into his data port and peeled back his synth-flesh, then she jammed the data cable into it, hooking him to the deck.

They'd done as much research as they could about Reynold and his augments; the only records they came away with referenced a recent visit to a
cosmetic surgery clinic in New Vegas. Still, everyone had agreed that he must
have a data port, and it looked like they'd been right. It was a nice-looking
port with an Aurora Systems logo on it, and Juliet hoped Angel wouldn't
struggle too much getting through it; she doubted he had a PAI that could
put up too much of a fight with Angel's daemons, though.

Juliet tucked the deck into Reynold's belt, securing it in place, before pulling her own data cable out of her arm and hooking herself to it, using it as a
bridge for Angel to do her thing. "Go for it," she subvocalized.

"I'm assaulting his PAI's ICE. Progress is good." Angel continued to give
her updates over the next minute or so, and then she said, "I'm in. I've suppressed his PAI and have full access."

"Okay, search his contacts and history. Find the person watching Ghoul's
sister."

"I have it. Reynold has been sending regular updates to a man named
Samuel Chance. His last message was, 'Just keep tabs on her. We have the
sister, and she's gonna break soon. Send me a pic of the girl tomorrow morning; something fresh to spur things along.'"

"Okay, send the following message along with one of the databases from
Vykertech: Sam, we broke her. You can leave off on the girl. I'm swamped
here and have a hundred things going on. Can you help me lighten the load?
I have a little analysis job for you, and I'll send you a bonus if you can help.
I'm attaching a database; break it down for me and write up your best guess
about its source or purpose. I'd tell you more, but it's need-to-know."

"Done," Angel said.

"Okay, now—" Juliet started, but suddenly, Reynold's body convulsed and
he rolled to his side. Juliet was kneeling to his right, and when he pivoted his
back to her and continued around, his right arm came up like he was going
to punch her. Juliet reflexively held up her wrist to block, but his arm split,
revealing a very high-end cosmetic wire-job. A foot-long, razor-sharp blade
snapped out of the cybernetic limb, piercing Juliet's forearm and continuing
into her chest.

The blade sank through the top of her right breast, through her ribs, and
into her lung. She grunted out a half-formed expletive, surprise and pain
overwhelming her ability to speak for the moment.

Juliet tracked the blade's progress in a detached, slow-motion realization,
suddenly feeling like she'd stepped out of herself and into a horror movie,

watching as Reynold's snarling face loomed before hers as he stood, lifting her off the ground—further ripping her flesh—and driving her back against the cement wall of the gloomy basement. "Think you can rape my mind, you damn little bitch?"

Juliet opened her mouth, but only a ragged cough emerged, spraying red flecks onto Reynold's too-smooth pale face. She kicked her boot against his shin, trying to knock him back, trying to get that horrible blade out of her, but Reynold didn't seem to notice, and a corner of her mind wondered what else about the man was cybernetic. "Angel," she subvocalized. Or tried to, but blood was thick in her throat.

"Juliet," Angel said. "Juliet, I've alerted your team. Hold on!"

"You silly bitch." Reynold twisted his arm slightly, sending sharp, horrible needles of pain through Juliet's arm and chest. "You think a ghost like me hasn't had some military-grade enhancements? My nanites ate that tranquilizer like a snack. So you fucked my PAI, huh? Kinda weird with no voice in my head after all these years.

"Can't chat more, love," he said, lifting his other arm. Juliet watched as this forearm, too, split, and another wicked blade shot forth. "I suppose you've alerted your friends, which means I need to do some killing."

Reynold's raised his other blade high like he was going to stab it into Juliet's eye, but then he convulsed. His body became rigid, and he hopped—no, he vibrated backward, his blade slipping free from Juliet's chest with a wet sucking sound. His face twisted in a paroxysm of agony and dismay, and then he fell backward, still vibrating like he was having a seizure. Was he having a seizure?

"I'm sorry, Juliet," Angel said.

"What?" Juliet sobbed, falling to her knees and trying to press her uninjured arm to the horrible wound in her chest.

"I couldn't wait any longer; I activated the dreamer program in the deck, connecting it to his PAI. He's no longer lucid, and the PAI is rapidly expanding its synth-nerve nanofibers through his nervous system."

Juliet breathed shallowly, trying not to cough while pressing her hand to the hole in her chest, and watched as Reynold continued to spasm. His blades retracted, and his eyes began to glow before they closed. He'd only been down a minute when Honey was suddenly looming in front of Juliet, whispering, "Oh God, hold on, Juliet." Her voice buzzed funnily in Juliet's ears, and a weird chuckle erupted from her throat.

Everything was strange; her limbs felt numb and heavy, and the pain from her wounds was distant, dulled. She'd heard of people getting tunnel vision as they lost blood or slipped from consciousness, but that didn't happen. Her view remained bright and clear, even as her eyelids grew too heavy to hold open. She heard Honey's voice buzzing in her ears again, tickling through her skull. "We need a trauma kit! There's gotta be something in the garage; Mags is gone with ours."

"I can come back!" Mags's voice sounded peculiar and slow to Juliet.

"I got it," Hot Mustard replied. "Coming now."

"Juliet? Juliet! Stay with me, okay?" Honey said, gripping the sides of her face and giving her a jostle.

"I'm here. Plug me back into that deck. My cord came loose when that jerk fell down."

"Forget it! We need to get you to a trauma center."

"No. Doc Sack. Sack . . . Tsakanikas!" She chuckled at how funny his name was, her head lolling forward. She didn't realize she'd started to slip under until Honey jostled her again.

"Stay awake, Juliet! Hot Mustard's almost here."

"Plug me in! Hurry!" Juliet breathed through clenched teeth, a sudden spike of pain running through her chest.

"Dammit," Honey groused, turning to find Juliet's data cable and then dragging on Reynold's boot until he was close enough that she could plug the cable into the deck. "Is he going to wake up?"

"Dreaming," Juliet said with an entirely inappropriate, bubbling, red-foamed giggle. "Angel, finish the job," she hissed, another knife of pain shooting through her as she began to cough, and though it hurt and she tried desperately, she couldn't stop. She gave in to it, allowing her body to try to get the blood out of her lung, trusting Angel to finish sending the personal messages with the Vykertech data to a bunch of Reynold's contacts.

She coughed for an eternity, or so it seemed, and suddenly Hot Mustard was there, sprinkling burning powder into her stab wounds and whistling softly. "Too bad he missed the plate in your vest by a centimeter." Juliet thrashed and screamed as the powder cauterized her vessels, and then she felt the sting and heard the hiss, and Honey shot her up with not one or two but three different pharmaceuticals. After that, everything was a blur.

She had vague, dreamlike memories of Honey telling the others she'd take her to the doc—it was up to Pit and Hot Mustard to strip Vikker's place of valuables. They all had the keycodes to the drone terminal, so Juliet had a fuzzy, comforting thought that her friends would be able to use them to keep watch until they were ready to move out in their rented truck. Meanwhile, she reclined in Honey's passenger seat and let the drugs do their thing; she was pain free and floating, hazily hoping she'd see Ghoul again soon, and that she'd be all right.

She felt Honey reach over and take her hand at one point, hearing her say, as if from a distance, "That was a smooth execution of a plan, right up until you got stabbed." Then Juliet, smiling in narco-bliss, closed her eyes and let her mind drift away.

38

///////////////////

EPILOGUE

Juliet kicked at her blanket and stretched, arching her back. Just as the stretch was getting good, she felt a straining of her flesh, a needle of pain in her chest, and cut it short. She huffed, flopping her arms down to the surprisingly comfortable gel mattress. "Can't even get a good stretch in," she yawned, looking around the spartan, white-walled room. Bright, diffuse light came through the frosted glass of the window, and again, she groaned. "Would it kill Tsakanikas to put some curtains in here?"

"Good morning, Juliet," Angel said. If Juliet closed her eyes, she could imagine the clear, pleasant voice coming from a dear friend sitting by her bedside.

"Hey, Angel. Any updates?" she asked, rubbing at her eyes. She only felt a minor twinge of discomfort as she twisted her bandaged wrist, putting some pressure on the bonded flesh.

"You have two messages—one from Honey and one from Ghoul."

"Really? Ghoul?"

"Yes, would you like to see that one first?"

"Ye—no. Give me Honey's first." Juliet was excited to hear from Ghoul but wanted to focus on it without worrying about what Honey had to say. A blinking tab appeared on her AUI, and she selected it, opening up a vid message from Honey. She was smiling, standing in a hallway that looked suspiciously like the one outside the room Juliet was convalescing in.

"Hey, Juliet! You were conked out, so I went to get you some breakfast and make some calls to the gang. They've had a productive couple of days, and I'll give you an update on everything they got up to when I come back. Don't worry; I've been keeping tabs on your good doctor, and everything seems up-and-up so far. He's kinda shifty, but I get a serious honor among thieves vibe from him; I think we're still good here for a couple of days. See you soon!" The vid stopped on a freeze frame of Honey's smiling, fresh face.

"I don't think so, Hon," Juliet whispered, shaking her head. "Heading home today if I have anything to say about it." She cleared her throat, about to ask Angel to play Ghoul's message, when an urge to cough hit her, which she did, *painfully*, for the next minute or so. When she finally got over the fit, her face was bright red, and her chest wound was aching.

"Don't worry, Juliet," Angel said. "The doctor cleared most of the blood from your lungs, but he said you'd have some discomfort and coughing for a few days."

"Yeah, I just don't wanna rip this cut open," Juliet replied, gently patting the gauze pad on her chest.

"There's little chance of that; the wound was sealed with a powerful bonding agent. It will hold together as it heals."

"Right, well, play me Ghoul's message, please." Juliet had woken up from surgery sometime around noon the previous day. Honey had been waiting for her but hadn't had any updates on Ghoul other than that Mags had gotten her to St. Mary's emergency room okay and was staying with her to learn more.

"It's a text message, Juliet," Angel replied, displaying the text in an opaque amber window on her AUI:

Juliet,

I hear you got hurt helping me. I'm so sorry about that and everything else. I know you think this is somehow your fault, that I was taking the blame for Vikker. You don't know the whole truth, though. That night, the night Vikker and Don almost killed you, they told me they were going to question you. They told me they thought you were a corpo rat. I argued a little, but I was kind of out of it. God, Juliet, I sat in a recliner drinking a craft beer while they fucked you over in the garage.

No, I didn't know they'd take it so far, but I could have stopped them; I could have come out to the garage to see how things were going, to make sure they treated you right. I was not unconscious, no matter what they said or what I said before. So you see? I deserved what Reynold was doing. I earned the shit that came my way.

Still, somehow, fate or the universe or God, I don't know, saw fit to give me another chance, put you in my path—a true friend, an actual good person in this filthy, dirty hell we've crafted for ourselves. I'm kind of a mess right now; my emotions are all over, and I'm still coming to terms with the idea that Reynold is no longer a threat. I'm going to trust that it's true, though. I'm going to believe your friend, Mags.

I don't deserve you or your friendship, nor do I deserve the sister Reynold found. I'd thought she was lost, and dammit, I need to make some things up to her. That's where I'm going to start. Start working to turn shit around in my life and become worthy of people like you and Allison, my sister. So, this is thank you and goodbye for now. I'll understand if you never want to see me again, but I will look you up someday and give you the chance to say it to my face.

I know sending you this text message is cowardly. I should have called, let you cuss me out. I would've sent a vid, but my PAI wasn't sure he could encrypt it as well as this text message—I really need an upgrade.

Take care of yourself.

Love,

Cassie

Juliet leaned back on her pillows and wiped at the tears that had sprung from her eyes when she'd read Ghoul's confession and had continued to flow as she read the rest. "Dammit, Ghoul," she breathed. She felt the urge to call her, to demand she come back, to scream at her for lying about Vikker, and to tell her she didn't care, that she could forgive her.

"I'm sorry, Juliet," Angel said, her voice soft and full of simulated emotion.

"Yeah, well, alone again, I guess."

"Not exactly, Juliet. You have me. You have Honey and the others who helped on your rescue mission. You have Sensei and his dojo, and someday, we'll get you clear of WBD, and you can reconnect with your older friends and family."

"Will we? It doesn't feel like it, Angel. It feels like I'm going to be hiding for the rest of my life, which, judging by the last couple of weeks, might not be very long at all."

"You've accomplished a great deal already, Juliet!" Angel's voice was emphatic. "You took down a quasi-criminal syndicate two nights ago! You did so by leveraging an immoral corporation and using them as a weapon. You subverted the goals and motivations of powerful organizations! If you can learn from this and continue to gain strength and reputation, I truly believe we can bring WBD down just as you brought Reynold down."

"Just as I . . . you think I can get other big corpos to turn on WBD?" Juliet's eyes were dry now, and she sat up in the bed, distant glimmers of ideas tickling the edges of her consciousness.

"That's one angle you might consider, but you should know from what you've accomplished so far that it wouldn't be impossible. You have a long way to go until you're ready for that fight, but you will be ready, Juliet. Ghoul wasn't wrong—there's something special about you, and there's much more to your exceptional nature than me."

"Well, Angel," Juliet said, wincing as she scooted her legs over the side of her bed, "you're pretty damn exceptional yourself. Now, c'mon, help me figure out where my clothes are; we have work to do."

Alec Kline frowned as he drove his Gault Motors Urban Charger over the winding, rough dirt road. The outskirts of Tucson were even worse than Phoenix. Open pit mines were everywhere, and the artificial hills and mountains built up from the tailings made getting anywhere without wings rather a pain in his very busy ass. "Tom, take a note."

"Yes," his PAI said, succinct as always.

"Remind me to call Yessenia again about getting access to one of the corporate fluttercraft."

"Time?"

"After breakfast." He rounded a bend in the dirt road and saw floodlights and activity ahead. He gently reduced pressure on the accelerator and coasted down the gravelly dirt road toward the two SUVs and the temporary barricade which seemed to be blocking access to a ranch house of some sort. As he rolled to a stop next to the fully geared-out corpo-sec guards, he let the black-tinted window roll down and displayed his WBD corporate security badge, holding it out toward the visored guard.

None of them had pointed their weapons at the sedan, and Kline took a moment to admire their professionalism. Vykertech did a few things right, and corpo-sec was one of them. "I'm here to see Mrs. Green."

"A moment, please," the guard replied, then his eyes went distant as he communicated through his PAI to someone, checking Kline's credentials, no doubt. Kline sat back and tucked his designer Nikko-vape between his lips, sucking the berry-flavored vapor into his lungs. As the nicotine coursed into his bloodstream, he felt like the lights outside got a little brighter, and the dial of his impatience wound back a bit. He'd been close to snapping at the guard to hurry, but now, he just inhaled deeply through his nose and drummed his fingers on the steering wheel.

"You're clear, sir. Mrs. Green will meet you at the house." The guard backed up, gesturing toward the gate, and it slowly trundled open. Kline put his window up and drove through, not sparing a glance for the guards; his eyes were too occupied by the massive forensics team Vykertech had deployed around the ranch property. He saw ten or twelve people in white cleanroom suits walking around purposefully, and two very large, very well-equipped box trucks with the Vykertech logo painted on the sides.

Kline pulled his sedan up to the ranch house, turned the H-cell off, and stepped out. He hadn't seen Tasha Green in nearly five years, but he recognized her right away, standing near the open front door. Tall with neatly quaffed black hair pulled into a bun so tight it looked like a plastic ornament. She wore a baggy white cleanroom suit, though he imagined she had on a sleek, high-fashion business suit underneath. He walked toward her, holding out a hand.

"Tasha! It's been too long."

"Kline," she greeted, her voice warm and smooth with the hint of an edge, a bit of a rasp from too many self-inflicted carbon inhalations. "You made good time."

"Well, you said you had something that would interest me, and you've never been one to joke around, so here I am. This is quite an operation you've got here—Vykertech moving into Tucson?"

"No, no. We had a bit of a breach, but I think we've tied up the loose ends. I think I found one for you, though. Follow me, if you will."

"Do I need to, uh . . ." Kline trailed off, pointing at her clean suit.

"No, we're past these now. I could take this off, but my shirt's soaked in sweat underneath; I wouldn't want to subject you to that."

"Been there and done that!" Kline laughed. "Had to wear one of those for nearly forty hours in Chicago. I couldn't salvage the suit I had on underneath."

"Don't say that, Kline! I'm wearing my favorite outfit!" She sighed, chuckled ruefully, and turned to walk down the main hallway leading from the living area of the home back to, presumably, the bedrooms. Kline followed her, noting the lack of furniture and the bare concrete floors; the place had been stripped clean. She surprised him by walking into a closet near the end of the hall, and then he saw her step onto a wooden ladder built from two-by-four scraps. "Down here."

"All right," Kline said, then, as he put his foot onto the first rung, he added, "You aren't leading me to my doom, are you?"

"Come on, Kline. You know Vykertech has people better suited for things like that."

"Yeah." Kline stepped down the ladder. "Just a bit of a joke." He looked around the small, concrete room, probably twenty feet by twenty, taking it in. The only furnishings were a small card table and two folding chairs. A man was sitting on one of them, his chest and face lying on the table like he'd fallen asleep, but Kline saw the data cable running from his implant to the little deck in one of his hands, and he figured the guy wasn't simply sleeping.

After glancing over the table and its occupant, he scanned the room, but all he saw was stained concrete. He wrinkled his nose at the smell of bleach or some other harsh cleaning chemical and said, "This guy got something to do with WBD?"

"Not exactly," Tasha replied. "He's of interest to us regarding our breach, but something about him raised a flag. Looking into it, I thought I'd extend the professional courtesy and let you know what we found."

"Go on." Moving closer to the unconscious man, Kline noted how his eyes fluttered madly beneath his lids and how a puddle of drool had collected on the table. "Drugged?"

"Dreamer," Tasha said with a shrug as if that explained everything.

"Please elucidate." Kline straightened up with a frown. "What's this got to do with WBD?"

"When we got here, the place had been stripped." She gestured around the room and up over their heads, indicating the ranch house. "We found a few people of interest and this guy, but they couldn't tell us anything, especially him. He's locked into an experimental dreamer program; his brain's half gone due to a malfunctioning PAI."

"Seriously? I haven't heard of a PAI causing brain damage in . . . God, it's been since I was a kid, I think."

"Yes, well, Vykertech doesn't have a statement for you at this time. Trust that we're handling the matter and will get to the bottom of things. We'll prosecute the guilty party to the fullest extent of corpo law." She held up a hand as Kline was about to speak. "Let me finish. So, someone scrubbed the place pretty damn well, but I found something while I was analyzing this fellow."

She walked over to the card table and, to Kline's fascination, reached up to her bun to pull out a hairpin about the size of his favorite pen. When she held it out, a needlelike blade sprang forth from the tip with a *snick*.

Tasha Green pointed her wicked little scalpel at the sleeping man's elbow, and with the precision of a surgeon, she inserted it into his flesh. Kline heard a definite *click* before the dreamer's forearm split, and a bloody, twelve-inch blade sprang forth, hanging out over his knuckles and the scuffed card table. "Do you have a med scanner?" she asked.

"In my car . . ."

"No need to run out and get it; you trust me, right?"

"To a degree . . ."

"You wound me, Kline," Tasha said, reaching a hand to her chest over her heart. "No matter, hear what I have to say, and then you can take your own sample."

"Go on," Kline prompted, leaning over the table to examine the bloody blade. "Damn fine work, that implant."

"Very fine. Much about this man was exceptional, but that's not the point of our discussion. As I said, the place was scrubbed clean, but whoever did the scrubbing didn't know about this man's dirty blade. Either that or they didn't care—we're not sure the blood is related to anything that has to do with the people who cleaned the place out."

"Okay, so, what's the deal with the blood? I assume that's the point of all this, considering you asked about a med scanner."

"I sampled it, and the DNA raised a flag. Your employer, WBD, wants the owner of that blood."

"Ah! And my name was attached to the case. Well, which one was it?"

"WBD corpo security case number A49.1."

"Juliet . . ." Kline breathed, looking at the blade and the thick, dried blood in a new light.

ABOUT THE AUTHOR

Plum Parrot is the pen name of author Miles Gallup, who grew up in Southern Arizona and spent much of his youth wandering around the Sonoran Desert, hunting imaginary monsters and building forts. He studied creative writing at the University of Arizona and, for a number of years, attempted to teach middle schoolers to love literature and write their own stories. If he's not out enjoying the beach, you can find Gallup writing, reading his favorite authors, or playing *D&D* with friends and family.

DISCOVER
STORIES UNBOUND

PodiumAudio.com